RACHEL ZADOK

Sister-Sister

Kwela Books

While *Sister-Sister* is inspired by European and African folklore
and superstitions, nothing within these pages should be taken as
historical or cultural gospel. As in any work of fiction,
much has been invented.

I have chosen to represent stuttering with an underscore
separating the blocked sounds, rather than hyphens.
To my eye, the underscore, with the visual space it creates between
sounds, better conveys the obstruction (or block) to speech faced by
those battling this speech impediment.

Kwela Books,
an imprint of NB Publishers, a division of Media 24 Boeke (Pty) Ltd
40 Heerengracht, Cape Town, South Africa
PO Box 6525, Roggebaai, 8012, South Africa
www.kwela.com

Cover design by publicide
Typography by Nazli Jacobs
Set in ITC Veljovic
Printed and bound by Interpak Books, Pietermaritzburg, South Africa

First edition, first impression 2013

ISBN: 978-0-7957-0472-7
ISBN: 978-0-7957-0473-4 (epub)
ISBN: 978-0-7957-0609-7 (mobi)

For Julian,
who has never asked me to get a real job

The road swallows people and sometimes at night you can hear them calling for help, begging to be freed from inside its stomach.

— Ben Okri, *The Famished Road*

No, no, go not to Lethe, neither twist
Wolf's-bane, tight-rooted, for its poisonous wine;
Nor suffer thy pale forehead to be kissed
By nightshade, ruby grape of Proserpine;
Make not your rosary of yew-berries,
Nor let the beetle, nor the death-moth be
Your mournful Psyche, nor the downy owl
A partner in your sorrow's mysteries;
For shade to shade will come too drowsily,
And drown the wakeful anguish of the soul.

— John Keats, "Ode on Melancholy"

Prologue
Dreaming-Dreaming

The woman dreams she approaches KwaNogqaza Falls, just as she did on the night of her initiation ceremony, twenty-five years before. She reaches the pool at the bottom of the waterfall and sinks to her knees to pray, but the sandy bank collapses and she slips into the water. The Inkanyamba swirls around her, dragging her down to the river bed where weeds dance with creatures half snake, half fish, and long-bodied crabs watch from crevices in the rocks, eyes like jelly-berries on silver stalks.

"Dig," Inkanyamba tells her. She buries her arm up to the elbow. Sand clouds the water, enveloping her in a storm of glittering grains. Her fingers close around two smooth stones.

The serpent-god takes her into his mouth and spits her out at the surface. She is no longer in the forest. A beach stretches out before her. The woman walks along the sand with the pebbles in her hand. Before long, she comes across a dead gull lying just above the tidemark. Two white chicks sit on the bird, picking maggots from its feathers. As she watches, the water subsides until there is a single blue on the horizon. Where there was ocean, there is only sand. The dune grasses shrivel. The trees in the coastal forest sicken, dropping leaves until they are nothing more than splintered grey trunk and branch. The world dies as the chicks grow fat on their dinner of maggots.

There is a searing pain in her hand. She opens her palm and looks at the pebbles, perfect white ovals, identical save for a scab that discolours the purity of one. She picks at the scab with her nail. Blood wells from the pebble and a sound like that of a mewling baby fills the air. The stone shudders and rolls away from her prying finger towards its twin. They merge, becoming one. She contemplates the single stone in her hand, but before she can glean meaning, it splits in two and her palm begins to bleed.

Someone shakes her. The woman opens her eyes and sees Sizane leaning over her.

"It's time, Mama," she says. "The baby is coming."

PART 1

Spookasem

One for Me and One for You

I stand at the edge of an overpass as another bleak dawn spills over the city stretched out below. Office blocks rise into the leaden sky like a jawful of giant's teeth. The wind swoops through, picking a fight with the caged trees lining the pavements, stripping the branches. Leaves dance down the street with plastic bags, paper wrappers and tin cans, a rumble-tumble of discarded things. Only the sunshine sway of a Shoprite packet stops me disappearing into all that grey.

The same wind that steals warmth from flesh and leaves from trees jives the yellow bag down the road. At the corner, it catches a sideways gust and jellyfishes into the air. I watch it float towards heaven, thinking maybe the soul of a plastic bag is a helium balloon, and I pray it makes it all the way up; but before it can reach the second floor of Capital Bank, the wind drops it back down to ride the pavement to and fro, to and fro, pacing-pacing like a strung-out whore.

Traffic lights perform acrobatics for the empty streets. Flick green, flip orange, flick-flack red. And behind me the highway, circling the city like a concrete snake, waits for us.

I turn my back on the slumbering city and wander down the curve of the overpass to the highway, where Sindi spent the night in a wreck at the side of the road. She's curled like a worm on the passenger side, on the only seat that hasn't been ripped out to find a new life as somebody's couch. The lace of one of her boots hangs loose, almost touching the road through a hole in the rusted floor. It must have come undone in the night; she hasn't taken those Hi-Tecs off since she lifted them from the Salvation Army charity shop when the soles of her sneaks wore through. Her coat she grabbed from the back seat of a careless man's car.

13

My sisi is a talented thief. I lay my hand against the once plush wool of the coat, now matted as her hair and glittering with frost like Next-Door-Auntie's eyelids on shebeen night. Her lips are a dead-man shade of blue.

"Blue lips to count blue cars," I whisper, pressing my finger to her mouth to steal an ice-cream kiss. The kiss is a memory of the time we lifted a Cornetto from Joe Saviour's fridge and lay on the grassed embankment above the highway, counting cars with stolen sugar on our tongues. Zooming-zooming streaks of red, zooming-zooming streaks of blue. Our greedy eyes gobbled the white stripes. We used to believe that the highway went somewhere, that over the horizon was escape, places we'd never been and thought we wanted to go.

Leaning into the junk through the missing driver-side door, I try to make out the time on the dashboard clock. The dash is retro, the clock analogue: just two hands and four lines at twelve, three, six and nine. It doesn't work, but I want to know when it stopped. I like to know that things stop, because sometimes it feels that we never will.

For Sindi, walking is better than standing still. When you walk, things change. Mama Moon slides from skinny sliver to bloated belly; as her baby grows, we circle the city. In summer, if it rains, sunflowers seed in cracks and sprout and bloom, and each time we pass, they've changed. The stems thicken, the petals brighten and the seed cluster grows blacker than a nest of hungry beaks. Then comes the day when nothing grows there any more, when all that's left of that yellow sun is a dried, brown husk.

Leaving Sindi to sleep, I drift over to the buckled crash-barrier and sit down. I sink into the dent, run my fingers over the rusted scars. If I wanted, I could sense what twisted the metal. Ghosts clamour in my ears. They want to tell me their stories, but I don't like to listen. Everybody's got a story. I have a story of my own.

Across the highway, the salmon-pink boundary wall of a townhouse complex jars against the barren embankment like a bright mirage projected onto the dawn. It hurts more than my eyes, so I turn to the safety of the grey road and block the complex out completely by shutting an eye.

One-eyed, I watch sunlight spike over the horizon, but before the orb appears the drone of an engine breaks the stillness and a b-diesel junk rolls into view. The driver hunches over the steering wheel, peering through a hole wiped clean in the condensed breath clouding the glass.

I don't notice the man standing on the shoulder of the highway until he bolts into the road and plants his feet into the concrete. I suck my teeth as the junk swerves to avoid him, but he just roars and raises a panga into the air.

Joe used to say that crazies have always walked this highway. Sometimes, while we sat on the grass counting cars, one of them would wander up to Saviour's Pit Stop. The first time we saw a crazy, we'd just turned eight. Sindi was ahead, eleven blue to four red, when a gogo came walking up the road. She wore a floral-print summer dress and shaded her head with a tattered umbrella, silver spokes glinting. She had only one shoe. Her face was hidden behind a net of tangled grey hair, but when she got close, she swept it aside and gave us a smile and we saw she had a mouth full of white teeth and skin like a baby, smooth-smooth. Curious that someone could be young and old both, we followed her to the Pit Stop and hid behind the pumps. Joe bought a family-sized bucket from Chicken Licken next door and, while she told him her story, they shared out the drumsticks and wings: one for me, one for you. Her story was probably sad, because Joe cried. Joe had cried for so many people, his tears had carved ravines in his cheeks. When there were only bones left in the bottom of the bucket, Joe led her to the men's room to freshen up, even though she was a lady. We waited for her to come out, until boredom made us brave enough to knock. *Knock-knock*. She never replied, *who's there?* After her, there were others, some scary, some nice like that first gogo, but none ever came out when we knocked.

Joe made lots of money from selling illegal b-diesel and renting out

15

zozo houses, but he wasn't like the other fat cats. I only ever saw him in ragged denim cut-offs and freebie T-shirts, XXXL, with company logos splashed across the front. Mama said he must have wanted to be a head doctor because he never did anything but listen to people's problems. Ben did all the real work at Saviour's: man's work, he called it. Sindi thought that was funny because Ben was soft, like a baby angel. He had round cheeks and full lips and always wore a black beret tilted at an angle, like the auntie that hawked paintings of shacks for big bucks on the side of the road. Ben said the crazies were harmless, just lost souls looking for the way home. "They are not going to hurt you, little sisters," he told us. "Trust me, I know things."

Ben knew things because he was from Nigeria, which is high up in Africa and therefore closer to heaven. "I've got God's ear, little sisters," he liked to say, tugging on an earlobe.

I wonder what he'd think of this junk-chasing crazy. He's naked except for bits of rag he's tied around his waist like a skirt. A black cape flaps out behind him as he runs down the highway, slicing the panga from side to side like he's trying to cut the sky into pieces. This one thinks he's a superhero.

The junk passes us by, backfiring greasy b-diesel farts that smell of fried chicken and remind me again of Joe. The crazy comes barrelling after, eyeballs popping like boiled eggs. Up close I see his superhero cape is an animal pelt. From the brown paws knotted at his throat, I figure it once belonged to a Rottweiler. And the rags aren't rags but a collection of dead things hanging from a belt. I spy the skin of a cat and a pair of severed pigeon wings.

The boom of backfire wakes Sindi. She bolts upright and hits her head on the bent windscreen frame. For one heart-stopping moment I imagine her skin hanging from the crazy's belt, but she crouches down as he passes, clutching her head. He doesn't even glance her way.

We sit against the salmon-pink boundary wall of the townhouse complex, watching the crazy chase a green electric up the highway. Electrics are slower than junks so maybe he'll catch it.

The electric fades into the distance and he stands on a white line, back straight, panga down, watching. His breath forms miniature cumulus clouds in the cold air. I wonder what sort of legend God has sealed into him that makes him chase cars he can't catch and skin creatures he can.

Joe Saviour once told me that every life has a legend. Before the soul comes down to earth, God seals a story inside it. To know your purpose, you need to unravel the mystery of that legend. He says it's a sad thing that most people only think about that mystery once they've walked to the end of the road.

Our story began on the dawn of a fresh new era. That's what the head-line of the newspaper article said, the one Mama kept folded into the cover of her ID book: *The Dawn of a Fresh New Era*. It was D-Day, the last day of the petrol-car amnesty, when everyone was meant to change to electric. We only learned that in history class when we were ten, though. Until then, I thought *we* were the dawn they meant, and I told any-one who teased us that we were so special our birth made headlines.

I've always had a big mouth. Mama said I came into the world squawk-ing like one of Gogo Nkosi's hens with a stuck egg. I made such a fuss, no one noticed Mama's labour pains hadn't stopped; thirteen minutes later, when my sisi followed, the nurse had to lunge across the room to catch her.

Two wrinkled doll-size gogos, exactly the same right down to our toes – but my sisi entered the room without a sound. Quieter than a mouse: she didn't even squeak.

For long, Sindi spoke to no one but me. Then we went to school and the teacher forced her. Even so, it was only me she spoke to straight. To any-one else, she had to spit out words like gum chewed so long it stuck to her teeth.

Mama named us the wrong way around, what with me being a big-mouth and Sindisiwe a stutterer. Maybe, like most people, she had a hard time telling us apart, even though we were tagged *Nxumalo baby 1* and *Nxumalo baby 2*. I know because, along with the headline, she kept our plastic hospital bracelets.

But that, like the petrol car, is history.

I step away from the wall like a piece of its shadow. Winter has seeped into Sindi's lungs. She sits, catching her breath in the sun, while I drift off to suss out the townhouse complex.

The complex is like lots of places on the south side of the city. Loops of barbed wire gleam down at me from the top of the eight-foot stop-nonsense, but there are no guards or cameras. Security with more bark than bite. All a thief needs is a foot up and a blanket.

I stand at the gate and stare through the bars at the houses beyond. An intercom, ten buttons equals ten houses, controls who gets in. The houses are all the same, five on the left mirrored by five on the right with a brick-paved road between them. I wonder if the people that live there were ever like me; if I might've turned out like them, given a half-chance. Maybe I would've married, walked down the aisle with a boy who knew the proper names of clouds, like Dumisile. Sindi might have married his brother. We would live in a place like this, locked up safe behind a gate. Maybe here, with a view of the highway. We'd be next-door neighbours in twin houses. And the cars parked in our garages would be proper electrics, not b-diesel junks. One red, one blue.

When I return, Sindi is staring at the rush-hour traffic. A piece of glass, probably from the windscreen of the wreck she slept in, is lodged in her hair. As I reach out to remove it, she turns her head. The glass catches the sun. I'm struck by how alive it looks, compared to her eyes. My fingers hover, ready to pluck it out; then I change my mind and leave it there.

Sitting side by side, we watch the traffic. Sometimes I forget why we walk this road, and I tell myself it's because we're looking for the beginning. Not of the concrete highway – it's not called the Ring Road for nothing – but for the beginning of the rush hour. Each day, we're at a different place when the cars slow down and sit, bumper-to-bumper, inching-inching. But I've never seen it, that first vehicle that blocks the lane and becomes the head of a multicoloured car snake, five lanes wide, unwinding along the highway forever.

Each day I look, believing my small legend, until I see a driver, impatient, stupid, raging, thrust into the oncoming traffic. Believe until I hear the metal scream as the cars twist into each other like wrestlers on WWE in a lock-up. Round and round they go, caught in a spinning vortex for an eternity of seconds and THUD, they sideswipe a barrier and THUMP, tyres squeal and burn black into the road and THWUMP, a nose smashes against the steering wheel, a skull smacks the windscreen, glass shatters, bone splinters. It's almost music, a melody of broken glass over a bass beat of bumper cars. *Thud, thump, thwump.* A wind-up traffic-accident circus song.

And after, in the short, shocked vacuum of silence, you can almost hear the hiss of the soul leaving the body.

Then I see the light inside Sindi switch. Her eyes glitter like the glass in her hair and she whispers, "Emi, oru, abiku, O," and I know, finding beginnings is not why we are here.

Thirteen cars leave the gate, among them three red and two blue. Game Thuli. I peer over Sindi's shoulder as she examines the intercom board with its shiny silver buttons all in a row. Next to each button, a strip of Perspex holds the occupant's name: Williams, Gxekwa, Sihoyiya, Abrams, Thwala, Walker, Makofane, Simons, Wynn, Sousa. I try to decide which to press, a random calculation based on nothing but gut. My gut says go with A: it's easy to say.

"Abrams," I whisper. Sindi pretends not to hear me and presses her palm against the board, sounding all the bells.

She waits three seconds before thumbing the buttons again, one-one, one-one, one-one.

The speaker fizzes and cracks and spits: "Hello."

Sindi steps back, as if she'd not expected anyone to be home. I nudge her with my elbow. She clears her throat. "Delivery," she croaks.

"Leave it in the box," comes the sigh-reply.

"It's too big."

"The madam said nothing about a delivery. Who for?" I smile.

"Mrs Abrams," I murmur in Sindi's ear.

"Uhm_m_M," Sindi peers at the board, "Abrams."

"Abrams? She's in number three, buzz her."

"She's nnn_not home." But by the time her words are out, the domestic's gone. Sindi kicks the ground with the toe of her boot, but still we hang about in the vain hope she'll buzz us in. After a minute, Sindi walks away. I follow, disappointed I won't get to see, close-up, the life we could've had. We haven't gone five steps when the motor clicks.

We're through the gate before it's wide, ducking into the shadows. Hidden behind a bush, we watch a car reverse clear of a driveway. The driver slicks lipstick over her mouth, checking her reflection in the rear-view mirror, before heading out into the world. Auntie, I think, didn't anyone ever tell you not to open the gate until you were right there? Unlucky for you, lucky for us.

Sticking to the shadows, we slip behind the houses on the left. A wide service path runs between the eight-foot boundary and another wall painted the same fishy pink; it's not as high, but we still can't see over. Wheelie bins stand sentry next to five metal doors, one for each house. We pass door number one: too easy to see from the gate.

At door number two, Sindi cocks her head. A TV blares a tune I know. It takes a second before I get it and flash back to lying on Next-

Door-Auntie's brown couch watching soapies until my eyes burned and my head throbbed. Next-Door-Auntie loved soapies, *Isidingo-Generations-Backstage-Scandal-7de Laan-The Bold,* she didn't have time for new-fangled nonsense. She'd started watching with her Ma when she was two bricks high and the starrings in those shows were like family to her. She knew their ins and outs going back decades; who was who, even though the casts weren't always the same as when she was a girl. Except for *The Bold.* Those starrings never changed. She said Ridge still looked the same as when she was four. Behind her back we called him Rigid.

There's an empty silence that says nobody home at number three. Sindi tugs the handle. Locked. At four, my nose fills with Surf Superblue scents. On the other side of the door, Kabelo's "Can't Kill Me Now" is playing on the radio. Someone sings along, out of tune and a beat behind. The song reminds me of the radio Mama once bought with her Christmas bonus.

"Don't touch," she said when she lifted it from the box. It stood on the kitchen table, shiny plastic casing unmarked by our greasy fingers until, one day at school, Dumisile told us there was going to be a three-hour "Legends of Kwaito" retrospective. That afternoon, me and Sindi jaiva'd jigga jigga around the kitchen table.

> *You should have killed me,*
> *You should have killed me, cos*
> *You can't kill me now.*

"One day," I told Sindi, "I'm going to win *Idols.* I'm going to be a starring."
"Woo, Sisi!" she said, "Woo woo!"
Mama came home, tired and beat, and found the battery doornail-dead and no soapie to go with her tea. We ran to Saviour's Pit Stop to beg a new one from Joe so we could restore her happiness, but he said Mama

had lost her happiness long before that battery died. I don't think he understood what that radio meant to Mama. It was a sign she might one day get out of there, and its death, no matter how temporary, reminded her that she never would. There was always a radio playing at Saviour's. Joe used to tune in to the golden oldies and croon out songs like a dog at full moon – until the Black Preacher began to fill the airways with his new religion. Joe loved those sermons. He'd sit in his chair and listen, chuckling to himself. Sometimes, the things the Black Preacher said made him laugh so hard, he'd fart.

One more door, then we have to cross the little road to get to the houses on the other side. I suck my bottom lip. Forever passes before the singer next door finishes hanging out the washing and her song fades into the house. Sindi eases the handle, leans into the door. The metal groans, shifts. I hold my breath. She pushes harder. The door gives. Holding it just wide enough for her eyes, Sindi peers in. My heart beats fast enough to blow, but I resist the urge to bump her up so I can see. There's a smell, thick and moist on my tongue.

Sindi slips through the gap, leaving me alone with the wheelie bin. I wait a moment, in case she comes back; then, against my worming guts, I step through the door.

We're standing in a small yard. The wall's depressing pinkness is broken only by a kitchen door and window. A gutter runs down one wall and spits a hunk of slime into a choked drain. On the inside sill, an avocado pip moulders in the neck of a jam jar among a clutter of coffee cups, dishwashing liquid and empty bottles. A dead moth, belly-up in a dirty glass, makes me scrunch my nose. I look away. If this were my house, I'd keep it nice.

Squeaking to mark each grinding rotation, a wash line turns in the breeze. Sindi slinks over and frees a raggedy T-shirt from its pegs. She holds it up against her. *FIFA World Cup* is printed in large letters across the front.

I sniff. Dog kaka litters the yard. I play a mental game of join-the-dots, my eyes leaping from turd to turd until I sight two plastic bowls, too yellow and happy for the place. One is half-filled with water, filmy with dust, the other with dry pellets. I glance at the door. There is a small flap at the bottom, not big enough for a pit bull or a Rottweiler – but mini-mutts are yappers, alarm dogs worse than police sirens for bringing the domestic out to see what's up.

I turn to Sindi. She's spotted the bowls and is moving towards them. At the window, she stops and looks in. The glass is a still pond broken only by her reflection, a ghost girl watching. She sinks to her knees and lifts a bowl to her lips. Water spills from the corners of her mouth and slides off the matted wool of her coat. She drinks half the water, then takes a fistful of pellets. They crunch like chicken bones in her teeth.

We used to share. Everything was one for me, one for you. On payday, Mama would bring home a quart of Black Label for her and Next-Door-Auntie and a packet of slap chips for us. We'd rip the greasy bag and savour the vinegar-soft, salty chips, one for me, one for you. Even the last lick of the bag we split, half-half. While all the other kids rolled oranges along the ground until the insides were a squash of juice and pulp they could suck through a hole, me and Sindi peeled the skin, stripped the spongy pith and divided the segments, one for me, one for you.

We stole sweets from Joe's shop. I leaned on the counter asking him stupid questions while Sindi stole up and down the aisles, sticking rolls of Triple-X and Lifesavers into her pockets. One time, she pushed a whole packet of Sparkles up her sleeve. She looked like she'd grown a goitre like the one on Gogo Nkosi's neck.

Sitting on our bed we divided our sweets, one for me, one for you. We split them by colour: orange, purple, green, yellow, red; any that didn't come out in twos we'd collect in a Consol jar. We didn't stick anything in our mouths that didn't have a twin, wasn't a one for me, one for you.

Remembering happy days brings me low. I drift over to the steps by the door and sit down. I stare at my baby-dolls, at the dust-clogged pattern of teardrops cut into the toes, and listen to Sindi's stomach growl. The sound hollows me out.

"Sisi's eating Epol, one for me and one for you."

She looks up, stops chewing.

"Sorry, Sisi," I whisper, ashamed of my song. "I was just teasing."

But it's not me she's looking at. The skin at the base of my skull pricks, sending a spike of cold down my spine. Slow, I turn my head. The flap on the dog-door points at us like an accusing finger, and the shaggy head of a white Maltese poodle pokes through.

I wave my hands. "Shoo," I say, "Shoo!"

Sindi hisses, spitting bits of stolen pellets. The Maltese bares its teeth. Eyes fixed on the dog, Sindi digs into the bowl, takes a handful of pellets and drops them into her pocket. The dog growls. She narrows her eyes, reaches into the bowl again.

"Sisi," I warn, but it's too late. The dog rockets forward. Sindi throws up her hands up to defend her face and the dog sinks needle teeth into the soft flesh of her palm. Her arms flap, but the dog is all over her and she loses her balance. Pellets scatter across the yard as the bowl is sent into a spin. The water bowl flips, but neither Sindi nor the dog notice. The dog snarls and bites. Sindi kicks and yells.

I run around waving my hands, but it does nothing to help. Their coats blur black and white and I'm thinking this is the end, the dog will rip her throat, when Sindi's foot connects. The dog yelps. A strange liquid sound that makes everything stop.

The dog takes a few wobbling steps, whimpers and sits down; but just when I think that dog is going to fall over dead, it jumps up again and shoots through the pet flap into the house, tail between its legs.

I want to get out of there, but Sindi doesn't seem in any rush. She dusts dog shit from her coat, carefully wiping the wool with the stolen T-shirt, then bends to gather the scattered pellets. Blood runs down the inside of her hand and drips off her fingertips, freckling the concrete. I scan the yard for somewhere to wash the wound, but there are no taps, and all that is left of the water from the dog's bowl is a damp patch on the concrete.

Long-Dead Worm Dinner

There was a time I used to dream, curled up warm in Mama's house that smelled of paraffin, Vicks VapoRub and Vaseline. A time I'd press my face into Sindi's neck and breathe in the smells that clung to her hair, spicy as the air in the takeaway where Mustafa sold slap chips and bunny chows and Black Label quarts wrapped in yesterday's newspaper. A time I'd close my eyes and drift, like a paper boat floating in rainwater currents between the pavement and the road. Drift into the soft mouth of sleep, where sweet dreams waited.

Now, I close my eyes and disappear. I close my eyes and I am gone and being gone feels like forever, though I never left at all.

We walk all day, tramping down the emergency lane. Trucks thunder by. We march past vacant lots bristling with scrubby grass, rusting cans and broken beer bottles. Sindi only stops to watch the evening rush hour. Even then, she stays standing, halfway up the embankment, mumbling, "Emi, oru, abiku, O." When the first cars shake loose she's off again.

By the time the roads unclog, Mama Moon is on the rise, but she's sucked her belly in and the night pours over us like fresh tar. Cat's-eyes, lumed up by the headlights of passing cars, stretch into forever like rows of licked lime Sparkles. One for me, one for you.

"Sisi, stop," I wail at the dark and the passing cars and Mama Moon. The soles of my baby-dolls feel like they're sticking to the road. I struggle to put one foot in front of the other, step after step after step. "Stop, stop, stop," I cry, frost-bitten, bone-tired. She keeps walking, but my legs are like lead, dead-dead.

Mist rises from the cooling concrete. Twisting white vapours swirl around my ankles until I can't see my feet. Soon that milky sea reaches my knees, trailing ice along my skin. I think of the deep earth in winter and my head fills with cold and damp and I want to lie down and sleep forever. I close my eyes and, in the dark space inside myself, I see a bare bulb swing, flickering on, flickering off. I follow its shadowy arc back to before. Mama is crying and Sindi stands by the door, wide-eyes. And then they're gone and I'm alone.

I open my eyes. "Sisi," I call, but my voice is mouse-squeak small. Memories flash and fade. With every step Sindi takes, another piece of me disappears until she is so far away I hardly remember her.

Something buzzes in the soles of my feet. I frown at the dark curve of road. The ground rumbles as if a giant truck is hammering down the highway, but the road's dark.

"It's the King of the Road, little sister." I hear Ben's voice in my ear, but no one's there. "He's got a belly long as the highway and five lanes wide, and no matter how much he eats he's always hungry. You better run."

I look down and will my feet to move. I don't want the King of the Road to eat me like roadkill, like an accident victim, but fear has made me lame. A hooter whines through the night. Passing headlights leave me blinded by white spots. I push my thumbs into my eye-sockets, then squint into the dark. A man stands in the middle of the highway, behind the barrier that separates the cars going west from the cars going east. He's a shadow, but his eyes are like coals in an oil drum. He holds my stare and heat pours into me. My toes zing with pins and needles and the road lets go.

I dash up the embankment and I don't stop running until I reach the top. The mournful warning of another car draws my eye back to the man. He drops over the barrier and stands on the same side as me. I scan the grey belly of the highway. Headlights float above the road like disconnected ghosts.

I can't tear my eyes away as he darts across, long legs running lopsided, veering left, veering right. The car cuts close, speeding-speeding. He's roadkill, I think, another soul sacrificed to the road's hungry King. Even from up high I can hear the King's stomach grumble. I close my eyes and plug my ears.

When I look again, the man is safe behind the yellow line. He gives me a narrow look and takes off up the road. I follow along the embankment.

The man has a strange way of walking: he takes long strides and careens from side to side, as if one of his legs is shorter than the other. And he keeps up a constant conversation with someone invisible, nodding like he's listening and pausing like he's considering the answers to questions. He's loony and I mock him, "Loon Man, Loon Man, your legs are lopsiiided!" He pretends he can't hear me, even though I know he can – he keeps glancing my way with his heat-projecting eyes.

Ahead of us, a girl walks into the train of Mama Moon's glowing indigo dress. She walks like she's asleep and dreaming. Loon Man calls out to her and she swings around.

"Sindi!" I yell, relieved to have found her, though for a moment my head is a fog of confusion as to how I lost her, if she was lost at all. I want to ask her where she's been, but she's focused on Loon Man. The air between them is tense. Sindi's shoved her hands into her pockets and pushed them wide, so she looks bigger than she is. Looking at Loon Man, bent double, wheezing, hands flapping like dying fish, I wonder why she bothers.

Loon Man's old. His face has collapsed in the middle like he has no teeth. A thin grey straggle spills from under his sooty trilby and sits unevenly on the shoulders of his trench coat. The coat gives him bulk, but his hands tell me that under it he's skinny-skinny. Still, he's tall, and his brogues are polished to a mean shine. What's a man with nice threads doing walking the highway at night?

As his breath slows, Loon Man straightens up and the years fall off him. I frown, trying to focus on his face. It's like watching a TV being fine-tuned, the screen warping back and forth. His face shifts through a lifetime – young, old and every age in between – but always his eyes remain the same. Hot cosmic eyes, deep as the moonless sky. His face fixes around sixty, but the shifting has left me dizzy. Loon Man slides a hand into his coat and Sindi cocks her pockets.

He smiles. "My child, I know you've got trigger fingers, but you don't have a trigger. Still, I understand where you're coming from." His voice reminds me of Next-Door-Auntie's boyfriend, too smooth for his mouth. Mama said Next-Door-Auntie's boyfriend spoke like an American televangelist, and that all preachers were tsotsis, you could tell by the designer suit. I cut narrow eyes at Loon Man, to let him know I've got his number.

"I'm not going to hurt you, my child. See?" He pulls out a hip flask that glows in the lunar light like the embers of a dying fire. "Just something to keep warm," he says, raising the copper flask to his lips. He knocks back a slug, shuts his eyes and shakes his head. His cheeks sound loose. "Church brew. Good stuff, blood of the Lord." He winks and with a flick of his wrist offers the flask to Sindi. She draws her right hand from her pocket and holds it out.

"That's fair," he says, dropping the flask into her palm.

As her fingers close round it, she steps out of his reach. Sindi doesn't trust men, not even Joe Saviour, whom we've known since we were four days old. She sniffs at the neck of the flask. Her nose wrinkles but she takes a sip. It makes her cough. She hacks until she doubles over. The flask tilts in her hand. A drop of Loon Man's golden brew splashes onto the road. One for the King.

"Watch it, that's the blood of Jesus." He snatches the flask as Sindi spits. The snail slides off the toe of his brogue, leaving a glimmering trail.

Sindi holds up her hands. "Sss_asorry, mm_man, sorry."

She backs away and I watch, wide-eyes, expecting his fist, but he just throws back his head and laughs. He laughs and laughs like it's the funniest thing that's ever happened, gesturing at his toe with the open flask. He doesn't spill a drop. At first, Sindi frowns at the sight of Loon Man playing the fool, but after a while his laughing catches and she smiles. I haven't seen my sisi smile since . . . I can't remember the last time. I hug my shoulders, wishing he'd stop. His laughing shakes me. It twists the world. It makes me fade and blur.

"Go away!" I scream.

The sudden silence throbs.

"We shouldn't hang around, my child," he says, pocketing the flask. "It's not safe." As he adjusts the lapels of his coat, the headlights of a passing car catch a copper gleam in his seams. Loon Man is a Believer, a tuned-in follower of the Black Preacher. "Joshua Piepper." He holds out his hand and fires his name into the night. "First Disciple of the One True Church. Pure of blood, pure of spirit."

"Loopy loopy Loon Man," I jeer, motioning circles at the side of my head.

"Sss_aSindisiwe." My sisi's fingertips graze his.

He frowns as people do when they notice her stutter for the first time. "Sindisiwe," he says, looking thoughtful. "Sindisiwe." He repeats her name as if she and it are two pieces of a puzzle. Before he can fit them together, she turns her back on him and walks away.

"Where are you going, Sindisiwe? Wait. You don't have to tell me. Looking at you, no offence, you look lost. You're looking for a family. I'd say you've got no one – but seek and ye shall find, the Lord says.

"Tell you a secret," he says when he catches up to her. "I can read people. It's a gift. Praise the Lord for it. I look at you and I know, you're heading for The Ascension. The Ascension of the Mothers for the New Mankind? Am I right? You know what I'm talking about."

Silence.

"Okay, I understand, you're nervous. And who could blame you, a young woman can't know what to expect. You worry that you won't be good enough. But I'm here to tell you, all God's creatures are perfect, the Lord made you perfect and you are. Am I right, my child, you want to be saved?" He pauses and pats his heart. It takes me a second to figure out he's checking for his flask. "Your name means saved. Sindisiwe, it means saved. Did you know that?"

They walk under an overpass. I hurry across the top, reaching the other side just as they emerge.

Loon Man is still jabbering. "I know I met you for a reason. The Lord sent you to me, so I could lead you to salvation. That makes me happy, for that is my purpose. Saving good girls and keeping them pure so they can be the Mothers for the New Mankind. So few untainted souls left in the world, so few."

He looks up at me and frowns, as if remembering something. "You are pure? I mean, your blood, it's clean?' He clears his throat and answers for her: "Of course it is. I can see into people and in you I see a pure heart, pure blood, a pure soul."

Sindi stops walking. She looks at Loon Man as if she's only just seen him. "What did you ss_asay?" Her voice crackles like a badly tuned radio.

Joshua Piepper looks at the road. "I'm sorry," he says, hunching his shoulders to ninety years old. "An old man can put his foot in it. I didn't mean anything by it."

Sindi narrows her eyes.

"My child, if you've got the sickness, don't worry. The Lord has a plan for us all, have faith . . ." He trails off, sounding disappointed. "The Lord has a plan."

She kicks the ground. "Before, what did you ss_asay?"

"Before?" He shrugs. "I said you should join our church."

She shakes her head, her hands balling into fists at her sides.

"Calm down, child. All I said was that you have a pure heart and soul, nothing meant to offend."

She blinks and the darkness, lifted earlier by his lunatic laughter, comes crashing down. In the faint moonlight I can just make out her eyes. Dead eyes. Colder than broken glass. "Soul." She exhales the word, so quiet only my twin ears catch the sound.

"My child, where are you going?"

Sindi clutches a clump of grass to steady her balance and turns to face him. We're already halfway up the embankment, but the old man hasn't lifted his soles off the road. Ahead, the dark wheel of the off-ramp winds around the hill and disappears into the night, reappearing high above us as Voortrekker Road, bright with streetlights and straight as a runway.

"Let's keep going, we can be at the church tomorrow morning. It's not far, just past Nasrec in the old refinery. My people are on the move, I know we'll get lucky and catch a ride. I foresee it. We'll be there tonight." Joshua Piepper pulls up the sleeve of his coat and brings his wrist close to his face. The eerie green glow of his watch light sinks deep crags into the flesh around his eyes. Loon Man the ghost.

The old man's fresh, but we've been walking since dawn and it's so late now I have to bend my neck all the way back to see Mama Moon. Soon, the sun's going to creep over the horizon and people will begin to leak onto the streets. While the night still wraps us in her blanket, we can shut our eyes for few hours in peace.

Sindi raises her hand to wave goodbye. Loon Man twitches. He looks at Sindi, looks at me, checks his watch again, face glowing green. "There's evil up there, my child."

I glance over my shoulder, wondering where the crazy from this morning went. Nothing moves. The wind whispers against my skin. "Leave him, it's cold," I murmur.

"Sss_asomething bad on the road," she tells him. "I s_asaw him this mm_morning."

She turns and continues the steep climb. After a moment, he follows. No one wants to walk the road alone. There are people who do, but they're sad and mad and talk to invisibles, warding off loneliness in the company of ghosts.

Loon Man's nervous twitching stops when we step into the milky glow of the streetlights, as if he thinks light can protect him. We follow the road as it crosses above the dark highway towards the racecourse. In the distance, the neon sign of the Casbah Roadhouse sparks and goes out. There's always something fresh in the bins at Casbah at closing time. Usually, we'd head straight there, but Sindi keeps going until she gets to the patch of grass by the racecourse gates. We once sat for hours on the concrete bench here, waiting for Mama and Next-Door-Auntie to win big so we could go home. They lost so much they couldn't pay the taxi fare. That was the first time we walked the highway.

Sindi leans against that same bench and yawns. I wonder if she's ashamed to go through the bins in front of Loon Man, or if she just isn't hungry. For the first time since we left the townhouses this morning, she examines her hand. Already, the flesh around the wound is red and swollen. She prods the area, sucks her teeth.

"You okay, child?"

Sindi nods and puts her hands in her pockets. Joshua Piepper takes out his flask. He offers it to Sindi but her eyes are closed. For a while he sits sipping at it, staring at nothing. Sindi's breathing slows, deepening the stillness. It's so quiet that when he speaks, I jump.

"Why are you here?" His voice like boots on wet gravel.

Long time after, when it begins to seem like the question never was, she pats the green blades. "The grass."

"No, my child, not here on this patch of God's ground, that's not what I'm talking about. I'm asking a bigger thing. Why are you *here*?"

The silence makes a hole in the night and it sucks me in.

"I was on the street too, long time ago now, but years, many years, so many I can't give you a number, but it was long enough for me to grow old. Truth be told, I lived between the streets and prison." He lifts his sleeve. The number 28 is tattooed on the inside of his wrist.

Sindi shifts, her eyes flicking behind their lids. She's too tired to be interested in bedtime stories. And me? I don't usually listen to other people's stories – everyone has a story, I have stories of my own – but his voice pulls me away from the silent hole.

"Everyone comes from somewhere. There's a beginning to every legend, some place we call home. Don't matter if it's a palace or a shack."

I've heard this sermon before, at Saviour's Pit Stop.

"There's very few that's born to the street. Even the street kids, they've got family out there. Whether they care or not, that's a different story. Point is, you've got to start somewhere to end up here. The in-between, from there to here, that's what I'm asking. Why are you here?"

A snore rolls in Sindi's throat. Loon Man doesn't seem to notice. He sips from his flask, his voice dipping until I can no longer follow – his lips seem to swallow the words just out of his mouth. Keeping mouse quiet, I slip closer and sit down on the bench.

He stops talking and frowns at me. "Why are *you* here? Why? Why? What do *you* want?" He reaches into his coat. His hand rests on his heart a minute, then draws out a piece of string tied around his neck. There's something on the end of it, something black, and he rubs it between his thumb and finger, muttering like a crazy.

"Now flee from youthful lusts, and pursue righteousness!" he shouts, making me jump. He lifts the flask to his ear and shakes it, testing the level. "Look at me now, I'm one of God's generals, but once I was a general of another kind. I was nineteen when I went to prison for the first time. I was a boy, but I thought I was a big man. Prison makes you realise you're nothing, and if you want to survive, you better find your balls." Loon Man slumps under the weight of his memories. He's getting like Mama on payday after a few quarts of Black Label. "I spent twelve years in prison. I went in a burglar with a two-year sentence, came out a killer. To survive, you follow orders. They tell you to kill, you kill. God was with me. Even as I shed the blood of another man." He stabs the air with an invisible knife. "I came out and I was going straight. Wife took me back and I did okay for a while."

He trails off and just sits there, staring at the past and sipping from his flask. He's beginning to bore me. I look at Sindi and wonder what she's dreaming. I long to sleep, to dream the same dreams as my sisi, but I'm afraid of the dark, of the empty place I go to whenever I close my eyes.

"In his pride the wicked does not seek Him, in all his thoughts there is no room for God!" Loon Man's roar knocks me off the bench.

"Janine got pregnant. Me, a father. I was happy, I was, but the pressure – didn't think I could do a kid. In prison I ran from nobody; out in the world, I was scared of a baby. The night Sonny was born, I started to run. But you can't run from the life God gives you, you can't run from your legend. If you try, He will find a way to turn you, to make you pay."

"Scaredy-cat man, scaredy-cat man, prison don't bite but your baby can," I sing, getting back on the bench.

"All I took was my gun, my phone and a bottle of whisky. I checked myself into the Carlton Hotel. A room on the twenty-eighth floor – twenty-eight, to remind me. I took a shower to wash the soot from my skin. My phone started ringing. I didn't answer, but Janine kept calling and I thought, I owe her a goodbye. She told me about my boy. She said he had ten fingers, ten toes, she said they were so small but they were perfect. Tiny and perfect and blue."

Loon Man stops talking. The silence buzzes, tense, waiting. I cling to the bench.

"Either make the tree good, and his fruit good; or else make the tree corrupt and his fruit corrupt, for the tree is known by his fruit." He slaps his thigh and I snap up straight, but I don't fall. "I don't remember anything else, just the sound of the air rushing in my ears as I fell. You know what it's like falling buck naked through the air, my child, balls slapping against your arse? The ground was far away, didn't seem to be getting any closer. I wanted to yell – not scream, I wasn't scared. I wanted to shout. I was angry, but when I opened my mouth my cheeks filled up like plastic bags flapping in the wind. God silenced me."

Loon Man sinks into his past, droning on about Sonny and twenty-eight floors and a life of sin, the words sliding round his mouth and coming out slurred and broken. He's mumbling-shouting, raving-moaning, crying for poor Sonny who never stood a chance. Then, sudden as a finger click, he snaps out of it. "Listen, my child, God has plans for all of us. I fell twenty-eight floors and when I opened my eyes again I was nobody. The next twenty-eight years I spent on the street. I didn't have the stomach to rob or kill any more. I wandered like Christ in the desert, looking for salvation. Almost thirty years. But I can offer it to you now, I can save you a lifetime of pain. Come with me, become one of my children and birth a Pure Child for God."

He reaches over, puts his hand on Sindi's shoulder and starts praying. "Jesus, save this child, bring her into our fold. Let her be a mother of your children, bless her clean blood and fertile womb. Keep her safe from unclean men, from infidels and Satan-worshippers. Save this child from the devil, don't let her wander the streets for thirty years. Save her from my pain. I wasn't strong, no Lord, I wasn't strong like Jesus. I deserved my suffering. I gave in to temptation, I gave in to the devil. Don't let this child escape You like I escaped You."

I dance to Loon Man's gospel raving. I sway and stamp and clap my hands, just like Sunday. "No Lord," I shout when he shouts. "Save me," I shout when he shouts. "Blessed be," I shout when he shouts.

Then, rapid as it came, the raving stops and he shoots me a look. "They say there's no place in heaven for babies with no name," he says. "My boy died before I gave him a name. Tell me, demon, do you know my Sonny?"

I shake my head and give him a wide grin, stretching my lips so far back my teeth gleam against the night. I jive, still full of gospel. "Sonny's dead, Sonny's long-dead worm dinner, Sonny's dead, long dead."

Loon Man narrows his eyes. "You," he says, pointing at me, his hand wrapped in string with the pendant tucked into his palm, "work out your own salvation with fear and trembling." He begins to pray, so soft at first

I can't hear the words; then, ever so slow, the volume rises. His words stroke me, wind around me, tie me up. I'm caught in the singing, swaying-swaying, and I don't suss his game until the ropes are halfway up my legs.

"You tricked me!" I shriek, but he keeps praying. I wriggle. I squirm, but his prayers are binding. The hole made of silence opens wide, like a hungry mouth coming to swallow me. "Please, I'll be a good girl."

He holds out his pendant. It spins on tattered string.

"That's just broken string," I say.

He glances at the string, taking his eyes off me for a second. I begin to laugh. I laugh and laugh until my laughing fills me up and I balloon, big as a house, big as the world and when I pop, the dawn breaks, icy and grey.

Bad Things

Sindi lies curled on the grass, frost lapping her coat. I kiss her cracked lips, dead-man blue, and she opens her eyes. She stares at the tiny ice crystals clinging to the grass, focusing on nothing, focusing on nowhere.

Dawn bathes the streets in a clinical light that reminds me of the corridors in Bara Hospital, late at night.

"Don't leave me," I begged them, "take me home, don't leave me alone." But they left me there, with all the people skinny-limbed and dying.

Sindi sits up and rubs her face. She looks around, brow creased, as if she's trying to remember if Loon Man was dream or reality.

"Everything's a matter of which way you're looking, and which day you're looking from," I tell her. It's true. What was real yesterday is today's dream, and it works backwards too. If you're lucky, you dream good things.

We're ready to walk when something catches her eye. I follow her gaze and there on the grass in a tangle is Loon Man's necklace. She picks it up and holds it in front of her face. A black cross dangles from the frayed string. The cross is hand-carved, the rough wood darkened by the rub of oily fingers. It looks like a shadow suspended in the air, a cross-shaped hole in the day. Even the beaten copper eye, set into its centre, eats light.

The cross spins as the tangle unwinds, back and forth, trying to decide which way to settle. It finally stops with its back to Sindi, looking at me. Inside me, in my guts, I know. Bad things come.

Three days we walk, going nowhere. During the morning rush hour on the second day, a lady with bloodshot lips and eyes winds down her window and shakes a clear plastic bag containing a sandwich and an apple at us.

"Where you going?" She smiles, displaying lipstick-smeared too-white teeth. Sindi takes the bag and sticks her hand through the window, pointing at a bottle of water. The woman shrinks back, afraid.

"Please," Sindi says, remembering her manners. The woman hands it over, winds up her window and stares straight ahead, as if she's afraid we're going to ask for more.

Sindi mutters her thanks to the glass, walks on. Later, when the cars are zooming again, she sits on the embankment and eats the sandwich. The apple she pockets for later.

On the third day, we come to the fence of the Reading Car Yard. It used to be a golf course until the government bought the grounds and turned it into a scrap yard for all the petrol cars they seized on D-Day. They fenced it in and posted guards in towers, but most of the cars still ended up back on the streets as b-diesel junks. Then some government clever wised up. Now the towers that punctuate the empty sky are rusting, and nobody watches over the pack of dogs they keep just hungry enough to bite.

We sit halfway up the embankment and wait for the rush hour, but it doesn't come and we know it's Saturday: Saturday and Sunday, the roads don't clog. If we were any good at counting, we'd know they were coming. But the days stretch without end; dawn comes, night descends, nothing happens, we lose count. MondayTuesdayWednesdaySaturday who cares. It wasn't always like that.

I stare at the highway winding round the city, at the trucks that work seven days, all hours. They slide onto the N3 and rush to the coast, leaving us behind. It's far from here to the sea, but we were there one time: on New Year's Eve, the beach jammed and crowded. I held Sindi's hand as the waves rushed between my legs and tried to suck me under. I want to go there now, hitch a ride with a trucker back to when we were eleven and still happy, but my memories pull back like the waves and all I can remember is the salt on my lips and the feel of Sindi's hand, slippery as a fresh-caught fish. And then it's gone, and thinking of the sea makes my mind black.

I stand behind my sisi like her disobedient shadow, staring-staring at the billboards mounting the roadside, windows into lives we'll never have; staring-staring at the ragged city sky and the cardboard-and-corrugated shacks where only children live because everyone else has died. And the clouds.

Sindi used to think that clouds were spookasem that had been blown off the stick by the wind. Next-Door-Auntie laughed when she told her that. "Ag child, that the dumbest thing you ever said. If clouds are made from candyfloss," and she pointed at the white filaments scraped across the blue, "why don't the rain taste sweet?"

Sindi stamped on Next-Door-Auntie's foot. Mama saw and she caught a slap. We ran away to the veld and sulked for the rest of the day. Later, when the sun went underground and the clouds turned pink, she said *see*, but I could tell she no longer believed.

It hardly rains any more. The cirrus clouds that wrinkle this faded sky are mean and meaningless. They leave the city to suffocate under the dust that creeps into everywhere, powdering our cheeks until we look like ghosts. With each passing season, circling this road, I feel how it sucks at our juice. We are being slow-baked, hardened like tar. In summer the heat plucks our flesh, stealing sweat and blood and tears; in winter the cold freeze-dries our bones. When we pee, if we pee at all, it splashes up onto our shoes. The soil doesn't want our water. There is nothing this earth wants from us, and we have nothing left to give.

The sun climbs the sky. Noon and too hot. Less than a kilometre from where we sit, the shadow of the overpass spills onto the road like a purple pond.

"Shade, Sisi," I whisper, but my voice is a breathless breeze. Sindi sits still as a lizard on a rock. Sweat beads on her top lip and her dusty lids sink over fever-yellow eyes.

In the distance, a motorbike breaks the flat line of the horizon. The rider hunches into his machine, going so fast the roar of the engine thunders over the concrete and warps the still air into a watery mirage after the bike has passed us by. Sindi hardly notices. A cloud blocks the sun and turns the air cold. Sindi drops her head onto her knees. I can almost taste the sweetness of her sweat on my tongue, a faint whiff like roadkilled dogs baking in the sun. Then the cloud moves on and for a time it's hot again.

The shadows are long when she lifts her head, face puffy from the stuffiness between her legs. She holds out her dog-bitten hand, pulpy as a rotten plum. She prods it, pushing and squeezing her palm until the pain stretches lips over gums and her fingers spasm. Nothing she does, not bending or pushing, not pulling or pressing, can make the claw back into a hand. I stare at the claw-hand that's too old and deformed to belong to my sisi but pokes from the sleeve of her coat, stare at the fingers that pulling can't make straight, stare at the black dog-tooth pits oozing.

And inside me, in my guts, I know. Bad things come.

The dusky light that borders night flattens the city and reduces the squatter camp across the way to a single row of shacks. Smoke from cooking fires winds upwards; the spirals twist together until the smoke is too fat and heavy for the air to hold and it sinks back like a sigh onto the low roofs. Cold drops on us.

Sindi's head rests again between her knees. I sit next to her, my palm pressed between her shoulder blades, concentrating on the whispering of her breath and the rising-sinking, rising-sinking of her back.

I watch the shadows move between the shacks: the shades of men drinking and women cooking, the shades of children playing and dogs sniffing. Everything's humming along. The smoke drifts, opening up their lives for me to see; then it wraps them up and hides them away again. The smell of shack life – of burnt wood, of samp sticking to the bottoms of pots, of meat shrinking in a gravy of water and cabbage, of people's shit and dogs' shit and rot and rubbish – drifts across the lanes, ignoring the concrete barrier that separates cars going west from cars going east, and sticks its fingers up my nose. Noises float over the highway and take me home.

Mama squatting by the government tap at the end of our street, talking to Next-Door-Auntie while she scraped plates with her fingers. Behind them, the queue swapping chat while a ten-feathers-chicken tikked at the crumbs of pap Mama flicked from her fingers, running circles whenever she turned on the tap to rinse.

"Whose hen is it?" Someone pointed at ten-feathers with a dirty pan.

"Daai anorexic ding?" The whitey who stood at the junction by the mall every day begging change shook her head. "Looks like Gogo Nkosi's chicken, they all scrawny like that one."

"Looks like Gogo Nkosi," came a shout from the back of the queue. Everyone laughed.

Across the highway, a woman screams. Someone shouts and bangs a pot against the corrugated wall of a shack, and the dogs in the camp pick up the commotion. A shot cracks, and two shadows break free from the haze and run down to the road. They bolt across the lanes, not pausing to look. Without slowing their pace, they vault the concrete barrier and make it almost all the way to our side before a man leaps clear of the line of shacks. In one hand, he holds a gun. He shuffles down the embankment, but he isn't as easy on his feet as the boys. Arms windmilling, he slides the last couple of metres to the road.

"You fucking shits, I'm going to kill you!" he yells, thrusting his hand forward. Gunshot fractures the air.

Sindi's head snaps up. She sees the two boys running up the embankment, she sees the man with the gun. She stands, too quick, and sways as the man fires again. The boys bolt past her. They're fourteen, maybe fifteen, about the same height as us; the one in the front wears a dark, oversized coat that flaps behind him. In the low light, Sindi might look the same to the gunman.

"Run, Sisi!" I yell, and she runs.

The boys are fast. They disappear over the top and we scramble after, not looking back to check if the man with the gun is following. As we crest the ridge, we see the boys pull back the KEEP OUT – GOVT. PROPERTY sign and slip through an open seam in the rusted car-yard fence. The fence rattles as the sign swings back, closing the gap behind them.

The fence stretches for a kilometre. We've walked it before, dragging a stick along the links until the guard dogs came, barking-barking, snapping and snarling. The man with the gun could pick off someone running along it, easy.

Sindi heaves back the sign and slips through the gap, but she doesn't duck low enough and a wire snags in her hair. I bounce on my toes. The man is coming. Clambering over the barrier in the middle of the road, gun tight in his grip. Sindi twists and turns, trying to pull free, but the wire works deeper into the mat of her hair and won't let go.

The gunman is coming.

She grabs her hair and rips it free, leaving a tuft for the wire as a toll. Grunting, she lurches into the scrap yard.

The ground swells around us in uneven mounds and slopes. The earth remembers the shape of the course, though the lawns are long dead and no one plays golf here any more. Ahead, a dark mountain of dumped petrol-cars rises into the deepening night, rusting and rotting, the biggest pile-up I've ever seen.

Sindi stumbles, already struggling for breath. Her skin, slick with sweat, looks plastic. The boys throw her a look and I wonder if they think she's the man with the gun. Behind us, the fence rattles.

"I'm going to get you, hear? I'm going to fucking get you."

I can feel the man's fingers twisting around the gritty wire like they're around my neck. Then, somewhere in the hollow space between the petrol-cars and the fence, the pack begins to bark.

The dogs are coming.

The boys run towards the car-mountain and veer left when they reach the tangle of slumped bumpers and gutted chassis. Sindi leans forward, trying to push herself, faster-faster, but her legs aren't listening and her feet smack the dust slow-mo. We both scan over our shoulders, checking for dogs, checking for the man, and in that second the boys vanish, like they're witchdoctors, spirit people, ghosts.

The pile-up stretches as far as I can see into the dusk. There's no way over, and the way around, left or right, would leave us open to the gun or the dogs. But the boys went left, and they're gone.

Sindi ducks left, hunching as she runs to look for the crawl-space, that magic door the boys have vanished through. The cars are jammed tight, some crushed flat as 2D by the tons of metal above. Each car is like a brick in a wall, the spaces between only big enough to stash a baby.

And the gunman is coming.

Frantic, Sindi starts pushing – pushing the bumpers, the squashed hoods, the doors of the side-on cars; running-running, pushing-pushing, looking for spaces, gaps, big or small, any place wide enough to crawl into and deep enough to hide in.

Because the dogs are coming.

I can hear them, snapping-snarling, and the man, swearing and rattling the fence. Sindi stops. Her breath heaves in, out. She stands, arms at her sides, fists clenched, and faces the wall of cars.

A third shot cracks. A dog yelps. Its life snaps away: in a finger-click it's gone. I hear the brother-dogs, the sister-dogs, crying-crying. Then they're on the move again, away from the fence and the man and the gun. And he's climbing; his weight sends a reverb down the wire.

The gunman is coming.

Sindi looks around, wild; looks left, looks right, looks left, looks up. A shadow shifts. I narrow my eyes. There's a dark gap, four or five metres above us, between a trailer and an old tanker, the round kind for transporting fuel or milk. The circular back-end of the tanker is facing us and juts out a little over the cars. The trailer is jammed into the pile just above, and the container it was carrying tilts at an angle, creating a triangular space: a narrow tunnel too small to stand in but big enough to crawl through on hands and knees. The boys must have gone in there. Maybe it leads all the way through to the other side.

Using bumpers and empty headlight sockets as steps and handholds, Sindi reaches the tanker quick-quick, coming up on its left-hand side. Up close I see it was once painted green, but the paint's faded and the company logo's covered in scabs of rust. On the right, the rungs of a ladder climb the flat back of the tanker. Sindi stretches for it, but it's at least twice as far as she can reach. I scan the grounds. I can't see the man but I feel his madness.

Sindi presses her body against the flat back of the tanker and edges along the bumper, arms stiff, fingers spread, desperate for something to grasp. Don't look down, I think, but halfway across, she does. The world turns.

Sisi's going to fall and the dogs are going to eat her.

A bead of sweat rolls down her face and plummets to the ground.

Sisi's going to fall and the man is going to shoot her.

Sindi lunges for the ladder. For a split second the top half of her body seems to disconnect from her hips. Her fingers graze one rung, then another, and she lifts one foot to give herself the extra reach she needs. As her hand closes over the third rung, her other foot slides off the bumper. She pivots on her wrist and slams into the ladder, yelping like that dog she almost killed. The sound of impact echoes through the hollow length of the trailer. For a moment she hangs, frozen midair; then she twists to face the tanker, settles her feet on the ladder and begins to climb.

I taste my heart as I inch across the bumper, praying the gunman didn't hear her cry out. We're easy targets: Sindi stands out against the pale-green paint like a bird against the sun. I'm sure he's going to pick her off, but she moves with surprising speed, wriggling into the tight space under the container before I reach the ladder. The hole swallows her.

By the time I stick my head into the space behind her, her feet have disappeared. The dark closes in, heavier than night-dark, than normal dark. It has a fatness, as if all the cars pressing down from above have squeezed it into something solid. We crawl into the car mountain like two blind mice. I can't even see the soles of Sindi's boots, though if I move too fast I bump against them. This is a place that has never known light.

The air is soupy with smells. Engine oil and the grit of rust are sharp in my throat. The stink of damp carpets, sun-perished seat leather and rotting foam rubber clots my nostrils like fungus spores. I can even taste the cigarette butts in the ashtrays. The space becomes tighter the further in we go. There are dents in the tanker and the unevenness makes the blackness shrink and swell. As we inch along, the tunnel pushes down, getting tighter and tighter until it scrapes against the top of my head. Soon, I'm forced to lie flat on my belly and pull myself along the porous metal, the skin of my palms hot with friction. I can't hear the dogs barking or the man shouting any more. Nothing penetrates the dense air. Even Sindi's breathing is thick, as if someone's stuffed a wet cloth into her mouth.

My head bumps against the soles of her boots. I lie there, waiting for her to move, ears straining against the ink. For a long time, there is only silence. Then I hear scratching, small at first, but rapidly increasing into a frantic scrabbling, fingernails on rust, and the stink of Sindi's panic closes around me and I know: the boys didn't come this way.

In the dark there's no way to tell how much time has passed, or if the hours move fast or slow. How do we know the clock is still ticking, or if the cogs are stuck and the hands, twitching-twitching, count the same second over and over?

In the dark it is cold. The icy night air seeps into the scrap mountain, between bumpers that jut at odd angles, through sagging windscreens, over bonnets and roofs where rust has eaten away hope and shine and Mama Moon's light glints off broken glass. The cold presses in, layering chill over chill until the metal shrinks and groans. It sinks towards us. When it reaches the tanker beneath us and the trailer above us, it swaps frost for body heat.

In the dark sounds are big and small, there and not there. The metal creaks and moans and complains. Our tomb speaks, saying things we don't want to understand, but do. It tells us it's easy to crawl into its belly. It says there is no way out. Around us things scratch, fall silent, scratch. Tiny nails scrape, tiny teeth nibble, small creatures burrow into the rotten seat stuffing. The mountain is alive. The mountain is dead.

I forget Sindi.

She's so silent, drifting in, drifting out, asleep, awake, afraid, afraid, dreaming-dreaming. The dark's a swamp. It drowns my mind and steals my memories. I try to hold on, but it's more than I am.

After a while, the dark pressing down on me begins to feel good, like when Mama squashed my face between her breasts and held me there until I couldn't breathe. The dark feels safe. I close my eyes.

I forget me.

Follow You to Your Drowning

"Fphst."

I sit on the bumper of a yellow electric, blinking. From my perch I can see an ocean of dirt rolling out beneath me, shadowed by the skeletal trees that push skywards like cracks. To my left, pines hunch in a sombre clump. I blink again. The light's so sharp I can see the crisscross mesh of pine needles carpeting the ground. To the right, the highway arcs against the horizon like a grey rainbow. The sight of it makes me feel empty inside. I look away, not wanting to feel like that when I'm on top of the world, light and free, floating-floating. I wonder how I got to be sitting on a sun-faded plastic bumper, leaning against the dented bonnet of a car. I turn my mind round and round, but all I find is a space, a big black hole, and it makes me feel bad.

"Fphst."

The noise sounds like someone with no teeth trying to whistle. I look down. Below me, two boys stand on the edge of an old tanker. One boy has his head shoved into the space between a trailer and some cars. The other boy wears a long coat. I stare at them, the funny feeling in my gut getting bigger.

"Hey bra, let's waai, maybe she not in there," says the boy with the coat.

"She is," says the other, pulling his head back into the sunlight, "I can see her feet." He wipes his nose on the back of his hand then pulls his beanie over his ears and sticks his head back in. "Fphst."

"That nywana dead, bra, you think of that?"

"How'd she die in here, huh?" His voice sounds like the second bounce of an echo. "No bra, she's alive, I see her move."

"Ag, you 'magined it, she dead bra, los it or we gonna miss last dish."

Beanie Boy pulls his head out. He shrugs. "Let's waai then, I'm hungry."

But they stand like statues, waiting-waiting.

I lose interest in them and scan the sky. A few blushing cirrus clouds streak against the blue. The sight of them makes the black in my head swirl and stirs something at the bottom of me. I kick the heels of my baby-dolls against the bumper. The hole spins, faster, faster. I feel sick. I think I might vomit. I open my mouth and a word pops out: "Spookasem."

It floats in front of my face like a tiny sunset cloud. I stare at it. I want to put it in my mouth, eat it, roll it around on my tongue so I can say it again, again, again. I clap my hands over it, but when I open my palms the fluffy cloud is gone and all that remains is a squashed mat of pink fibre no bigger than a piece of chewing gum. I put it in my mouth. A burst of burnt sugar fizzles on my tongue and is gone. I burp.

On the tanker below, the boys look at each other. "You hear that?" asks Beanie Boy. Sticking his head back into the space, he shouts, "Sista, can't you speak?" He pauses to listen, but there's no reply. "She can't speak, maybe she can't speak."

"If she can't speak, she's dead. Let's waai," says the boy with the coat.

"Sweet, waai. What about Ma Wilma? What you gonna tell her? No, sorry Ma, we chafa a girl and now we lost her. Ma Wilma going to be kwata."

"Aggg! I don't know why you told the ouledi we got a nywana in the first place. Why you do that, huh? Move, let me look."

They shuffle sideways, swap places. The boy in the long coat sticks his head into the space. "Okay, sista, no worries, we going to get you out!" he shouts. He takes off his coat. Without it, he looks skinny-skinny and too tall. He gives it to the other boy, then wriggles into the space until only his feet stick out. I watch the bottom of his shoes kick up and down, like swimmer's feet. Swimming through cars, a swimmer in a car dump. The thought of it makes me laugh.

"Marlboro, pull bra." His voice is muffled, metallic, like one of the rotten cars is speaking.

I laugh harder. The laughing catches and I can't stop. I laugh so hard I begin to cry. Tears roll down my cheeks, dripping off the end of my face. I watch them drop, like tiny stars falling from the sky. When they hit the ground, they explode. *Sisi's going to fall and the . . .*

I stop. The weird feeling in my guts is back. I clutch my belly. Something stirs, pushes against my hands. It's like I've swallowed a snake and it's trying to chew its way out. "Help me," I try to shout, but my voice is hoarse. I can only manage a whisper.

"Rilexa, sista, we helping you."

Below me, the boys begin to pull something from the dark hole. They work as if the thing is fragile. Maybe they're helping a butterfly from a cocoon – but if you do that, the butterfly will never be strong enough to fly. And if a butterfly can't fly, it will fall and shatter on the ground.

Sisi's going to fall and the . . .

A girl emerges. They sit her down on the ledge and hold on to her shoulders. I watch them for a while, relieved that she isn't a butterfly. After a few minutes, the boys begin to climb down, lowering the girl between them. The snake in my belly squirms. I push down harder, trying to squash it, but each time they drop a car, my abdomen jerks like it's trying to follow. It jerks so hard I fear I might fall. I let go of my belly and wedge my fingers into the crack between the bonnet and the windscreen, but the pull is strong, dragging me down.

I look at the clouds and the trees and the grey rainbow. I want to stay up here, float above the world forever. The ground is bad, I've been there before. Down there it's dark and cold and you can hear things scratching. Then the girl looks up, straight at me, and I see her face, sharp as the pine needles. The face is my face, mine but not mine. Her name creeps up my throat onto my tongue. I whisper it, "Sindisiwe," and saying it makes me know my own name.

Her gaze, hot and spiky, pricks my mind slowly – like a pin stuck through sellotape into the skin of a balloon. My memories hiss out and I begin to know myself. In her head and in her heart she holds the pieces of me, and her gaze glues me back together.

Then she looks away and, with a last glance at the twilight dusting the blue, I slide to the ground.

Streetlights flicker through the trees. The boys lead us past the mountain of cars towards the quiet suburban streets that lie on the other side. Three guard dogs come from nowhere and walk alongside us, but the boys don't seem bothered. The dogs whine, lonely as lost souls, and lick the boys' fingers.

"Chila," the one in the coat says, "these hounds been well fed." He laughs like he's cracked a joke.

The boys are the same two who ran from the shacks. They're called Booysen and Marlboro, though Marlboro says his name like he's not so sure of it. He's the one wearing the beanie. Booysen, in the coat, is taller and looks older. He has a circle tattooed on his neck, just above the collar.

"Next time you need a spot to hide, sista, check out this g-string," he says, bouncing on the boot of a white BMW. There's a click and the latch releases. They let Sindi sit on the mouldy carpet in the boot for a while, "to get straight". She sits with her legs hanging over the bumper and her head in her hands. Her right hand looks like a boxer's glove, but the boys, if they notice, say nothing about it.

Marlboro paces, glancing sideways at Sindi. I can tell she makes him nervous. He takes off his beanie and runs his fingers through grimy blond hair. It stands straight up, stark and surprising against his tanned skin. He sits next to Sindi a second, then springs up again. He bounces on the balls of his ragged sneaks a while, then leans forward and wipes his sleeve across the scratched white paint of the BMW. "This was my daddy's car."

Booysen laughs. "Sho! You, bra? You think your daddy's a fat cat now? You wish." He gets Marlboro in a neck hold and rubs his knuckles across his head.

Marlboro struggles free, cheeks flushing red. "Fo sho, I know the plate. This is my daddy's car, from way back, when I was a laaitie."

Booysen leans against the BMW, pulls a packet of Stuyvesants from his pocket and lights one. He drags, slow and long; smoke escapes from the corners of a sneaky smile. He points the cigarette at Marlboro. "Foshizi? Okay, chizboy, tell us then, how long 'go your daddy own this car?"

Marlboro shrugs. "How must I know exact? I was just a laaitie."

Booysen nods like he doesn't mean yes. The air between them is electric, and I sense a fight about to spark. "This scrapheap been here years," he says.

Marlboro tilts his head, sniffs, "So?"

"So, bra, how old you now?"

Marlboro shrugs, looks at his sneaks. Booysen whistles and shakes his head. "You don't know how old you are? You some kind of stupid?"

"I'm fifteen, you know I'm fifteen. What's your problem?"

"You can't count, that's my problem. You can't even lie good." He slaps the car. "This g-string runs on petrol, bra, you know what is petrol? This died before you born. All these transis run on petrol, this heap started after D-Day. You know when is D-Day? If you weren't so thick, you'd know."

"So? Not all these cars been here since then. That one up there," Marlboro points to the yellow car I was sitting on earlier, "that one a 'lectric. That car can't be more than four years old."

Booysen laughs. "Wanya, you speak out your bum. That 'lectric here because some stupid like you rolled it. That car on the top, *this* car on the bottom. Your daddy must have plenty zak to waste back then, cruising round in a petrol car after D-Day. If he was such a fat cat, why he chuck you in the bin?"

Booysen and Marlboro stare at each other, eyes dark. Booysen flicks the butt of his cigarette at Marlboro's feet and cracks his knuckles. I ball my hands into fists, my cheeks tight with glee. "Fight, fight, fight, fight," I chant.

Marlboro glances down, lifts the toe of his sneak and snuffs the glowing cherry. He turns to Sindi. "You good yet, sista? It's late-bells. Time to make tracks."

Sindi stands slow and the boys glance at each other, their faces blank. For the first time since they rescued us, I wonder what they want. I chew my bottom lip, trying to suss if they're bad inside. What did they do that made the man with the gun want to kill them? I reach out to take hold of Sindi's arm, to keep her from going with them, but the three of them have already disappeared into the shadowy nest of trees.

Night smudges dusk. We walk in a tight fist of silence, Marlboro trailing behind, kicking at the blackjacks growing between the cracks in the pavements. Soon, the bottom half of his jeans are covered in black specks. I hate the prickly seeds and worry they'll stick to my socks, but none attach to me. The streetlights come on and we walk through pools of light into darkness, light into darkness for five blocks. We pass houses with warm windows. The muffled sounds of life filter through the brick and glass and curtains and they make me think of Mama and Auntie and sharing slap chips with Sindi on Fridays. They make me want to go home.

Booysen stops at a chain-link fence that spans a gap between two houses, There's no streetlight in front of the fence, as if someone wants to keep the place it protects secret.

"Check coast, chizboy."

Marlboro narrows his eyes but he does as he's told and scans the road.

"All clear," he says.

Booysen peels back the fence. Someone and their bolt-cutters have been to work on it. A gash, tall as Booysen, runs up the centre. Marlboro climbs through, slipping down so low on the other side that only the top of his head shows at street level. Booysen nods to Sindi. She ducks through.

We drop into a storm-water drain. The walls are bone-dry, but years of rain have seeped into the concrete and the scent of water is strong. The place is full of ghosts; their hands reach out and touch me as I pass. Wet hands, dripping-dripping. I want to run, but Sindi and the boys are making for a massive concrete pipe. Where she goes, I follow.

The banks above the sluice must have once been lush and overgrown, though all that remains now are thirsty trees. Still, their branches close over us, cutting us off from the light completely. The boys' feet tap out a steady, unfaltering rhythm. It seems they've walked this drain many times before and don't need eyes to know the way. Booysen calls out: "You good, sista?" His voice raps against the walls, fading on the last word. *Sista, sista, sista.* The echo reverberates though me, sinking in like damp. I can't help rapping my own voice to the wall. But the walls don't hear me, and I have to sing my own *Sista, sista, sista.*

The mouth of the pipe looms like a hole in the night. The air feels dense and my eyes struggle to find points to focus on. I can only make out black and shadows, but they're vague and unreal, shifting-shifting.

I think of poor Dora. *Dora Xplora vetkoek floating.* We all thought Gogo Nkosi's lodger was such a nice man until Dora washed up dead in the vlei. Dora's mama wrote her name on her schoolbag with black marker. That was the only reason we knew it was her, because black marker doesn't wash out. At school, we made up a skipping song so it wouldn't happen to us. I sing it now, to ward off the bad in the pipe:

> *Dora Xplora didn't go home*
> *Her fat ouledi called the gata on the phone*
> *He drove up and down in a banana-kaar*
> *Shouting Dora Xplora tell us where you are.*

At the mouth of the pipe, Booysen lights a smoke. He takes a few deep draws and the cherry flares bright red and burns down fast. He tosses it and steps into the darkness. Marlboro and Sindi follow. I watch the glow fade out. With my heart bumping and my skin creeping, I let the dark hole swallow me.

Dora Xplora vetkoek floating.

I can hear dripping, as if somewhere there's water bleeding from the concrete. Not likely. I can't remember the last time it rained. Still, I crouch and run my fingers over the bottom of the pipe to check.

Dora Xplora dead in the drain
Waiting-waiting, waiting for the rain
One week, two week, three four five
Auntie prays that Dora's still alive.

Walking down the centre, I can't touch the sides. The black air sucks and pulls. I could lose myself here, easy, but the boys give off a funky fug and my nostrils cling to their stink.

Dora Xplora blue and bloating.

Furrows and gulleys cut into the pipe by water erosion make me stumble. I count my steps to help me keep focused. After one hundred and five, we turn left. The dark begins to shift. There's a circle of light ahead. Soon, we're walking under a row of bulbs strung along a raggedy wire like giant Christmas-tree lights. The pipe ends, and we step into a cavernous circular space. The boys keep walking, but me and Sindi hold back to suss the scene.

Fire drums flicker orange over mattresses and blankets crammed around them like lump-animals looking for warmth. The place is thick with whispers and the funk of piss and bodies. Smoke spirals into the night through three open manholes high above us. Metal rungs climb the walls towards them. One ladder is wired like the passage, but the glow the bulbs give off doesn't come down far enough to brighten the place. It's like looking at stars: their twinkles don't count because they're part of a different world.

"Sista, you just gonna stand there or what?"

Hunched forms press against the walls, their eyes flicking fire. They've been watching us, quiet, but when Booysen speaks they erupt into excited chatter.

"Shut it."

The noise switches off. I squint into the dim space, trying to find the speaker. My eyes flick over the mouths of six dark pipes set into the wall before I spot her. She steps heavily out of one of the pipes and shuffles toward us, knobkerrie rapping against the hush. She looks like the Oros Man's ouledi, but she's grey like meat boiled too long. Rolls of fat spill from the sleeves of a T-shirt the same colour as her skin – I can't tell where the cotton ends and flab begins. If she weren't walking I'd take her for dead.

She stops at a fire drum to warm her hands – skinny and delicate, like the fingers of a hungry child. The firelight throws her eyes into deep shadow, but it doesn't bring colour to her swollen face.

"Well, what gift have my boys brought me today?"

She angles her face towards us and beckons Sindi with a stolen hand.

Her smile speaks of the cold hours of winter nights when it seems dawn will never come. I put my hand on Sindi's shoulder to hold her back.

Shame-Shame, All the Same

All eyes slide from Sindi to the woman. Everyone's waiting to see who'll be the first to give. Sindi takes a step backwards and some small child, nerves wired, giggles. A murmur runs through the watchers. Booysen and Marlboro spring to their feet and scurry towards us, flashing spite at each other as they pick their way over mattresses and people.

Marlboro reaches us first. He takes Sindi by the elbow and, with a smug grin, drags her into the centre of the room. "Ma, this the sista I told you about."

I look at Booysen. He sucks his lips, says nothing. The oros woman folds her arms across her chest. Strong arms, solid slabs of hard fat, like Mama's. "Well, girlie, you got a name?" she says, voice full of sugar.

Sindi sways.

"My name's Wilhelmina, but you call me Ma Wilma like the rest of them. What you want us to call you?"

Sindi studies the toes that poke from under Ma Wilma's skirt.

"Don't she talk?"

Marlboro shrugs. "She talk, Ma, but not so much. I think maybe she's tired. She been inside that heap of ou transis all night till I pulled her out."

"Sho, bra, you lie."

Ma Wilma snaps around. Her thick steel-coloured braids whip across her face and settle on her shoulders like spiteful Siamese cats. "Shut it, Booysen. This isn't a competition," she snarls, caramel tones burnt bitter. "For all I care a 'copter airlifted her here. You boys aren't heroes. Yesterday you were all for boasting how you knew where to find little ones, now you want a kiss for bringing me this. You better hope she's clean, otherwise the mess is going to be yours. Now both of you fok off and mind yourselves 'fore I give you a klap."

Both boys slink into the shadows.

"And you, girlie, you a bit of a vuil pop. You need a wash." She grabs Sindi by the arm and leads her away, shouting over her shoulder for Rissik and Bree to bring a bath. They disappear into the tunnel she emerged from a few minutes earlier.

As soon as she's out of sight, the watchers start laughing and making kissie-kissie noises and I realise: they're all children. And all girls, as far as I can tell, except for Booysen and Marlboro and two other boys around their age. They look like street kids, with their matted hair and dirty faces, but their clothes are clean enough and though they're not fat, they're not starving either. I do a quick headcount: about thirty girls. The smallest looks five or six; the oldest, a blonde girl, is maybe twelve. It's hard to tell the ages of street kids exactly – they're small from being hungry and sucking glue. Sometimes you meet a boy that looks ten and he tells you he's sixteen. Maybe true, maybe not: it's like that. The streets are full of lies and invisible kids nobody wants.

I find Sindi in a pipe lit by a single bulb. A double mattress, with a sink-hole in the centre that tells me it's Ma Wilma's bed, sits at the edge of the cold blue circle cast by the bulb. Next to the bed is a cardboard box containing a few dog-eared magazines. Beyond the lick of light, a white dress hangs like a lonely ghost on a clothing rail. I wander over and rub one of the lacy cuffs between my finger and thumb. Crispy, like crumbs of burnt toast.

I turn from the dress and look at my sister. She sits shivering on the mattress. Ma Wilma stands in front of her, holding her coat. Without it, Sindi looks small-small. I can't remember the last time she took off the coat, but her jeans, belted with string, remember the width her waist used to be. Her jersey is faded and full of holes, the New Tiyang Primary colours stolen by sun and dirt. The sleeves are too short and sit halfway between her wrist and elbow: Sindi's getting longer and thinner. Two girls come in carrying a washtub between them. Water slops over the sides as they set it down.

"Watch it," Ma Wilma snaps. "Next time you waste water like that, I'll bleed you to replace it. Take this and get rid of it." Ma Wilma holds out Sindi's coat. Neither girl moves. "Problem?" she asks, arching her brow. I see she doesn't have any eyebrows or lashes. They shake their heads like their ears are glued together. "You girlies aren't princesses either. Remember where I found you? I can put you back there."

"Ja, Ma," they say with one voice.

"Now get, and send Loveday with some clean clothes."

The girls skitter out with the coat and Ma Wilma turns her attention back to Sindi. "You sick, girlie?" she asks, tilting Sindi's head back. She pulls my sisi's lower eyelids down. Sindi's eyes roll, but she doesn't pull away. "You got the sickness or what?" Sindi shakes her head. Ma Wilma looks hard at her face. "How old are you?"

"Thirteen," I say.

"I asked you a question," she says, shaking Sindi.

"I'm fift_teen."

"Liar, liar pants on fire!" I shout.

"You ever been with a man? You got a boyfriend?"

Sindi shakes her head. Ma Wilma grunts and shuffles over to the cardboard box. She takes out a sewing needle and a white plastic stick about the length of a pen. The black swirls towards me when she stabs the needle into my sisi's finger.

"Okay, okay," Ma Wilma soothes. She twists Sindi's finger so the drop of blood beading on the end of it drips into a small window in the plastic stick, then drops the stick into her pocket. "What happened to your hand?"

"A dog bit m_m_me."

"Ah, a whole sentence. Good, I was beginning to think you were simple. Loveday will get that cleaned up, then we'll get you something to eat and find you a bed."

As if summoned by her name, a lanky girl with a shock of hair as blonde as Marlboro's enters, carrying a bundle of clothes. Ma Wilma and the girl speak in low voices. I hover around my sisi. She's shivering, hugging herself to try still the shakes. Ma Wilma leaves the pipe, her skirt hissing like a snake. When she's gone, Loveday tosses the bundle of clothes onto the bed.

"Ma Wilma says for you to wash. She want me to do it, make sure you get properly clean but no way. You wash yourself, neh. I'm happy to look out for the laaities, make sure they gets cleaned up once a week, but you not a laaitie. You got years on me fo sho. And you stink worse than the ouledi's blumas." She flops down onto the mattress, takes a magazine from the box and flicks through it. Sindi doesn't move. Loveday shoves her with a foot. "Look, sista, don't mess around. Ma Wilma's going to come back now-now. She's got other uses for that knobkerrie, she's not as old as she looks."

When she still doesn't move, Loveday stops paging and gives her a hard look.

"Jissis, moegoe. Move it." Loveday drops the magazine, grabs Sindi by the arms and pulls her to her feet. The girl looks like a stick of the pampas grass that grows in the barren stretches of veld along the Ring Road, all white fluff on top of a thin reed, but she handles Sindi towards the washtub as if she's a paper doll.

Sindi's head jerks back from the shock of cold water splashed in her face. The glaze lifts and she looks at Loveday like she's only just seen her. "I can wash m_m_myself." She strips and uses her T-shirt as a washcloth. Loveday drops onto the bed and begins paging through the magazine again.

When Sindi's done, she wrings out her T-shirt, then turns her jeans inside out and gives them a good shake. A few coins and the collected dregs of our life on the road fall from her pockets.

"Don't do that, sista, you'll spread fleas and lice," Lovedays says, eyeing

Sindi's stuff. "Los your kak and get dressed, or we gonna miss last dish. I'll sweep it up later."

Loveday watches Sindi dress with a sly face. "You know Ma hates Believers." She pauses like she's waiting for this fact to sink in. "Ma hates them. Give her a box of etchies and a bottle of b-diesel and she'd burn the whole church to the ground with every Believer in it. If one of them come in here," she swipes her fingers across her throat.

There's spite in her voice. I put my face close to hers. She's pretty but her lips are thin and lines have already formed around her mouth, like an old lady's mouth, like Gogo Nkosi's mouth. I know, looking at those bitter creases, that Loveday is brewing trouble.

"Why does she call you Loveday?"

Loveday frowns over the top of the magazine. "It's my name, neh, everyone got a name, even you."

Sindi wrings water from her shirt. "There's a ss_astreet called Loveday."

Loveday sighs. "Ja, there's a street. Ma Wilma names all her girls after streets, sometimes the street where she pick them up, sometimes just sommer. Depends."

Sindi stands in the washtub. Light from the naked bulb snags on every bump on her body, casting purple shadows. It makes dark hollows of her cheeks and the sunken spaces between her collarbone and neck, runs a line of light along her ribs and cheekbones. She looks like a negative, an X-ray, a shivering-shaking X-ray.

Loveday leans back. "They find you by the old golf course, huh? Maybe Ma'll call you Reading."

"M_m_my nn_name's sss_asSindi."

"Ja well, it's not like you can say your name so maybe now it's Reading. Ma don't like anyone to be called by their real name. If nobody knows your real name, nobody can find you. No one come looking anyway. 'Cept one time this ou mlungu come looking to recruit us to his church. Fokken Believers. Ma went spare, she moered him stukkend, snapped his leg like a twig. Booysen and Oxford drag him out and leave him on the street. That was at the warehouse. Nobody ever find us here, but we can't stay here in summer, just in case it rains. It don't, but the Long Dry got to break some time. Better safe, neh."

"Where are we?"

"This?" Loveday looks around like she's not sure. "Ma says this a ou storm-water reservoir, part of the waterworks. We safe enough down here, the city got no use for this reservoir long as the dry hold."

Dora Xplora blue and bloating.

"Out there, the big round room, that was where they stored the water before treating it, but we call it the dorm. Makes Ma jumpy to think of all the water that filled it once."

Dora Xplora face-down in the vlei
Barefoot, no socks, her shoes got washed away
Her satchel strap still wrapped around her throat
Daai ding kon nie swim but vetkoek floats.

Loveday hands Sindi a long-sleeved T-shirt and a pair of jeans that are wide at the waist and too short, but they're clean and Sindi looks grateful. I glance at my dusty New Tiyang Primary uniform and wish she'd give me something new too. When Sindi is dressed, Loveday bandages her hand, pulling the strips of rags tight. Then she collects Sindi's old clothes and leads her back to the dorm. The air stinks of boiled cabbage and burnt pap.

"Just in time for last dish," she says. She points out a mattress and leaves my sisi standing next to it, staring at the crowd gathered at the mouth of a lit-up pipe, holding plates.

By the time Loveday returns with food, Sindi's curled up on the mattress, asleep.

"Wake up, girlie, you can't sleep all day."

I lift my head and look over the mound of my sisi's shoulder at ankles, thick as diseased tree trunks, and driftwood feet with chipped yellow nails. I don't need to see her face to know who they belong to.

On the road, you learn that it's better to play dead than to give in to panic and bolt. Sindi's quickening heartbeat tells me she's awake, probably squinting at Ma Wilma's feet through slit-eyes while sifting through her memories, trying to place us in time and space. But remembering's hard. The world's an ugly place and memories aren't something to unwrap like birthday presents.

I can feel Sindi's exhaustion in the heaviness of her limbs. After a few minutes of playing dead, she falls back into sleep. Ma Wilma clicks her tongue but she leaves us alone. I press my face into the back of Sindi's neck. We curl together like two spoons in a drawer, but Ma Wilma's visit has made me restless. I leave my sisi sleeping and climb the ladder strung with lights. I perch on a rung halfway to freedom and pretend to be an angel, watching.

Ma Wilma is the first of Sindi's visitors, but she isn't the last. Others come. Loveday leaves a plate of food. Later, she returns and takes it away, uneaten. Booysen stands over her, looking worried. He shakes his head, but I'm not fool enough to think he worries for her. Young girls come, giggling-giggling, and drip water into her mouth and ears.

Their tricks make me mad. I wrap my arms in wire and spark until everyone is asleep. Then I'm the only one awake and I feel cold and alone.

Dawn filters through the manholes and Ma Wilma's kids begin to stir. The dorm fills with breakfast chatter that soon drops away as kids disappear up the ladders and into the pipes. By mid-morning, only Ma Wilma and a few little ones are left. I stay on my perch and watch the dull fade of the afternoon slide over Sindi. By the time twilight comes and the older kids pour back into their hole, I'm lumed up like a light bulb, but Sindi still sleeps.

That night, I slip into her mind and dream her dreams. I see myself, Thuli, strange and disconnected and the wrong way round, like I'm stuck in a mirror. We walk across the patch of veld to Saviour's Pit Stop, our arms crooked at the elbows and linked together. The sky is silver-blue and the propeller on the Legend winks as it turns slow in the breeze, fanning our cheeks. The colour of her dreaming is sharp, as if our lives then were so much brighter, but rapid guilt oozes over the dream. Emptiness eats at happiness and the black blots us out.

Sunshine spotlights the floor. It's the kind of sun that traps you in a lazy daze, unable to do anything but stare at dust motes. Everyone is drowsy, as if the sleeping sickness that has taken hold of my sisi is contagious. I almost expect them to drop, one by one, onto mattresses and curl into their dreams. The air is thick with unsatisfied expectations, a gift we brought. Someone new, and everyone waiting for the small changes in their lives that new things bring. But Sindi sleeps on, dragging them all into our limbo.

Ma Wilma shuffles across the floor, the tap of her knobkerrie soft, as if she doesn't want to disturb anyone. She steps into a sun spot, blinking at the brightness, and stops. "Marlboro," she calls, rapping her knobkerrie to make him hurry. They exchange a few words; then he crosses the floor to where Sindi sleeps and drags her mattress from its shadowed recess into the light.

Ma Wilma is like a moth with no wings, pacing up and down in the harsh glow of the bulb. Three days have passed since we last saw her, since she stooped over Sindi's sleeping body, nudging her with the knobkerrie while sunlight played over my sisi's face and brought her back to life. In those three days only Loveday came near us. She brought porridge and bread and, once, a tub of hot soapy water and clean rags for Sindi's hand. She refused to speak to Sindi, keeping her eyes down as she unwound the dirty bandage. The stink from the wound brought a sour kiss to her lips. That was the only time her stony mask slipped.

Then Ma Wilma sent for us. Now we stand, hands behind our backs, waiting for her attention. Her pacing makes me think of Miss Booley, our grade five teacher, even though Miss Booley was ruler-thin. Miss Booley once made us stand in front of the class, hands behind our backs, eyes reading the floor while she paced, up and down, up and down, up and down . . . until, without sign or warning, she snapped around to face the class with their blank eyes and their straight necks.

"Look," she hissed, her finger pointing at us while her spiky features faced the others. "They're not clean children, not clean the way children in my class should be." And they looked at us, at our uniforms that weren't clean enough. Our second-hand uniforms, too short and not clean.

"No, ma'am, not clean."

They looked at our baby-dolls, our scuffed and worn baby-dolls, and they laughed and pulled their lips thin over their white teeth; and inside me, hate grew. Hate bubbled and boiled until the rage clenched my hands into fists. I wanted to bash Miss Booley's face. I wanted to take her head and smash it into the wall, into the whiteboard and the desk, to wipe that face away until there was nothing left but blood and mess and no face. No, ma'am. No face. No clean face. Just fat bloody lips and broken teeth.

Tears brimming, I cut a look at Sindi to see if she was ready to smash Miss Booley. But Sindi's eyes were dancing, her nostrils trembling as she swallowed the giggles. She was laughing. Laughing at Miss Booley. And as I looked at her I-don't-care face, my fingers went soft and my anger dissolved and the laughing caught and it snorted out my nose, a pig grunt laugh and then Sindi couldn't swallow any more and we were both laughing-laughing, laughing-laughing, and Miss Booley was raging-raging and we were "OOUUUT!"

But we didn't care. No ma'am, we didn't, because second-hand dresses and worn-out shoes don't matter. Teachers and classmates don't matter. Sisters matter. Only sisters. Sister-sister, sister-twin, twin-sister.

"I thought the sickness was on you, girlie, even though you tested clear. The way you slept, like the dying sleep. Coma, I said to the boys, that one's got the coma of the dead on her. We've seen it before. Many times we bring girls in, older girls that have been on the street for years and they roll over and die. Stink the place up like dogs. Then my boys have to move the body, dump it somewhere. It's looking for trouble, shifting corpses. So no more older girls, I says to them, no more. Bring me little ones and we can look after them until they're old enough, but only if they haven't been fiddled. Not easy to find little girls nobody's fiddled with these days, everybody thinks a little girl's going to save them."

Dora asked a skollie for a sugar sweet.

Ma Wilma leans on her knobkerrie. "But then my boys told me you was a beauty. Bit skinny, but a beauty. They said you'd clean up good. They told me how they'd watched you crawl into the cars and not come out. They're good boys, but they can make trouble. I couldn't have it on my conscience, such a beauty trapped in the cars." She spits on the ground at our feet. "Now it looks like I've rescued one of *them*."

Dora flashed pink blumas in the street.

She pulls something from the folds of the clothes and holds it out. Her hand wrapped so tight around it her knuckles show white through her skin.

Dora kissed Jack-rola an' now she's dead.

A spiteful smile twists Loveday's lips and she pushes Sindi so she's within punching distance of Ma Wilma's fist. Sindi flinches, but Ma Wilma just opens her hand. Something falls to the floor.

66

Dora's not in heaven cos her vetkoek bled.

Loon Man's cross lies there in a tangle of string. I look at it and I know, bad things have come.

The boys strip her of her new clothes and she cowers in front of them while they stand around talking about her titties and her bum. She tries to hide behind her arms, but they pull them down and hold her wrists. They say she's too skinny, but she has a pretty face and in a few weeks they can make her fat. They look at her. She looks at the floor.

"Think about something else," I whisper, because I know how it is.

I know because of the day we went to the sea. When we caught a taxi to the swimming beach, Sindi and me and him, while Mama went shopping for a tombstone. I think about the waves and how we clung to him, holding on to his thin arms to keep from being swept under. Then he showed us a place they used to call the Golden Mile before the water rose up and flooded the fancy hotels.

Shame-shame, Thuli's shame, all the same, shame-shame.

They paint her lips the colour of blood and smear the same waxy stick onto her cheeks to cherry them up. I've never seen her with make-up before, it makes her look like a clown, just like Mama used to say it would. It makes her look like she's been punched in the mouth. They say the colour suits her.

They make her wear the white dress. The lace crackles when they zip it up. The camera flash flares against the fabric, against the shiny sweetheart cups that stand out proud while her titties try to hide. The dress is so bright, her skin so dark it seems the dress is a person and she its shadow.

Shame-shame, Sindi's shame, all the same, shame-shame.

I stood on the lid of the toilet seat, staring at the lock. The echoing drip from the cistern kept time steady while his breath came hot and fast-fast. On the other side of the door, I heard Sindi singing quiet to herself. I thought it was strange, Sindi didn't sing. Then I realised it wasn't her singing. It was me.

"You're a good girl, Thuli," he whispered in my ear.

After, we stood in the damp shadows of the ladies' toilet and changing room, peeling our wet vests away from our bumpy skin. The pads of my fingers were wrinkled, as if the sea had made me old. They felt numb and strange, like somebody else's fingers. The changing room smelt of pee, wet concrete, splintered wood and the thick-bleach salt smell of him. We turned away from each other then, no longer the same. I watched her dress in the mirror, but her face was a closed door and she wouldn't look at me.

Shame-shame, Thuli's shame, all the same, shame-shame.

"Smile, sista," they say and poke her in the ribs, tickling her like this is a joke and everyone's friends. They take picture after picture, crowding around her image on the tiny screen after each flash.

"There are some good ones," they say. Ma Wilma smiles and says to tell the Commissioner to sell her cheap.

PART 2
Z3

Something Bad

Something bad had happened, or maybe it was going to. The creases around the stranger's eyes said so. They were like the scribbles in the margins of Sindi's new exercise book where someone had tested a pen, ruining the perfect blankness of the page. They gave his eyes a downward turn that told her the stranger wasn't smiling inside, even though his full lips were pulled wide enough to see gums.

"Why didn't you visit before, Uncle?" Thuli asked. Her voice was bold, her direct gaze demanding. She placed a mug of tea and a newly opened tin of condensed milk in front of him.

The stranger looked away and laughed, a *he he he* that sounded string-tin-telephone fake. He cocked his head to the side, took off his sweat-stained trilby and put it on the table. "Before, there was no reason. You see, I come from Eston." He made arcing movements with his hand, indicating that he'd travelled over many hills to get to them, which presumably meant that Eston was far away. "And the taxi fare!" he whistled through his teeth. "But now your grandmother . . ." He trailed off.

Sindi dropped her eyes from his face to his thin hand reaching for the tin. He ran the tip of a finger over the sweetness oozing from the ragged cut in the lid, then along the jag of the opener, before sticking it into his mouth. Liar, Sindi thought. Mama would've said if they had an uncle or a grandmother. In fact, Mama had told them they had no family. Even Auntie-Next-Door wasn't a real aunt. Mama was an orphan, and they were half-orphans with no father.

The kettle sat on the primus stove, bottom blackened. In the time it took to boil water for the strange man's tea, the kitchen had become muggy and the oily smell of b-diesel closed them in. They weren't supposed to touch the stove or the row of plastic Coke bottles containing the flammable fuel, except to take the empties to Joe's to be refilled. Mama would be angry when she came home, angrier than that day three months ago when they ran the radio's battery down. Sindi imagined Mama standing by the door, eyes heavy with exhausted disapproval, nostrils narrowing to new moons as she considered what fresh nonsense the twins had brought her this time. Sindi stiffened, thinking of the beating that would tenderise their backsides into swollen cushions of blue and purple.

Sindi could say she'd been in the toilet when the stranger knocked, and that when she'd returned from her business he was sitting at the table while Thuli busied herself making tea. It was true, and she could say it, but she wouldn't. They didn't do things like that. You didn't sell you sister out, no matter what. She crooked her pinkie fingers and linked them together under the table. "Sister-sister, sister-twin, twin-sister," she whispered.

What should she do about the man? His presence in their kitchen made her stomach churn, it made her palms damp and stole her voice. She knew she should tell someone about him, maybe Auntie-Next-Door, but she didn't want to leave Thuli alone with him. In case. Something bad could happen, something very bad.

Thuli's exercise book lay open on the table. Sindi slid it closer and flipped the pages. She stopped at a worksheet on clouds: blurry photocopied images, like dirty finger smudges, labelled in Thuli's backward-slanting handwriting. The exercise was months old, but Sindi still remembered all the names. They'd spent hours reciting them, strange words that rolled off the tongue like abracadabra.

Cirrus. Cirrocumulus. Cirrostratus. Altocumulus. Altostratus. Nimbostratus. Stratocumulus. Stratus. Cumulus. Cumulonimbus.

All the clouds belonged in one of two groups. There were heaped clouds and layered clouds, cumulus clouds and stratus clouds. Sometimes, the girls lay on their backs and stared at the towers of cumulus cloud shape-shifting above them.

"See that dog."

"There's a dragonfly."

"And that fat one's Ma Elias, look, upside down, just her head and shoulders."

"Cauliflower," Thuli always said when she got bored.

But Sindi thought the fat fluffy clouds looked more like the puffs of spookasem Joe sold in his shop. Spookasem – they'd picked up the word from Auntie. They liked that: spookasem, ghost breath. As the sugar melted on their tongues, they pretended they were ghosts and *boo-whoo-hoo*'d passersby.

When she was much smaller, Joe convinced her that the sticky blue machine behind the counter was a cloud catcher, sucking clouds from the sky with a juddering whirr when he pressed the button. She frowned at first, unsure of whether to believe him.

"Hurricane," he said, pointing to the metal logo bolted to the machine, "that's what it says, right there." Sindi had seen hurricanes on the TV news at Auntie's house. Swirling cloud masses that moved from the sea onto land, bringing lashes of rain, knocking down houses and flooding the lobbies of beachfront hotels. She believed him then, but never again after that.

Sometimes men did worse things than lie. Sindi thought of Gogo Nkosi's quiet lodger and shuddered. She'd liked him, everyone had. He'd read to her from the newspaper sometimes, once even from a book. He'd made her feel important.

"Did you know," he'd told her, "that your heart is the same size as your fist?" Then, to demonstrate the size of his affection for her, he'd made a fist and held it against his chest.

It could've been her. After the police arrested Gogo Nkosi's lodger, Sindi stayed away from men, in case her luck ran out.

Thuli was the opposite. As soon as Thuli heard the *Star Trek: After the*

Rapture theme tune – which meant that Auntie's boyfriend was there, because it was his favourite programme – she'd dash next door and offer to fetch him a quart of Black Label from Ma Elias. Then she'd pour the beer carefully, tilting the glass the way he'd shown her so it didn't make too much foam, and take it to him. She liked it when he patted her on the bum and said, "Eh, Thuli, every man should have a daughter like you."

Thuli had a way of sauntering up to men, smiling her bright smile and asking wide-eyes questions that made them want to tell her things. She stored their words and recycled them later, to give her arguments weight with the other kids in the schoolyard.

Sindi had spent her entire life on the edges, struggling to spit out words while Thuli tried to push her into things. All Thuli's attempts at gaining them entry into one of the playground cliques ended up with someone breaking the embarrassed silence by mimicking Sindi's stutter, and Thuli, quick-tempered and ever-protective, would retaliate with her fists. Sindi had long ago accepted that she'd never have a best friend that wasn't her sister. She pretended it didn't bother her. When they saw groups of girls walking arm in arm down the road, gossiping at the tops of their voices about boys who would never notice Sindi, they'd link their pinkies together and whisper: "Sister-sister, twin-sister, sister-twin." Sindi knew she'd never be pinkie-linked to anyone else.

The b-diesel fumes had dissipated, leaving Sindi's nose free to absorb the smells the stranger had brought with him. Oil from his hair and skin darkened the felt of his trilby in pungent stale layers; the greasy scents leached from the hat and gave the air an acidic sourness like the scour of Vim on burnt milk. And the stranger's suit smelled scorched, like a just-ironed sheet with the dust of a windy day pressed into it. Sindi bunched her fists in her lap, the hard edges of her fingernails biting into her palms. Something bad.

She hadn't seen many hats like his. In church, one very old man who stood at the back would hold a hat like that against his chest during hymns. And that crazy old white guy who stood on the back of a slow-moving bakkie with a megaphone, shouting about the end of the world and the beginning of a Pure Mankind – he also wore a hat like the stranger's, though his was as black as the grainy b-diesel residue left on the bottom of the kettle. They called him the Black Preacher.

The stranger didn't look as old as the man from the church or the preacher, even though he wore a hat and suit. She couldn't tell his age. The whites of his eyes were yellowed like a dagga smoker's but his cheeks were smooth, the skin stretched over his cheekbones like clingwrap on sandwiches. His gaunt face was unlined except around his drooping eyes and in the space between, above the nose.

"Cumulus," Sindi whispered. "Cumulus, cumulus, cumulus." Repetition stole meaning from the word. "Cumulus" was no longer the name of a cloud but a series of sounds, breathy knocks on the door of her mind. An abracadabra, sim-sala-bim, open-up-and-let-me-in magic word that opened an escape hatch to her inner landscape, and the only person who could follow her there was Thuli, if she'd just . . .

Sindi looked at her sister talking to the man, smiling her bright smile. Her words buzzed and hummed like flies dancing on guitar strings, sing-song and happy.

"Stratus," she whispered, placing the word on Thuli's moving lips. "Stratus, stratus, stratus."

The shadows had folded in on themselves by the time Mama shuffled through the door and brought Sindi out of her daydreams.

"There was a jumper on the track today," she sighed, hanging her coat on the wire hanger behind the door. She adjusted the shoulders so it hung straight, smoothed the creases, plucked a bit of fluff from the brown wool. The girls watched the homecoming ritual in silence, wondering when she would notice.

"Some poor lady," she said, turning to face them. As her eyes fixed on the man, the words dropped from her lips. Mama's eyes narrowed, her nostrils flared. Skin prickling, Sindi glanced at the stranger. The jovial mask he'd worn all afternoon didn't change. It was like the face of a doll, the smile plastic and pretending.

Thuli slid from her chair. "Uncle's come to visit," she said. She slipped her hand into Mama's and tried to draw her towards the table. The stranger stood, the legs of his chair scraping against the floor and setting Sindi's teeth on edge.

Mama slapped Thuli's hand away. Her eyes darted from the stranger to the empty chair beside him. When she finally spoke, she sounded as if her breath had been stolen. "What do you want here?"

He held out his hands. "It has been a long time," he said. "Eleven years, your daughter tells me."

Mama pulled Thuli towards her, pushed out her chest and stepped forward, placing her body between man and girl. But Sindi was too far away for Mama to protect: Sindi saw the distance in the wideness of her mother's eyes. Fear twisted her guts. Something bad. Sindi sat, sucking her teeth, unable to move as the scene in front of her played out. It was like watching TV at Auntie-Next-Door's, except this was real. Something bad was going to happen and it was going to be real.

"You have no right to come here. Get out."

"We need to talk, I need to talk to you."

"There is nothing I need to hear from you."

"Sisi, I did nothing wrong."

"You did nothing, and that alone is wrong. Get out now, or I swear, Jabu, I will scream and the whole neighbourhood will come running."

The stranger swallowed. "I will come back tomorrow, when you've had time to calm down." He gathered his hat from the table and held it against his chest like the old man in church, as if waiting for Mama to change her mind. When she did not, he left, touching Sindi gently on the shoulder as he passed her. "Stay well, my sister," he said. Mama didn't reply.

That night, Sindi dreamed she lay staring at the clouds on the grassy verge close to Saviour's Pit Stop, where shiftless men sometimes sat drinking. On the highway, fifty feet below, cars sat bumper to bumper. It was late afternoon and the sky was the ocean, she knew from the deep, sad colour of it, though she'd only ever seen the sea in pictures. Clouds, like giant kernels of popped corn, drifted across the blue. She took Thuli's hand – sensing, without looking, that her sister would be there.

"There's a mouse," she said, pointing out a rodent-shaped mass.

"Uncle," Thuli said.

Sindi turned to her sister, a flutter in her belly.

Thuli's face wore the same plastic expression as the stranger's, the same stuck-on doll smile. "Uncle," she repeated, without moving her lips. Her voice was cartoon, squeaky as a squeeze toy. She turned her gaze to the heavens and her arm jerked skyward, her splayed fingers rigid. "Uncle!" she squeaked.

The grainy texture of Thuli's hand in hers chafed Sindi's skin. She pulled her hand away and sat up. Lying in the grass among the cigarette butts and discarded bottles, Thuli looked abandoned, like an oversized doll that had outgrown its owner. Sindi had a strong urge to throw the Thuli-doll over the edge, onto the highway where it would be smashed under the wheels of a truck, but she couldn't bring herself to touch her sister's hard plastic skin again.

"Uncle," Thuli-doll said. A shadow the colour of week-old bruises covered her face and the temperature dropped.

Gooseflesh raced along Sindi's arms and up her neck. With the burn of ozone in her nostrils, she turned to the sky and saw that it had come down low. Turgid nimbostratus clouds, bloated and ready to burst, hung over her head. In their purple contours she saw his taut cheeks, his fleshy lips.

"Uncle, Uncle, Uncle!" Thuli-doll cried as the lips came down, puckered for a kiss. They opened and swallowed her whole and Sindi felt a wrench in her soul.

She woke shivering and afraid and smelled the rain. A sideways wind blew wet into the room through the open window. She tiptoed across the worn-out carpet to close it and saw, in the blue light of the streetlight, a triangle of damp on the carpet. Bad luck. It would moulder and make the room stink. She shut the window and stood staring at the rain.

The damp from the carpet made her colder, but she wasn't ready to return to bed and her dreams. She scanned the road, almost expecting to see someone staring back at her from the window of one of the houses opposite, or leaning against the pole of the washing line in the yard. Maybe the stranger was out there, in the deep shadows between shacks. Maybe he could see her. The thought made her blood speed and she almost cried out when a dog weaved into her frame of vision, its fur rutted with rain.

Dragging the soles of her feet across the carpet to dry them, she made her way back to bed. Thuli had pulled the blankets over to her side and they'd tangled in her limbs. Sindi tugged them free, hoping to wake her twin so she could share the dream and diminish it, but Thuli just groaned and rolled onto her side.

Sindi slipped into bed and rearranged the blanket. She curled into her sister, keeping an inch between them so she could just feel Thuli's body heat, and making a fist so her icy palm wouldn't come into contact with skin when she rested her arm on Thuli's hip. In the ghostly glow of the streetlights, she could make out the tight braids she'd woven into Thuli's hair earlier that week. As her body warmed she shuffled closer, pressing her nose into the nape of Thuli's neck and inhaling her dusty Vaseline scent.

Across the room, the mattress springs creaked. Usually Mama snored loud enough to rattle the window glass, but now her breathing was silent and Sindi knew that she, too, was awake. Sindi closed her eyes, but Mama's worry agitated the air and kept her from sleep.

When the stranger had gone, Sindi thought Mama would beat them blue, but she hadn't been angry – just hugged them to her. For a long time

Mama had sat at the table and stared at her hands, as if she could make them stop shaking with her eyes.

Later they went next door. The twins ate baked beans from a tin in front of the TV while Mama and Auntie sat in Auntie's kitchen, discussing the stranger in low voices.

"Do you think that man was really our uncle?" Sindi whispered during an advert break. Thuli shrugged and stared hard at the woman selling Omo washing powder on the flickering screen.

Sindi pushed the man from her head and snuggled closer to her twin. Outside, dogs barked and howled and fought and growled. In the distance, she could hear the music at Ma Elias'. She drifted on the bass beats, then made them into steps and climbed into Thuli's dreams.

Mama left the house at seven the next morning, but returned ten minutes later with airtime and called in sick. The twins hung about, chancing their luck, but she made them put on their uniforms and said she'd walk them to the school gate. Halfway there, she turned and hurried them back.

By lunch time, Sindi wished she were stuck behind a desk reciting multiplication tables or the names of struggle heroes. Mama refused to let them leave the house, so they sat at the kitchen table paging through old magazines and drinking coffee until Sindi's palms were sweaty from nerves and too much caffeine. If one of them needed to pee, which was often because of the coffee, Mama made them all traipse down the road together to the cinderblock toilets they shared with the other families in the street. They thought about disappearing while Mama was in the toilet, but her mood was so black it wasn't worth the trouble.

Black moods were rare and usually came after a night spent at Ma Elias' with Auntie. They were quiet storms, signalled by silent glares and stale-beer-and-nicotine burps. They strung the air with so much tension that the twins tiptoed around the house, praying Mama would send them for the cure: a two-litre Coke and a packet of Grand-Pa Headache Powder.

Some days the cure worked, but other days it was like adding fuel to fire. Often, the twins just bought sweets and stayed out until dark. If luck smiled on them, they found Mama snoring when they came back. Most times, she was waiting, angry as a stood-on snake. Still, it was better than spending the whole day flinching, and the sugar on their tongues made up for their stinging cheeks.

Through the kitchen window, the balmy day goaded Sindi. A perfect day to swipe sweets. Joe would be basking in the sun like a lizard, the shop would be wide open. Thuli knew it too: she stared out the window at the mocking blue that came all the way down between the houses. The sight of it brought on a sulk, and it wasn't long before Thuli started to whine. Sindi stole a glance at Mama, not brave enough to add her voice to the pleading. Mama looked tired. Her eyelids were like the soft brown patches on bruised apples, but they narrowed quickly and Thuli shut up.

The knock came at four thirty, an hour and a half earlier than the time Mama normally arrived home from work. Thuli hopped to the door and had it wide before Mama could push her chair back. The stranger stood in the street, holding his hat to his chest like someone had died. In his other hand was a bag of groceries. He stepped forward but Thuli blocked his entry, an action that might have been more useful the first time he'd come.

"You alone?" Mama asked.

The stranger nodded and held out the bag. "I brought some things for supper."

"You weren't invited."

"I need to talk to you, Sizane. I am your brother, not your enemy."

"I lost my brother eleven years ago."

"Don't say that."

"A brother would have done something."

The stranger sighed. "Must I stand in the street while we discuss family matters? Do you want your neighbours to know our business? I am no stranger, can I not come in?"

Thuli looked at Mama and, on her nod, stepped back and let him pass. He put the groceries and his hat on the table. Through the bag's taut skin, Sindi could see a box of tea and a quart of Black Label. She watched Thuli unpack the rest of the things he'd brought: a loaf of bread, two tomatoes, an onion, a packet of powdered soup. It seemed a meagre gift to win them over: no chocolate, no sweets, not even an apple.

"Why have you come?" Mama shot the question at him as soon as he was seated.

"A cup of tea would be nice, Sisi. I walked from the hostel, there is dust in my throat." He paused, as if waiting for Mama to get up. When she didn't move, he shook his head slowly and sighed. "I have a wife now. Thembi, you remember her? Do you not want to know how I've got on, these past eleven years? Are you not curious about your brother's life?"

"What do you want, Jabu? You haven't come all this way to tell me you married a goat." She frowned. "How did you know where to find us?"

The man cleared his throat, demonstrating how dry it was, and Thuli stood up to light the primus. Mama flared her nostrils.

"We've known for years. You remember Ntokozo, who worked at the Spar in Mid Illovo? She has a cousin who lives nearby. She saw you."

"I remember, it was five years ago. I thought she'd kept my secret."

"There are no secrets in Eston."

"I thought if you knew, she would come . . ." Mama stopped and looked at Sindi. "Girls, let me talk to your uncle. Go out and play."

Outside, the day's heat had rolled back. Sindi reached for the sky, stretching out the tension that had coiled into her spine during the long wait. The day was almost over, but they could still spend a precious hour free from the confines of Mama's black mood. The thought buoyed her squashed spirits. It seemed nothing could wipe away Thuli's sulk, though. She hunched against the wall, her face puckered like Gogo Nkosi's when her hens laid no eggs. Sindi laughed.

"What's so funny?"

"You. Why you so cross?"

Thuli rolled her eyes, which Sindi knew was supposed to make her feel stupid.

"Ah," Sindi said, "you want to be with *that* man. Thuli's got a boyfriend, Thuli wants to hold his hand!" Hands on hips, she waggled her bum and made kissing sounds.

"Stop it. I just want to know what he's doing here. He's our uncle, our real uncle."

"Says who? Mama says we've got no other family. It's just us."

"You heard, Sindi, don't be so stupid. He said he was Mama's brother."

"So?"

"So, she didn't say, 'I don't have a brother'."

"So?"

"So? So are you saying he's a liar? That Mama's going along with him for fun?"

Sindi shrugged. She wasn't going to agree with Thuli, just because. But Thuli was going to get into a real twist if Sindi didn't stop teasing, and anyway, standing and arguing was a waste of time. Sindi pressed a finger to her lips, crept to the open window and peered in.

"Get," Mama growled. Sindi ducked, but the blow caught the side of her head.

Thuli burst out laughing. "Now that's funny, that's really funny."

Sindi didn't know whether to laugh or cry. It wasn't so sore, but the humiliation of catching a smack while trying to be a clever set her cheeks on fire. She was considering passing it on, punching the smile off her sister's face, when Thuli lunged at her and pulled her away from the window.

"Pas op." Mama shook her finger at them.

The bedroom had two windows: one in the front, the twin of the kitchen window, and a long narrow one at the back, higher up. Both had been left open to dry the carpet. Auntie sat out on her front step, hunched over her toenails, painting them the colour of scabs. If the girls tried to climb in through the front, she'd rat them out.

Sindi waved as they slipped between the two houses.

"Hello, Auntie," Thuli called out. Auntie grunted, but didn't look up.

The ground around the house was not yet dry. As they crouched beneath the window, figuring out how to get in, their shoes sank into the mud. On her toes with her arms stretched, Sindi could just reach the sill. She looked for something to stand on.

"Make a step," she said.

Thuli shook her head, "You make it."

"It was my idea."

"So?"

"So, I'll tell you what they say. Make a step."

Thuli folded her arms across her chest. "Ching chong cha."

"Okay." Sindi thought of paper and made a fist behind her back. "Best of three."

Thirty seconds later, Thuli got down one knee, like Gogo Nkosi's lodger that time he pretended to propose, and linked her fingers together.

The window was above Mama's bed. The sill scraped against her ribs as Sindi hoisted herself up and over. She hung half in, half out for a moment, unable to turn around in the small frame, then tumbled headfirst onto the low bed. She tried to hold her feet up off the bedspread, but as she rolled off the bed onto the floor her shoe caught the edge.

"Cha!" she exhaled through her teeth. Rubbing the mark made it worse. Jik would clean it, or Vim, but both were in the kitchen cupboard with the cloth and bucket. She tucked the muddied edge of the spread under the mattress. Hopefully Mama wouldn't notice before Sindi could deal with it. Otherwise, Mama would strip the skin off her backside.

And if she did? Sindi shrugged at her reflection in the wardrobe mirror.

The only sounds coming from the kitchen were the hiss of gas and the clang of the kettle on the stove, as clear as if they were in the same room.

All that separated her from them was a curtain strung from the wall to the wardrobe. She should hide, just in case. She dismissed the idea of crawling under their bed. She'd have to squash between the suitcase and the boxes stored there, and there were spiders. Mostly dead ones, long legs curled around their bodies, the broken strands of their webs thick with dust.

The wardrobe was creepy too, but she'd never seen a spider in the wardrobe. Huddled into the corner with the door shut, she was surrounded by the smell of shoe polish, mothballs, the sharp armpit chemistry of Mama's work blouses. The wood muffled sound, but when Mama spoke, her voice was clear enough.

"I can't believe you married Thembi. Remember how we used to tease her when we were children? We said her father was a goat. Does she still huff like an angry ram?"

"That is my wife you are talking about."

"Your wife, I can't believe it. What did Mama do when you told her? What I would've given to see the look on her face."

"Believe it or not, they have made their peace. Mama is different now. These past ten years have softened her. Why don't you come see for yourself? Come home with me, bring the girls to meet their family."

"Jabu, this is my home now. After Sandile died, I swore I would never return. There is nothing for me to go back to."

Sindi tensed, holding her body as still as she could, so the small rustling sounds of the clothing moving against her skin and hair would not drown out any of Mama's words. All she knew of their father was that he was dead and the twins had his mouth. They knew because Mama kept a photo of him folded into the sleeve of her ID book, along with the newspaper article from the day they were born. His name was written on the back of the photograph along with a date four days after their birth. Until Auntie set the record straight, they'd thought he'd run away, like most of Auntie's boyfriends eventually did. "At least your daddy died before he could run," she'd told them, as if death was an easier loss to bear.

Mama never spoke of him. He was less than a shadow in their lives, the fading photograph the only evidence that he'd existed at all. Sometimes they snuck Mama's ID book from her handbag and laid the article and photograph side by side. Thuli would read aloud from the article while Sindi slid the tip of her finger up and down the crease that ran the length of their father's face. The crease split over his nose, opening it up so that it looked squashed, like a wrestler's on *WWE SmackDown*. Perhaps that was why Sindi imagined he'd died in a fight.

Sindi pressed her cheek to the back panelling of the wardrobe, as if to bring her ear closer to Mama's mouth, but it was Uncle who spoke next.

"Your heart has turned to stone. Our mother is dying. Have you no forgiveness for an old woman? Please, Sizane, she is asking for you."

Sindi's chest tightened. The only family she'd ever had was Mama and Thuli. Now it seemed they had a grandmother and she was dying. It wasn't fair.

Mama laughed, but it was a laugh devoid of joy. "Really, Jabu, old? How old can she be, fifty, fifty-one?"

"Fifty-five."

"Fifty-five is not old. You're trying to trick me."

There was a clunk, an innocent noise like a mug being put down sharply, but the long silence that followed set Sindi's heart hammering. She held her breath. Something bad.

"No trick. Mama's health is not good. Illness has taken a heavy toll on her. She looks one hundred. You won't believe, Sisi."

"If she is ill, it's because God is punishing her. She's a bad woman, Jabu, she has the devil inside her."

"Sizane, that is unkind. Her life has not been easy."

"Unkind? Do you think it's kind to put soil in a baby's mouth, to cut off her breath? Jabu, do you? Or do you think that is evil?"

"Sizane! That was a long time ago, she's sorry. And the girl is fine. There is nothing wrong with her. Can you not put the past to rest?"

"Nothing wrong? She has no tongue in her mouth. Her sister, she talks to everyone, she's friendly, outgoing, but that child, Jabu. You saw when you were here yesterday. Did she say two words to you?"

Uneasiness fizzed in Sindi's abdomen. Her mouth tasted of rusted nails. She held the stifling garments away from her face and pushed the wardrobe door with her foot. It opened a crack and the light bled in. Her fear let go a little.

"Sizane, she's just shy. Some children are shy. You can't blame Mama for that. She made a mistake, she is sorry."

All the air seemed to have been sucked from the wardrobe, and the metal on her tongue was becoming more intense.

"She tried to kill my child."

Sindi's cheeks tightened painfully, as if something had been pushed into her mouth. She pressed her palms to her face, flat, but inside it felt as though the skin would split.

"Why are you laughing?"

"Sizane, you gave your girls the wrong names. Thulisile means 'quiet one' but she talks, talks, talks, and the other one has no tongue."

Something wet and sticky slid to the back of Sindi's throat. She gagged.

"That is nothing to laugh at. I named her because she didn't cry when her sister was suffocating. Not one sound. And Sindisiwe, she was so close to death when the nurse found her. Jabu, how can you laugh?"

Sindi clutched at her throat. She made small hic-ing sounds as her lungs tugged for air. The darkness tilted. She reached for the door, but everything had shifted and her hands closed around Mama's pink nylon housecoat. It slid off the hanger.

"But the nurse saved her, Sizane. And there is nothing wrong with her now but shyness. Please, come see Mama."

Sindi closed her eyes. A white dot spiralled through the dark towards her, growing bigger and bigger. *Cumulus*, she thought, *cumulus, cumulus, cumulus*.

That Man is the Devil

Darkness gave way to grey. Sindi opened her eyes. Strange shapes floated in front of her, unfocused ghosts in a tight, grainy space. Mama's housecoat covered her face, the nylon mesh giving everything a pink sheen. She pushed it away, releasing a crackle of static that ran along the fabric in thin blue flashes. A slice of light drew a line down the edge of the wardrobe door. She remembered climbing into the wardrobe to eavesdrop . . .

When she thought about what she'd heard, her head began to throb like it did when she competed with Thuli to see who could last the longest on a single breath.

Sounds filtered through the wood. Voices. Mama's and Thuli's, the strange man's.

"Thuli, where's your sister? What's taking her so long, is she sick?" Thuli mumbled a reply she couldn't make out.

How long had she been in the wardrobe? She wanted to push the door wide and spill into the bedroom, where the world was normal and she could feel safe. But she was not safe. If Mama discovered her, she'd be in big trouble. She took a deep breath, opened the door and peered out. There was no one there, but someone must have come in while she was in the wardrobe because the light was on. The front window was a black square reflecting the lit room. It was dark outside. No wonder Mama was asking for her. A ripple in the reflection alerted her to movement. She shrank back and pulled the door shut.

The wood vibrated as the curtain swung against the side of the wardrobe. She held her breath, listened. Someone entered the room on light feet. It had to be Thuli, but she couldn't be sure.

"Sisi?" said a soft voice.

Sindi opened the door and stuck her head out. "I'm here," she whispered, relieved.

"That's where you're hiding? What you doing in there? You've been gone forever."

"I think I fell asleep."

Thuli rolled her eyes. "I knew it, you can't do anything right. You should have let me do it. Now Mama's asking for you. I said you went to the toilet, but she's going to look for you if you don't come back soon."

"Is it safe?"

Thuli shrugged. "I'll try keep her in the kitchen. You climb out the window and come in the front."

"Someone will see me."

"Check first that there's no one there," Thuli said, dragging out her words as if she was speaking to an idiot.

When she was gone, Sindi scrunched Mama's housecoat in her fists. Cow, so full of herself. Nobody's perfect, not even Thuli. She tossed the housecoat aside, setting off an angry crackle, and slipped out of the wardrobe.

Sindi stood at the front door, feeling like she did when she'd walked out the shop with something up her sleeve and knew she was clear. No one had seen her climb out of the window. Still, her heart beat so hard she was sure anyone could see it knocking in her chest. She reached for the handle. As her fingers connected with the metal, the door swung back and she tilted into Mama's belly.

"Where have you been?"

Mama's full-moon face was pulled tight. Maybe she should make a run for it, Sindi thought, but then Mama would know she'd done something wrong. Mumbling something about the toilet, she tried to push past.

Mama shifted her weight from one foot to the other. "Sindisiwe, answer me. Where have you been?"

In the kitchen, Thuli joked with Uncle. Sindi heard her sister giggle, and imagined her squirming away from his tickling fingers with the top half of her body while she twisted her hips towards him, like she always did with men. Uncle's hoarse laughter dissolved in coughing.

"I was . . ." she scrambled for a story but came up empty. "I, m_m_mmy sss_astomach . . ." Had Auntie been sitting on her doorstep in the dark? Perhaps she'd ratted her out and was in the kitchen with Thuli and Uncle. She strained for Auntie's voice, but Uncle's coughs drowned out all other sound.

She should have let Thuli do the spying; she was a much better liar.

"Show me your shoes."

Sindi gave Mama what she hoped was a blank stare.

"Ah." Mama placed her hand on the back of Sindi's head and drew her close. Flesh closed around Sindi's cheeks as her face was mashed into the space between Mama's breasts. Her nose pressed against sternum. She squirmed. Mama tightened her grip. Mama's damp cleavage smelled like guavas fermenting in the sun. That pale-ale perfume stung Sindi's nostrils every time Mama went to Ma Elias'. It was a sign her mood, like her sweat, had soured.

Mama let go of her head. Her hand slid down to Sindi's shoulder, where it rested a moment before seeking out her ear. She began to knead Sindi's earlobe, gently squeezing and releasing, a sensation that might have been pleasant if it hadn't been for the angry heartbeat thrumming against Sindi's cheeks.

She used to worry Mama would get shot working at the Checkers in town: it got robbed so often. But time passed and nothing happened, and she began to believe a bullet could never penetrate Mama's fat breasts. When she laid her head on Mama's chest, she usually couldn't hear her heart like she could hear Thuli's. Her sister's life tapped right up against her ear, just below the surface, red and unguarded and made of glass. Mama's was buried deep, and the sound of it heightened Sindi's fear.

The kneading stopped. "Why is everything that comes out of your mouth a lie?" Mama pinched her earlobe so hard Sindi felt sure the thumbnail would pierce it. Sindi bit her lip to stop from crying out. She knew Mama would hurt her more if she didn't cry, but she didn't want Uncle to hear.

Thuli began to sing a Zulu wedding song they'd learned in school for the end-of-year concert. Sindi thought the concert was stupid, mainly because Dumisile played the groom and Nandi his bride while the rest of the class had to get down on all fours and pretend to be singing cows. "Nginesiponono sase Thekwini," Thuli sang.

Mama twisted and tugged and pinched, but her sister's voice cushioned her from the pain. Mama could rip her ear off and it probably wouldn't feel much worse than hitting her funny bone.

"Sizane, what are you doing?" Uncle's voice was too close.

Mama let go of Sindi's ear and pushed her away. "Pas op."

Blood rushed into her throbbing lobe, making it feel pumpkin-sized. She was relieved it still fitted into her palm.

Uncle peered at her over Mama's shoulder. "What's going on, Sizane?"

"There is nothing going on."

Sindi stared at her feet, but she could feel the heat of Mama's glare. She lowered her hand and turned her face so Uncle could not see her ear. What would he think of them?

"What have you done to her ear?"

"What's it to do with you?"

"Ai, Sizane, have you not yet learned to control your temper? You pinched me when we were children, but a child pinching a child is not the same thing as an adult pinching a child."

"I don't believe this. You're telling me how discipline my children?"

"I'm just concerned, Sisi. Your children are my nieces."

"Your concern is eleven years too late."

Sindi snuck a glance. Standing like that, with Uncle behind her, made

Mama look as if she had two heads. Sindi hadn't noticed before, but Mama and him had the same face, like they were boy-girl twins. Both had wide noses with nostrils that wobbled and flared with each inhaled breath, and womanly mouths. They weren't identical twins. Uncle's lips had cracked and he'd nibbled at the flakes, and their eyes were different. Mama's slanted while Uncle's protruded through heavy, fleshy lids. And Uncle was thin.

"I need cigarettes," Uncle said. "Maybe the girls will go to the shop for me."

Mama's nostrils dilated and she gave Uncle the look. The look meant she wanted to smack him. Sindi had seen Mama punch a man before, at Ma Elias'. He'd hit the ground with a thud and lain there for such a long time everyone thought she'd killed him.

"Have you lost your mind, Jabu?" Mama turned, ruining the two-headed monster effect. "Can you not see it's dark? What kind of mother would let her babies go off to buy cigarettes at this time of the night?"

Uncle sighed. "I'll go with them and keep them safe. I don't know the way. Sizane, please, let the girls show me."

The unlit paths between the shacks were littered with junk that ambushed bare legs and snagged on clothes. Sindi followed Uncle through the inky darkness, his breath the only sound. Where were the barking dogs, the screaming car alarms, the airless pop of backfiring exhausts and trigger fingers? She bent down to free her skirt from a rusty wire and lost sight of Thuli and Uncle. Through the corrugated walls of a nearby shack, she heard the first strains of the *Generations* theme tune. She unhooked the wire, wishing she was at Auntie's watching TV, and lurched after them.

"It'll be cool," Thuli had whispered, eyes flashing. They'd told Uncle it would take an hour to go the other way, following the grid of well-lit municipal roads, and that on these darker paths there was less chance of encountering tsotsis. Really, they wanted to avoid the Spaza shop, where Uncle could buy his cigarettes but there was no chance of pocketing anything at the small service window. Sindi had immediately begun to regret the lie: although they took the same route whenever they went to Joe's, in the dark her feet forgot the way and even shadows seemed to trip her up.

It took almost twenty minutes to get to the veld that lay between the township and the road. Mama was going to flay them when they got home.

"Come on, we're almost there." Thuli pointed across the veld to Saviour's blue forecourt lights, but Uncle placed a hand on her shoulder, holding her back.

"Are you sure it's safe? There might be tsotsis lying in the long grass, waiting for us."

Thuli squirmed from his grasp and ran off across the inky grass, *pwack pwack* chicken noises bouncing from her lips.

"What do you think, Sindisiwe, are there tsotsis?"

Sindi didn't know how to answer. There were children who sometimes camped in the veld, orphan gangs that would take your schoolbag off you. They usually only rifled through it for food and money, leaving everything else. She'd never heard of them mugging a grown-up, so the answer was probably no. She shrugged, cursing Thuli for leaving her alone with this man. The fact that he was her uncle did nothing to shrink the dread lurking in the pit of her stomach, a feeling that rose to her throat when he slipped his hand over hers and began to pick his way across the bleak no-man's-land.

Saviour's Pit Stop lay on the far side of the road. Fluorescent lights spilled onto the forecourt, tainting everything with a frigid glow and turning the neon-orange Chicken Licken sign dried-blood brown. A dog hung around the bins, waiting for someone to chuck a few stripped bones her way. She was a mean street-mutt with a missing leg that Joe called Tripod.

Joe sat on a lawn chair at the entrance to his shop, head lolling against his chest. He'd be half asleep when he served them. There was no sign of Ben. Perhaps he only worked during the day – Sindi had never been to

Saviour's at night. She shivered. It was too quiet, with no one around but Joe and the pumps. The pumps were bad enough during the day. Like all very old things, their squat robotic forms had a presence. She sensed a lurking mechanical intelligence observing her from behind the small rectangular window where the numbers spun, counting out fuel in rands and litres. Silent sentries, the pumps watched her every move. They knew what she was up to and they were biding their time. One day, the rubber hose-arms would reach across the forecourt, force a nozzle into her mouth and cut off her breath, and she wouldn't be able to cry for help.

It wasn't just the pumps that were old. The whole place, from the greasy counter to the oil-stained forecourt, sagged back into a time of gas guzzlers like the ones abandoned in the scrap yards. A time Joe spoke of with reverence, when everyone drove a car and there was big money in flogging fuel.

Joe had a vintage Mercedes-Benz parked in the yard around the back, hidden behind rusting sheet-metal gates. It sat on bricks, going nowhere, but he kept its pale-yellow hull polished up and gleaming. When they were younger, he'd lift them into the red-leather driver's seat and give them a view of the past. They weren't allowed to touch the wheel or any of the levers or knobs, but the feeling of being so high up and having so much space was enough to make them nag to sit there. It was more bus than car. You could fit six people in the back, easy. Sindi couldn't imagine a time when the roads were full of cars like that. The lanes on the highway now weren't wide enough for the Merc: it would be like trying to squeeze two Mamas into a single aisle at the supermarket.

No, Saviour's Pit Stop wasn't like other service stations. Joe was a diesel pirate, one of the last. No one knew why the police turned a blind eye to the still behind the Merc where Ben refined the thick brown oil from Chicken Licken's deep-fat fryers. There were rumours. Some said the police chief had shares in Joe's business, others that Joe was married to the chief's daughter. Sindi believed neither story. The place was falling apart and she'd never seen a Mrs Saviour.

Sindi liked the Merc and the free sweets she sometimes managed to lift from under Joe's nose, but her favourite part of Saviour's Pit Stop was the Legend: the old Shackleton bomber that sat on the forecourt roof like a gigantic, exhausted goose. It had a scarred and battle-weary look. Once, the body of the plane had been painted white and cobalt blue. The undersides of the wings had been yellow, with two custard stripes arcing down the belly. But the Legend wasn't lovingly buffed on a weekly basis, and the paint had long ago dulled. The cursive script spelling out *The Legend* was a shadow, and a snatch of sky could be glimpsed through one of the wings where rust had chewed a hole.

Some days a torrid wind picked chaff from the veld and blew it across the street. As if to protest the dusty assault, the propellers would rotate arthritically, squeaking out four different tunes. It set people's teeth on edge, but no amount of complaining could convince Joe to get out the Q20. He told anyone who'd listen that, with every turn, something happened out there in the world. The squeaking was the song of passing time and the end of the world would have to come before it could be silenced.

Everybody knew it was really because Joe was too fat to climb a ladder.

Sindi led Uncle up the road to where Thuli waited, and saw that the Legend had disappeared. Only when she squinted could she see its hulking shadow against the new-moon night; even then it faded in and out of her vision, refusing to solidify.

A bakkie and several minibus taxis rounded the corner at speed, drawing her attention from the now-you-see-it, now-you-don't mystery of the Legend. The bakkie screeched to a halt in the centre of the forecourt, jerking Joe from dreamland and sending Tripod skittering. Two men in black suits stepped out of the cab, followed by a square woman in a kaftan. The older man wore a hat like Uncle's. The taxis parked at untidy angles in front of the station, blocking Sindi's view. Doors slid open, people spilled out. Everyone in black.

Sindi had heard that followers of the Black Preacher kept radio receivers in their pockets and could tune in to his sermons wherever they might be; that they sewed copper wire into their clothing to pick up the Voice of God. As the people crossed from the shadows into the neon brightness, she saw from the glints on their dark jackets and skirts that it was true.

An amplified whine murdered the quiet. Sindi snatched her hand from Uncle's sweaty grasp and covered her ears. The air thickened with clicks, with *testing, testing*, with *one, two, three*, with the rough clearing of someone's throat.

"What's happening?"

As if in reply to Uncle's question, a voice rang out: "Brothers and sisters, let us bow our heads and ask God to bless this gathering."

While Uncle leaned against a taxi, smoking a cigarette he'd bummed from the driver, the twins circled the mass of dark bodies around the bakkie, looking for a way in. Auntie said the Black Preacher was the devil. Mama said that Auntie thought anyone who wasn't Catholic was the devil. Auntie countered that she'd met him once and got a shock when she touched his sleeve, which proved he was associated with dark and unnatural goings-on. Since then, Thuli had begged Auntie to take them to a meeting of Believers: she wanted to feel the dark and unnatural goings-on for herself. Auntie refused. "Stay away from those Believers," she warned. "They're up to no good."

The square woman stood on the back of the bakkie, straightening her kaftan, while the three men it had taken to haul her up there mopped their brows. The congregation waited in silence. Sindi bit down hard on her fist, eyes brimming with laughter. How could they just stand there, when she couldn't even look at her sister for fear they'd both burst?

Then the woman began to sing. Her melodic voice drew each syllable out before stringing it on to the next to create a single long note. Sindi's fist dropped from her mouth.

Auntie had once told them that she felt transported when she listened to hymns in church. She'd shut her eyes and swayed when she said that, even though the only singer present was a dog barking in the road. For weeks after her revelation, the twins had swayed past her like drunks whenever she sat on her doorstep rubbing Vaseline Intensive Care into her arms. Now, Auntie's rapt expression flashed into Sindi's mind as she closed her eyes and let the words of the song wash over her. At first she struggled to decipher meaning, catching only an odd phrase here and there, but by the third verse her ear had relaxed and the beauty of the woman's voice could no longer shelter her.

All children are born blessed with the pure blood of Christ
But your sinner's veins are tainted black with devil's vice.
Your mothers bear babies that die on the breast
And your fathers spread sickness, disease and hate.
You will sicken and die like trees in drought
While the Earth becomes hell and heaven closes its gate.

The desire to join Thuli in her quest to touch the Black Preacher vanished. Perhaps Auntie had been right and these people with their dark clothes and grisly music were up to something bad. She reached out, meaning to draw Thuli away from the crowd and convince her to go home, but as her fingers connected with her sister's elbow, the square woman picked up the tempo and began to stamp out a clang-and-rattle rhythm. Following her lead, the crowd snapped their fingers and clapped their hands. Gentle hip undulations swivelled into gyrations as men and woman came together, grinding pelvises as if they were on the dance floor at Ma Elias'. The Believers spun faster and faster, eyes rolling, spit frothing at their lips. Copper flashes darted across the frenzied mass.

Thuli grabbed Sindi's hand and dragged her along the outskirts of the crowd. Sindi tried to pull out of her sister's grasp, but Thuli, intent on breaking through the mesh of flailing arms and stamping feet, held on. Glassy-eyed women gave them slanting, over-the-shoulder glances. They ducked to avoid elbows and jumped to keep their toes from getting crushed, but they found no gaps. The twins didn't belong and nobody wanted to let them in.

Then, as if a switch had been flicked, the singing stopped and the congregation turned to face the bakkie. Heads bowed and hands came together. Many of the faithful fell to their knees, careless of the hard, oily concrete. The megaphone tortured the air and a man began to pray. Then he stopped short – someone was still clapping and singing. Thuli giggled and elbowed Sindi in the ribs when she saw who it was.

Joe, surrounded by kneeling Believers, was swaying from side to side, eyes closed, belting out *Kumbaya my Lord* at the top of his voice.

Sindi smiled and turned to look at the wide-open door of the shop.

The slab in her hand was family-size, as long and wide as a brick. Inside the foil, the chocolate slid away from her fingers, escaping to the far corners of the wrapper. They were all like that. The shop's tin roof had never been insulated, and the unclad asbestos walls inhaled the day's heat and exhaled it into the shop at night, ensuring a constant milk-souring temperature. It was why Joe spent most of his time outside.

Eating the sticky mess would be gross – the melted chocolate would glue her tongue to the top of her mouth – but Sindi had never lifted one of these slabs before. They were too big to slip up a sleeve, the rectangular bulge a dead giveaway even Joe couldn't miss. She dropped it into the carrier bag she'd taken from behind the counter and cocked her head. The preacher's voice was tinny: the megaphone turned his voice TV. With practised calm, she picked up a roll of Triple-X and slipped it up her sleeve. It was good to polish her sleight of hand, even when she didn't need to. Thuli stood lookout at the door. She crouched behind the news-paper stand, only partially hidden. Not that it mattered: the crowd out-side was in raptures. Someone would have to scream blue murder to get their attention.

A moth the size of Sindi's hand perched on the stack of yesterday's *Daily Voice*, wings pulsing slowly. Sindi dropped another slab into the bag. Time was up. Thuli hadn't noticed the moth yet, but when she did, she'd yell loud enough to wake the whole city.

Moths flew at Thuli all the time, as if there was a light inside her head. Like cats that sought out people allergic to their fur, they sensed her distaste and wanted to rub up against it. She hated them. She said it was the whirring of their wings, the powder they left on her skin, their clumsy bodies. But it was more than disgust. Thuli's reaction was ex-treme, as if she thought contact would scorch third-degree burns into her skin. Once, to prove it was harmless, Sindi caught a moth, cornered her sister and tried to force her to touch it. At first Thuli screamed and pleaded, swore and threatened. Then her eyes rolled back until only the whites were visible and Sindi felt her slip away a little. She'd never done it again.

She grabbed Thuli's hand and dragged her out the door. After the heat inside the shop, the night air hit her full in the face like a slap from Mama in winter. Her skin buzzed; her blood zipped in her veins. She loved the way the pulses in her neck began to throb whenever she left a shop with something up her sleeve, like her head was about to explode.

What if it did? What if her brains splattered on the reverent crowd? Imagining their startled faces gave her the giggles. She was about to burst into a full laughing fit when she saw the girl leaning against one of the pumps, watching. She nudged Thuli with her elbow.

Thuli narrowed her eyes. "So what?" She gave the girl the finger. "It's just Nandi."

Some Place Else Called Home

Three days later, without any warning, the twins came home to find their door chained and padlocked. The curtains were drawn and they could see the houses across the street reflected in the windows. Sindi placed her hand over the lock. The tips of her fingers and thumb just reached the shiny chrome edges. Brand new and bigger than her heart.

"We've been evicted," said Thuli. "Joe's kicked us out."

Sindi rattled the chain. The clatter of metal on metal set dogs barking. The man across the road looked up from polishing his shoes. She flushed.

Whenever there was an eviction, Sindi would stare at the ground, unable to meet the eye of the forlorn tenants sitting on the street with their things. Sometimes they sat for hours, waiting for a kind neighbour to offer to watch their belongings while they went looking for new accommodation. Few were keen. A search could take days and most people's homes were cramped.

"You girls are late." The window next door opened and Auntie's head popped out. "Your ma expected you back from school at two. Where you been?"

"Where's Mama?" Thuli asked, ignoring Auntie's question.

Auntie pursed her lips and fixed a curler into her hair. A sneer rode up her nose and settled between her eyebrows. Sindi glanced at Thuli and tried not to giggle. With her sour face and her set curl, Auntie looked like one of Gogo Nkosi's hens today.

"Come wait inside," she said. "Don't go no place else."

Sindi sat at Auntie's kitchen table across from Thuli, rasping her thumb along the chipped yellow Formica in time to the scratch and hiss of Auntie's emery board. A suitcase sagged in the corner. It was the one from on top of their wardrobe and it looked a hundred years old. The latches had long ago lost their snap, and Mama had wrapped a leather belt around the middle to keep it shut. Still, the suitcase could not be muzzled: its sides refused to come together, as if it were trying to spit out their clothes.

Auntie sat opposite manicuring her nails in nothing but her underwear and a towel. The towel gaped – once, wide enough for Sindi to see a strange misshapen bulge between her legs, like the goitre on Gogo Nkosi's neck. After that, she could not help looking, but all she managed was a glimpse of the blemish above her knee that Auntie called her death-mole, and dark curls that spread from the elastic of Auntie's panties onto her thighs. She imagined Auntie's fingers wrapping the hair round tiny curlers to get it tight. The thought made her stomach ache.

Auntie's maternal grandmother was a Griqua, or so she claimed, and she liked to show off the caramel skin tone she called her legacy. "Didn't get nothing else from that side," she said. On sunny days, Auntie would sit on her front step in a short skirt and bra rubbing Vaseline Intensive Care into her arms. If a man walked past, she'd hold out her arms to admire them and say, "Cappuccino," but she'd been sitting out so long nobody looked any more.

Thuli lifted the saucer Auntie used as an ashtray and held it under Auntie's chin to catch the ash from her cigarette. "Auntie?"

"Hmm?"

"Where are we going?"

Auntie twitched and squeezed one eye shut against the smoke. "Home," she said, out the side of her mouth.

Sindi watched Uncle pass their faded suitcase to the driver squatting on top of the minibus taxi and thought about *home*. Once in a while, a taxi would come and load up boxes and cases and shabby bags while a family stood in front of their shut-up house, dressed in their best. When you saw them, you knew. They were going home. Home was a place visited only once or twice a year, over Easter and Christmas. It could be anywhere: Limpopo, Buffalo City, Mpumalanga; anywhere but the house you lived in here. Everybody Sindi knew came from someplace else. Everybody except them.

Squinting into the sun, she watched the driver rearrange the load. Their suitcase was too big to go on top, so smaller things had to be taken out of the stack to make a space for it. He had to stand to hoist their suitcase into place, the veins on his arms cording with the effort. When he rattled the handle to check its stability, everything seemed to tilt. The driver restacked the load and secured the lot with washing line, looping it through the handle of their suitcase, then down to the roof rack and back again. Sindi worried it wouldn't hold. If their suitcase came tumbling down, it would spill its guts and everyone would see their panties – and worse, Mama's gigantic bras. Against the sky, you couldn't tell the suitcase was meant to be blue. Next to it, even the taped-up cardboard cartons looked new. She glared at the scuffed toes on her school shoes. Maybe Miss Booley was right about them.

Auntie, who'd dressed to see them off, gave the driver a glass of water. He gulped it down in three while she fingered the top button of her blouse. Then he opened the door, revealing a cram of sweating passengers. Sindi let the others get in first, her eyes lingering on the only home she'd ever known. Most of her life had been lived within a five-kilometre radius of that house; it was the nucleus of her world. The driver sniffed and cleared his throat, but it was only when Mama barked her name that Sindi turned from the house and stepped up past him.

She jammed her bum into the tight space between Mama and the side panel, wriggling to make contact with the seat. She bit her lip as the door rolled closed, latching with a sigh that sounded like forever. The engine wheezed, but the brief flicker of hope the sound sparked in her was snuffed out when the motor caught. She stared at their shut-up zozo. The windows stared back, reflecting the outside world.

Thuli sat on the other side of Uncle, two bellies away. When she could no longer crane her neck and see their house, Sindi glanced across the abdominal expanse and caught her sister's eye. Thuli beamed at her. None of the apprehension Sindi felt about going home to their grandmother was visible in Thuli's glowing face; but then, what did Thuli have to be afraid of? No one had tried to kill her. Sindi returned her twin's broad grin with a wan smile and sank into the cramped space between the window and her mother's arm, contracting her stomach muscles as hard as she could to squash the flutter of disquiet.

Since the day in the wardrobe, she'd dreamed of suffocation. Every night, as she drifted on the first waves of sleep, she became aware of a presence in the room. Shadows shifted across her lids as if someone stood over her, but she was always too tired to open her eyes. As the warm glue of sleep sucked her down, she felt a weight pressing against her breast-bone and the grainy sensation of soil in her mouth. At first, the pressure was gentle but it gradually increased until every breath she took was an effort. Finally, when she could no longer expand her lungs against it, she'd bolt awake. There was never anyone there except Mama and Thuli. Nuzzling against her sister's back in the aftermath of the dream, she felt bruised and too afraid to get up for a glass of water to wash the sweet mineral taste from her mouth. A taste like the smell of earthworms after rain.

"What did they say?" Thuli had asked on their walk to school, the morning after she'd hidden in the wardrobe.

"Couldn't hear properly," Sindi'd lied, not knowing why.

Inside the taxi, it was starting to cook. Rearranging the luggage to accommodate their suitcase had taken so long they'd ended up hitting the rush hour. All the windows that could be opened were wide. Sindi's was jammed shut. Dark circles seeped around armpits and sweat loaded the air, turning the taxi's interior humid and rank. Sindi pressed her nose to the steamy glass to escape the old-sock stink.

The wool of Mama's skirt itched sweaty-damp against her leg. Sindi wondered why Mama had put on her church clothes for the journey. She wondered about all the passengers, dressed in suits and smart jackets, the aunties in their hats, when even the summery fabric of her school dress made her feel like a potato baking in tin foil. Ten or eleven hours it would be, depending. That's what Uncle had said. She glanced again at the scuffs on her school shoes, and now she was glad that they hadn't gone straight home from school. Mama had spent so long looking for them, they'd had no time to change.

They eased down the on-ramp into the glut of vehicles. She'd only ever viewed the snarl of traffic from above, perched on the embankment by Saviour's. Level with the road, it was an entirely different game. Sindi watched in fascination as three women in the car next to her bounced up and down, lip-syncing to a song on the radio. Sindi could only just hear the music. Boxed in behind the window, she pretended she was watching TV with the volume turned down low.

The singers' car lurched ahead. Sindi willed the taxi forward but their lane was stagnant, going nowhere. She sighed and stared at the car that had taken its place. The solo driver was a disappointment. She sat up primly, as shiny as her red car. One for Thuli.

Feeling the heat of Sindi's stare, the driver turned towards her. Sindi dropped her eyes, embarrassed at being caught peeping. By the time she felt brave enough to look again, a white car had slipped into the space next to them. Before Sindi could scrutinise the new driver, the taxi slid forward and they caught up to the prim woman again. As they passed, she inserted a polished pearly-peach fingernail into her nostril. Sindi stared hard to make the woman look; when by some magic she did, Sindi stuck two fingers up her nose and jammed her tongue through them.

"Sindisiwe," Mama growled.

By the time they queued at the second tollgate, the day had shut down. She'd counted twenty-two blue cars, eighteen red cars, six singers, three nose pickers, one driver reading a book while he steered and a man raging at the traffic. She'd been too afraid to look at him for more than a few seconds in case he looked back.

With the light gone, she could no longer see into other cars and her thoughts turned to their destination. Uncle said they were going to the family kraal, the place where he and Mama had grown up. He referred to it as "home", as if it were their home as well as his. She tried to picture a welcoming homestead with chickens pecking the ground and a tethered goat, just like the drawing of a Zulu kraal in their history textbook. But when she peopled it, all she could see was the looming figure of her grandmother.

An informal settlement sprawled in the bitten veld flanking the toll plaza. Smoke from the shack-dwellers' cooking fires blanketed the road. It stopped the beams from the taxi's headlights short and turned everything hazy. As they neared the toll plaza and began to slow down, a man emerged from the smog ahead of them. He was walking down the middle of their lane, his back towards them. The car in front of them swerved to avoid him but he kept marching down the road like he owned it, oblivious to the angry honks.

"Look at the crazy," Thuli said, craning to see. He did look crazy. He wasn't dressed like a normal person. The tail of the pelt he'd tied around his waist dragged in the road behind him, and his shoulders were draped with black furs from some dog-like creature. As they neared him, she saw he had a belt of mice, flattened as if they'd been trodden on, and linked by their tiny shrivelled feet like a row of paper dolls. She wondered if he'd sewn them together like that, or if, in death, they'd reached to each other for comfort.

Unlike all the others she'd stared at on the journey, he did not turn to meet her gaze, but as he passed her window he reached out and tapped the glass with his index finger. Then he was gone. The image of the rhino beetle wrapped around his finger pulsated in her mind.

Under the toll-plaza arches, the air stung. The woman who took the toll looked tired and poisoned, and Sindi felt listless just looking at her. The cold booth light washed the tones from her skin and turned the rims of her eyes to fluorescent strips. She counted change, then nodded them through. Sindi felt like they'd crossed some kind of border. She'd never left the city before, but she didn't need the *Thank you for visiting* sign to tell her: this was the end.

When she opened her eyes, the rhythmic roll of the taxi that had lulled her through the long, cramped night had stopped again. Another passenger must be getting out. She'd lost count of the number of times she'd been jostled by someone lifting her seat to squeeze past, whispering apologies. Not all had reached their destination: most just wanted to stretch their legs or relieve their bladders while the driver climbed onto the roof to untie luggage. Through eyes thick with the remnants of a strange dream, she'd watched a man pee off the edge of the road into the inky black. How dark it is beyond the city, she'd thought, how dark.

This time, though, it was the engine dying that had woken her. This time, no one stuck their bum in her face trying to get out; this time, she opened her eyes to the cast-iron dawn and saw they were the only ones left.

The others still slept. Mama's head had sunk into her shoulders and her chin rested on her chest like a dozing pigeon's. Sleep softened her face and ran a thumb over the permanent frown that creased her brow, erasing it. She looked younger, like a girl not much older than Sindi. Asleep, Mama was a stranger.

The driver was up on the roof working the knots of the luggage ties. His tugging rocked the vehicle and Mama's head rolled from side to side. Sindi eased out from under Mama's arm and, quietly so she didn't wake the others, clambered over the seats to the front and out of the driver's open door.

Free from the stink of stale perspiration and artificial-lemon-scented freshener, she gulped the crisp air and rubbed life into her limbs. The taxi had stopped in a deserted parking lot; there was a superette, with a sign proclaiming it the Mid Illovo Spar. The shutters that came down over the windows were rusted. She knew it was too early for the Spar to open, but looking at the dejected building, she couldn't help thinking that maybe it never did. She walked to the entrance and peered through the security bars. The whole front stoep was enclosed, making the place looked caged in. Postboxes had been set into one wall. Some were open; on some, the doors hung from single hinges, like broken bird-wings. The cavities of the open boxes were deeply shadowed. She squinted, trying to see into their depths. Small creatures made their homes in spaces like those. Small creatures with watchful, beady eyes and lots of legs. There might be colony of them in each box, living on top of each other, squirming sightlessly. The shadows twisted, as if the things in the boxes were pushing forward, woken by the light. Or perhaps it was her presence. She did not wait to find out.

Though she'd been stuck in the taxi all night, she needed to sit to still the wobble of fright in her calves. At the far end of the parking lot, she spotted a bench under a tree. She'd never seen a tree like it before. Branches covered in thorns as long as her hand, and smooth green bark, like a tree from a dream where the colours were all wrong. She picked up a thorn that had fallen to the ground and tested the point against her finger. A yolky sun cracked onto the undulating hills. The patchy altocumulus blushed the colour of sour apricots instead of the suicide red of a city sunrise. Even the air was different, heavy and a bit briny, like a Lucky Star pilchard tin after the fish had been eaten and the tin rinsed out. She sucked her teeth and pressed the thorn into her skin. The sight of her blood, crimson, expected, comforted her.

Standing at the bench with the battered suitcase, they watched the taxi tilt away.

"Well," said Mama, blinking at the brightening sky, "eleven years doesn't change much."

"Too much, Sisi, too much." Uncle loosened his tie, shrugged off his jacket. "Ready?" he asked, angling his trilby so it shadowed his eyes. Mama nodded and lifted the suitcase onto her head. Steadying it with one hand, she set off as unevenly as the taxi. The twins stood side by side and watched Mama and Uncle go. Sindi thought Thuli might say something, but then she skipped after them without a word and Sindi had no choice but to follow.

An hour later, the last wisp of cloud had evaporated and the sky seemed deep and close and forever. Sindi was used to heat – summer temperatures in the city climbed just as high; but this heat was different. This had weight, as if a steaming dishcloth had been placed over her face. Every breath she took felt thick and wet, although dusty fields flanked them on both sides.

They walked without speaking. The silence rubbed against Sindi's exhausted nerves until she felt raw and exposed. Despite the suffocating heat, she walked with her arms folded across her chest, trying to focus on the road at her feet. So far she'd counted six. Six skeletons lying in the fields. Cows, probably, going by the horns. She didn't want to count them; she wasn't doing it for fun or to pass the time like when she counted cars. Counting was a compulsion. She tried counting rusty tractors instead, but after a while the axles, stripped of their tyres, began to look skeletal too, like the ends of chicken bones with the grizzle chewed off.

It wasn't the first time she'd seen death. She'd seen plenty chickens lose their heads to Gogo Nkosi's axe, but that was part of life somehow. This was different. This made her feel strange, hollow in the pit of her stomach, like the time she watched a group of boys stone a rat. She'd been waiting for Thuli outside Joe's when the rat was driven from the drains by the first hard thunderstorm of summer. It had crawled, half drowned, onto the pavement a little upstream from where the boys were releasing newspaper boats into the gush.

For weeks she'd dreamed of that rat's death, waking each night with the same empty pitch in her gut, but slowly the memory had faded and the dreams had stopped. Now, miles from home under a broiling sun with the sweet stink of rotting cattle in her nostrils, she remembered the un-controlled way the rat jerked after a well-aimed stone had broken its spine, as if an invisible hand held it by the tail and cracked it like a whip. She'd been unable to tear her eyes away. Even when the boys surrounded it, pelting it with stones, she'd tried to see through the gaps between them.

After they'd abandoned their sport, after the rat had stopped twitching and its blood had rinsed to a pale pink wash against the grey paving, she'd crossed the road and crouched over it. It lay on its back, eyes glassy pips, mouth slack, its long yellow incisors exposed and cartoonish, like Bugs Bunny. With rain running down her neck, she'd dug her fingers into the rat's fur. Still warm, the limp body pliable.

"How much further?" Thuli broke the silence with a whine.

"Not far," said Uncle, but he stopped in the scattered shade of a tree that looked as parched as the fields, and suggested they rest. After he'd helped Mama lower the suitcase from her head, the two of them used it as a seat while the twins sat cross-legged in the dust. Mama took the hand-kerchief Uncle offered and mopped the sweat from her brow. She stared at the desolate field and Sindi saw a shocked sadness in her eyes.

"Why did you not tell me?"

Uncle patted her knee. "What did you think, Sizane? This is what ten years of drought looks like."

"Yes, the drought, I expected the drought, but it's so quiet, so very quiet. Where is everyone?"

"Some people moved to the city to look for work, but most are gone."

"Gone?"

"Yes, Sisi, gone. When the drought came it took the last of us, just like Mama said it would. They wanted to burn her house, after what she did." He glanced at Sindi. "They said she was a witch. They wanted to burn her."

Despite the heat and her thirst, saliva filled Sindi's mouth and she tasted metal, like she had that day in the wardrobe.

"Jabu, what has this to do with anything?"

"She was right, Sisi, we are cursed and everyone is gone. The drought took the cane first. The year the drought began, the cane grew only to my waist. Without rain it turned yellow and by the second year, when we should have been harvesting, we were burning fields just to clear them and start again. But there were no setts to plant and the farmers had to buy. That year, the cane did not grow. One by one the farmers began to clear out; they abandoned their farms and us. Then the clinic closed. Now people must go to the hospital in Maritzburg to get medicine – but with no work, who can afford the taxi? Sisi, we are cursed and everyone is gone."

"If that is what you believe, I should not have come back here." Mama pinched the bridge of her nose. "I had a heavy heart when I left here. A life in the city without a family was not a life I wanted for my children. My heart was like a stone because I knew what had been stolen from them. My babies only have each other, Jabu. When we were children, we had many mothers, many fathers, many brothers and sisters, but they only have each other."

For a while the only sounds in Sindi's ears were the vibrating heat and her own sticky breath. When Uncle finally spoke, he sounded distant and mechanical, like a radio newsreader. "They were lucky, then. If you'd stayed, they might not even have had that. You know, Sisi, seeing your neighbours waste away until there is nothing left makes a man desperate. This thing, it eats you from the inside, it makes even good people do bad things."

Sindi looked at Uncle, at the jut of his cheekbones and his hollow eyes, and wondered what it was that ate a man from the inside. She thought about the dark postboxes and the creatures inside them. Did they crawl into your body through your open spaces? Your mouth and nose and ears, maybe even into your down-there places, and chew on your organs and meat until there was nothing left of you but skin drawn over bones? Is that what had happened to the cows?

"What are you saying, Jabu?"

"When the clinics closed, people had no one to turn to. Some say we must return to the old ways if we are to save ourselves. They say the only way . . ." Uncle trailed off. He could not look at them, his eyes shifting over their heads until he focused on a point high above them.

"They say the only way is to sleep with a virgin," Mama's voice was sharp. "Is that what they say, Jabu? That old lie? Nobody says that any more, people know better. Please, Jabu, tell me they don't say that here."

Uncle nodded.

"And what does Mama say? Is she one of those?"

Uncle did not reply. He looked up again and Sindi followed his gaze. The sky was no longer blank. Dark birds circled against the blue. As she watched, one broke away and spiralled downwards, landing on a carcass in the field opposite them. It was the biggest bird Sindi had ever seen, sharp-beaked, sin-ugly. Oily brown feathers puffed around the base of its neck like a coat collar turned up against the wind.

As if, like the car-drivers, it felt her stare, the bird tilted its bald head towards her. Its dull black eye reminded her again of the rat. The bird blinked slowly, thrust its beak at the carcass and tore a strip off the hide.

The sun drew long shadows behind them as they trudged up the hill to three huts that sprang from a scar of earth. Dusk had blued the light but the heat had not abated. Mama dropped the suitcase and collapsed onto the stool that stood against the trunk of stunted tree. The tree's branches were tipped with shrivelled orange petals that curved over each other like fingernails grown too long.

Nothing like Sindi had imagined.

The only structure besides the three dilapidated huts was a large, fine-meshed shade-cloth stretched between two tall wooden poles. A plastic gutter ran along the bottom of the cloth, feeding into a clay pot that squatted in the dust at the foot of one pole.

"What's the net for? Flying fish?" Thuli giggled, her excitement seemingly undiminished by the exhaustion that crushed the others.

"It's a fog net," Uncle said. "It catches the mist that comes in off the sea in the morning. When the river dried up, they came and erected them all around the village." He went on to explain how water droplets from the fog were trapped by the shade-cloth; as the droplets swelled and became heavy, they dripped into the gutter and ran into the pot.

"All it needs is a thick mist and a small breeze, which are the only two things we have left." He dipped a cup into the pot and held it out to Thuli. "Don't waste it, we don't have an abundance."

By the time Thembi arrived, it was dark. Like Uncle, she was doorknob-shoulder-thin. One of her incisors came out of her gum at an almost ninety-degree angle. Sindi could see the tip even when Thembi's mouth was closed, slightly lifting her lip so she looked like she was constantly sneering. Mama pushed Sindi towards her aunt for a kiss, but when that horizontal incisor nibbled her cheek she pulled back – and saw her own disgust mirrored in the wrinkle of distaste drawn across Thembi's brow. Mama said you shouldn't judge a book by its cover, and Sindi knew it was wrong, but her aunt's rasping chin-hair and sour breath was repulsive.

Thuli, on the other hand, greeted their new aunt with an enthusiasm that was immediately returned. "Look at you," Thembi said, pinching Thuli's cheeks. "You are so beautiful." She drew Thuli into a hug.

No, the kraal was nothing like she'd imagined. There were no chickens, no tethered goat, no life at all. It was a dead place. A slight stirring of the muggy air cooled the sweat on her skin as if the kraal had read her thoughts and wanted her to know it lived. Sindi shivered.

Things that Eat a Man from the Inside

Sindi's first thoughts, upon waking from a dream in which the sky had sunk low again, were of fish. Her skin felt clammy, as if the clouds that pressed against her while she slept had only just evaporated. She lay still, trying to hold on to the dream, but all she could recall was a cumulo-nimbus mass made up of thousands of flapping pewter arrows crammed together like sardines in a tin.

She pushed the rough blanket away and sat up. The twins had slept on reed mats, and there was a tingling in the side of her body that had pressed against the floor. With pins and needles hot in her fingers, she massaged the cramp from her ear, and looked around at the hut Thembi had prepared "especially for you, Sizane, and your girls". She'd been too exhausted the previous night to take anything in. It was bigger than she'd imagined a hut could be. Bigger, she thought, than their zozo, but maybe it only appeared so because there were no walls dividing the circular space.

Mama snored gently in a bed that looked like it came from a hospital. Under it was their blue suitcase, still bound by the belt. An enamel basin and a candleholder, the candle in it burnt down to a stub, sat on a three-legged stool to one side. There was no other furniture in the room. Like the kraal, the hut felt dead.

A large crack ran from the floor to the top of the wall. Smack in the centre, someone had started a repair job, then hung a framed picture of a beach scene over the patch as if ashamed of the unfinished handiwork. The picture was from a magazine, the torn edge of the page ragged as a ripped fingernail against the black plastic rule of the frame. The only other ornamentation was a row of sheep jawbones and picked-clean smileys, grins interrupted, shoved between a wooden roof-beam and the slanting thatch. They reminded her of Thembi's broken smile.

There was nowhere to pee. All night she'd ignored the pressure building in her bladder, but if she didn't relieve it soon she'd be unable to walk. Still, she wasn't keen to venture out alone in case she ran in to Thembi.

"Thuli," she hissed. Her sister groaned and pulled the blanket over her head.

After another hard shake, Sindi gave up and hobbled out into the morning alone, dead leg zinging. Mist had settled over the kraal, dispersing the sun's rays into a blinding blanket of white. After the hut's gloomy interior, the brightness made her eyes ache. She could see nothing. Figuring if she couldn't see them, they couldn't see her, she stepped to the side of the door and squatted in the dust. Her pee drilled a hole in the sand. Still squatting, she peered into the luminous glow. All was silent. She was the only one awake. Emboldened, she walked into the mist.

Walking in the white felt like floating, like dreaming. In the bleached expanse with the rest of the world hidden, she forgot her aching leg, her thirst, the spectre of her grandmother. She twirled around, watery traces streaming from her fingertips like ribbons. Dizzying, disorientating, but so perfect, perfect, unmarred and clean . . . she twirled and twirled and only stopped twirling when a shadowy shape spiralled towards her.

She tilted unsteadily. It was the tree with the shrivelled orange flowers. She looked up. Only a single bloom on a low branch was visible. The rest of the tree had vanished, as if someone with a giant eraser had rubbed it out. This is like being in a cloud, she thought; Thuli's missing out. She turned her back on the tree and hurried into the white, determined to wake her twin and bring her out before the mist disappeared. Already it seemed thinner, though she could see nothing beyond her outstretched arms.

The tree loomed in front of her like a trickster leaping out from behind a door. Was it the same one? It couldn't possibly be, she'd been running away from it – but she remembered no other tree in the kraal. Standing still, she realised her mistake. Spinning had made her giddy, something she hadn't noticed while moving quickly through the mist with nothing to focus on. She'd run in a circle. Again, she turned her back on the tree. This time, she took slow, careful steps. No longer solid as a wet bed sheet, the mist had curdled, become grainy. She could almost see through it to a monochrome hint of the world it concealed. Soon it would be gone and Thuli would never believe.

Fists at her sides, she stared at the tree leering from the milky swirl. The clawed blooms seemed to jiggle above her, as if the tree was laughing. She wondered then if she was still asleep and the mist a dream. She reached out and touched the trunk. The bark, rough and real in the nothingness, sent a jolt of adrenaline coursing through her veins.

Heart kicking, she turned and fled – straight into the fog net. Flailing, she stuck her hand through a rip in the shade cloth, fingers tangling in the plasticky threads. Blind with panic, she thought first of giant spiders, then of things that ate a man from the inside. She kicked out. Something slammed against her ankle. Cold soaked her feet.

The clay pot rolled away, water spilling from its lip, and shattered against a door. She stumbled forwards, gulping down her sobs.

Back pressed against the door's painted planks, Sindi held the mist out. In the white, her pupils had contracted to pinpricks, and as they dilated in the hut's low light, shadows ballooned towards her. She closed her eyes and counted out a full minute, inhaling and exhaling every third second, to bring her fear under control.

The dark shapes weren't scary like outside was scary. She tiptoed towards the centre of the hut where her mat lay, scanning the floor for things that might trip her up. She did not want to risk waking Thuli. If Thuli saw she was upset, she'd want to know why. In the hammering of her heart she could hear Thuli's mocking, *scaredy-cat, scaredy-cat, pwack*

pwack chicken noises. She just wanted to climb back under her blanket and feign sleep until the mist evaporated. Thuli need never know.

Something wasn't right. She sniffed: dust, a sweet herby fermentation like Ingram's Camphor Cream gone off, and shit. A wrinkle, half puzzlement, half disgust, rode the bridge of her nose as she stared at the blue walls while rotating the soles of her feet against the candle-wax texture of the ground beneath them. This was not the rough grain of dried mud. She stood not on a bare floor, as she had before she ventured into the mist, but on reed mats woven with coloured thread that jumped at the eyes.

A red, black and white cloth hanging on one wall drew her attention. It was stretched wide to show the image of a spitting cobra, reared and ready to strike. Under it was a collection of paraphernalia she couldn't easily make out. She took a few steps towards it to take a closer look. A rope was strung between the wall and a wooden pole, and slung over it were gourds, bags and a variety of animal pelts: a spotted fur, striped tail long and flat; a snakeskin, brittle edges curling; a hank of reddish-brown hair from an animal she couldn't imagine. A small table, draped with red cloth, stood on a raised platform. The platform was covered in jars and bottles, their contents indiscernible. The table was bare save for a leather-bound Bible and some long strings of white beads. Her gaze trailed over a drum, knobbly gourds, a severed tail bound at the end with leather, a knobkerrie, a long forked stick, shells, animal horns, dried plants and a stack of bright plastic tubs – glaring and out of place.

"You are not me."

Sindi froze. Slowly, she turned her head and squinted into the gloom. There was a bed against the far wall, a hospital bed much like the one Mama was sleeping in. Light from a small window set into the wall above the bed illuminated its occupant.

Sindi's eyes travelled from the bulge at the bottom of the bed, barely high enough to be made by feet, towards the head. Halfway towards the pillow, she saw a hand: knot knuckles, kinked fingers. The skin of the arm seemed to melt from the marshmallowy nightgown sleeve into which it disappeared. A stripe of daisy-print sheet topped the blankets tucked neatly under the woman's armpits. Her face, a shrivelled pecan, turned towards Sindi, rheumy eyes the only sign of life. The bed looked just made, the woman displayed against the pillow like a corpse for viewing.

"I thought you were me. So like me when I was a girl, but your eyes . . ." She trailed off. "Come closer." Her hand made small, agitated circles against the blanket.

Sindi met the woman's wet gaze and her gut tipped. Here was her grandmother.

Gogo Nkosi's lodger once told her that when you faced your fears, you saw they weren't as big as you thought. She added that to the list of lies Gogo Nkosi's lodger had told. Fear didn't evaporate when you saw its face. It churned inside you, turning your stomach acid and your tongue bitter. An earthy taste filled her mouth: compost, earthworms, rain. Her saliva began to run, her throat clogged. She could do anything to the immobile scrap in the bed. She could fill her hands with soil and stuff it into the old woman's mouth until it frothed, red like blood, from her nostrils.

Somehow she had crossed the room, was at the head of the bed. A cold shadow moved over her face, dissolving her vision into a thousand black dots. She felt a pitch of vertigo, like falling in a dream, and thrust out her hands to steady herself.

"When you have finished trying to murder me, perhaps you can give me some water."

The voice, like scrunched cellophane expanding, brought Sindi to her senses. She lurched backwards, trying to say that she hadn't meant to, that she didn't attack people, especially ones she'd never met before, even if that person had tried to kill her. That she was just trying to stop herself falling. The words twisted and issued from her throat as a drawn-out groan.

Sindi wanted to slink into the shadows and disappear. With her grandmother actually in front of her, what she'd heard in the wardrobe seemed like something she'd dreamed. People don't just stuff soil into babies' mouths, they don't. People did bad things, like Gogo Nkosi's lodger did bad things. Sometimes they even did bad things to babies: the papers were full of kidnappings that made Auntie shake her head and say things like, "Those kids are dead, man," or "Ag sies, the poor little thing, she's going to end up as muti." Yes, the world was full of bad people. But gogos didn't do bad things. She must have dreamed the whole thing up.

She backed into the chair beside the bed. The wooden seat slammed into her coccyx. Tears stung her sinuses, threatening to sharpen her humiliation. She squeezed her eyes shut, but the pain was acute and the tears came. She couldn't reach up and wipe them away without drawing attention to her crying, so she stared at the ground.

"Some water, please," Grandmother repeated – this time slowly, as if addressing someone funny in the head.

Sindi glanced at her and saw a mocking glint in the woman's eyes. She knew it well. *Say something clever, something Thuli might say.* But she wasn't Thuli. She had no way of explaining that there was no reason for her grandmother to talk so slowly, despite what Mama or Thembi or Uncle might have said. *There's nothing wrong with me*, Sindi wanted to tell her, even though, deep down, she didn't believe it herself.

She reached for the earthenware jug on the bedside table and removed the doily that had been placed over the top. Without Thuli's voice, her only hope lay in her actions. She shook out the doily, dislodging a fly that was trapped in the mesh. It fell onto the table and spun frantically before taking off with an angry buzz. She placed the doily to one side, folding it in half and aligning the beaded edges with her fingers. Her tongue ached as the water splashed into the glass, but, afraid to further insult her grandmother by drinking uninvited, she pressed her lips together and held out the glass.

Grandmother clicked her tongue, a disapproving sound so like Mama's yet smaller, a slight *tac-tac* in her dry mouth. For a long moment they stared at each other, then the wrinkled hand began its agitated circling again and Sindi realised her mistake. Placing the glass back on the bedside table, Sindi grasped her grandmother's shoulders and pulled her into an upright position so that she sat supported by Sindi's arm. Underneath the clammy cotton of her nightie, Sindi could feel the rub of skin against bone. She hoped her face wasn't visible as she put the glass to the old woman's lips and tipped it hastily. She allowed her grandmother a few noisy swallows before she pulled away, her fingers curled in disgust.

The woman dropped back. Water dribbled out the corner of her mouth and was shrugged off by the oil stain on the pillow. It rolled away as if it also wished to escape. Sindi watched the drop until the cotton absorbed it, then stared at the moistened spot until it evaporated completely.

"I thought you were me."

Sindi, unsure of what was expected of her, sat down and waited. Minutes passed in expectant silence, the only sound in the hut her grandmother's laboured breathing. Sindi coughed, like she always did when something made her uncomfortable.

"Ghosts visit me all the time now," Grandmother whispered, jolted from her reverie. "My grandmother, my teacher. The only ghost that does not visit me is the ghost of my mother. I think, perhaps, it is because she was a Christian." Her lips twitched, contorted into a half smile or a grimace, Sindi wasn't sure which. "I thought you were the ghost of my child self, come to punish me. But life is punishment enough, it seems. I had thirty years when my grandmother lay dying in this bed, and I too struggled to touch her. How much harder must it be for an eleven-year-old girl to touch death."

Sindi looked down, her cheeks hot.

"No, no, indodakazi, do not feel embarrassed. The young cannot look upon the old without being reminded that they too will one day rot. This is the natural cycle of things." She sighed and closed her eyes again. "You are not me at all, but perhaps you have come to hear my confession. My mother would like that."

Sindi sat for a while watching her grandmother sleep. The tension she'd carried in her shoulders since that day in the wardrobe let go, and she relaxed back into the chair. Her grandmother's words had been strange, but they were softly spoken, gentle words, her smile kind. The conversation between Uncle and Mama was definitely a dream. No one had ever tried to kill her. She grinned, pleased she'd lost her way in the mist. She couldn't wait to tell Thuli that she'd met their grandmother. She was going to be Gogo's favourite, she was sure of it. Didn't Gogo say that Sindi reminded her of herself when she was young? Thuli would be so jealous.

She pushed back the chair, but before she could stand, her grandmother's hand snaked out and snatched hold of her arm.

"You say nothing," she hissed, her nails biting into Sindi's skin. "What is wrong with your voice?"

Sindi scrabbled at the clawed fingers, surprised at the strength of their grip.

"Speak, or your silence will expose you for the devil you are."

Sindi fled across the reed mats, her eyes fixed on the door. It had taken all her strength to pry her arm away, but she knew she was free only because her grandmother had released her.

The Dead Don't Care

Sindi opened the door and ran out of the hut without slowing. Too late she saw Thembi kneeling at the threshold, picking shards of clay from the steaming ground. She hurtled over her aunt and slammed face-first into the ground. The impact pushed her teeth deeper into her jawbone, sliced a gash in her bottom lip. For one synapse-crackling second, she felt suspended, the only sensation a zinging in her ears. Then the pain thundered in. The force with which she'd hit the ground had knocked the wind from her lungs. She rolled onto her back and lay gasping, a fizz of dirt and blood on her tongue. A keening filled the endless blue-white of sky and scissored clouds tilting above her. It vibrated in her ears, adding to the clatter inside her bruised skull.

"What happened here?"

Sindi was pulled to her feet. The world swam in front of her, a zigzag of blurred colour and sharp noise.

"That girl is cursed. Just look at what she's done to my hand."

Sindi took a deep breath and steadied her gaze. She looked at Thembi's hand, then at the bloodied jags of the pot's broken lip.

"Thembi," said Uncle, "it was an accident. The girl is injured too."

"Twins are no accident." Thembi began her keening again: "Jabu, why did you bring them here? I told you not to! This girl will bring us nothing but bad luck!"

"Thembi, be quiet. You're going to wake everybody up."

Uncle's warning came too late. Mama emerged from their hut, half-dressed, still snapping the catches of her bra. Water dripped from her face and she clasped a towel in one hand. "What's all this commotion so early in the morning? Sindisiwe, what have you done?"

Before Mama could assess the damage for herself, Thembi began listing her complaints again. "This girl," she pointed at Sindi with her bloodied hand, "first she tears the fog net and breaks the collecting pot, wasting all this water. Then, while I'm picking up the pieces so I can fix it, she kicks me in the chest and before I can stand up, she bites me on the hand. She is a devil."

Mama's eyes cut from Thembi's hand to Sindi's mouth. Her nostrils flared and Sindi knew by the flat, shut-down look on her face that there was no point in trying to defend herself. She didn't resist when Mama took her by the arm and dragged her across the yard to their hut. All the way, they could hear Thembi shouting, accusing Sindi of causing a variety of injuries to her person and belongings. Even after Mama kicked the door shut behind them, they could hear her howling.

"What's going on?" Thuli sat up on her mat.

"Go back to sleep," Mama barked. She propelled Sindi to the washing bowl and bent her over it. Sindi braced, but instead of the expected hiding, Mama filled her cupped hand with sudsy water and threw it into Sindi's face. Soap stung her eyes and the gash in her lip, adding a burning sensation to the uneven rhythm of pain that throbbed in the bones of her face. The water's icy slap brought the tears that shock had held back, but they did nothing to inspire Mama's sympathy. She carried on splashing until Sindi's blood swirled through the grey in the bowl like an overcast sunset.

"Now, rinse your mouth."

Sindi did not immediately understand. The only water was the filthy mixture of soap and blood in the washbowl, and surely Mama did not expect her to drink from that. What if she got cancer? Auntie-Next-Door had once made Thuli eat soap because she'd called her a bad name, and when Mama found out she'd accused Auntie of trying to give her baby cancer and refused to speak to her for a week.

"Rinse!" She pushed Sindi's head towards the bowl.

The edge of hysteria in her voice made the hair on the back of Sindi's neck prick. She dipped a hand into the water and, glancing at Mama just to be sure, took a small sip. Soap greased her teeth. The caustic taste of it sucked the moisture from her tongue, her gut tipped. She spat. She'd done nothing to deserve this, nothing.

"Again. Rinse again."

Sindi shook her head. This was worse than a hiding. At least when Mama hit you, she hit you once and it was over.

"Do it." Mama's chest heaved as she tried to swallow a sob. "Thembi is Z3."

They were six the first time Sindi saw someone who was Z3. Measles swept through their school and, like most of their classmates, the twins succumbed. They lay on Auntie-Next-Door's brown couch, toe to toe under a blanket. Every day, Mama would be relieved to return from work to find them still alive. The papers were full of stories of kids who'd died of measles encephalitis and babies that had gone blind. Sindi worried about her eyesight. The flash of the Auntie's TV hurt her eyes and she rubbed them until her lids felt raw.

After a week it became clear that Auntie's sweet tea and *Isidingo* wasn't going to cure their fever, so Mama took the day off work, and she and Auntie carried the twins to the clinic.

Auntie smelled of cigarette smoke and Vaseline Intensive Care in the yellow bottle. Sweet and bitter, like granules of tinned coffee. The aroma, combined with the lolloping rhythm of her stride, might have put Sindi to sleep if Auntie hadn't been so bony. Sindi struggled to find a comfortable resting place for her head on Auntie's shoulder. She spent the entire journey shifting her cheek between the point of Auntie's shoulder and the ridge of her collar bone.

Auntie's skin was lighter than Mama's; up close it looked thinner too, like the brown paper Mama used to drain the oil from chips, almost transparent when you held it up to the light. Under it, veins bulged blue, and a lump in the centre of her throat moved up and down when she swallowed. The veins were unexpectedly soft, collapsing under the lightest touch, but the lump was hard and made Auntie growl when Sindi touched it.

The clinic, a purpose-built bungalow hunkered in a patch of dirt, was overrun. Beyond the fence, people sat in the dust waiting to be called. Some were lucky enough to have found a seat in the thin wedge of shade cast by the overhang of the tin roof, but the rest of the crowd were exposed. The sun glowered onto the heads of dull-eyed children lying in their mother's laps, glared at maternal hands spread to shield feverish cheeks. Mama and Auntie nodded at neighbours, but few returned their greeting. Stunned by heat, their blank faces reacted only to the appearance of the nurse calling the next patient in.

The guard at the gate instructed Mama to register at the desk. Auntie untangled Sindi's arms from around her neck and let her slide to the ground. To be thrust suddenly onto solid ground was like stepping off a trampoline. Sindi clung to the fence, riding a wave of dizziness. Leaning against the chain-link fence, Auntie freed a squashed box of Peter Stuyvesants from her bra strap and lit one.

"She isn't mine, you know," she told the guard, exhaling smoke into his face. "I'm not married."

They'd been there an hour before Sindi noticed that the guard was directing some patients to a side door. There, patients entered and left without waiting. She tugged Thuli's foot and pointed at the door.

"Mama," Thuli asked, "why don't we go in that door?"

Auntie replied before Mama could open her mouth. "You better wish you never have to go in that door. Those that go through that door are all Z3."

The following Monday the twins went back to school. Their classmates returned in dribs and drabs and, by the end of the month, the playground was once again full. Everyone came back. Everyone except Mr Edwards.

Sindi knew the sunken-eyed Mr Edwards by sight alone; he'd never taught her and never would. During break, there was much speculation about his disappearance. Someone said he'd died of measles, but surely measles couldn't kill a man. Babies and small children died, not grown men. Sindi refused to believe the rumour until Dumisile overheard his mother talk about that "poor Mr Edwards", to which his father replied: "Poor nothing. Mr Edwards died from measles because he was Z3, which just goes to show you can be a teacher and still be stupid."

Speculation began afresh, this time as to what it meant to be Z3. Somebody said Dora was Z3, but Dumisile said she was too fat to be Z3. "Look at Mr. Edwards," he said, holding up his index finger. "Skinny-skinny."

Sindi didn't think it was true: not everyone who went in the side door at the clinic had been thin. Then someone said Z3 meant you'd bought a House In Vereeniging, which didn't mean an actual house but was just a way of saying you had the sickness with the three-letter name.

"ABC, ABC," Thuli sang, "don't buy a house in Vereeniging or a red BMW Z3."

Sindi flung a leopard-print blanket over a low branch and picked up the short straw broom. She tested its weight in her hand as if it were a weapon, then swung it over her shoulder and brought it down on the blanket. A cloud of dust exploded in front of her and Sindi cursed the tree. She'd spent the morning cursing everyone and everything in the kraal. Thembi and Mama bore the brunt of her bad will, but she hadn't forgotten the part the tree had played in her humiliation.

"Serves you right," she muttered as the dust cleared and her eyes settled on the weeping cuts in the tree's trunk where Thembi had demonstrated her sjambok while reciting a list of chores for Sindi to carry out. The thin wounds exposed the tree's pale wood. Sindi smacked the blanket again. One thing was certain: Thembi was looking for a reason to use the sjambok on her. It would slice much deeper into flesh than bark.

Not that she hadn't got used to bleeding. The crust around her bottom teeth leeched a coppery taste onto her soap-numbed tongue and her split lip seeped. She wanted to lie down and close her eyes until the throbbing in her head subsided, but Mama had decided she should make it up to Thembi by doing anything her vinegary aunt asked.

"I'll teach her how a good Zulu girl behaves," Thembi told Mama and Uncle as they headed off to visit the neighbours, leaving the twins in her care.

Mama had not wanted to go. "I didn't come to pay courtesy calls on old neighbours. I came to see Mama."

"Today is not the best day to go and see her," Uncle had said. "I told her only this morning you had arrived. Allow her a day to prepare herself."

Sindi doubted a day would improve the crazy old woman's temperament. She folded the leopard-print blanket, took another from the pile and threw it over the branch. This time, as she brought the broom down, she cursed Thuli. Angry tears stung her eyes. If the situation was reversed, if it was Thuli suffering this unfair punishment, Sindi would help her. She would not sit there twisting plaits into the enemy's hair while Thuli bent over the short broom sweeping the floor. No, Sindi would stand by Thuli and take on the punishment as if it were her own. She would sweep and wash floors and beat blankets until her palms blistered.

Curse Thembi, curse Mama, curse Thuli and curse the shrivelled thing lying under her daisy-print sheet.

She pushed the door to Thembi's hut with her shoulder, the pile of folded blankets balanced across her arms. Once her eyes adjusted to the dimness, she saw Thembi's head still rested in Thuli's lap. Her twin tied off a plait with nimble fingers and wound thread around it until the frizz disappeared into a nub of cotton. Then she raked two fingers through the remaining hair and divided it into three pieces. As if they were sisters.

Sindi spread a blanket over the bed, breath shuddering in her chest. When she dared steal a glance at the two playing hairdresser-hairdresser,

she caught Thembi's sharp gaze. Sindi knew she was looking for a reason to unleash a fresh stream of criticism. In her aunt's eyes, she could
do nothing right. Earlier, with a long list of chores stretching in front of
her, Thembi's scrutiny would have bothered Sindi, but now she didn't
care: once she'd made the bed, she'd be free. She tucked the last loose
corner of the blanket under the mattress and turned to face her aunt.
Thembi sniffed and closed her eyes. Her head dropped back into Thuli's
lap and, after a moment, her mouth went slack. Sindi shook her head in
disgust.

"I hate you," she mouthed, hoping her swollen lip did not obscure her
meaning. Thuli ignored her but Sindi knew she'd seen. Still, to ensure
Thuli knew the words were directed at her, she linked her pinkie fingers
together and, slowly, so they made a snapping sound as they separated,
pulled them apart.

Satisfied, Sindi turned to leave the room. She'd not eaten all day. Her
head was floating but the fury burning in her gut fuelled her.

"Sindisiwe."

Sindi clutched the door handle. "Auntie?" she enquired. Rage clipped
her stutter.

"There is still time before supper. Go and sweep out your grandmother's
house."

In the encroaching dusk, the collection of jars and animal remains gave
Sindi the creeps. The rays of afternoon sun filtering through the small
windows lengthened the shadows, and the snakeskin and hanks of animal
hair seemed to dance on the periphery of her vision. More than once she
swung around, heart pounding, convinced that something had moved. In
contrast, the figure in the bed lay still as death.

Sindi skulked from one side of the room to the other, skimming the
grass mats with the tip of her broom. She was terrified the *shush-shu* of
sweeping would wake her grandmother, but equally afraid that if she took

too little time Thembi would know she hadn't done the job properly. The only way to count the right amount of minutes was to simulate sweeping. She was so focused on the arm-aching effort it took to keep the broom an inch or so above the ground that she didn't notice the stack of bright plastic tubs until she'd backed into them.

In the pregnant hush after the last tub rattled to a stop, Sindi held her breath. She felt her grandmother's feverish gaze upon her. She considered simply restacking the tubs and leaving without even glancing in the old woman's direction, but the thought of Thembi's sjambok cutting thin welts across her backside stopped her from rushing to the door. Sindi squinted into the grainy space between herself and the bed. Grandmother hadn't moved but there was now a watery flicker of light around her eyes.

"I knew you would come back."

Sindi wanted to say that she'd not returned by choice, but fear held her tongue. She massaged her wrist, trying to dispel an echo of her grand-mother's grasp, but the heat from her palm seemed only to remind her skin of the friction of that grip.

"Where is your mother? I thought she would come today."

Sindi shrugged. She picked up her broom and began to sweep in earnest. Dust rose from the mats, tickling her throat and making her eyes itch.

"You tell your mama to come soon. The spirits of the dead wait for me. Ask them if I will not soon join them. They lie thicker than the dust in this room." She began to wheeze. "Stop that."

Sindi ignored her. The quicker she swept, the sooner she could leave.

"I said *stop*." A sharp pain rang across Sindi's knuckles and she dropped the broom. The sting disappeared before the broom hit the ground, but the top of her hand felt oddly numb, like when she pressed her index finger to Thuli's and rubbed them both with her other hand. Dead-man's finger.

"Leave it." Grandmother hissed as she bent to pick it up. "How many times do I have to tell them, I do not want anyone sweeping in here. It disturbs the dust and I cannot breathe. Have you come to kill me?"

Sindi turned towards her grandmother. Her cheeks flushed. It was a trick, a mean trick. "Auntie Thembi told . . ."

"The tooth of the dog that bites is sharper than the tongue that commands it." Sindi wasn't exactly sure what that meant, but she understood the reprimanding tone well enough.

"Thembi! That goat poisons me while my son is not here. And now she sends you to steal my breath. Do not deny it. You cannot conceal who you are, your voice gives you away." She clutched at her throat. "Your birth brought nothing but bad luck to our people. And now you are back. What is it you want, devil child of my child?"

Sindi backed towards the door. She'd take her chances with Thembi's sjambok.

"Since you were born, we have had illness and drought without end. Now you come to peck over my bones like the vultures pecked your father's eyes."

Sindi stopped. She'd always imagined their father died in a fight. Made brave by curiosity, she looked directly at her grandmother for the first time since entering the hut. Grandmother stared back, and her face seemed to soften. She sighed, patting the bed covers. "Come, sit here with me, indodakazi. Forgive me my outbursts."

Sindi remained where she was.

"Please, indodakazi, death knocks at my door. Give me a chance to unburden my soul."

Sindi shook her head. The memory of her grandmother's cast-iron grip was still fresh in her mind. She wasn't about to place herself in reach again. The light around the bed seemed to grey, as if a cloud had passed in front of the sun. It turned her grandmother's skin to putty.

"Please, water." Her breath came in shallow asthmatic gasps, her fingers scrabbling at the bedcovers.

Sindi shifted her weight from one foot to the other. She deliberated for a full minute before she bolted across the room to the bed.

The sharp edges of Grandmother's shoulder blades pressed into her arm. Sindi kept her gaze fixed on the water level in the glass; as soon as it was empty, she lowered her grandmother to the pillow, pulled her arm away and stepped out of reach.

"Thank you." She seemed not to notice Sindi's sudden withdrawal. "Perhaps you are not what I once thought, indodakazi. Perhaps I sinned against you."

Her eyes glowed in the ashen twilight. Although she looked directly at Sindi, she appeared to be focused on some point behind her. When she spoke again, her voice carried a quaver of regret, like a child about to cry. "Before you were born, I dreamed of birds. I dreamed I walked on a beach until I came across a gull sitting on a nest. It wasn't the first time I'd dreamed of the beach or the bird. I had been plagued by strange dreams for several nights. I knew the dreams had meaning, but I could not decipher them. Still, I sacrificed two hens I had been saving for the cooking pot as an offering to the amathongo.

"But my ancestors could not be so easily appeased and I dreamed of the birds again. This time, the gull had laid two white eggs. In seconds they began to hatch. As soon as the first chick had fully emerged from its shell, the mother bird attacked the second. She stabbed at it, snapped it up in her beak. The first chick began to cry, *eurl eurl eurl*, for its murdered sister. The cries became more frantic until the mother leaned over and fed the dead chick into its sister's gaping mouth. It had hardly swallowed when it began to shriek again."

Her voice was a soft rasp now, and Sindi had to lean towards her to hear what she said. "The sight turned my stomach. Then the sea rose up and a great wave washed onto the beach. I was certain the evil birds would drown, but when the waters receded, the nest was still there. Both the mother and her daughter had been cleansed of blood. Fish flapped around the nest and the mother began to feed them to her squawking child.

"The night you were born, I dreamed of the birds again. This time the chicks picked maggots from their dead mother's feathers while the world shrivelled up. Sizane woke me from that dream to tell me she was in labour. I did not have time to ponder the meaning of the dream. It was only after she'd birthed her twin daughters, you and your sister, that I realised what the amathongo were telling me. For the first time since I was a girl, I went to Father Vic's church and I prayed. I prayed for many hours and I would have prayed all night had I not been asked to leave. Even with splinters in my knees and the dust of hymnbooks in my nose, I could not hear the voice of Jesus. The god of my Christian mother would not help me.

"That night I spilled the blood of two good laying hens, one for each of my granddaughters. I did not sleep. At first light, I filled a leather pouch with soil. I chose soil from the sugar-cane fields because I thought it would be sweet. I went to the hospital and sat with my daughter, speaking of motherhood until her eyes grew heavy and she fell asleep with a baby at her breast."

Grandmother had not glanced at Sindi since she'd begun speaking. Now she studied Sindi's face as if trying to remember who she was. Sindi shifted under her gaze, unable to turn away. "I did not want you to suffer cold on your tongue, so I took the pouch from my pocket and warmed the clots of earth in my palms. Then I pushed them into your mouth. I plugged your nose before you could splutter and I hid your small body, swaddled in the blanket I had crocheted for you, under the bed.

"The police came, but after Sizane fled the hospital and took you and your sister, they did not charge me. My neighbours wanted to burn my house, they thought me a witch. They would have turned my bones to ash had your father not tripped and hit his head on a sharp stone. The child who found him said two vultures sat on his head, pecking his eyes."

Her words were like hooks designed to unpick the stiches that held

Sindi together. She wanted to stop her ears with her fingers, deny them entry, but it was too late. The photograph of her father flashed into her mind, but she saw empty sockets where his eyes had been and torn flesh in the crease where once she'd imagined a wrestler's flattened nose.

"Your birth brought bad luck to our village. After they found your father, the neighbours came to me and asked me to help them. They realised I had been right. The birth of twins would bring illness and misfortune if we did not appease the ancestors. But what could I do? Sizane had taken you. If only I had waited until you'd stopped breathing before I left the hospital, the nurse would not have found you and given you back your breath. Then I could've poured water on your grave to bring the rain. If only I had waited, your father, a good man, would not be dead."

Sindi squeezed her eyelids together to hold in her tears.

"Instead, like the chick that ate its sister, you grew fat while the flesh melted from our bones."

"Mama!"

Sindi had not heard her uncle enter. He crossed the floor and stood behind Sindi, placing a hand on her shoulder. "What have you been saying, Mama?"

The old woman glared at him, and made a show of clamping her lips together.

"What have you been telling Sindisiwe?" Uncle's voice was sharp.

"That is her name," Grandmother spat, "Sindisiwe." She pronounced each syllable with a force of hatred that made Sindi's fingers curl into her palms. "Does Sizane think if she gives a soulless thing a name, that thing will be welcomed in heaven by Jesus and saved?"

"Mama, what is wrong with you?"

"What is wrong with me? This thing that is wrong with me, that is wrong with you, that is wrong with this whole village of ghosts started the day these twins were born. Did I not tell you long ago that we must find them and appease the ancestors?"

Out the corners of her tear-blurred eyes, Sindi saw Uncle shake his head. "You cannot blame these children for everything bad that has happened to us."

"Don't be a fool. The blame does not lie with her, but with us for not listening to the amathongo. The dreams were clear. That this girl lives insults your forefathers."

"That is enough." He clenched Sindi's shoulder so hard it hurt. "Think of the damage you have done this girl already. At your hand, she lost her voice."

"I have little breath left, Jabu, but I will not die falsely accused. The other one, the first-born, she speaks?"

Uncle nodded. "But you did not . . ." He looked down at Sindi and shook his head.

"Soil did not steal her voice. She has no voice because she is empty. It is not our lips that speak, Jabu, but our souls. The ancestors tested us, and we failed, but you can set it right. There is still time for you to save yourself."

Sindi looked up at Uncle's tight lips, his wide nostrils, and prayed he would say something to reassure her: that the words spilling from her grandmother's lips were false, that he wouldn't do as she said. But he could not meet her eye.

"Now I understand why Sizane did not want to come back," he said softly. "If she hears you speak like this, she will never forgive you. Look at the pain in this child's eyes, Mama. Look at what you have done. Even if she finds it in her heart to forgive what you did eleven years ago, she will never forgive you for what you have said to this child today."

"All children turn against their mothers, it is the way of things, Jabu. No mother believes her baby will turn against her, but they all do in the end. Some are born turned, like this one. Some, like you, harden their hearts late in life. It is a lesson I should have learned from my own mother, but I thought I was not like her. I would have sacrificed my life for my children, but Sizane sacrificed us all."

With those words following her across the reed mats, Sindi allowed Uncle to lead her to the door. At the threshold, she hesitated. Behind her, her grandmother continued to whisper hate. Through the door Uncle held open for her, she could see the silhouettes of her family hunched around the cooking fire in the fading light. The crackle of the flames fused with a sparkle of Thuli's laughter, and she felt the vast distance between them. The air buzzed against her wet cheeks.

"Come, Sindisiwe," Uncle said gently. On stiff legs, Sindi walked towards the fire. She stopped just outside the circle of light cast by the flames and watched Thuli stir the pot while Thembi and Mama talked.

"Thuli is such a good child, look at how beautifully she has done my hair." Thembi patted her head, preening. "You are so lucky to have such a daughter, Sizane."

"I am lucky," Mama said. "God gave me two the same."

Alone in the hut, Sindi crawled behind the blue suitcase, tears racing down her hot cheeks. She'd been dogged by bad luck. Even things that at the time seemed good turned out to be bad. Like the urge to make a fist, then a flat hand, then a V with two fingers that led to her stepping on Mama's bed with muddy feet before climbing into the wardrobe, where more bad luck would have her fall asleep. Bad luck followed her again on exiting Joe's shop that same night when she'd been spotted by Nandi – a goodie-two-shoes Believer who, sure as Joe loved chicken, had ratted her out. She'd been jinxed before she was born. Why else had she travelled down the birth canal a full twenty-three minutes too late? Her delayed birth had given Thuli everything, while Sindi lacked a proper voice and an entry to heaven. And even Dora had gone to heaven.

Sindi was nine that bright Saturday morning when the bus came to New Tiyang Primary to transport the pupils to Regina Mundi Catholic church to attend Dora's funeral. Like all Dora's classmates, Sindi knew nothing about Dora except that she was fat and lived in an RDP house that her father had renovated. The renovation made the already unpopular Dora an even greater pariah: everybody knew that if you were rich enough to renovate, you shouldn't have received an RDP house.

Standing at the back of the church with the rest of her classmates, Sindi listened to the priest commit Dora's soul into the arms of Jesus and struggled to recall her face. She could conjure a clear image of Dora's sausage fingers, calculate the width of her boneless wrists compared to her own thin ones, see the place just above her knees where her thighs mashed together, but no amount of concentration could bring her face to mind. The only whole image that sprang into her head was of a hunched figure sitting alone on the outskirts of the playground during break, staring into her lunchbox.

Sindi couldn't imagine what had held Dora's fascination each day. She'd never seen her eat. No one had. Dumisile said she stuffed her face locked in a cubicle in the girls' toilets. Though he never offered proof, everyone assumed he was right: before lunch, Dora's stomach could be heard growling over the scratch of pens, while after lunch it was silent.

They shuffled past the pink coffin in single file. Earlier, her teacher had handed out white carnations. As Sindi placed the flower on the lid, she leaned forward and listened for her snorting breath. In its absence she began to understand death.

In life, Dora had no friends. Yet after the service, while the teachers and parents drank tea in the church hall, Dora's classmates huddled together in the sun and spoke of her in hushed tones. No one called her Vetkoek. It was all Poor Dora this and Poor Dora that. They revised their memories of birthday parties and playground games. In each whispered telling, Poor Dora's imaginary antics became funnier, more daring. They put words into her dead mouth her living tongue had never spoken, repeated jokes they said she'd told that she'd probably never even heard. In the yellow sunlight, the cold girl in the pink box got the sympathy Vetkoek had never received.

134

Sindi didn't know what to make of these things. It seemed she was alone in her struggle to fit the new picture of Dora into her memories. The strange magic that revised Dora in everyone's mind had even cast a spell over Thuli. "Dora was a good friend," she told Mama and Auntie.

Sindi had studied her, looking for the lie in her eyes. When she could not find it, she reminded Thuli that she'd once said she'd rather die than talk to Vetkoek.

She caught the back of Mama's hand for that, and she'd run to Saviour's in tears. Sitting at Joe's feet, she stammered out her troubles. He'd contemplated her over the top of his mirrored sunglasses, exuding his sebaceous stink of stale chip-oil and fried chicken. Then, adjusting his shades to conceal his eyes, he said that the stories people told about the dead Dora were not lies but prayers. He said that prayers were the bricks of paradise and their stories built a heaven for Dora's soul.

"Besides, the dead don't care how they're remembered, as long as they're never forgotten. Now go home before your Mama comes looking for you."

"What's a sss_asoul?" she asked as she stood to leave.

"The soul is the piece of you that lives after your body dies. It is the part of you that goes to heaven."

"Does everyone have a ss_asoul?"

He didn't reply and, unable to see his eyes behind her double reflection, she didn't ask again.

Their small procession came to a standstill at the edge of the unfenced field, halted by the sight of the headstones that littered the landscape. Uncle removed his hat and, expecting a prayer, Thuli pressed her palms together and closed her eyes. Their grandmother, wrapped in her daisy-print sheet, slumped in the wheelbarrow while Uncle dabbed the sweat from his brow with a hanky. Then he heaved the barrow onto its wheel and set off across the field, leaving the praying Thuli behind.

Sindi had not expected the dead to take up so much space. Where once there must have been sugar cane, there were only graves. As their procession picked a wobbly path between them, Sindi read the headstones. She whispered the names of the dead into the humid air, calculating the length of each life by subtracting the date of birth from the date of death. Most of the graves had been there for less time than she'd been alive. Halfway across the field, she stopped reading.

On the other side of the firebreak, fewer graves were marked. Some families had bound sticks with wire to form crude crosses and placed them at the heads of graves, but the rest were bare. The paths between the graves narrowed, and the whiff of rotten eggs wafted up from the ground. Sindi played a grim game of hopscotch, trying not to step on any of the graves, but when she accidently did her footsteps sounded hollow, like tapping a damp wall.

An hour after they'd left the kraal with Grandmother in the wheelbarrow, they came to the hole Mama and Uncle had dug the day before. Here, mounds of red earth rose from the ground like boils. A straggle of children waited for them, perched on grave mounds a safe distance away. They watched the family lower the body into the ground, then slunk away. It seemed they were only there to make sure the old woman was dead.

The sharp edge of the shovel cut into the heap of excavated earth beside the grave. Uncle grunted as he heaved the spade into the air, arms trembling. Sweat trickled into his eyes. His lips moved as though he meant to speak, but the combined weight of iron and earth tipped the spade and sent a pattering of soil onto the daisy-print sheet. It shaped an arm in the cotton and the sight of it made Mama weep. Her grief sounded like denim tearing.

The funeral was brief. No one besides the immediate family attended. There was no one to stand around after, drinking tea and building a heaven for the old woman, and for that Sindi was glad. Dry-eyed, she stared into the dark recess, blinking at the dust rising like a blood mist from the swaddled body. Thuli, who'd never laid eyes on the woman until she was a corpse, stood clutching a lanky spray of fabric flowers by their bent plastic stems, eyes welling.

After they'd filled in the grave, they placed two rocks at the head so they'd be able to find it again. Mama said she'd pay for a headstone and they all agreed to return in the new year to erect it. After that, there was nothing but sunstroke to be gained by standing around in the heat, so they turned from the grave and began to make their way home. Only Sindi lingered.

She knelt beside the fresh mound. Glancing quickly to make sure no one was watching, she rolled first one rock and then the other away from the grave. Satisfied that her grandmother's grave would go forever unmarked and unremembered, she stood and dusted her dress. Then she picked up Thuli's flowers and ran to catch up to the others, concealing the posy behind her back. Somewhere in the middle of the first field, she dropped it.

That night, she lay awake listening to her sister breathe. If she reached out she could touch Thuli's back, yet the gap between them felt like a chasm. When she finally drifted off to sleep, she dreamed they walked hand in hand into the picture on the wall. Waves washed over them, the sun smiled. But the water made Thuli's skin slippery, her hand impossible to hold on to.

The wall of water came without warning, churning with angry foam. It snatched her sister's hand from her grasp and carried her away. Sindi, struggling to stay afloat in the seethe, could only watch her sister's bobbing head until it was nothing more than a freckle in the blueness of sky and sea.

She woke with the salt of tears on her lips. They'd fought before, but in the past their arguments were quickly forgotten. This was different. They'd never been divided before, never taken sides with someone else against each another, like Thuli had with Thembi. Now they barely spoke, communicating only through resentful glares full of blame and spite. Sindi didn't know how to cross the dark space between them, didn't know if she even wanted to.

As she lay in the dark, trying to shake off the funk settling over her, her thoughts turned to her dead grandmother. She went over the old woman's story in her head, trying to find a key that would turn it into a lie, but she couldn't. She recalled the pity in Uncle's eyes, the disgust that Thembi no longer bothered to hide, and she knew: the only lies were the ones that Mama had told.

When sleep finally claimed her, she walked again into the picture on the wall, but this time she was alone and her hands were full of soil.

Mermaids Lined up All in a Row

Two weeks after the funeral, Sindi stood in an abandoned changing room down the strand from New South Beach, staring at her distorted reflection. There were three basins in the changing room, and each had a thin sheet of metal fastened to the wall above it. Not real mirrors. Not her real face.

Her eyes flicked over the tarnished surface to the corners. She counted the domed rivets punched through the metal into the damp brick. There were supposed to be four rivets in each mirror, one in each corner, twelve in total. This one had all four. She scanned the next mirror. The bottom edge had warped and those rivets were gone. She stared at the black holes. Something bad.

"Twelve minus two equals ten," she whispered. "Twelve minus two equals ten." She repeated the equation, her gaze travelling up to the empty hole in the top right-hand corner of the last mirror. "Ten minus one equals nine. Nine," she whispered, "nine."

Nine was the number of days since Christmas. She'd hoped they'd be home by then. With the old woman dead, there seemed little point in staying, but the days passed hot and blank and Mama never mentioned going back.

Then came Christmas, the worst Christmas ever. Mama didn't even get out of bed and there was nothing special to eat and no presents. *No presents for her.* Thembi gave Thuli a red plastic comb, and she stuck it in her hair and paraded around like a starring from TV. She looked more like Gogo Nkosi's rooster, and not just because of the handle sticking straight up like a cock's comb. It was a rubbish present, but Sindi couldn't think of that red comb in her sister's hair without angry tears.

The changing room smelled like a rat's nest. Stagnant water pooled around the basins and toilets and mosquitoes clung upside down to the toilet seats, drifting upwards when she pulled the chain to flush.

Five toilet cubicles, one locked. Sindi could hear Thuli singing behind the door, her voice soft, quavering. That left four free cubicles. Maybe she should lock herself in one, just in case.

There was a big gap between the doors and the floor. You could see a person's legs almost all the way to their knees when they sat down to do their business. She knew because, when they'd first come into the changing room, there'd been a lady in the first stall. She'd farted so loud the twins got the giggles. Hanging upside down like toilet mosquitoes, they'd looked under the door and seen the woman's stubbly legs, the v-shaped flip-flop tan line across the top of her feet, the sand in the creases of her toes, her pink bikini panties around her ankles. It had been like old times, almost.

She could lock herself in a toilet stall and stand on the seat, like people hiding from baddies did on TV. She chose the stall furthest from Thuli's, but the lock wouldn't turn. In the stall next door, the lever displayed red, but the catch was gone like someone had forced it and the door hung open.

"Two," Sindi whispered, "two times two is four. Four minus two is two."

Four was the number of free toilet cubicles and two was the number of broken locks. Two was also how many hours it took to get from the Mid Illovo Spar to town by taxi.

They'd waved goodbye to Thembi at lunch time on the second-last day of the year. This time, walking past the dead fields with their ugly birds and cow skeletons, Sindi had felt like skipping. She was so relieved to be free of her aunt, even the tension between her and Thuli couldn't dampen her spirits.

They'd reached the Mid Illovo Spar just as the hills swallowed the sun. There were a few groups of people camped out on blankets in the parking lot. Everyone headed to the beach to bring in the new year, Uncle said.

There used to be more families. Still, it took forever to find somewhere to lay their blanket, what with Mama and Uncle stopping to chat to all the people that were there. Sindi was dog-tired by the time she finally curled against Mama's leg, but she struggled to fall asleep. Excitement made her restless. Uncle had promised to take them to the beach. He'd said they would swim in the sea.

One and one is two. One was the number of women in the changing room when the girls first entered. Two was the number of hours.

The next day, it had taken two hours to get to the outskirts of the city by the sea. The overcast sky crammed between dirty buildings, everything grey and decaying. The taxi sped along, over a flyover that looked like it went right up into the clouds. "Stratus, stratus, stratus," she whispered, but they crested and curved towards another highway long before they reached the sky. Halfway back down to earth, Sindi saw a sangoma dressed in red, black and white cloths like the ones in her grandmother's hut. The sangoma had set a plank across two oil drums in a bus shelter. Sindi craned her neck for a glimpse of what lay on the makeshift table – *a spotted fur, a snakeskin, a hank of reddish brown hair from an animal she couldn't imagine* – but they passed by too fast to see.

By the time they disembarked in town, the sun had burned the clouds away. Mama bought them vests and panties at Pep; then they left her at Bird and Sons Funeral Services, where she had to see about a headstone, and walked with Uncle down to New South Beach. All the way, Sindi worried about that headstone: that when they went back to the grave-yard and couldn't find Grandmother's grave, Mama would look at her and know that she was to blame.

They swam in the sea for the first time at New South Beach, where they had to pick their way to the water's edge between towels and umbrellas and sun-worshippers. Sindi was embarrassed by the near-nakedness of the people: women in bikinis, men in bright board-shorts or, worse, skin-tight briefs that bulged like Auntie's panties. She feared the drag and pull of the waves, feared bumping up against the other bathers, recoiled at the thought of their oiled skin rubbing against hers. She was relieved when Uncle said he wanted to show them something special further down the beach.

They'd followed him away from the lifeguard station, where two red flags marked the swimming area. Sand the colour of hens' eggs stretched ahead of them, ending at a headland beyond which was only ocean. They walked for a long time before they rounded the bluff and saw the ladies' toilet and changing room, just above the tidemark. She frowned: it couldn't be that. It looked long abandoned, the bricks crumbling and darkened at the bottom by damp. But between the sand dunes behind it she caught a glimpse of sun-bleached hair and the bright splash of a surf-board.

"Look." Uncle pointed across the water.

Sindi stared at the ships moored in the harbour, but it was not until she looked beyond them that she'd seen the special thing.

One was how many women were in the ladies' room when they first entered.

She hugged her knees. Outside in the hot sun, her wet vest and panties hadn't bothered her, but in the dank changing room, the fabric chilled her skin. She looked under the door. Their Checkers bag-for-life with their clothes slumped in the middle of the changing-room floor where Thuli had dumped it when they first came in. She bit her lip and reached for the lock, but then Thuli cried out and Sindi clamped her hands over her ears and closed her eyes.

Two was the number of red flags marking the swimming area they left behind, where lifeguards would save you if the waves pulled you under.

They'd stood on the bluff, staring across the water at the ships in the harbour, and beyond them to the drowned part of the city, where build-ings rose from the water like the tail-spikes of a prehistoric sea monster.

"They used to call that The Golden Mile," Uncle told them. "Those buildings were the hotels along Marine Parade. When I was a small boy, my mother cleaned rooms in one of those fancy hotels."

"Who lives there now?" Thuli asked.

Uncle shrugged. "No one is supposed to, it's not safe. The water undermines the foundations and one day they'll collapse. The government wants to demolish them all, but crazy people have squatted the higher floors and refuse to move. If you listen carefully, you can hear the concrete groan."

They'd swum again on the deserted beach, clinging to Uncle while the waves broke over them. Uncle had suggested they change out of their wet things, all three of them in the ladies' because the men's had been washed away, but then the woman was there and he had to wait outside.

One woman in the first cubicle. Two sisters hanging upside down, like old times, almost.

Alerted by a sharp prick, she opened one eye and squinted at the mosquito on her knee. It was so close she could see where its proboscis entered her skin. She took her hand off her ear to slap it, heard grunting and panting like someone running. She blocked the sounds and watched the mosquito drift away, wishing the woman in the pink bikini would come back.

Eleven was how old she was, eleven years and five months. Eleven was the number of hotels she'd counted.

Sindi lowered her hands. The grunting had stopped.

"You're a good girl, Thuli," she heard Uncle whisper, "a good girl to help your uncle."

Sindi prayed that he would go, just go. She didn't want to do bad things with Uncle like Thuli had, because she wasn't like Thuli. Sindi didn't bat her eyelashes or fetch beer for Auntie's boyfriends or let anyone pat her on the bum.

Footsteps echoed across the concrete. She held her breath. The door clicked. She counted the seconds up to sixty, then started over at one. Her head began to throb to the drip, drip rhythm of a leaking cistern. She counted to sixty three times to be sure. Then she exhaled and slid the latch.

The cistern trickled, mosquitoes whined, but the only human sound was her heart, thrumming in her ears. The door to the beach stood open. Through it she could see a strip of sunlight and his footprints, but not him. She tiptoed across the floor, pulled it shut and bolted it. She rifled through the Checkers bag-for-life with shaking hands, separating her things from Thuli's. Holding her dry clothes between her knees so they didn't touch the floor, she peeled off her vest and pulled on her T-shirt. The cotton dragged against her damp skin, refusing to cover her nakedness properly. Her jeans pulled up over her dry legs easily but resisted when they reached her bum.

Shivering, she rolled her wet things into a ball and stuffed them and Thuli's clothing into the bag. It was just like Thuli to go back out without covering up so that men could look at her legs and her nipples poking darkly through the wet cotton. Even on the beach, among all the scantily dressed bathers, Sindi had been embarrassed by her body's betrayal and had walked with her arms folded across her chest. But not Thuli. Thuli stuck out her bum and slipped her hand into Uncle's like they were boyfriend-girlfriend.

Behind her, the cubicle in which they'd done it sucked and pulled, trying to make her turn around and look. Tears stung her eyes. How could she? And with Sindi right there. How could she? In the dank piss smell of the changing room? She hiccupped, swallowing painful fists of rage until her chest hurt.

The tap spat rust-dyed water into her hands. She splashed her hot cheeks before examining her face in the warped mirror above the basin. She looked like a monster. Beyond her distorted features was the cubicle. A girl hunched on the toilet seat hugging her knees, her skin mottled and bruised by the tarnished metal.

"You better get dressed," she said.

The girl didn't move. Sindi's heart raced. She looked at the basin, the watermark like an old bloodstain in the cracked porcelain bowl. When she looked again, the girl stood next to the Checkers bag-for-life, dressing. Had it not been for the vest and panties that lay stuck to the cement, a vest and panties identical to the ones she'd just shoved into the bag, Sindi might have been able to tell herself that the girl was not her twin-sister, sister-twin, sister-sister. She looked away then, and did not look at the girl again.

Sindi did not remember the walk back along the sand to New South Beach, but she looked up and they were among sunburned holidaymakers with their pink smiles and pinker ice creams, then jostling along the promenade where everything was for sale: rickshaw rides, bead necklaces, baskets and buxom girls with worn-out eyes and too much lipstick. Earlier, everything had been sunshine and festive, but now it hurt her eyes just to look at it. The music spilling from restaurants slammed against the pavement, booming, discordant, angry. She wanted to curl into a ball, shut her eyes tight and stick her fingers in her ears.

Dazed, she trailed Uncle, half wishing he'd lose them so Mama would punch him in the face like the man at Ma Elias', but every time he disappeared into the throng she sped up until she spotted him again. She didn't know if Thuli was behind them until Uncle went into a shop to buy cigarettes and she saw Thuli's reflection floating among the souvenirs displayed in the window, the buckets and spades and boogie boards.

Two boogie boards, one blue, one orange, three red buckets, three red spades, one green bucket, one green spade, seven plastic domes containing seven mermaids sitting on seven rocks, nine polished brown shells with white spots.

"Thuli?" Uncle stood behind them. When had he come out? In the glass, she saw him take Thuli's arm and press something into her slack palm. Curious, she turned and looked directly at her sister for the first time since she'd emerged from the cubicle. In Thuli's hand was one of the plastic domes. Uncle folded her fingers over it.

"Shake it," he said. Thuli blinked like someone waking from a trance.

"Go on, shake it." He tilted her wrist one way, then the other. Beach sand slid up the sides of the dome. When he let go of her arm, her hand continued to flop listlessly, clouding the liquid with sand until the mermaid disappeared. Uncle lit a cigarette. While he smoked, Thuli tilted the dome one way, then the other, like a metronome.

"Come, your Mama will be wondering what's happened to us." He tossed his smouldering butt onto the pavement and took hold of Thuli's free hand. Sindi watched him lead her away; then she glanced one last time at the things in the window, at the buckets and spades and the mermaids lined up all in a row behind the cowrie shells, trapped in plastic bubbles, and she was glad Thembi and Uncle didn't like her enough to give her presents.

Mama sat on a wooden bench in the reception room of Bird and Sons Funeral Services, with that shut-down, black-mood look on her face. She clutched her handbag in front of her like she was afraid someone would steal it.

"You look tired, Sisi." Uncle said.

She nodded. "A headstone will take two weeks. I told him I only had today. He said he could sell me one of the bronze plaques from the display room."

"Expensive?"

"Ai, Jabu, too much."

Sindi's gut tightened. She wished there was a coffin or something to look at, an open one so she could see inside, not just the outside like Dora's, but there was only a desk and chair and grey carpet squares covering the floor. There wasn't even a person sitting at the desk. Her eyes flicked from the doves stencilled on the wall to the shadow under the bench. She couldn't see the bronze plaque. Maybe Mama hadn't bought it.

"It gets worse. The workshop is closed so I carried it three blocks to a jeweller. That man," she nodded towards a closed door, "he wouldn't help me, and it's mounted on a black stone. Granite, he said." Mama dabbed at her eyes. "I only had enough money left to engrave her name."

Sindi bit her lip. They wouldn't be able to carry it all the way to the grave if it was very heavy. Then she remembered the wheelbarrow. She was in big trouble: Thembi's sjambok for sure.

"Mama would be pleased that her name is on a brass plaque, like the mayor." Uncle squeezed her shoulder and Mama gave him a sad half-smile that made Sindi hate him even more.

The door opened and a broad-shouldered man in a tight suit, presumably *that man*, came out clutching a parcel. Wrapped in newspaper and tied with string, it looked like nothing more than a stack of school exercise-books, but its weight became obvious when he handed it to Uncle. *That man* ushered them onto the pavement, muttering something about the holidays and closing early and how he'd already stayed open far longer than he'd planned. Mama clicked her tongue, and *that man* rolled his eyes and said she should be grateful for the favour.

Uncle went to find a taxi to ferry them back to Eston. They stood on either side of Mama, waiting for him to come back. Sindi eyed the package at Mama's feet. She'd probably never speak to Sindi again.

"How was the beach? Did you like the sea?" Mama's tone was falsely jovial.

Sindi cut a sideways glance at her. What was she meant to say? She supposed she could get back at Thuli and tell Mama what they'd done, how they'd made her listen while they did it, but she wasn't a rat, even though she no longer trusted that Thuli would do the same for her. She shrugged and kicked the pavement.

"Hey, Thuli, I asked you a question. Did you have a nice time?"

Thuli dropped the mermaid dome. It cracked when it hit the ground and the liquid leaked out. Eyes blank, she picked it up and shook it, one way, then the other.

"What's wrong with you?" Mama clicked her tongue like she had at *that man*. "Maybe Thembi's right, I should teach you some manners."

By the time they got back to Eston, the evening star hung off a misshapen moon. Sindi did not relish the prospect of walking to the kraal in the dark. At the kraal, she heard noises at night when she left the hut to pee: whispers like wind rustling leaves on still nights, and once a pitiful yowling she was sure was the sound of something being eaten from the inside. One night she took the candle, even though she wasn't allowed. Squatting just outside the door, where she relieved herself after dark in spite of Mama's pleas to keep Thembi happy and use the stinking outhouse, she wasted what was left of the matches before the short wick caught. The flame's halo made the surrounding night blacker, shifting the darkness no further than her hands. She stared into its amber brightness and listened to the murmuring things. They sounded louder, closer than ever before. She saw herself from the outside, face glowing like a beacon.

At the Spar, a woman and two girls waited at the bench. Sindi pressed her nose to the taxi window and stared at them. The girls were dressed the same, but they weren't twins. Even in the dark, Sindi could tell. Why couldn't she be like them? Or better still, one of them?

The driver wound down his window to ask where they were going. Sindi didn't need to hear their reply to know they were headed somewhere far away, the red suitcase and two boxes sealed with layers of brown tape told her that, but her heart skipped when she heard the destination.

"Tonight?" Mama enquired.

The driver glanced at her over his shoulder. "People need to get back to work and it's a good night to travel. Not much traffic."

Sindi nudged her sleeping sister, forgetting their fights in a moment of hopefulness. Thuli's eyes flickered behind her lids. She hunched further into herself, tightening her grip on the broken mermaid dome.

"We should go," Mama said.

The negotiations to take them all the way to the kraal first were quick. Once there, Sindi skipped around gathering their things while Mama packed them into the blue suitcase. Thuli's comb lay next to the enamel basin. Sindi put it in her pocket. When Mama took the suitcase out, she climbed onto the stool and stuck it behind the framed picture of the beach. The red teeth stuck out the top, not too obvious, but one day Thembi would notice.

Then it was time for goodbye. Uncle promised to lay the stone at the old woman's grave and Sindi almost smiled when she thought of Thembi and Uncle hunting for the two rocks in the hot sun.

Thuli stayed in the taxi through it all, curled into sleep like she had no intention of ever waking up. When all the passengers had finally been collected and all the luggage loaded, and the taxi hit the highway, picking up speed, Thuli's fingers relaxed and the mermaid dome dropped from her hand, rolled under the seat and was gone.

Sindisiwe Means Saved

Nandi came knocking three days after they'd returned from Eston. They'd been out shopping for school shoes and Sindi was in the bedroom with Thuli, stuffing wet newspaper into the toes of her brand-new baby-dolls to stretch the leather, when Mama called them to the door for a visitor. The sight of Nandi standing there, clutching a Bible to her chest, made Sindi go cold.

"What do you want?" Thuli snarled, pushing Nandi into the road.

Thuli had been spoiling for a fight ever since she'd woken up in the taxi, nine hours after they'd left her precious Uncle and Thembi in Eston. She'd even kicked the man at the school-uniform outfitters when he went down on one knee to help her with her shoes.

"I saw you," Nandi said primly. "I saw what you did."

Sindi glanced at Mama through the open door. Mama sat at the table, staring into her mug of tea, wearing that distracted look she'd picked up in Eston.

"Saw what?" Thuli stepped into the space Nandi occupied, forcing her backwards so they were no longer in Mama's line of sight. "We didn't do anything."

"I saw you that night at Saviour's, coming out of the shop with a bag full of stuff."

"So?"

Nandi sucked in her cheeks and gazed at the sky above Thuli's head. "It's a sin," she said.

"Are you going to t_t_tell?"

Thuli scowled. "She's not going to tell, stupid. You're not going to tell, are you?"

Nandi gave Sindi a secretive smile that said neither yes nor no. "Don't you want to be good?" she asked. "Don't you want people to like you?"

"We don't care." Thuli clenched her fists. "Now get out of here before I hit you."

That night, Sindi lay in bed wondering whether Nandi had a boyfriend. She didn't know what made one girl attractive and another not, but she was almost certain boys didn't think Nandi was pretty. She was wide around the bum and thighs, with shoulders that, if not exactly slight, were disproportionally narrow to her hips. And she moved in a lumbering way, in no hurry to go anywhere. If she were an animal, she'd be a cow. A cow with a human face, but a made-up one: a collage of features cut from a magazine. Thick lips, deep-set eyes and a sharp nose that didn't go with anything else. But when Sindi thought about that smile, a warm glow spread through her lower belly until she itched in her secret place. She fell asleep imagining Nandi in the bed next to her, snuggled up and spooning, a new sister.

She dreamed of the beach again. Waves hissed up the shore, but this time Thuli was not there. Sindi stood a little way up from the water with the sun yellow on her face. In the distance, someone stood at the edge of the world against the panorama of drowned hotels, a shapeless figure whose outline she could not bring into focus even when she squinted. At her back, something slick and cold pressed against her. Afraid of the thing behind her, she ran towards the headland where the person stood, heart speeding, a breath not her own panting in her ears. The figure did not lose its formlessness until it was too late. Then she was struggling against the current with her grandmother's fingers clamped around her wrist. *You're dead and you can't touch me.* The daisy-print sheet billowed as they sank beneath the foaming black water into the stillness.

On the first day of the new term, she awoke entangled in Thuli's limbs. In the fog of confusion between sleep and waking, she was flooded by love both familiar and empty with loss – before she remembered and shrugged her twin off.

Sitting on the edge of their bed, she cut a resentful sideways glance at her sister. Thuli's eyes were open. For a few brief seconds, Thuli's sleep-dilated pupils were locked into her own and something passed between them, the ghost of a whisper too soft to decipher. Before she could decide how to respond, Thuli lowered her lids and shut her out.

She dressed quickly while Thuli pretended to sleep. Cursing her sister's backstabbing fingers under her breath, she ran a comb through her hair, then wet the resulting wild fluff down in an attempt to tame it. Maybe Auntie would help her braid it after school. In the kitchen, she gulped her too-hot tea and porridge, ears attuned to the soft thud of her sister's feet moving around the bedroom.

The walk to school seemed to take much longer with no one to talk to. The curious stares of neighbours they usually greeted together made her feel disfigured. She started when Thuli appeared beside her – only to realise she'd jumped at her own shadow. After that, she kept her eyes on the road and counted cracks in the tar.

At the school, she leaned on the fence, trying not to meet anyone's eye. She spotted Nandi in a gaggle of popular girls. She watched them a while, eyeing their short skirts and painted nails, the straps of their satch-els angled across their chests to accentuate their breasts. Then she ad-justed the strap of her bag so it lay at the same angle and crossed the courtyard. When she was close enough to hear their conversation, she dragged her feet, hoping to be noticed. Nandi did not look up.

Disappointment sank into the pit of her stomach and stayed there through assembly. All around her, they whispered. She hunched her shoul-ders, stared at her new baby-dolls, and counted first the teardrops cut into the leather – ten, five in each unscuffed toe – and then the stitches around the sole, still pale because they were new. Forty-six on the left shoe. Fifty-one on the right. Her stomach clenched. Unnerved by the mismatched totals, she lost focus for the first time in half an hour and the principal's voice rushed in: "I wish you all a good year. Do your best, make your parents proud. Dismissed."

She stood with the others and shuffled towards the door, trying to spot her sister in the bottleneck. Thuli was nowhere to be seen; nor were any of her other classmates. Panic beat against her ribs. She hadn't heard which teacher her class had been assigned.

"Hey, nom popi." Dumisile grabbed her by the shoulder and fell into step next to her. She blushed. He'd never touched her before, never mind called her doll. Once, he'd sat next to Thuli and held her hand through the entire morning, but at break he'd told everyone she sweated like a pig. Even though Sindi had been incensed on her sister's behalf, she had to admit she was a little bit glad they weren't boyfriend-girlfriend.

"Hi, hi, hi, Dumis_s_s," she stuttered.

"Oh, it's you, Double Trouble. Nice fro. Where's your other half?" Dumisile spun past without waiting for a reply. She followed him; at least he knew where to go.

The cacophony in the new classroom reminded Sindi of the day the three-legged stray got into Gogo Nkosi's henhouse. The teacher had not yet arrived, but someone had let the students in and missiles flew through the air: pens, crumpled-up bits of paper, half a sandwich. She stood at the door and studied the layout, trying to figure out her next move. Four rows of desks, five in each row; the numbers had not changed. Twenty, same as last year. And her classmates were all sitting in the same seats as they had in grade five. She eyed the empty desk two rows from the back. She could casually flop down somewhere else before the rightful occupant arrived, but without anyone to back her up she didn't have the nerve.

Reluctantly, she sat where she and Thuli always did. With nothing to do but keep her head low and wait for the teacher, she read the graffiti left by her predecessors. They'd scrawled the usual symbols and declarations of love, this time for Ketso, Danny, Sipho and Jesus. X's had been struck through the names of the first three and, in the same red pen: *Khazi shows her kuku behind the prefab toilet every day at first break.* The author had gone over each letter several times, turning the words into welts of hate. She wondered which of the boys Khazi had kissed; it must have been a kiss to make someone write such a thing. She was still comparing the scratches of Ketso, Danny and Sipho to the scars of Khazi when Nandi sat down next to her.

"What's up with you and Thuli?"

Eyes fixed on the red sentence, she shrugged.

"I know something's up, everyone does. You can tell me."

"There's nnn_n. . ."

"Don't say nothing," Nandi interrupted. "She's sitting over there and you're over here. First time in history. Something's going on."

"It's nnn_n. . ."

"I get it, Sins, none of my business. I'm just being friendly."

Sindi wanted to scream. She bit down on her fist, hating herself. What was she going to do without Thuli? She was such a *nothing* she couldn't even spit out the word.

"Hey, don't do that. Look here, write it down." Nandi opened her exercise book and slid it across the desk. Sindi stared at the page, at the thin blue lines dividing it into spaces where words could knit seamless sentences. No one had ever cared enough about anything she had to say to ask her to write it. She took out a pen and pressed it against the paper. Ink bled from the nib, staining the new blankness with a permanent blue dot. Her gratitude faded. Nandi had never bothered to speak to her before, and now she was "Sins".

No, she wrote.

Nandi narrowed her eyes. "Okay," she said, "I get it, Sins, but since she's not sitting here, can I?" She smiled her secretive smile.

Sindi looked at the *No* on the page, and nodded.

Nandi didn't speak to her again during class that day. Her books and stationery never crossed the invisible line that divided the desk in half. Still, she took up too much space. Sindi struggled to focus on anything beyond the chubby thigh almost pressing against hers. She counted every pane in the bank of windows lining the classroom wall, but still her hand crossed the line and brushed against the stiff polyester of Nandi's tunic. She snatched it back, forced her fingers to take hold of a pen and began to calculate the number of tiles it took to cover the floor. She couldn't see them all from her seat, but by multiplying the width, eighteen tiles, by the length, twenty-four tiles, she concluded there were four hundred and thirty-two.

That equation was the only thing written in her exercise book when the final bell went. She gathered her things. Four hundred and thirty-two seemed like a lot of tiles. Too many. She must have worked it out wrong.

Nandi was waiting in the corridor outside the classroom when Sindi finally exited the classroom, the last to do so. She was still thinking about the tiles when Nandi spoke. *Four hundred and thirty-two*, she thought she heard Nandi say. She hid her surprise with what she hoped was a blank stare.

"I said, do you want to come to my house after school?"

Apprehension clutched her gut. What did Nandi want with her?

"My parents are at work. We'll have the house to ourselves." Nandi turned and walked slowly away without waiting for a reply.

Sindi hesitated a moment, then followed.

Nandi lived with her parents, grandmother and aunt in a neighbourhood where shacks didn't crowd the houses and the toilet was inside. When Sindi stood on the beige carpet in the hallway, she was glad of her new baby-dolls – the ones she'd cursed all day for the blisters the rigid leather rubbed onto her heels. The shoes were shiny enough to let her pretend she belonged.

The lounge lay just beyond the hallway, and all the furniture was arranged around an OLED display mounted onto one wall. The paper-thin screen was almost flush with the plaster; if it had been the same colour as the wall, Sindi might not have seen it at all. A bowl of potpourri on the glass-and-chrome coffee table saturated the air, but under the pungent aroma of lavender and rose was a disturbing hint of something familiar. Uneasily, she thought of her lunch, a greasy combination of Lucky Star pilchards and buttered bread, and hoped it wasn't her breath and skin infecting the air. She tucked her hands under her arms. Nandi would never invite her again if she left dirty marks, which was likely since she'd neglected to wipe her shoes on the doormat. She lifted one foot.

"Do you want to watch TV?" Nandi dropped her bag and flopped onto the leather settee. Sindi did. She desperately wanted to wave a hand in front of the screen to turn it on, then swipe one finger through the air to flip through the channels, like she'd seen in the adverts. She eyed the pristine white doilies draped over the back of the couch, and shook her head.

"Oh, okay." Nandi stood, dislodging a doily. "Let's go to my room." Leaving her bag where she'd dropped it, she lumbered down the passage. Sindi followed, sniffing the air as inconspicuously as she could. Without the mask of potpourri, the house leached the chemical acidity of cleaning products, but there was something fetid under the bleach and ammonia.

Nandi stopped at the first door. "Hello, Gogo," she called into the room. She turned to Sindi. "This is my granny."

Sindi put on her best smile and stuck her head around the door. An old woman sat in front of the window, knees covered with a crocheted blanket that matched her lilac shawl. The room was neat, the woman well-groomed, though her hair stood straight up as if she'd combed it out and then forgotten to flatten it. Sindi hoped her hair didn't look like that. The woman was looking straight at Sindi, as if waiting for the respectful greeting someone her age deserved. Sindi raised her hand, but the woman's eyes didn't shift; after a few uncomfortable moments, she lowered it again.

The flesh cascaded from the woman's cheekbones as if she'd recently had the fat sucked out her, though she wasn't skinny, not yet. Her lower eyelids looked as though they'd been turned inside out. As Sindi scanned her eyes for a spark, she heard an unmistakable rumble of flatulence. The smile dropped from her lips and she took an involuntary step backwards. Although they looked nothing alike, the smell issuing from the old woman was the same as in the hut where her own grandmother had lain dying.

Nandi grinned. "Sorry, I should have warned you. Gogo had a stroke last year. That's when my aunt came to stay. She's a nurse. Auntie Doreen says Gogo's a vegetable, but Daddy says she's not and we have to talk to her."

"Sss_assorry, her eyes freak me out."

The tip of Nandi's tongue poked through her lips. "Auntie Doreen says it's called ectro-something palsy, lots of old people have it, even if they've never stroked. Come."

The next door opened to reveal a messy bedroom. The chaos of books, clothes and toys put Sindi more at ease, though she was not comfortable enough to venture too far into the room without being invited. She stood just inside the door and watched Nandi hang her jacket on the almost empty rail inside the built-in-cupboard before kicking off her shoes and placing them neatly together next to three other pairs, all black. Sindi squinted into the empty wardrobe, surprised at the care Nandi took with her jacket and shoes when the rest of her clothes lay in a crumpled heap on the floor. The T-shirt on top of the pile was yellow and emblazoned with red sequined lips. She'd assumed that Nandi, being a Believer, always dressed in black, but this was more Thuli's style.

"I'm donating my old clothes to the church at the next Ascension. You should come."

"I . . ." she angled her face away, embarrassed at being caught staring. "I don't know. M_m_my m_mom ss_asays religion is bullshit. "

"Don't swear, it's a sin. Your mom doesn't have to know. You want a sandwich?"

"Okay."

"Okay what? You want a sandwich, or you're going to marry God and become a mother for the new mankind?"

"Uhm, I . . ."

Nandi laughed. "Jokes, I'll get us something to eat. Get comfy so long."

When she'd gone, Sindi sat on the edge of the bed and looked around. She hadn't imagined the walls in the room of a big-boned girl like Nandi would be painted such a delicate shade. It made her think of stolen strawberry-and-cream Cornettos melting onto her hand and not-quite-ripe guava pips and the just-revealed pinkness of gums in Nandi's secret smile. Maybe a Nandi colour after all. She hadn't thought of anyone in terms of colour before, except for Auntie-Next-Door, but that was about Auntie's skin thing so it didn't count.

Sindi would have been happy to just sit and stare at the walls while flavours leaked from her memory – if it wasn't for the creepy old white man in the black suit. Nandi had hung pictures of him all over the room, and the way he squinted at her out of every frame made her feel like she was doing something wrong just by being there. Shifting uncomfortably, she examined the skirt of her uniform for bits of fluff, then turned to the rest of the room for something to draw her focus.

Her gaze alighted on Nandi's bedside lamp: a clown doing a handstand with the bulb fixture clenched between his oversized feet. She flicked the lamp's switch, on and off, on and off, on and off. The bulb cast a cool corona of light, creating a faint lilac balloon on the pink, but it was not enough to distract her. She could still feel the old man looking. She eyed the things on the bedside table: a heart-shaped jewellery box and a piece of fabric Nandi was embroidering with wool. Mama crocheted and had once offered to teach them, but Thuli had said no way. Sindi opened the box. Empty.

"Who cares what Thuli thinks." As she pulled the embroidery towards her, a book that had been folded inside it fell to the floor.

158

Fingering the short lengths of red and black wool on the reverse, she opened the canvas over her knees. She wasn't sure what it was supposed to be. Maybe an eye. But why would anyone make a picture of an eye out of wool? She folded it and put it back, then bent to retrieve the book. After sharing a desk for a day, she recognised Nandi's handwriting. At first, she thought it was an exercise book, one from the previous year; it had fallen open to a page near the back, and she could see it was full of writing. But then her eye snagged on the first sentence: *Sindisiwe means saved.*

She frowned. The book was covered in the kind of wrapping not allowed on schoolbooks. The shiny pink foil said it was something personal, private. Something she shouldn't be reading.

Sindisiwe means saved. She is the one. GOD wants her. I told Nombise at skool that I figured out which twin was the light one. But she laughs and says I am crazy since my family joined the New Church. I told her she was going to HELL!!!. She says the black preatcher is the devil. I wish she would stop calling him black preatcher, his not even black!!

What did she mean by "light one"? She listened for Nandi. She could tell by the clatter of cutlery that Nandi was still in the kitchen. Oversized people are often clumsy and Nandi was no exception: she'd knocked her pencil case off their desk at least once every hour. Sindi flipped through the diary, looking for her own name. There was a lot of bitching about the girls in their class, mostly the girls Nandi was meant to be friends with, with occasional references to the twins.

Pumi is going to Hell. She says her mom says I must stop saying that or else. I told her its GODS word and she should stop wearing such short skirts or else. The twins are still gone.

A few pages back, she also mentioned them:

The twins stoped coming to skool. I found out from Dumisele where they live. He says they rent a Zozo from Joe Saviour cauz their mom doesn't want to live in a shack. He says their mom thinks she's better than that, but shes not, shes just a cashier at checkers and she doesnt pay skool fees. I went there.

Its a bad hood and there was a lock on the door. The lady next door said they went home. I didn't think she was very nice she only had a bra on.

A bad hood? Sindi clicked her tongue. Since when was Nandi so gangsta? She was tempted to rip the pages out. Nandi had no right to say those things. She turned back the pages, no longer caring if Nandi caught her prying.

I saw those twins at Joe Saviours garage tonight. I felt dizzy from the dancing and was sitting by my self listening to Father Pieppers sermon. The Father says the place has reznance because lay lines cross there, but Joe is a weirdo. Then those twins came out from the shop carring a bag of stuff they stole. I know they stole it cauz they dont have any money. I was going to shout but then I saw a light around one of them. one of them was light one of them was dark like a black hole. I think it is a message from GOD but I dont know what it means.

Sindi closed the diary and slid it under Nandi's embroidery, wishing she'd never opened it.

The rest of that afternoon was a blur. She remembered struggling to swallow the sandwich while Nandi told her that her aunt, the nurse, slept with lots of men and was going to hell. She remembered that Nandi let her listen to headphones plugged into a radio receiver in the pocket of her black Believer jacket. She heard nothing but static, even after Nandi took the small copper plate out of her pocket, changed the battery and fiddled with the tuning knob. She remembered being introduced to Nandi's mother when she returned from work and thinking she looked too thin to have produced such a cowlike daughter. Mostly, she remembered the shadow of her grandmother's words settling over her life with icy permanence. Even with the old woman dead, she could not escape the truth. Nandi had seen. Sindi had no soul.

PART 3

Sister-Sister

Pwack, Pwack, your Chicken's Dead

We dreamed of white dresses once. Paging through the *True Love* magazine I lifted from Next-Door-Auntie's coffee table, we came across two women. Identical-as-peas, same-boned brides standing side by side in white dresses that frothed from their hips like upside-down teacups made of lace. Sindi traced her finger over the pink words at the top of the page, over the pink roses that sprouted from the curly-twirly letters. *Double Date Down the Aisle.* We linked our pinkies together and swore: *Same day, same church, same dress, same flowers.*

The boys leave. They take the heat of their breath, but their mockery raps through the pipes. Camera flash has whited out my vision and all I can see is a dim circle of concrete-coloured light and the bright edges of things, but I know Ma Wilma is there. The fat stink of her greases my mouth like butter gone bad.

"Get that dress off her, chop-chop. And I don't want to find a rip in it like the last time."

"Not my fault the dress too small for Queen, Ma, one size don't fit all."

"Don't cheek me, girlie, a dress like that costs – more than your life's worth." Fabric swishes against the floor, fades out. "If you look for me, Loveday, you'll find my fist."

A figure moves across my line of sight. I ball my fists into my eye sockets and her edges flare against my retina. Loveday in neon. She thrums in my head like a strobe, getting smaller and smaller, a pinprick of brightness; then it's gone, and the darkness slides in.

My eyelids snap open, pupils dilating, grasping at light. It comes in a flood that makes me reel and cartwheel, hands over feet, feet over hands.

I land upright, legs wobbling, staring straight into the fear-dark eyes of my sisi.

Her gaze cuts sideways, trying to eyeball the grubby fingers sliding over her shoulder and along her collarbone. Loveday grunts. Her index finger pauses on a pulse in Sindi's neck, like she's trying to still it; then she rests her hand against Sindi's throat. I sneak a peek around the back of my sisi. Loveday is tugging at the zip of the wedding dress. My hands twitch with the urge to snatch a hank of dirty blonde hair and rip it out by the roots.

"Not my fault if this tear," she growls, teeth tight. "This thing so ancient the zip's rusted. The ouledi should buy a new dress with the zak she gets for you." She's managed to open the zip to Sindi's waist, but it refuses to budge further, as if it wants to protect my sisi's dignity. Loveday sinks to her knees, gripping the dress where the zip has stuck with one hand and yanking the pull tab with the other. Finally, it gives and hisses down. "About time, fok."

Loveday stands, dusts her jeans. She takes Sindi by the shoulders and turns her so they're face to face. She's so gentle, anyone watching would think she's full of love, but her cold blues tell a different story. They say that girl's as hard as broken glass and twice as sharp. She lifts Sindi's arms and shimmies the sleeves so they slide off without turning inside out, then shuffles the dress down to Sindi's hips and holds it open. My sister crosses her arms across her titties.

"Sista? Today."

"My sisi don't listen to you," I say.

"Come now, move it."

"You can't keep me here, I want to leave."

Loveday snorts. "Ah, the sista wants to leave. Okay, go. Step out the dress first, then you can waai. Ma Wilma's gonna be pissed if you java her wedding dress."

Sindi shakes her head.

164

"Come, sista, I don't got all day to be playing dress-up with you."

"I'm going, you can't sss_astop me."

"Ja, you said. Where you g_g_going to g_g_go? Down to the seaside? Or maybe you want to go crawl back into the hole Booysen pulled you from? Wake up, sista, there's nowhere for someone like you to go. You better off being some larney's pet. Least he feed you, if you keep him sweet."

Sindi grabs Loveday's wrists and pulls her closer, like they're sisters and she wants a kiss. Loveday still grips the dress in her hands. "Sss_asomeone like m_m_me? I'm the ss_asame as you, I'm free. Nnn_nobody owns me. You don't own me. Let me go, or I'll rip your dress."

Loveday laughs, but her ha ha ha sounds forced. "N-n-nobody owns m-m-me." She inches forward, cheek to cheek, and whispers. "No, I don't own you. Ma Wilma owns you. Didn't you hear, sista, nothing in this life is free. You eat Ma's food, you sleep in Ma's bed, you even take her nice clean clothes and you say *ta* for that. Didn't nobody tell you, *thank you* isn't enough. Even the laaities pay their way, but you, you think you don't have to bring cake to the party. You sleep all the time and you eat like you never seen food before. Now you owe her the only thing you got. We all got only one thing, and it belongs to Ma."

Sindi tightens her grip until the veins in Loveday's hands bulge.

"Listen, sista, this life's not so bad. Better than living on the street. On the street you end up so hungry you sell your kuku to anybody. At least Ma'll take good care of you. She won't sell you to just any man. The ouledi's customers are clean, and they looking for clean girls. They won't make you sick. Ma's hard on the outside, but inside, she not a bad person." Loveday drops the dress.

"She's bad, she sss_asteals children and she sss_asells them."

"She don't steal them. She found every one of us on the street, and she takes good care of us. Those laaities out there, nobody wants them. Ma feeds them till they old enough; then, if they pretty, they get to be a bride. The rest go work for the Commissioner. He runs a clean house, the ouledi makes sure of it. She's like any mother, she just wants the best for her kids."

"She's not m_my mm_mother."

Loveday's thin mouth twists. She shoves Sindi, breaking her hold. "Sorry for you, then. Some mothers' sweeter than others, but us, we're all the same."

"Eat up." Loveday holds out a plate.

Sindi has been lying curled like a worm on the mattress. She eyes the mess of cabbage and gravy, looks away.

"I'll chow that if she doesn't want it." The boy is called Oxford. He looks hungry enough to jump the plate. Loveday scowls at him.

"Look, sista – eat, don't eat, I don't care, but it won't change nothing," she says. "You not gonna starve to death before they come for you, you might as well go with a full belly. Besides, the ouledi say if you don't eat, she's gonna come in here and force-feed you again."

How much time has passed? Three weeks, a day, one hour? They keep us separate from the others in the pipe with the dress. We huddle under the dim globe as if its feeble light can protect us, but the shadows sneak up the walls and curve over us like a cage. The smell of damp seeps from the concrete and mixes in my nostrils with the bitter stink of our fear until I can't tell one from the other.

The boys keep watch in shifts. They sit in the mouth of the pipe, blocking the way to the dorm, but they can't block sound. High-pitched voices drift past them to remind us that the children are still there, living underground lives in their burrow. Only Loveday comes, to bring food, and once Ma Wilma, to push pap into Sindi's mouth with grey fingers. The rest keep clear, leaving us to the boys. I miss their curious stares pressing in on us. I don't blame them. Sometimes it's best not to look too far up the road ahead.

No one guards the dark end of the pipe. Maybe they think we won't run, or maybe they just figure they can catch us quick if we do. There's a chance it leads nowhere, though every road leads somewhere. Loveday said the drains mapped the city like underground streets. Still, I don't want to dip my toe into that darkness to find out. I could get lost in that deep hole. I could be trapped under the city, forever.

It's easy to drift inside your head in this place, too easy. I look at Loveday kneeling in front of Sindi, who's sitting on the edge of the mattress now. How long have they been like that? Three weeks, a day, one hour.

"Listen, sista, I know this makes no difference to you, but if you don't eat, the ouledi blame me. So, I'm going to ask you nice. Please, you getting out of here, but I have to live here four more years, least."

She balances the plate on Sindi's lap. "I leave it with you, you eat it soon, neh."

As soon as Loveday stands, Sindi pushes the plate away and lies down again. The plate slides to the floor, landing upside-down like fallen plates always do.

"Ag, fok, sista." Loveday makes a fist but before she can use it Marlboro pushes past Oxford, blues flashing.

"What with you?" Loveday turns to him, lowering her fist. "I thought Ma sent you out."

Marlboro nods, shakes his head. He bounces on the toes of his sneaks, tugs his beanie, pulls it off, twists it in his hands. His hair springs up, Day-Glo electric. A vein throbs in his temple. "The Commissioner here."

Loveday frowns. "I thought you was going to the house."

"I did, but the chiskop's got business to discuss with the ouledi, so he came back with me. But," he looks at his sneaks, "I saw Queen."

A smile flashes across Loveday's face, turning her into an angel. "Queen Elizabeth? Serious? Where? Is she good? What she say?"

Marlboro swallows hard. "I saw her at the house, Day." Loveday's hands close around his shirt and I catch a flash of fright in his eyes as she shoves him past Oxford into the dorm.

Something's up. I eye Oxford, hoping he'll follow, but he's focused on scraping dirt from under his nails with a tin-can blade, like this kind of commotion happens all the time and isn't worth his attention. I stand as close to him as I dare, straining for bits of conversation, but all sounds from the other side blur.

Sindi lies on the mattress, dead still. She's squeezed her eyes so tight shut her face is pinched. I sit down next to her and stroke her hair to pass the time. Three weeks, a day, one hour.

"Heita, bra, Ma want the sista."

I don't need to look up to see who it is. I'd know Booysen's snarky voice anywhere.

Oxford slips the blade into his pocket. "Come on, nom popi, show's starting."

Sindi doesn't respond. He slaps her cheeks with light fingers, pulls her standing. Her eyes roll to white.

"Sho, bra, she don't look so cool. The Commissioner's not going to want her like this."

Oxford shrugs and pushes her in Booysen's direction. "Not my problem. You found her, you take her."

The dorm's been cleared. All the mattresses are stacked at the edges of the space and the girls are nowhere to be seen. A tall boy they call Highway hangs in the shadows with a man I haven't seen before, rat-faced in a sharp suit. I spy Marlboro and Loveday in the pipe where everyone lined up for their dinner the day they first brought us here. Loveday is crouched behind a fire drum with her head in her hands. Marlboro stands over her, looking at her, looking away, looking at her. He reaches down to touch her, but before his skin and her hair connect, he snatches his hand away like he's been burned. I feel a twist of glee. Loveday's crying. I want to snap over there and sing *crybaby crybaby*, but my sisi needs me.

Booysen leads Sindi to the middle of the dorm, where two plush armchairs and a couch huddle in the glow of the fire drums. I don't know where they've been hiding the furniture, or how they managed to get it down here in the first place, but I've stopped being surprised by all that goes on underground. Ma Wilma sits in one armchair and a man hunches into the other, his face camouflaged by the dance of flame and shadow. His scalp gleams through the thin strands of his comb-over.

"Well, boy, what you waiting for?" Ma says. "We don't have all day."

Booysen shoves Sindi onto the couch and flops down next her.

Ma Wilma's lips twitch. "Don't you have something better to do, boy? Me and the Commissioner got business."

"I find the girl, this business mine too."

Ma Wilma says nothing, but her eyes pop and her lips pull so tight I can see the nubs of her teeth.

"Fight, fight, fight!" I bounce on my toes, punching air. Booysen thinks he's such a playa, I want to see her smack him down. Then I change my mind: I want the oros lady to get it. No one moves. It's a stare-off, no action. Booysen loses and he walks away, spitting air.

"That moegoe gets more cocky every day. Thinks he's a big man. Thinks he's got what it takes to run this business."

A hand floats from the shadows and settles on Ma's thigh like a jaundice-brown moth. Gnarled fingers squeeze flesh. "Calm down. The boy's just trying to assert himself. Every dog wants to be the alpha. Don't let it get to you."

Ma's cheeks pink up. I sidle to the back of the man's chair and give him a sniff. He's thick with smells: stale cigarettes, rancid hair-oil and vinegar.

"To business then, shall we. This is the girl?"

"This the girlie. Pretty as any, don't you think, Commissioner?"

"Not the prettiest, but attractive enough. She reminds me of the girl in Gauguin's painting, *Nafea Faa Ipoipo*. You know the one?"

"I know you like your arts, Commissioner, and this one pretty as a picture, like you say."

"She's a little on the thin side, and she looks unwell. You sure she's not contaminated?"

"Questioned her myself. Says she never had a boyfriend, never been with no man. I can tell a liar by the eyes, but a pretty girlie like that, I don't take chances." She shakes out the contents of her pocket – old tissues, a crumbling biscuit, a roll of Wilson's XXX – and holds the white plastic test stick out to him. "See for yourself."

"Perhaps she's got something else. I don't like . . ."

"This girlie clean, she just got a little fever. A dog bit her and the wound got infected, but we cleaned her up and fed her. She's good as any I raised myself. Now, we both know there aren't too many girls like this out there, and I don't got none else that's of age."

"Fair point, Wilhelmina, but you're selling cheap. I just wonder why."

"What can I say, Commissioner? The girlie's a Believer. I want shot of her before that lunatic preacher come knocking on my door. Once your customer's been with her, Joshua Piepper won't want her back."

I look at Sindi. Her dilated pupils suck in firelight and turn her fear orange. She shrinks into herself, trying hard to disappear.

"Tell you what, to help you out, I'll give you five thousand for her and the other girl."

Ma Wilma frowns. "I don't have another girl."

"No? I think you'll find you do. I gave her to you, or have you forgotten it was I who discovered the blonde nymphets in the park, lying under the trees like unfinished works of art? I think it's time to collect. She's grown up to be quite as lovely as her sister."

"You talking about Loveday?"

"Loveday, is that what you called her? Nice choice. Yes, Loveday, the willowy Loveday. She'll fetch a good price once we wash that hair."

"I don't think so, Commissioner."

"Don't tell me you're saving her for someone else. I don't like competition."

"Course not, Commissioner, but that girlie's not even thirteen."

"I have someone in mind – a long-standing client of mine has developed a taste for rare fillet. He has enough money to buy every girl in your cave, and he's untouchable. No chance of anything blowing back in my face. Five grand will be enough to feed your brood for some time, I expect."

Ma Wilma shakes her head. "No way. If I sell Loveday before she's sixteen and the rest of them get wind of it, they disappear faster than I can say skedaddle."

"Seven thousand."

She snorts.

"Okay then, make it ten, but that's my final offer. Ten thousand, and I'll take the skinny Believer off your hands."

I can't watch any more. I drift over to the kitchen to see what Loveday's crying about. She's leaning against the wall. The edges of her nostrils match her bloodshot eyes.

"Crybaby, crybaby," I jaiva jigga jigga around her.

"I'm sorry, Day, but I know what I saw. It was Queen."

"But how?" She swallows a sob.

Marlboro shrugs. He shifts his weight from one foot to the other, then takes a step backwards, away from her. "She was very thin, sick I think. She looked sick."

"No way," say Loveday's lips and her head says it too. "No way. Ma said the Commissioner had a customer who wanted to marry her. She told us she wasn't going to work in the house."

"I know what I saw, Day. You calling me a liar?"

"You calling Ma a liar?"

Marlboro shoves his hand into his pocket and pulls out a bracelet. He holds it out. A woven band of pink and white beads, a cheap trinket, but the sight of it makes Loveday's tears come hard. "I wanted to go in the room, but they wouldn't let me. They said she wasn't in there, said she was married and I made a mistake. But she was there, Day, I know my own sister. I want to see, I told them. By the time they let me in, she was gone. They moved her, Day, they stalled me so they could move her out. I asked the other girls if she was there. None of them would look at me. And I found this by the bed."

Loveday holds the bracelet to her cheek. I thought seeing her cry more would make me dance more, but it makes me sad.

"What you crying about?"

All three of us swing around.

"Well?"

Loveday pockets the bracelet, blinking back tears. "Nothing, I'm not crying. It's just onions."

Ma sniffs, but if she notices there's nothing cooking, she doesn't let on. "Listen, girlie, I want you to pack your things. The Commissioner will be coming back tomorrow, and you'll go with him."

"What?" Marlboro bursts out, "You sold her? She's only twelve, you can't sell her!"

"I didn't sell her, boy, I wouldn't do a thing like that. Queen Elizabeth wants to see her, that's all. Her husband said Loveday could visit a few days. A little holiday for you, girlie. I told you the Commissioner find Queen a very nice man." She smiles, baring jagged grey teeth.

We'd just turned nine when the rain bucketed down and washed poor Dora out into the vlei. Some kids were playing sticks when she popped out the storm-drain culvert, unblocking it and releasing a gush of water that propelled her and their sticks to the opposite bank. It was the first time Dora ever won a race.

Three days later, the police came and arrested Gogo Nkosi's lodger. Everybody shuddered. We'd all thought Jimmy Normans was the nicest of the men who'd lodged in Gogo Nkosi's backyard shack. Nobody ever saw him kick a dog, and the day Gogo Nkosi decided that her ten-feathers chicken, the one that had never laid an egg, was going to the pot, he ran from her yard as if the axe she was sharpening was for him.

Me and Sindi didn't hang with the crowd of kids gathering at Gogo's fence to watch the chicken run around her yard with no head. We thought it was more fun to chase the lodger. He led us a back way through the shacks to Ma Elias' shebeen. While Ma Elias went off to fetch his quart, we folded our arms in half and danced round his table. Elbows flapping, we mocked him: "*Pwack, pwack,* your chicken's dead, Gogo took her axe and chopped off its head!"

The lodger poured his beer and took a sip. Then he tilted his glass at us and winked, the pink tip of his tongue flicking at the foam on his top lip.

The lodger always seemed to know what it was you wanted before you asked. In that way he was like Joe. We sat down and waited for him to say something about ten-feathers, but he just angled his bottle and stared into the neck. After a few long minutes of silence and staring, I kicked Sindi under the table. She glared at me, snake eyes.

"Ask him," I hissed. The lodger was Sindi's friend, one of the only people she spoke to, but she shook her head and studied the table. I rolled my eyes. "Why did you run away?" I asked.

"I hate to see God's creatures suffer," he said. Then he ordered a smiley and we watched him pick the meat off the grinning skull with thin fingers.

"People like that man," said Mama, "are the reason they need to bring back the death penalty."

Next-Door-Auntie clicked her tongue, but we all knew she was agreeing. She just couldn't say so out loud because her boyfriend was against executions, and would give her a smack if he heard her disagree with him. Nobody in our street understood his point of view, which he was willing to share with anybody who asked. We asked more than once, and each time he turned the volume on the TV down and leaned forward, as if he was about to tell us a secret.

"State-sanctioned killing is no better than murder." He rubbed his stomach, burping beer into the room. "What kind of example is the government setting for you kids if they go around killing people?"

"There won't be children to set an example to if we don't hang men like that," Mama told him. She also said (but not when Next-Door-Auntie or her boyfriend could hear) that the only reason he didn't want the death penalty to come back was because one day there'd be a rope around his own neck.

Lots of people in our neighbourhood blamed Gogo Nkosi for what happened to Dora. They said she'd cast a spell over "that nice man" so she could use Dora for muti. There was talk of getting a party together to go and necklace her. Someone spray-painted BURN IN HELL WITCH across the front of her house one night. Next-Door-Auntie said she wouldn't want to be in their shoes when the spirits told Gogo Nkosi who'd done it. Mama said Next-Door-Auntie should keep her superstitious nonsense to herself.

Three days after the police took him away, *The Daily Voice* ran a story about all the girls that went missing from the neighbourhoods the lodger had stayed in before he came to Gogo Nkosi's backyard shack. The next day the lodger confessed, and *The Daily Voice* ran headshots of the victims in neat rows across the top of the page. A girl called Shelly-Dee was in spot number one, and three rows down, on the far right, was Dora. Last again.

"See," said Mama, "poor Gogo Nkosi could have been murdered because of people like you."

"Just because she wasn't involved this time, doesn't mean she's not a witch," Next-Door-Auntie told her.

After the confession, the trial moved quick-quick. The whole country was screaming for him to hang. Then the papers ran a picture a court reporter had drawn of the lodger smiling in the dock and people stopped shouting at the TV, got off their couches and took to the streets. There were marches in every city, town, location and squatter camp in the country. By the time we were ten, the death penalty had marched back into the constitution and Jimmy Normans, a.k.a. The Storm Drain Strangler, had the honour of being the first man to be executed since the end of apartheid.

The night before Gogo Nkosi's lodger was to hang, me and Sindi lay awake, whispering in the dark.

"What do you think it feels like, knowing that tomorrow they're coming for you?"

Did he want the night to be over chop-chop, or did he wish it would last forever? We lay face to face, heads on one pillow, and listened to the kitchen clock ticking off the seconds of his life.

Pwack, pwack, your chicken's dead, Gogo took her axe and chopped off his head.

Somewhere deep in the pipe there's a drip, quiet and steady, with a murmuring echo that counts it out: *one, two, three* . . . It wasn't there before, or maybe it was and I just never noticed. I lie on Ma Wilma's lumpy mattress watching my sisi pretend to sleep and the drip gets louder. It begins to seem as if it's always been there in the background of our lives, counting seconds: *thirty, thirty-one, thirty-two, thirty-three* . . .

Booysen's feeling spiteful. I can see it in the pinch of his nose, the dark scowl that shadows his eyes. He stands over Sindi, mouth twisting. "Hey, sista, how 'bout you give me your cherry. Better me than a wrinkly fat cat. I make it sweet for you." He prods her with his foot. Her chest stops moving up and down. Her stillness makes the pipe feel airless, like the wind's forgotten to exhale. Booysen kneels next to the bed and slides his hand towards Sindi's secret place. I stare into the dark pit of the drain. *Hundred and one, hundred and two, hundred and three* . . .

"Take your hand off m_me or I'll scream."

I glance at them out the corner of my eye. His hand hovers at her thigh. Waves, deep and blue, wash over my head and I taste the salt and the shame of silence.

Don't tell anyone, or else. His bony fingers creeping up my leg. Good girl Thuli, don't make a noise.

My scream, too late to save me, rises from my belly and pours out of my mouth. It whips through the city's waterless veins like the wind, howling-howling, waking the ghosts and river devils sleeping in the drains. They rush into the pipe, knocking Booysen off his feet and filling the place with the scent of mud and drowning.

His eyes flash fright, his skin goosebumps, but his mouth is as twisted and hating as ever. "You lost your chance, sista," he spits. "'Least I would be gentle. You be lucky if you can walk after they finish with you."

Five hundred and one, five hundred and two, five hundred and three . . .

There's a time, in the early hours, when the clock hand is past midnight but the sky hasn't begun to turn from black to indigo and the stars still burn a bright silver-white against a velvety darkness that has no edges. A time when night shifts. My bones feel it. The earth exhales yesterday's stale air and the new morning begins to settle.

Above ground, on the embankments that border the Ring Road, diamonds glisten on the seed-heads of the rough grasses that cling to the slopes. Then the frost bites my sleeping bones and reminds me I will never be warm again.

I can't see the frost from our underground prison, but I feel the shift. The cold reaches through the earth and settles her icy tomorrow on us. Soon the light will come, and with it the end of the road.

"Booysen, wake up."

Booysen's been dreaming twenty minutes when Marlboro arrives. I feel my sisi sink into a pit of hopelessness so deep it makes me want to close my eyes and let the darkness swallow me.

"Wakey wakey." Marlboro shakes him.

In a flash, Booysen's on his toes with his hands balled into fists. If that had been Sindi sneaking past, she would be black-eyed and bloody.

"Jissis fok, what you doing sneaking up on me?" Booysen drops his fists but his face stays black.

"Not difficult to sneak up on a person that's sleeping."

"Fok you, don't you go spreading lies, nobody sleeping. Check my ears, chizboy, they fine-tuned. Maybe my eyes closed, but my ears wide awake."

Marlboro shrugs. "Nobody hear nothing from me," he says.

My hair crackles with static. "Fight, fight, fight," I chant, but they stand in silence, waiting for the buzz between them to settle.

"You got a gwaai for me, bra?" asks Booysen.

Marlboro shakes his head and stares at the ground. Booysen clicks his tongue and stalks out.

With him gone, Marlboro turns to Sindi. "You good, sista?"

She gives him a blank look, closes her eyes. The sun stopped shining for Sindi a long time ago, I don't remember why, but deep down there's still a small spark, burning-burning, waiting for her to breathe again and fire it up. As her lids come down, I feel that flame flicker. I know, when morning comes, it'll go out.

Twenty thousand nine hundred and ninety-two, twenty thousand nine hundred and ninety-three, twenty thousand nine hundred and ninety-four . . .

The drip seems to make Marlboro more fidgety, like his pockets are full of ants. He sits for a second, then leaps from his chair as if it's loaded with drawing pins. He stalks the pipe, up and down, up and down. Just when I think he's about to spin out, he bolts to the entrance of the pipe and stands there, listening-listening.

Sindi seems unaffected by all his pacing. I can tell by the even rhythm of her breath that she's escaped into dreaming. I want to curl up behind her and close my eyes, let myself sink into the ground, into the dark, but Marlboro's energy buzzes like clouds of hungry mosquitoes and I can't settle.

He slips a pack of cigarettes from his pocket. Tendrils of smoke rise to the top of the pipe, clouding in layers like broken ghosts. I run my fingers through the haze, and they take on a bluish hue and turn into wispy ghost-fingers. I suck smoke into my lungs and breathe out my name. It dances towards the ceiling, swaying slow like Mama's hips late on Friday night. I see my letters twist and drift, until my name is stretched out like cirrostratus. Mama used to say that if we were good we'd go to heaven. If I went up to heaven I'd stretch out thin and float, I'd be a cloud high above the world, a cirrus strip in the endless blue.

Marlboro tosses his cigarette and stamps it out, half smoked. He frowns at the squashed butt, like he's trying to decide whether to pick it up or leave it there. Not a big deal, even if Booysen sees it, but Marlboro's staring as if it's the most important decision he's ever had to make. Then he turns, and in two steps he's across the pipe and kneeling next to my sisi, shaking her awake. Her eyes snap open, wide-wide. He clamps his hand over her mouth, as if he's afraid she'll scream.

"Sista," he whispers, "Sista, I gonna help you."

The dorm is layered with sleep sounds. At the bottom, a vibrating snore drones like a buzz saw. One level up, it's a peppering of child snorts, whistles and grunts. Together they make a sweet even rhythm of breath, broken only by the roll of a fart or the whimper of a little one as they run from the monsters of their dreams. These petty sounds flatten us against the wall, frozen by fear for infinite seconds.

My heart grows wings and beats against my ribs. It's impossible to tell blanket from human, and some kids sleep so close together they're like giant octopi, arms and legs sticking out, a minefield with fingertip triggers. I think of what Marlboro said after he'd explained his plan:

"Look, sista, no jokes. I'm going to help you get out, but if someone sees us, you trying to escape and I'm just catching you. That's what I'm going to say, and you can't say different. Okay?"

It was easy to agree – what else were we going to do? Now, inching around the mass of sleeping bodies, his plan seems crazy. Through the uncovered manholes far above me, I see the sky is turning, growing lighter with each passing minute. What if this is a trick and he wants us to get caught? If Ma catches us, we're dead, then the deal would be off and Loveday wouldn't have to go. We shouldn't have trusted him, but it's too late to go back.

We stand at the bottom of the ladder, looking up. It must be the oldest of the three ladders, maybe as old as the storm-drain system. It's half rusted away and I've never seen anyone use it. But it's set into a dark recess – if someone wakes, they probably won't see us. The first rung sticks out from the wall about three feet above our heads. Below it, holes dark as thieves' eyes stare out of the concrete where the lowest rungs were once bolted to the wall. Sindi opens her hands and looks at Marlboro.

"Jump," he whispers.

I go first. The waterproof paint has blistered and peeled, revealing the rusted metal beneath. The rungs feel porous in my hands, like a rack of fragile, sun-dried ribs. Not the stairway to freedom Marlboro promised, but a bone ladder descending from the surface into Ma Wilma's underground hell.

Sindi bends her knees, leaps upwards. Her fingertips graze metal, hands snapping around air as her feet thud down. We become statues of ourselves waiting for blankets to flap back and kids to explode towards us like startled pigeons in the park. Her breath jags, hard-fast, sawing through the sleep sounds. Nothing happens. Marlboro widens his eyes, nods for her to try again. She inhales deeply, crouches all the way down. She misses again, stumbles backwards and almost steps on a sleeping kid. Marlboro grabs her and they stand close as boyfriend-girlfriend. The girl rolls over and pulls her blanket over her head.

"Okay?"

She nods. He links his fingers together and gets down on one knee, making a spy-step like I did that time Uncle came to visit and Sindi climbed into the back window. The extra height puts the ladder within easy reach, but Sindi hangs on to the rung, too weak to go further. Without warning, Marlboro stands and thrusts her upward. She grabs a higher rung with her bad hand and pain flares across her face.

"Come on, sista, move it."

She jams a knee between two rungs while she gets her foot onto the ladder. Then she begins to climb. The rusted metal flakes under my sisi's hands and sends a blizzard of brown tumbling downwards. It freckles Marlboro's stark face as he hops like a frog caught in a bucket, the ladder just out of his reach.

And what do we feel, watching him leap and miss, leap and miss? The boy who led us into this hole, then helped us get out again. Soon Ma will wake and when she finds us gone, she'll take her knobkerrie and beat him until his brains leak from his skull like porridge. What do we feel? We save our feelings and climb the ladder.

Marlboro grunts. His fingers latch. He hangs there, getting a feel for his weight before hauling upward, his feet scrabbling against the wall. I look down and see his blues, innocent as a baby's, staring up at us. We're half-way between the sky and hell but he's behind us in seconds, breath furious.

"Kick him," I hiss over my shoulder.

We grasp blindly into the darkness, praying all the way up that no rung comes loose and sends us back to Ma Wilma, me and Sindi and our blue-eyed saviour. When at last we push through the manhole, relief comes in sobs.

Sindi and Marlboro lie on their backs on the cold concrete, gasping and giddy. I lie on my stomach, peering into Ma Wilma's hole. Far below, a little girl cries in her dreams.

"Run," I whisper, because I know the monster they run from in their nightmares is nothing compared to the monster they call mother. And, like a dream made real, I hear the drumming of feet on concrete and I turn to see a boot connect with Sindi's head.

Eye of the Believer

"Fok, Day, what you do that for? You could've killed her."

"Who cares about her?"

"What's your problem, huh?"

"My problem? I didn't have a problem till now. Why you bring her?"

"I felt bad for her."

"Why, B'ro? You never felt bad for any girl before. Why now?"

"Queen."

Silence. It buzzes in my ears like TV static. Then she slaps him. "You think bringing her gonna help Queen? B'ro, it's too late to help Queen. You fokken stupid, you know that, B'ro, fokken stupid."

"Why, huh? Why am I stupid? Just because I can be nice, Day, don't make me stupid."

"No, nice don't make you stupid, stupid makes you stupid."

She folds her arms across her chest, turns away. This time the silence is stony and cold. "We need to move."

"What about her?"

"Leave it already."

"I won't leave her. Ma gonna kill her if she finds her."

"So?"

"So, I don't want somebody to die because of me."

"Queen gonna die because of you."

"That not fair, that not fokken fair. How can you say that?"

"Life's not fair, didn't nobody tell you?"

"I'm not leaving her."

"Bad enough we running, but if Ma think we take her, she won't sleep till she find us."

"She won't find us."

"No? You think? Fok, B'ro, you so stupid."

"I'm not. I have a plan. I've thought 'bout it. We can leave the city, head for the coast. If we make for the N3, we can find transi easy. We get a ride on a truck, next day we on the beach. Ma'll never look for us there."

"That's a stupid plan. You stupid, man, stupid."

"Well, what plan you got?" He crouches over Sindi, slaps her cheeks. "Wake up, sista, wake up."

"She's not your sister."

"Can you stand, sista? We need to move?"

"Ag fok, grab her arm, I'll grab the other. Once she gets moving, she'll come right."

And just like that we're back on the road with dawn creeping up the sky, cementing the new day. We puff miniature cumulonimbus clouds into the air: they're the words we don't say as we track the deserted suburban streets, walking in a tight huddle that speaks of friendship with a liar's tongue. Birds chirp and chatter, hidden in the naked branches of trees that haunt the winter gardens. It's that time of morning. Under the earth, beetles and worms wake, and below them, Ma's gang stretches and yawns.

"We got to find somewhere to hide. They gonna be looking for us soon." Marlboro blows into his cupped hands, scans the houses.

"Let's just keep going, catch a transi at the N3, like you said."

He shakes his head. "When they suss we gone, the ouledi will get the Commissioner's crew to scan the highways. First we need to hide for a few days, till they give up."

Loveday balls her hands into fists. That girl's always sparking to fight. "This is all your fault, B'ro. We could be halfway to the seaside by now."

"My fault?"

"You the one who bring her."

"You the one who kick her in the head."

Sindi and me sink onto the edge of the pavement: ringside seat to another argument. She rests her head between her knees. I stare at the cracks in the tar.

"Please, B'ro, what we gonna do?" Loveday's tone has shifted. Marlboro pulls his beanie low. "Ag fok, B'ro, think."

"I'm thinking. Maybe we can hide in one of these houses."

"These houses? What we gonna do? Go ring the bell and say, we running away from our Ma who sells girls? If she finds us, she's gonna kill us, can we hide in your house?"

She has a point. Knocking on doors is just inviting another kind of trouble. People don't even like sharing pavements with beggars and street kids, they aren't going to ask us in.

"What about The Ascension?"

They squint at Sindi like they're surprised to see her sitting there.

"You said M_Ma Wilma hates Believers and all the Believers will be there. It's their festival. I mm_met a Believer a few days ago and he told me it was in the old refinery just past N_N_Nasrec. M_m_maybe she won't look there."

Marlboro nods, his jaw set tight, but the idea doesn't sit so well on Loveday's face. "That's a stupid idea. Ma'll kill us if she finds us there."

"She'll kill us anyway."

Loveday looks down the empty street at the lampposts lined up along the pavements like a row of tall gogos waiting to cross. Her thin shoulders curl to imitate them. I remember what it's like to think you're special, only to find what you thought was love is something else, something with a hard heart and black plans.

"You know that time that ou mlungu come to the warehouse one year, and Ma take to him with her knobkerrie?"

Marlboro nods.

"Before she beat him, he told me that when the day come that Ma wants to sell me, I should go to his church. He said I wouldn't miss it, that the roof shines like the sun. Said it was wired with gold. I told him to get lost. Ma won't sell me, I said. What kind of mother sells her children?"

Marlboro kicks the tar with the toe of his sneak, glances up at the brightening sky.

"Nn_nasrec's not far," Sindi says, heaving off the pavement.

"No, not far," Marlboro says, "just five kays down the highway. But it's down the highway."

"I knew this was a stupid idea. Why you bring her, B'ro?"

"Not so stupid. The Black Preacher's big in this neighbourhood, these streets is thick with Believers. Come here any day and there's a copper collar on every corner preaching Jesus. Some of these houses will be empty. We just got to case a few till we find one."

We leave Sindi and Loveday hunkered down in front of a recessed garage door while I go with Marlboro to find us a safe house to squat. The neighbourhood is laid out in a grid. Most houses are only just visible through chained gates, and surrounded by stop-nonsenses topped with barbed wire or spikes. They might be Believers, but they don't have faith that Jesus will save them from murderers and thieves.

Marlboro zigzags up, around and down street blocks with his hands in the pockets of his hoodie, trying to look like he takes a stroll at six am every morning. He takes loose steps but keeps close to the wall side of the pavement, checking over his shoulder as if he's scared someone's going to drive by and snatch him. Anyone spots him, they'll call the police.

We've gone three blocks with no chance of getting past a gate, never mind close enough to suss if a place is empty, when Marlboro stops in front of a one-storey bungalow. The perimeter wall is high, but this house is more run-down than its neighbours. Black paint flakes off two wide metal gates that open inwards on ancient mechanical arms. Judging by the rusted shafts, they haven't worked in years. There's a chain looped around the centre of the gate, holding it shut, but there's no padlock. All bark, no bite.

With quick hands, Marlboro slips the chain off and pushes the gate. It squeals in protest at our invasion, but gives easy. I follow him up a gravel drive crowded with blackjacks, glancing nervously at the irregular blue flash in a window facing the garden. I wonder what Marlboro's thinking, coming into the only house with any sign of life. Maybe he figures the owner's as tumbledown as the house, someone easy to sneak up on and overpower, like a pensioner. Underneath the dirt and drought-proof weeds, I can see the remains of flowerbeds laid out around a tree. Maybe the owner is an old lady, like Gogo Nkosi with her herbs and cabbages and roses. The thought of what Marlboro might do to her makes me shiver.

The drive runs along the side of the house. Following Marlboro's lead, I press my back against the wall. The rough face-brick bites. He sidesteps to the window, looks in. I do the same. Through a torn lace curtain behind the glass, I spot a TV sitting on a wooden tomato crate. Angled so I can't see it flat-on, the screen warps between picture and snow.

The only other furniture in view is a worn-out armchair. It's empty. The place feels like a cemetery where the dead were buried so long ago, no one living remembers them. There's nobody home. Still, I can't shake the feeling we're being watched. I press my face to the glass and squint into the gloomy interior. On the wall behind the TV, someone has painted a black cross. It spans the wall's height and width, and in its centre is a red eye. Copper wire wound tightly around nails hammered into the iris makes a pattern of lines and triangles that catch the flickering light and twist it so the eye gleams wetly.

There's something moving in the iris. The empty space at the centre of the spiral of wire, where the pupil would be, seems to swell and shrink, up and down like breathing. I'm staring, unblinking, trying to draw a shape from the shadow in the eye, when it lifts off the wall and hurtles towards us.

A large moth batters against the glass. Its wings make tiny dust devils in the air and powder the glass, exposing greasy fingerprints on the other side. Then, quick as the moth flew at me, it retreats.

The white noise buzzes against my face. Through a tunnel of static, I see the moth land on the TV. A voice blasts from the speakers: "Work out your own salvation with fear and trembling."

"Jissis fok!" Marlboro backs away from the window.

My vision dissolves, shuts off. I feel like I'm falling, down, down, down. I hear the gravel crunch under Marlboro's sneaks, the clang of the metal gates. I turn and flee blindly from the house.

We lean against the wall and watch Marlboro try to jimmy a window. Though the owner didn't bother to lock the gate, the windows are shut tight against us. He steps back, twisting his beanie, and shakes his head.

"You useless." Loveday pushes him aside. Before he can stop her, she's lifted a loose brick lying next to a gutter and put it through the pane. "Easy," she says, sliding the latch. The window opens towards us, but our way is still barred by the security grille bolted onto the inside sill.

"Could've been an alarm."

She snorts. "You think, stupid? This place is a dump."

"We still can't get in," he says, as if his way would've got us further.

She shrugs and walks away like it's no longer her problem. Just when I think she's heading for the road, she turns and does a Bruce Lee like in the movies Next-Door-Auntie's boyfriend used to watch, but with synced lips. Her foot connects with a bar so hard it leaves a dent. There's a communal sucking of teeth, but if it hurt she doesn't let it show. She kicks again and again, not even stopping when Marlboro joins in. Minutes later, she grips the grille in both hands and gives it a shake. The bolts drop. We hear them land and roll away, trailed by a trickle of plaster dust.

"Not so difficult, neh?" She tosses the grille into the room, ripping the lace curtain from its railing. The clatter reverbs; the lace billows down, a slo-mo ghost, and shrouds the metal.

"Jissis, B'ro, Ma's right, these Believers are pigs," she says, clamping her hand over her nose and mouth so she doesn't breath in dust from the falling curtain.

I look at Sindi. The way she shakes her head reminds me of Mama. Mama would've said this girl was looking for a smack, but I'm beginning to admire her violence.

We step into a room piled high with boxes. Sitting bang in the middle of the floor is a small desk littered with splinters of copper wire and broken bits of electrical circuits. A single bed is pushed against one wall. The mattress is bare and frayed and dark in places, and I think of all the people skinny-limbed and dying, the last of their life seeping into the sheets. I close my eyes and I'm back on the ward with the nurse closing the curtain around my bed.

A rustle like feet on dry leaves draws me back. I hold still, listening-listening. The gate groans against its rusty arms. I tiptoe to the window, stick my head out in time to see it bang shut. No one there. Just wind. Or ghosts.

Careful not to touch anything in case it tries to pass dark stories to me, I cross to the door. The passage is narrow and smells of mildew and cat pee. I creep past two doors, peer in. The first leads to a bedroom with a double bed made up in off-white sheets and grey blankets, the second to a bathroom.

I step into the bathroom and listen to the toilet sing a trickle to itself while the showerhead counts the beats, dripping into the cracked enamel bathtub. I lean over the tired basin, over the cup holding a toothbrush and a man's shaving razor, and grin into the murky mirror above it. I show it all my teeth, but it's lost my reflection.

I find the others in the room with the TV and stand in the doorway, looking for the moth. If it's still there, it's well-hidden. I step tentatively into the room and join my sisi. Somebody's turned the TV off and it no longer flashes static. Along with the armchair, there's a couch. The painting of the eye looms over the room. It creeps me out, but Loveday stands like roadkill caught in headlights, swaying slightly.

"What is it?"

"Eye of the Believer," says Marlboro.

"It's like the sun," she whispers. "It glows, just like he said."

We settle in the lounge in front of the TV, stripping blankets from the beds and ransacking the wardrobe for more. No one wants to be alone, the softness of a real bed no comfort when every sound makes fear bubble in our veins. My sisi stretches out on the couch while the other two curl into each other on the floor like snakes. One by one, their eyes lose focus and their lids come down and shut me out. Long after their breath becomes even and shallow, Marlboro keeps twitching. Even asleep, the boy can't relax.

My sisi doesn't dream of me. Something has shifted, she's moving away. I want to follow, but every time I try to slip in next to her, a door slams in my face. "Don't leave," I whisper to the rhythm of her breath, but the words fall from my lips without a hiss.

I sit on the worn carpet waiting for someone to wake and rescue me from the whispers of the lonely house. I know from the walls that this Believer lives alone, but he once had a cat that lost its mind. I see the cat's blank-eyed ghost cross the threshold and stand staring-staring at the sleeping strangers. The carpet fibres release ammonia memories when it comes into the room. It rubs up against me and I scratch its back, then it turns and stalks away, glancing over its shoulder like it wants me to follow. I stay where I am, kneeling over my sisi. The echoes of the prayers that wind through the house fill my head. The cat yowls and I stick my fingers in my ears to block out the noise.

Day sinks into afternoon and a ray of cold light, filtered through grimy gauze, catches the copper-wire eye and turns the dust motes orange. They twist at me, a laser beam of accusations, sucking me into the swirl. I struggle to break free of that orange spin. When I finally pull away, its stare bores holes into my back.

The eye has a presence that is more than physical. It worms into my mind, throbbing-throbbing. It whispers hate.

Not clean, no, not clean. Dirty, dirty.

The mocking murmur drives me into the narrow passage. I pace its length for eternity, up and down, until . . .

"This potato softer than Ma's backside."

I turn towards her voice and find myself in a small kitchen. Loveday's raiding the vegetable rack while Sindi and Marlboro rifle through drawers and cupboards.

"That all?"

"There's an onion as well," Loveday holds up the shrivelled vegetable. It's black with mould.

We stand around the table and stare at the only food the kitchen has to offer. Three tea-bags, an almost empty packet of sugar, one rotten potato, one mouldy onion and an egg. Sindi picks up the potato, rolls it in her palm. The sprouting black eyes break off and fall onto the tabletop, pitter-patter. "We can't s_astay here," she says.

Loveday snorts. "For days I bring you food and you don't eat, now you want to waai because the food's not five star. Bow down, B'ro, our friend here is a real princess."

Sindi puts the potato down and angles a look at her. I know that look. She's sizing her up, trying to find a weak spot. In Ma Wilma's underground, Loveday was protected. Out here, in the real world, our feet stand on the same ground. There's no one to step in and help her. But I know, and I think Sindi does too, that Loveday doesn't need help. If Sindi hits that sly face, she'll have to hit hard enough so that Loveday goes down.

Marlboro steps between them. "Sho, sistas, chila. She's right, Day, we can't stay here a week with just this to eat and still make it to Nasrec after. It's five kays and we need to walk it fast. Can't do that after no food."

"So what we gonna do, huh?"

"One of us has to go out and get food."

For once we all agree. Someone needs to go. But who?

"Me or you," says Loveday. "I don't trust the princess. She goes out, she don't come back. And if she gets caught, she won't think twice to save her skin and bring them here."

Sindi shrugs. It's true. Even though Marlboro helped us, we owe him nothing. He paid off his guilt by saving us, but it doesn't mean Jesus will welcome him in heaven, and it doesn't mean we're grateful.

"I'll go," he says.

Marlboro picks his way down the drive fluid as water. Usually he's a boy wound tight, a compressed spring. Even when he sleeps, he twitches and jerks, legs kicking out like his nerves are plugged into an electrical socket. I watch with narrow eyes for all that pent-up energy to burst and turn him into a whirligig – he'll explode before he reaches the gate, I bet. But he slips onto the street like an alley cat's silhouette, the sneaking shadow of a gutter rat.

We sit in the lounge, waiting-waiting. Sindi and Loveday choose spots on the floor in front of the three-seater. Hugging their knees, they curl into commas, dark and light, punctuating each end of the couch. I sit cross-legged in the centre of the sagging cushions, plucking the lines of tension that run from Sindi to Loveday and back again. I twang, filling the air with angry reverb. The sound blocks the endless spiral of prayers that seep from the walls and blur my edges.

Long past midnight, Loveday speaks. "You don't stutter so bad any more, you notice?"

Sindi nods.

"Why?"

"Don't know." She touches the back of her head. "Maybe since you kicked me."

Loveday snorts. "You think?"

"Maybe."

"I don't feel so bad then."

"You felt bad?"

Loveday shrugs. I look from her to my sisi. They smile, shy grins that pink Loveday's cheeks and sugar the air between them. "Look, about before," says Loveday.

"It's past."

I hiss. Sindi always forgives too easy. Except me, she never forgave me. I snap at the strings, but they've turned from wire to spun sugar and the sticky tendrils trail silent from my fingertips.

Without the crackle of their dislike, the stale prayers fill my head. They call the mad cat and it stalks into the centre of the lounge where it stands, back arched, tail strung, and adds its yowling to the noise.

Filthy girl, dirty, dirty, unclean.

I clamp my hands over my ears and shut my eyes. But still, it drags me back. Back to standing on the closed lid of the toilet seat while he rubs against me. The smell of pee and sweat and sickness, the taste of salt and sea, the grit of beach sand between us. The voices are right. I'm a dirty, dirty girl.

I blink and it's morning. Loveday and my sisi are asleep. During the night, they've drifted across the carpet and now they're nestled together like spoons in a drawer. Spooning together like me-and-you, like dreamers dreaming the same dream.

Sister-sister, sister-twin, twin-sister.

I lean over them and take a hank of dirty blonde hair in my hand. It's slippery and smells of stale cooking oil and musty carpet. I wind it around my fist and put my lips to her ear. "Your brother's dead," I hiss. And I pull her hair as hard as I can, ripping that thieving girl out of my sisi's sweet dreams.

She sits up, sees the morning light, feels her empty heart.

"What's wrong?" Sindi touches her shoulder.

"It's B'ro, he's not back. Something bad's happened."

I perch on the edge of the bath and trace our names onto the steamy tiles above the taps: *Thuli + Sindi 4 eva.* A distraction to stop me looking at my sisi, sponging warm water onto Loveday's shoulders.

All day Loveday paced, up and down, face hard, lips sealed against the voice of her fear, but when the night came down dark, it flooded out hope. No point waiting for a boy who will never come. Is she crying still? I can't tell if tears run down her broken face or if it's steam condensed on her cheeks. I reach out to trace a liquid heart onto her forehead, but she looks at me with lipstick eyes and I draw back, afraid to touch her. But I may as well have run my hands over her body, because she tells her story anyway.

"Funny thing about my real ouledi, she didn't call us by our names either. We were her numbers. I was number three, three of four kids, and B'ro was the boy. I was small, maybe six, when my toppie fell into a stamp mould at the plant. When they phoned, I was hiding in the stairwell, sucking on a cigarette Queen was holding. I remember the tune of Ma's cell, and the filter squeezed flat between Queen's thumb and finger. It was the colour of mustard."

She reaches out and grabs the rim of the bath, as if steeling herself against the memory. The movement is sudden, unexpected, and before I know what's happening, her fingers have brushed my leg and the familiar hospital tang of antiseptic and copper invades my nostrils and I'm dragging my restless feet along polished tiles in the corridor outside my toppie's room, with the lurch of my ma's grief in the pit of my stomach. The rubber soles of my shoes go squeak-squeak. There's a sharp, white glare when door swings open, releasing a grim-faced nurse. Before it shuts, I get a smeary glimpse of red and white and Ma's good floral print dress and a line of legs.

I pull back, but Loveday's stories have been buried too long and rush at me with the force of a truck. We collide head-on.

We're in a taxi, just me and Ma, going to fetch the toppie's things from the hospital because I'm the only one brave enough to hold Ma's hand. There is nothing left of him but a shattered watch and blue overalls dyed purple by his blood. I take the watch home. Ma takes a cough.

Then I'm standing next to Queen, waving at the taxi that's come to take Ma and her cough back to the hospital. After the taxi drives off, we go back into the house and I catch a glimpse of me and Queen in the hall mirror. Queen's taller and her hair is longer, and we're both thinner than we used to be.

Then it's night, a short time later. Queen looks the same, but her clothes are different. I'm at the top of the stairs, listening to Queen tell the rent man to come back later when Ma will be here. Ma is not coming back. I know, even though no one has said so. *Get your things,* Queen tells me. We pack what we can carry into plastic bags. The toddler stands in the cot, crying, her arms stretched towards me. *Bye, bye, have a good life*, I say. Queen kisses her on the head but I'm scared to touch her in case I can't let go. We leave the front door open and slip a note under the neighbour's door.

She's got a chance of getting fostered, says Queen, *but us lot will end up in a home. That's worse than the street.*

"Maybe you should get out, the water's getting cold," Sindi touches Loveday's cheek, my cheek. I cling to her voice, a safe island in the flood of Loveday's stories.

"Nights was a dark place, not just out there, but in here." Loveday taps her head. "I used to sleep with my hand wrapped around the neck of a broken bottle. 'Stab for the eyes,' Queen said, 'don't wait for a reason.'"

Sindi slips away from me. I try to grab on to the drip, drip, drip of the tap, the song of the leaking cistern, but these sounds can't protect me from Loveday's whispers.

"Queen had these two books. Ma's books. Romance rubbish full of kissing, but Queen said we should learn reading so one day, when we get off the streets, we can make good. She almost finished grade seven, so she tried to teach us, but we didn't want to learn, not then. Most times, she just read to us."

She sucks me down, down, down into a warm day at the beginning of spring . . . B'ro leads us through gates painted green into a park where there are flowers and benches and a sculpture of two squat iron men with helmets riding a motorbike with wings. A security guard warns us not to touch the art and stay away from the gallery, but he doesn't bug us if we lie on the grass at the far end of the park, away from the larneys.

Jump-cut to a different day, but the place is the same. Queen is reading a kissing story out loud. We've stolen strawberries and polony and we're pretending we're just normal kids having a picnic. The strawberries are sour and burn the ulcers in my mouth. I look up and spot a larney talking to the guard and pointing at us. We leave, but all the time we're gone, we talk about when it'll be safe to go back.

Next time, Ma Wilma's sitting on a bench, crumbling bread between her fat fingers for the pigeons. She offers us Coke and sandwiches, but we never take anything from her. Street kids disappear all the time. There are stories. Then one day she pulls a book from her bag. *Book can't hurt you, girlie.*

"What are you talking about? What book?" Sindi squeezes Loveday's hand, pulling me out of her. I reel away from the bath, out of Loveday's reach, but just because I'm free of her skin, doesn't mean I'm free of her tongue.

"She took us in. We thought she was a good person. We believed her when she said she was sending the older girls off to get married. We thought she was our only chance at making a good life. When we found out some girls went to work for the Commissioner, we didn't care: she'd never do that to us. We were her special girls, too beautiful to waste. Who else is gonna look out for a bunch of kids nobody wants?" She looks at Sindi with pleading eyes. "She gave us new names. Queen she named for the first bridge we live under, me for a street near there. Why she call B'ro what she did, I never knew, but sometimes she was random like that. Funny thing, I know Queen's name before was Sara, but I don't remember what name our real Ma gave *me*. Just 'Three.'"

"You going to get sick if you keep sitting in that water." Sindi opens a blanket and holds it out. Loveday's skin is waxy as white candles.

"I don't got anyone left. B'ro's dead and Queen got the sickness. She'll be dead soon, if she's not already."

"You don't know your brother's dead. Maybe he'll still come back."

"I know."

"How can you?"

"It was like a light went out inside me. Just like that," she snaps her wet fingers, "I felt him switch off. Everything feels different now, emptier." She makes a fist against her heart. "There's a hole, here."

I know she's lying, she felt nothing but me whispering in her ear, but as I stare at her lipstick eyes, her cherry nipples, the only bright bits of her, I believe her.

Sindi sticks her hand into the water and pulls the plug. "I felt nothing," she says, "I didn't know she was gone until the doctor told us. We were twins, and I used to feel everything she felt when we were small. But I broke that. I wasn't a good sister, not like you. If your brother's dead, he is with God. One day you will go to heaven and you'll see him again."

"You think?"

She nods.

"Then you'll come too, neh."

"No," she says, "I'm a bad person. I have no soul. A person needs a soul to go to heaven."

"Everyone have a soul."

"Not everyone. Some people are empty. Like twins, they're really one person, their shadow just came loose. I'm the shadow. Inside me, there's nothing."

"What happened to your sister?"

"I did a bad thing and she . . ." She takes a shuddering breath.

Loveday reaches out and places her hands over Sindi's. Their fingers intertwine like boyfriend-girlfriend.

"I'm going to put it right," says Sindi. "I swear I will. I'm going to hitch a ride to heaven and put it right."

"You can't hitchhike to heaven, it don't work like that."

Sindi pulls away. "You can. If you find a soul, you can." She takes a breath and begins to sing: "Emi, oru, abiku, o, catch a emi by the toe, hold on tight and don' let go if up to heaven you wish to go."

Sindi's song makes my head spin. I lurch to the basin and retch, but nothing comes up. Maybe I'm empty too. I'm Sindi's twin and if she's empty, them so am I. *Twin-sister, sister-twin, sister-sister.*

In the mirror above the basin, I watch Sindi wrap the blanket around Loveday. My sisi looks up and frowns at her reflection, like she's surprised by what she sees. I study her face, my face but not mine. She's different somehow, but before I can figure out what's changed, she slips her hand into Loveday's and leads her from the bathroom. And I'm left staring into the blank glass.

Ants trickle from a hole in the gummy sealant between the wall and the kitchen sink. I watch them crawling-crawling along the water-dulled steel, over the greasy stove and down the spattered tiles, carefully avoiding the patches where oil has dried to a sticky trap for their tiny legs. They trail across the linoleum and disappear into the crack of night under the back door. Then they come back again, hurrying along their chemical highway, pausing only to tell each other stories.

I know about chemical ant-stories from Miss Booley, but I can't read them. One time, for homework, we had to write a report on how ants behaved when their trail was broken. Miss Booley told us to find a line of ants and wipe a five-centimetre section away with vinegar. The ants ran in panicked circles, trying to pick up a trail. It didn't take long for most of them to make a new line and carry on like nothing happened. Some of the ants, though, took off at ninety degrees to the broken path and I knew that, like drunks stumbling from Ma Elias', they'd never find their way back. I grew bored and began to squish the stragglers. Sindi said it was mean but I told her they were dead anyway, I was doing them a favour. Without a nest they'd starve or something would eat them – whatever eats ants. It was funny then, it made me laugh, but I'm far from home myself now.

I place my thumb into the path of the ants crawling along the sink. By some trick of the light, they seem to disappear on one side and reappear on the other, as if they're going through me, and that makes me feel like a nothing, small-small, tinier than an ant and totally unimportant.

Over at the stove, Sindi fishes the egg out of the water, peels it and throws the shells into the sink. She cuts it into four and feeds the quarters to Loveday, one by one. Then she stirs all the sugar into a cup of strong tea and makes her drink it. But the girl still shivers, lips and fingernails and the dark circles under her eyes bruised by cold.

Sindi takes a sip of her own tea, and though she ate nothing, she's warm. Her eyes shine, not the glassy feverish glitter she gets when cars crash, but a softer glow. Something flows between them. They whisper to each other, secret things that silver the air and fence me out. I stick my fingers in my ears and circle their shiny new barbed-wire harmony.

Later, Loveday lays her head in my sisi's lap and Sindi falls asleep stroking her hair as if it were mine. I sit cross-legged on the floor and hiss into Loveday's face. Her wide eyes are two blank coins of sky and I get lost inside them. I'm a cirrus cloud wisped to nothing by the wind of her breath.

When I pull back, she's no longer there. I find her in the room with the broken window, sitting cross-legged on the floor with a heap of black books on her left and a neat stack of them on her right. All the boxes in the room have been opened. Most are empty but some contain electronic components. With the worn carpet rough against my knees, I peer at the pile of books. They're all the same, slim pocket-sized volumes with plastic covers, pretending to be something expensive. Fake, like Next-Door-Auntie's leather pants. There's an eye on the front. I tuck my fingers under my armpits. I don't want to know what those books have to say about me.

Loveday's lips move as she reads the tiny words printed on the thin pages. She reads only a single page from each book, then stacks it neatly on her right before taking another from the heap on her left. Night crawls towards dawn.

"What you doing? It's cold in here."

For the first time in hours, Loveday looks up. "Been reading," she says, pointing with the book she's holding at the piles around her. "All these books."

Sindi eyes them. "Aren't these all the same?"

"The Eye told me, read the books and you find the answer. I been reading them. I can find him."

"Who?"

"The man. The man who live forever."

"What are you talking about?"

"The man in the books. There's a saviour who walks the earth. He can do anything. He can save you. If we find him, he can give you a soul."

"You mean the Black Preacher? Loveday, the preacher's just a man, like anybody."

"No, no, no, not the preacher, the Black Preacher just a prophet. I'm talking about the other one. We need to find the other one. We need to walk the road."

A man hunches at the window watching us, his expression black as his suit. Loveday has her back to him, but she reads the sudden fear in Sindi's face. "What's wrong?" she asks, before she spots the shape of him in Sindi's eyes. She scrambles, but she's hardly on her feet when a second man grabs my sisi from behind.

"Run!" Loveday screams, but there's nowhere left to go.

We sit in a row on the couch while a slope-shouldered sack of a man prowls the length of carpet in front of us. He sags in the middle like a pouch of potatoes, potbelly and chin racing to escape the rest of him. He has the same bitter eyes as the three-legged dog that used to scrounge the bins at Chicken Licken next door to Saviour's, always watching for stones.

The other man is one hundred percent gangsta. He's tall and broad as a five-lane highway and dresses the part in a sharp black suit, black shirt and black tie. A real playa. The sheen on Sack Man's suit screams fong kong: the day Next-Door-Auntie's boyfriend went to court, he wore a suit like that. Mama warned us not to marry a man in a shiny suit or scuffed shoes. She said men like that had no pride.

The day Gogo Nkosi's lodger hanged, we sat on Next-Door-Auntie's brown couch with her boyfriend and watched it on TV. Mama had said we weren't allowed to, but she'd gone to work and Auntie wasn't there to stop us. The lodger shuffled towards the gallows, face blank. Next-Door-Auntie's boyfriend said that some people face death silently, shutting down inside before it arrives. It steals the pleasure their suffering brings to the killers.

I glance at my sisi, at her vacant eyes, and wonder if she remembers.

Other people go fighting, Auntie's boyfriend said. They spit and claw, ripping at the throat and eyes. They drag their nails across cheeks, sink their teeth into flesh. He stubbed out his cigarette, exhaled blue smoke. "Lots of women are like that," he said. "They're not aiming to escape, they know they can't." He pulled up his sleeve and ran his pinkie finger over the livid scar that ran from his elbow to his wrist. "They just want to leave a mark, something to remember them by."

Sack Man mutters something about seeing to the damage and leaves the room.

"Big man like you get a kick from hurting girls?" Loveday's hands twist in her lap. "Must make you feel strong. Bet you play with yourself after, neh?"

One Hundred Percent raises an eyebrow. Loveday sniffs, looking pissed. I don't think that was the reaction she was after. Then she smiles. "I not seen you with the Commissioner before. Or your funny little friend. You new?"

He doesn't reply and she stands.

"Sit down."

"Make me."

He laughs. "You're in enough trouble, little sister, don't make it worse. Just sit down."

"Or what?"

In the single step he takes towards her, he seems to grow so much bigger it's like he was standing a kay away before.

"Go to hell."

"I don't think so, little sister. Not me."

"You'll go to hell for all the killing you do. You'll go to hell for my brother." She spits at him.

"You got the wrong man."

"Figures. Your funny little friend cut people up while you hold them down? Think that keeps your hands clean? God sees you," she says, pointing at the eye.

"I don't hide from God."

Sack Man chooses that moment to return, as if revealing himself to God's eye too.

200

"Not too bad," he says, "except for the window. And some boxes opened."

One Hundred Percent nods. "What you want to do, Brother?"

Sack Man shrugs off his jacket, lays it over the TV and begins to roll up his sleeves. I ball my hands into fists. This is it. The end. Loveday knows it too, but she's not about to go without a fight. She rockets off the couch and launches an attack on Sack Man.

He stumbles, awkward on his feet. The TV crashes to the floor and sends his jacket flying. It lands on the carpet and falls open, seams gleaming. One Hundred Percent lifts Loveday off his friend. He pins her arms to her body, but her feet pedal the air.

"Stop!" Sindi yells. "They're Believers."

I hunker down in the back of the Believers' black bakkie while Loveday and my sisi huddle together in the cab. Brother Absalom, that's One Hundred Percent's real name, starts the engine while we wait for Brother Moses to finish talking to the neighbours. It turns out the rustling leaves and swinging gates weren't ghosts after all – although the commotion Loveday made breaking in would've rattled the dead.

Still, those Believers would be dropping us at the nearest pig-pen if it wasn't for Loveday's sugar tongue, so I don't kick up a fuss that it's not me snuggled up warm next to Sindi. She has a talent, I give the girl that. She can turn on the tears and sob out a story better than any starring on *Generations*.

When they heard we escaped from Ma Wilma, they sat up and paid attention. "Ma Wilma raised you girls?" Brother Absalom cut Brother Moses a sideways look.

"From small," Loveday said.

They thought she meant all of us and we didn't set them straight. Their teeth gleamed when she said we wanted to go to their church.

We speed down the highway towards salvation. The ride whips me into a different shape, stretching my fibres until I'm like spookasem spun in Joe's Hurricane machine. But I'm not sugar and spice, I've never been nice. By the time the bakkie veers off the Nasrec road and bumps over dirt and stones, I've been stretched a hundred metres from my clinging fingers to my toes. My hair is exhaust fumes and red dust and spiky legs and cellophane wings. Splattered insects shouldn't make a girl.

The dirt road twists through a thicket of blue gums. We drive through their menthol shade and stop outside a huddle of rotting prefab huts cringing beneath a three-storey patchwork of corrugated iron, stolen street signs and advertising hoardings. The old refinery. Under the eaves, the windows are glassless. The place looks as derelict as all the other abandoned factories on the industrial outskirts of the city.

"This it? This your church?" There's a waver of uncertainty in Loveday's voice.

"Let's just say, we don't like uninvited company. This keeps most out."

"But the preacher, he said it shines."

The sun peeps out from behind a cirrus cloud and lights up the copper wire mounted just above the roof's rusting sheet-metal, echoing the pattern of its corrugations. Miracles on demand. I follow the copper paths, up down, to an antenna hidden in the blue gum's dirty foliage. Sweet, I think, TV. I slither to the end of the flatbed. My feet are further away than they should be. They hang off the edge, touching the ground. My knees fold in on themselves. I hold out my arms, they're too long and skinny-skinny. All of me is blurred, transparent, as if I'm dissolving, becoming nothing. I pick bits of insect from my hair, trying to remember what shape I'm meant to be.

"You girls coming?"

I stand to follow, but my legs buckle, and I crumple in a heap on the floor.

"Don't leave me, Sisi!" I cry.

For one hopeful moment, Sindi hangs back. Then Loveday calls her name and I know, that girl has crammed her scrawny self into the sister-space in Sindi's heart and shoved me out.

202

Hand in hand, they grow small in the shadow of the old refinery, leaving me alone on the ground with my knotted knees and tangled elbows. "Don't leave me," I say to the dirt and the tyre tracks pressed into it, to the sharp-edged stones and the chaff of ground-up leaves, but my voice, like my body, has stretched out thin. I stare at the space where I last saw Sindi, until my eyes ache. My skin fizzes, and for a moment I'm part of the vast blue blank above me. Then all colour leaches away.

Stations of Purity

Something sparks electric. A triangle of blue sizzles, fizzes out, leaving a fading purple impression on the blanket of darkness. I ball my fists into my eye sockets, then scan the black. I can just make out the faint outline of a building. The air around me buzzes. It tweaks my nipples, prickles along the nape of my neck, blocks my ears like they've been stuffed with cotton wool. I try to wrap my arms around my shoulders, but instead hug empty space; I wonder if I even have shoulders, or arms.

Everything pitches and tumbles. My mind is a mess of inky swirls. Another spark runs along the roof of the building, briefly bluing up the night. When it disappears it leaves a solid blackness that snuffs out my breath. So dark I don't exist, part of nothing, going nowhere.

My lids drop and I hang in a sliver of black until the clouds lume up and the trees are etched in silver. Black bleeds to indigo and Mama Moon, her belly full, labours up the sky. Milky light spills off the sloping roof onto a huddle of slumbering huts, and a memory floats to the surface. Someone walked into that building and left me behind. I try ID the walker, but she's a shadow's shadow, and all I can think of is the berry burst of a purple Lifesaver, *one for me,* or the zesty zing of a lime Sparkle, *one for you.*

That brings me low. I close my eyes completely. I want to sink back into forgetting, but something collides with my face and drops into my lap. The air shimmers. Dust settles on my parted lips, coats my tongue with the taste of long-dead things.

I track the moth's movements on the fabric of my dress, unable even to pull my hands from my lap until it brushes against my thumb. Pin-thin legs tickle my skin as it crawls onto my palm. For a moment, forever, I sit with it cupped in my hand. Then I scream.

The moth shudders and lifts lightly into the air to hover in front of my face, mercury-winged in Mama Moon's light. I see myself trapped inside its black orb eyes, my fear reflected back at me in fractions. I shrink back and it whirrs past, ghosting my cheeks with grey powder.

The night was still, but now it vibrates with the beating of a thousand imagined wings. I swat the air, hands dancing like mad puppets, and the kiss of my fingertips on the back of my neck makes me lurch to my feet.

Holding my fear tight, I run towards the building, focusing on the reflected flicker under the eaves, the only light. I scan the wall, but I can't make out a door in the mish-mash of rusted sheet-iron, advertising hoardings and street signs. I pick my way around, fingers strumming the corrugations, and almost cry out at the sight of a pallid glow spilling from an open doorway.

Insects spiral in the exhausted halo of a solar lamp that stands just inside a raised loading door. The room beyond it seems to be a coat check. Jackets in all shades of night and navy hang in rows on wall-hooks, lie piled on the floor. A factory locker room, maybe.

I skirt the lamp, with its eddy of moths and mosquitoes, and enter. A strange electrical drone surrounds me, as if I've stepped into the speaker of a badly tuned radio. It seems to come from everywhere at once. Underneath the hiss, I can hear talking. A voice, smaller than a voice should be, but the kind that makes you sit up and listen.

"Hello," I whisper. No answer. The hum sizzles, buzzing-buzzing and the voice gets louder until it's 3D. Surround sound.

Brothers and sisters, wives, my children, tonight the moon is in her fertile phase . . .

It fades. At the far end of the room, I spot a man slumped in a chair, asleep. He's dressed from woollen cap to shiny boots in black. Perfect camo among the gloomy coats. Behind him, a knobkerrie rests against a door, partly obscuring a sign. I squint, trying to read the words, but they blur in the low light. I need to get closer.

I've tiptoed halfway across the floor when the watchman snorts. I drop and assume the please-don't-crack-my-skull position. I kneel forever, praying-praying, until his snores zigzag through the ambient hum. Then I peer through splayed fingers at his lolling head, the hand in his lap and the arm hanging at his side.

I stand on shaky knees, swallowing sobs. Why am I here? All I have is a snapshot of a girl disappearing into this building. I have to find her: maybe she can help me remember. All I have to do is open the door and step over the guard's leg. Trembling, I reach for the handle. My eyes flick over the sign.

LET ALL WHO ENTER BE PURE IN HEART AND VEIN,

THEIR BLOOD UNTAINTED BY SIN,

LEST THEY BE CAST FROM THE KINGDOM OF HEAVEN.

The words taste heavy. I bite my lip. A twitch runs through the guard's body, as if he can sense me hovering over him. I jump, but he breathes easy. Something silver gleams in the hand hanging at his side, too shiny to be the steely edge of a knife, too box-like to be a gun. I spot it just before it slips from his grasp and clatters to the floor.

The watchman sits bolt upright, spitting curses. I slip sideways and conceal myself behind some jackets. I'm only partly hidden, but I dare not move: even the tiniest shift causes the jackets to crackle. The watchman hunches in his chair, hands clamped over his ears. Two wires run from the box on the floor and disappear into his woollen cap, one on each side of his head. Gripping both wires in an angry fist, he pulls headphones from his ears and drops them on the floor. They squeal like a slit-throat goat.

"Damn receiver."

The receiver is right next to his foot. All he has to do is reach down and pick it up, but his hand sweeps the floor in wide circles until his fingers graze the wire. He stops, fingertips investigating, then following the wire down to the receiver. As he picks it up, a sentence bursts from the headphones: . . . *girls have chosen to give themselves over to God* . . .

The watchman stands and begins to sway from side to side, holding the radio up in the air. Every now and then the hiss of white noise solidifies . . . *followed the calling in their hearts* . . . squeal . . . *discard their old selves and step through the door* . . . hiss . . . *home* . . . crackle . . . *wives of the Lord* . . . hiss . . . *God's embrace* . . .

"Stupid homemade transistors," he mutters, bending down to place the receiver next to his foot. "Don't get angry with an old man, Brother Moses," he says, though there's no one else there but me, "accidents happen." He two-steps and brings the heel of his boot down on the receiver with a sudden violence at odds with the laughter in his voice. I gasp.

The watchman swings around and looks directly at me. "Who's there?" His eyes flick from side to side like they're honing in, but his irises are milky, white-white. I press my back to the wall. "Someone there?" He cocks his head and reaches for the knobkerrie. The constant murmuring seems to stop: everything is holding its breath, waiting for him to see me.

"No one there, no one there," he mutters. His twirls the knobkerrie and sets it tip-down on the ground. He taps a path across the room. "Another dud for you to take home, Brother Moses," he says, tossing his jacket onto the pile on the floor. It falls open, revealing a blue silk lining veined with copper wire. I watch him search through the hanging jackets, testing the width of the shoulders, until he disappears from my line of vision. I want to keep him in my sights so he can't spring a surprise attack, but if I move, the release of static will give me away. I have to wait until he sets off a loud crackle before I shift my position.

I'm starting to worry he'll work his way all the way around the room to me before he finds a jacket that fits, when he finally slips one on. The arms are a little short but it's loose at the shoulders and he seems satisfied. He taps a path back to the chair and plugs in. After a few minutes, he slumps. I listen to him rasp snores for ages before I'm brave enough to sneak towards the door again.

Ignoring the sign, I grab the handle. My fingers zing through the metal and disappear into the wood panelling. I snatch my hand back and hold it up. For a moment, I imagine I can see the door through it, like I'm fading. Fear that this means something bad grips my guts, but some sci-fi theme tune from TV comes into my head and pushes the fear away. I can't remember the name of the programme or the starrings, but my brain cycles through sci-fi speak, looking for a word that fits the door that isn't a door: black hole, warp speed, intergalactic, stun-gun, hologram.

Beam me up.

Grinning at the clever trick, I press my palm against the wood and watch it sink below the surface. My arm looks like it's been chopped off at the wrist. I pull my hand back, afraid I might find it gone. It reappears, skin itching like I've dragged my hand through splinters. "So long," I whisper to the guard, and step through the door.

I stand in a narrow room, blinking-blinking. After the constant hum, the silence spooks me. A single fluorescent tube flickers on the narrow strip of ceiling above me. The floor is concrete, and I can just make out footprints where people have tracked in red dust from outside. They all point towards a shuttered roller-door spanned by a red eye. It's crudely painted, two lines arcing over and under a spiral that radiates from a central disc, but I still feel like I'm being watched. A thick pulley-chain hangs down the side of the door. I don't think I can raise the door alone, but I reach up and grab the chain anyway. Cold steel bites. My palms come together, passing straight through the links.

Quick, I pull my hands away and examine them. In the faltering neon light they look almost transparent, like lace curtains. I pinch the loose skin above my knuckles.

"I'm real," I whisper. My voice sounds strange and far away. "I'm real," I say louder. I hum the sci-fi tune to reassure myself, and place my hand in the spiral at the centre of the loading door. Then I close my eyes and take a big step forward.

My ears fill with the drone of breath and electricity. When I open my eyes, I'm standing at the back of a cavernous warehouse, and there are people everywhere. They lean against the walls, sit cross-legged on the floor. Even halfway up the walls, they're crammed onto the rusted pipes and tarnished ventilation ducts, higgledy-piggledy. I can only escape the sight of them by looking at the vaulted ceiling. They're all dressed in black. A thousand heads – ten thousand heads – bob on a sea of dark clothing.

A runway of fluorescent tubing hums overhead, all the way to a raised platform at the front where a man preaches gospel. He lurches across the stage, dragging one leg, lopsided. His voice is the one from the watchman's headphones, the same voice that was murmuring in the room full of jackets, but it no longer has the tin-can quality. It booms from a bank of speakers surrounding the stage, reverberates over the crowd and crashes straight into my skull.

"I do not come into the presence of God cleansed by my own work. I do not come into the presence of God purified by my own work. I come into the presence of God as a sinner, dressed in sinner's robes."

I feel like he's wired into some sort of internal stereo – like I'd be able to hear him even if I plugged my ears.

"I come to the presence of God in sackcloth."

I stare, open-mouthed. Behind the stage, a giant eye gleams. It's the same as the eye painted on the loading door, but made entirely of beaten copper. Branches of copper wire lash outwards from the eye and snake towards the ceiling. A jungle of electrical vines, sparking-sparking. They cover the walls in decorative swirls, turning the blue fluorescent glow to sunset. Below the stage, lined up like sentries, is a row of nuns. Their long black habits are woven with copper, their eyelids painted gold. Glinting nuns with glinting eyes.

The preacher leans towards the crowd. Everyone's waiting-waiting and the preacher looks loaded, about to explode, but when he finally speaks again his voice is hushed: "My children, there are those amongst us who still wear sinners' clothes. There are those amongst us who have not thrown off the garments that tie us to the earth. There are those who come into the presence of God in silks and velvets."

The crowd hisses.

"Now is the time!" he thunders. "Now is the time to throw off those sinner's clothes, to stand naked in front of the Lord and give yourself over to His work." His voice drops again. "God has a plan for you. We all know that women carry inside them the gift of creation. Once a year, God brings new life into our fold. Women whose purity has singled them out as worthy. Women whose cleanliness has singled them out as God's chosen mothers. Now is the time for those women to stand and realise their destiny." He lurches across the stage and points into the crowd. "Now is the time!" he bellows.

A ringing silence follows his voice over the heads of his expectant followers. There's a shuffling in the rows close to the stage and people nearer the back crane their necks to see. The preacher's gaze swings over his flock, like he's searching for the chosen one. Their excitement vibrates in my limbs and I want to jump up and show myself. I want him to choose me.

Near the front, a girl stands. She wears a light blue, almost grey, dress, but against the sea of black she's a beacon. Shoulders hunched, she sways like a naughty schoolgirl forced to stand for whispering in assembly. She stares at the floor and a wave of shame rushes over me, drowning out the thrill.

Somebody sitting on a ventilation duct bangs their heels against the metal; somebody starts to clap. Another girl stands. Soon the sound of clapping-clapping and stamping-stamping is deafening, but even the noise of all the hands and feet in the hall is made small by the preacher's voice.

"Now is the time to stand up and fulfil your destiny!"

One of the nuns rushes forward. She grabs the arm of the grey girl and ushers her towards a door at the side of the platform. The others move into the crowd, smiling schoolteacher-wide.

210

"Go with our sisters," the preacher instructs. "They will take care of you." Dozens rise to their feet and begin to straggle towards the door. I catch a glimpse of dirty-blonde hair among them. My heart lurches. Is she the one?

Before I can reach into my scattered mind and pull her out, someone bangs a drum and a fat woman in a long black dress walks onto the stage. Her voice, clear and haunting, picks me up and sends me someplace past, but before I can settle there the song's over and I bump back down with the greasy smell of engine oil in my nostrils. The preacher steps off the stage and a thousand hands reach out to touch him like he's Jesus. He walks into the crowd and is swallowed by black.

Up on the stage, the fat woman is singing again. Her song throbs. The congregation writhes. Hands reach into the air, clap to the rhythm of the drums. Everyone's dancing-dancing, swinging their hips and swaying. I give myself over to the music, twirling and bouncing. My spirits lift and I float towards the vaulted ceiling.

And I could stay up here forever, above it all, part of the copper sunset, but I look down and see myself glance up. Me but not me, standing in a queue by the side door. My face, but not mine, among the girls giving themselves to God. Just a glimmer of me, like a reflection in glass.

Then she looks away.

I scramble towards the front, ducking into the tight gaps between thrusting hips and shimmying shoulders. The music tugs, telling me to swirl until I'm black-black and nothing at all. I plug my ears with two fingers and focus on her face.

I'm almost there when I feel the burn. I swing around. The preacher man's behind me. Up close, his face is mapped with wrinkles, but his eyes are black as a moonless night, his gaze hot as the devil's.

"You!" His hand flies to his neck, and the faded memory of a spinning cross dredges up dark thoughts.

I scowl at him, a song on my lips: "Loon Man, Loon Man, your legs is . . ." But before I can sing *lopsided*, his followers surge around him and swallow him up. By the time I reach the door, the me-that-is-not-me is gone.

Most of the girls lined up along the wall look between the ages of twelve and seventeen. A nun stands at the door like the bouncer at Ma Elias', letting them pass through one at a time. Inscribed on the lintel are the words:

STATIONS OF PURITY – CLEANLINESS IS NEXT TO GODLINESS

I jump the queue and slip past the nun, easy.

I follow a girl through a narrow passage full of whispers. I think it's haunted until I stumble against a pipe and hear someone laugh. No ghosts, just hollow pipes full of echoes. The passage opens out into a wide room, divided into sections by thick red lines painted on the floor. Arrows direct us towards a tent constructed from poles and washing-line hung with white sheets. A sign is posted in front of the room:

STATION 1 – PURITY OF LOVE

Inside, a nun sits at a desk. A bright lamp turns her into a shadow puppet and the furniture – desk, chair, bed – into a stage set. "Next," she raps.

A girl, blonde hair cropped at the shoulders, pale eyes fringed by colourless lashes, takes a nervous step forward.

"Come on, God doesn't have all day."

Hand trembling, the girl parts the fabric at one corner of the room and slips between the sheets. I catch a glimpse of the nun standing to greet her, the copper in her skirt glinting, before the flap swings closed.

"Take off your clothes, please."

I watch the girl's shadow undress, her long silhouette fingers struggling with the buttons on her blouse. She pulls it half undone over her head, then slips her skirt from her hips. She lies on the bed, shadow legs elongating as she bends her knees, then shrinking to nothing when she opens wide. *Shame- shame.*

The nun's shadow-fingers stiffen a shadow-glove. Her hand disappears

212

between the girl's legs. There's a sucking of teeth, a 3D sound in a world of flat shadows. I look at my feet, count out a minute and start again.

A bell rings, and the girl emerges holding her clothes. All her colour is in her eyes: they strike out, too green, in the bloodless shock of her face.

STATION 2 – PURITY OF BLOOD

I follow her around to the back of the tent, where goose-pimpled girls stand all in a row, elbows over nipples, hands concealing cake. *Shame, shame, all the same.*

Except for two near the front. They're older than the others, twenty maybe, and seem relaxed in their skin. They're chatting, not staring at the ground like they want it to swallow them. "I don't know why they just didn't ask me if I was a virgin," says one.

"Everyone lies," shrugs the other, "and a virgin will bear the Saviour's child, so they have to be separated."

"You think she'll be the one?" She sniggers, and points at a big-titty girl sitting at a desk.

The nun opposite her talks in hushed tones, but her voice travels along the pipes and spreads the girl's secrets. "This is just so the others don't feel we're treating you special," the nun whispers, smiling as she squeezes the girl's finger. "Personally, I don't see why we bother testing virgins, but the council thinks one rule for all is best." Big Titty winces at the prick of the pin. "Easy peasy," the nun says, twisting Big Titty's hand so the glistening ruby gathering on the end of her finger drops neatly onto one end of a white plastic stick.

The nun places the stick on the table between them and looks at Big Titty expectantly. Big Titty looks at the stick. I don't think she's much of a talker. The nun likes to chatter, though, and she attempts to draw Big Titty out by asking about her home life and her family. After five mumbled one-word answers, the nun gives up.

"Cleanliness may be next to Godliness,' she says, "but friendliness goes a long way in heaven too." She places her hands together like she's praying and focuses on the test stick.

The queue is beginning to fidget. The nun raises the sleeve of her habit and checks the time on a gold wristwatch. "Just ten more minutes," she says, smiling through her teeth. Less than two minutes later, she's raising her sleeve again. The girls in the queue shift from one foot to the other. The shoulders of some of the braver ones relax away from their ears. Their erect nipples glare at Big Titty.

Fifteen minutes later, the nun rings her bell and holds up the stick for everyone to see. "Pure!" she shrieks. "Next."

I don't want to take that test. I know I'll fail.

Big Titty lumbers off, sucking her finger. I follow her to a door with a sign above the lintel.

STATION 3 – PURITY OF BODY

The door opens to a smoky room that smells of soap and burning bluegum leaves.

"Jewellery in here, clothes over there."

Big Titty takes off her earrings and drops them in the basket the nun of the third station holds out. At the pile of cast-off clothing, she hesitates, her expression drawn into a questioning frown.

"You don't need the bonds of your previous life any more. God has chosen you." The nun's voice is flat.

Big Titty drops all but her skirt onto the pile. Stroking the fabric between her fingers, she looks again at the nun. The nun rolls her eyes, but she reaches out and touches the girl's shoulder. "I understand," she says, "but you must let go. God has chosen you."

The nun directs Big Titty to a blanket and places a stone bowl containing three glowing coals in front of her. She crushes some leaves and drops them in the bowl. "Breathe in the smoke," she tells Big Titty, and tents another blanket over her head.

214

I sit on the pile of discarded things and stare at the rows of smoking wigwams. The nun walks up and down between them, closing any flaps that have fallen open or been parted by a sly hand. Minutes pass, nothing happens. I grow bored. I pull Big Titty's skirt from under my leg and run my fingers along the silky fabric. If it were mine, I'd keep it even if God chose me. I hold it to my cheek, enjoying the soft rub, and dig into the pile with my other hand to see what else I can find. My fingers graze scratchy denims and cottons and polyester – and bingo. Velvet. Softer than the skirt. I want it, whatever it is. As my hand closes over the buried treasure, it moves.

I leap from the mound, swatting the moth with the skirt. I have to get out. The room is too hot and the acrid smoke makes my head spin. I weave between the tents, looking for an escape. Thin blades of light cut a rectangle in the gloom ahead. It has to be a door. I stumble towards it.

The moth clatters in front of my face, blindsiding me. I veer left and almost collide with the nun as she lifts a blanket. A young woman, skin slick with sweat, rises from the smoke. The moth careens into her. She takes a swipe at it, her hand moving though the air slo-mo, like she's drunk. There's a dusty explosion and the moth tumbles away, leaving a grey smudge on her palm.

The smudge begins to glow, softly at first, then brighter, brighter until it burns a hole in her skin. A fine silver thread unwinds from her shining wound and tracks a path towards me. As it enters my body, a light inside me switches. I glow lunar bright, like a child grown in Mama Moon's belly, like a star, and step into a room full of forgotten things. An exercise book lies on the floor. It's covered in brown paper and labelled: *Sindisiwe Nxumalo – Grade 6*.

I flip though the pages and stop at a smudged worksheet on clouds. I read the names written underneath the blurry pictures in forward-slanting handwriting: *cirrus, cirrocumulus, cirrostratus, altocumulus, altostratus, nimbostratus, stratocumulus, stratus, cumulus, cumulonimbus.*

215

"Sindisiwe," I whisper, and saying her name makes me know my own. "Sisi." I rush towards her but she steps back. "Sisi, it's me."

"Thuli?" The colour drains from her cheeks. "Thuli?"

Smiling, I reach for her hand. As our fingers touch, her eyes roll back and she falls to the ground, legs kicking, arms thrashing. I kneel beside her, trying to hold on. Fear squeezes my chest as she jerks and jerks.

They carry the limp body of my sisi to one of the prefab huts outside the old refinery and lay her on a bed. They cover her with a sheet that sinks into her hollow belly and gropes her damp breasts. From the neck down, my sisi is a white papier-mâché sculpture, but her face is clay. They leave Brother Absalom to guard her, and for a time he watches, but her stillness lulls him to dreaming and leaves my eyes to mark the shallow rise and fall of her chest alone.

A long time passes before anyone comes. Past twelve, past one, past even the time when the earth breathes cold. Away from the refinery, the frenzied music is muffled. Only the bass beats escape, travelling through the ground and vibrating in my feet. My toes are tap-tapping when they finally come: the preacher, the watchman and the sister-thief. I hiss at her.

Brother Absalom wakes when they open the door, rubbing their palms to hold off the cold. And me? I sink into the shadows behind the bed, not knowing what it is that makes me afraid.

"Any change, Brother?" the preacher asks.

Brother Absalom stifles a yawn, shakes his head.

The preacher leans over Sindi. "I know this child," he says, "I met her on the road. Thought she was tainted, but Sister Xoli tells me she passed all the tests. She's a virgin of pure blood." He frowns at the wall, forcing me to crouch so low to avoid his gaze that my nostrils fill with the mentholated dust of crushed blue-gum leaves swept under the bed by the wind's broom. He lays the back of his hand on her forehead. "She's burning up." The preacher turns to Brother Absalom. "I saw a demon in the church tonight. The same demon I saw the night I met this child on the road. You see something, Brother?"

"I don't have that talent."

"Sindi a good person neh, she not a demon." Loveday pushes between the two men leaning over my sisi and pulls Sindi's hand from under the sheet. "She just have a fever, a dog bite her. Look at her hand, you'll see."

"Calm down, my child," says the preacher, "nobody's calling your friend a demon. But sometimes even good people fall into the clutches of Satan's minions. This girl has a hole inside her, I can feel it." The preacher runs his hands over her body. "Here." He takes Loveday's hand and directs it to Sindi's left palm. "You feel that?"

"I don't feel nothing." She snatches her hand away and glares at him.

"Your anger closes you, my child. You must learn to control your temper. There is no place in God's kingdom for a hothead. Now go wait outside, you can see your friend after we heal her."

Brother Absalom opens the door and, to my surprise, Loveday obeys.

"You watch that one, Father, she's fierce. She almost scratched Brother Moses' eyes out when we found her."

"Jesus tamed the wild beasts – I think I can manage a little girl. Now, Brother Jacob, find me this demon."

The watchman slips off his glasses and scans the room with white eyes.

I slide under the bed and push myself against the wall. I squeeze my eyes shut tight, and sing quiet to myself: *Thula thula mntwana, thula sana . . .*

"I can see it, Father, it hides in the shadows."

uMamuzobuya ekuseni . . .

"A creature of darkness," says the preacher. "Join hands, brothers, let us pray to free this child's soul from the bonds of Satan."

The bed's iron legs scrape against floor. I scramble to stay hidden and avoid big feet as someone shuffles into the space behind the bed. Their prayers mingle with my song, beautiful, frightening, tugging at the cord that binds me to my sister. Their words wrap around my fear, cushioning me from it.

Slow, I am drawn from my hiding place. I float, up-up and away from the dusty floor and the dead leaves, through the mattress kapok that sticks in long fibres to the rusted springs and makes me think of spookasem.

Then, I'm surrounded by the burning heat of my sisi's flesh. It envelopes me, a cocoon, a woollen winter blanket that pulses and throbs and tells me I'm too silent, the skin I wear too still.

But what does it mean to have no voice in a world of noise? Before I can grasp the answer, I'm pulled from her sweating stinking body. The night air sucks her hotness from me, and suddenly I'm colder than I've ever been. I want to go back, sink into my sisi and stay inside her. A crack opens up above me, like a bolt of lightning cutting up the night sky. I hear a voice, thick and throaty and familiar.

Come, Thuli, it calls. *Thulisile, come home.*

"No," I say. The light burns brighter than the sun, whiter than stars. "I don't want to go." I turn my back on that light and the voice that calls my name. "No," I say, linking my pinkie finger to Sindi's. "Twin-sister, sister-twin, sister-sister."

The preacher man begins to shout, and with a snap, our fingers pull apart and I float further away. Below me, I can see Sindi lying under the white sheet, not moving, surrounded by the men. I can hardly hear them, as if an invisible wall lies between us, but I can see their prayer words, spiralling upwards, pushing me away from my sisi. I grab the silver cord and pull myself towards her, but they make their words sharp blades. A curtain of darkness closes over them. I can't see my sisi, or the men, or the room. I hover, clinging to the shreds of silver draining from the cord. They flicker in the blackness like dying fireflies, fizz, go out.

In my hands, the cord is cold and lifeless, dead-man-blue. Then even that fades and there's nothing.

PART 4

Lost Soul

You're Dead and You Can't Touch Me

"Happy birthday, girls. You're becoming such beautiful ladies, soon the boys are going to be lining up to kiss you."

"Haibo, don't you go putting ideas in their heads."

"They're thirteen, Sizane, they already have ideas." Auntie fished a Bic from her pocket and lit the twenty-six birthday candles rising from the icing in sets of two.

Mama always did that, doubled the candles but only bought one cake. "Who's going to eat two cakes?" Mama snapped when Sindi asked for her own.

Sindi frowned at her sister over the bright pattern of the special-occasion tablecloth. She hated having to share everything. They weren't kids any more, dividing a bag of Sparkles by colour and putting the odd ones into a Consol jar. She had her own friends, her own life, but Mama acted like they were Siamese twins. Why pay more when you could squeeze a two-for-one deal out of everything, bed to birthday cake?

Sindi eyed the stack of gaudy cardboard party hats. She'd only invited the sgqebhezanas because it was expected. It stung that none of them had shown up, but only because she told Mama they were coming. She was happy not to share Nandi with a bunch of vain pops. She relished Fridays when the others went to Maponya Mall to commit the double sins of shop-lifting and making eyes at boys, and she got to hang out at Nandi's. Just the two of them. She wished that Nandi could sleep over, but even if her parents allowed it, there was nowhere for her to sleep. Sindi desperately wanted a bed of her own, and not only so that Nandi could stay over. Thuli had begun to sweat like a pig in the night. Mama said it was just hormones, but Sindi didn't sweat like that. It was disgusting.

The fact that she had a friend while Thuli sat alone at break like a skinny version of Dora no longer made Sindi feel bad. Thuli had it coming. For years, Sindi had believed that her outgoing sister would be popular if she hadn't had to drag a stuttering twin around, when it was really Thuli's attitude that stopped anyone befriending either of them. It was like Nandi said. Thuli pranced around and made eyes at all the boys, even when they were going with someone else. As if any boy would think *she* was hot stuff.

Mama switched off the lights and Nandi took Sindi's hand under the table. They sat in bruised shadows, watching the candles flicker, and then Mama and Auntie began to sing – Auntie's deep voice cracking like a teenage boy's because she was trying to sing soprano. Sindi swallowed a giggle; she wasn't sure she could do this. She cut her eyes sideways at Nandi: her expression was sombre, like she was at a funeral not a party. How did she keep such a straight face?

Mama was singing in Zulu now, Auntie humming along because she didn't know the words. Sindi's mouth twitched. If Nandi didn't give the signal soon, she'd laugh and it would be game over . . . Then Nandi gave her hand three sharp squeezes. They stood up and blew the candles out.

Mama's voice died with the candlelight. Auntie kept on humming a moment longer, then stopped. Sindi let out a snort of laughter and Nandi let go of her hand and sat down.

"What are doing, Sindisiwe?" Mama snapped the light switch. "And you think it's funny? Say sorry to your sister."

In the glaring aftermath of their trick, guilt threatened to wipe the grin from Sindi's face.

"Forget it, Mama. It doesn't matter." The legs of Thuli's chair screeched against the floor. She stalked from the kitchen, swiping aside the curtain to the bedroom.

Mama shook her head, Auntie clicked her tongue. The curtain rapped against the wardrobe like the tap of irritated fingers. Even the house was waiting for Sindi to follow with an apology. But what would Nandi think if she did?

Nandi was her only real friend. The other girls had only allowed Sindi into their circle as a favour to Nandi. She was tolerated, rather than liked. Secretly, she'd nicknamed the others "sgqebhezanas" because of the slutty way they hemmed their school dresses, so you could just about see their panties, but she never said anything bad about them in Nandi's presence. Sindi couldn't understand why Nandi, in her black Believer garb, continued to hang out with the empty-headed mini-skirts, although she'd been friends with them since grade one. They seemed interested only in competing for the attention of the boys in their class. Too much lipstick, too much bum-waggling, too much like Thuli. Nandi's explanation – that it was a great sin to abandon the ones you cared about to the devil, rather than stick by them and pray for their salvation – hardly rang true. After all, Nandi was against any suggestion that Sindi make up with Thuli. Sindi chose to ignore the double standard because, in the end, it came down to a simple choice: Nandi or Thuli. And her sister had cast her vote in Eston.

To escape the atmosphere of accusation in the kitchen, Nandi and Sindi went to sit on Auntie's doorstep in the blue light of the streetlights.

"What are you doing next Friday?"

Sindi broke a bit of birthday cake off the shared slice that lay on a plate between them. "N_nothing." She scooped some icing onto her finger and popped it into her mouth.

Nandi took a deep breath. "I've been chosen to sing at next Friday's service. I really want you to come."

Sindi sucked her finger. Mama said Nandi's church was bad news. She would never allow Sindi to go to there, Nandi knew that. "Who else is going?"

"No one. I don't want anyone else to come, just you."

Sindi considered her friend. Although Nandi liked to tell everyone they were going to hell, she didn't talk about church like Auntie did. She'd once said the Believer services were secret, though Sindi suspected she held her tongue because she didn't like people laughing at her. The sgqebhezanas already teased her endlessly about her black clothes.

"Sure, okay. I'll come."

"Seriously?"

Sindi linked her pinkie finger through Nandi's. "On m_my life, I promise. But don't tell anyone. If Thuli finds out, she'll t_t_tell Mama and . . ."

"Oh my God, it's going to be so great."

Sindi smiled, and didn't point out that Nandi had just committed the sin of using the Lord's name in vain. Not that she'd have been able to get a word in if she'd tried. Nandi was chattering with the same enthusiasm as the sgqebhezanas had the day they saw a starring from *Generations* at Maponya Mall. She was speaking so fast her words seemed to blur. In that moment, Sindi felt as close to her as she once had to Thuli, except this time it was real, not just because they were twins.

"The Father says everyone has a legend written on their soul. You, me, everyone."

Nandi's talk about soul made Sindi uneasy. As they'd grown closer, Sindi had sometimes worried about how to explain what Nandi had seen that night at Saviour's, but Nandi had never mentioned it. And Sindi had let herself forget. Eston was a distant memory. On the rare occasions Sindi thought about her grandmother, she was able to dismiss her words as the ravings of a crazy old woman. Some nights, she would wake with the sensation of being pulled under, and would find Thuli clinging to her; but the dreams had mostly faded. Now, though, Sindi tensed.

"And there are people at the church who can look inside you and tell you what God wrote there before you were born."

Sindi felt sick. The sweet icing made her jaw ache, saliva flooded her mouth. Nandi's voice crackled in her ears.

"It's a special talent, only some can do it. I can't do it yet, but I think I did it once so I'll be able to when I'm older. Father says it only comes to you when you turn sixteen. Hey. We can get someone to look into your soul on Friday. That would be cool."

Sindi's vision dissolved into a thousand pulsating dots. The ground tilted, and she slid off Auntie's doorstep. A mineral taste mixed with the sugar on her tongue. She retched.

Sindi awoke with the caterwaul of the alarm clattering in her skull. She clung for a moment to the blank remnants of sleep, her pulse quickening as the sound dragged her upwards. The dread hit before she opened her eyes.

You're dead and you can't touch me, you're dead and you can't touch me, you're dead and you can't touch me. On the third *you're dead* of her old mantra, the memory of her birthday party landed. She groaned and pulled the bedding over her head. What was she going to do? If someone with the talent looked into her eyes on Friday . . .

The alarm battered on. "Switch it off!" she yelled. The only reply was its continuing nasal whine. Dragging the sheet, she lurched over to Mama's bedside table and brought her fist down on the off button. The silence was immediate and whole, a solid thing that left her unsteady. She flopped onto Mama's unmade bed. Maybe she had a fever. If she had a fever, she might be too sick to go with Nandi on Friday. She pressed her palms to her temples and prayed for some illness to swoop down on her, like the brain fever that killed Siphokhazi two doors down, even. Auntie said they had to bury the poor girl in a lead coffin so she didn't infect anyone from beyond the grave.

"Nothing gets out of a lead coffin," Auntie said.

If nothing got out, then nothing got in. Not even worms. Without worms, Sindi imagined that Siphokhazi would be forever preserved in her leaden tomb, at least until archaeologists dug her up in a thousand years. Shrivelled, like a very old raisin in a drawer, but still there, the Tutankhamen of her time. The archaeologists that had dug him up had all died of a curse, which Miss Patterson said was more likely to have been some kind of bacteria released when they unsealed his tomb. Which is exactly what would happen to whoever dug up Siphokhazi preserved in lead.

One thousand years in a lead coffin. It didn't seem so bad compared to the friendless fate that awaited her when Nandi found out she had no soul. Rather a millennium in lead than go back to having no friends and sitting alone at break like Thuli, like Dora. Which would happen when Nandi found out.

If.

If she found out.

If Sindi was dead, she never would, and Nandi would remember her best friend with breast-stabbing fondness, like when someone died on *Generations* or *Scandal* or whichever soapie. It didn't matter, they were all the same: someone always died, leaving some people gloating – in her case, it would be the sgqebezhanas and maybe Thuli – and loved ones stabbing their hearts with invisible knives: hopefully Nandi, definitely Mama and maybe Thuli. Not that she cared what Thuli did.

Was her temperature high? She couldn't tell. Her hands felt as hot as her head. She eyed the clock's digital face as if the number displayed there could tell her: 7:03.

She should get ready for school, otherwise she was going to be late. Even if she was coming down with something, she'd have to go. Mama only ever let them off school if they were almost dead, which with any luck she would be by Friday. She lay on Mama's bed, wishing she was the kind of mother that tucked you in and spoon-fed you soup at the slightest sniffle, like Nandi's. Another minute clicked over: 7:04. Sindi frowned and slid her hand into Mama's bedding.

With the sheet still wrapped around her, she pushed the curtain aside. Usually Mama would be standing over the stove while Thuli spooned porridge into her fat mouth, but the primus was as cold as Mama's sheets. Someone had set the alarm an hour later than usual.

She returned to the bedroom, opened the wardrobe and filed through the hangers. Thuli's uniform wasn't there, nor were Mama's work clothes. Where had they gone so early? And without telling her. She imagined them dressing, then resetting the alarm and tiptoeing out while she slept, stifling giggles. Thuli had always been Mama's favourite. She'd been everyone's favourite, until Nandi chose Sindi. Now the schoolyard was Sindi's territory, a place where she was liked more than her pretty twin. Though that was about to change.

She snatched her uniform from its hanger and kicked the wardrobe door shut. This was actually a good thing. With no one to check up on her, she could skip school and stay in bed. Mama would never know. She tossed her uniform on the floor and lay down on her bed. Her eyes stung, like they did when she was about to cry, but she wasn't a crybaby. Who cared if Thuli and Mama were out somewhere doing secret things? Besides, even if she did cry, it wouldn't be because of them.

She pulled the sheetless bedding over her head and lay for a while in artificial night, breathing into the woollen blanket until her face itched and anxiety began to gnaw through her anger.

What if something bad had happened?

Tsotsis could have broken in and kidnapped Mama and Thuli. Break-ins happened all the time, so it was possible, but why hadn't they taken her too? Maybe they hadn't wanted her. Men were always pinching Thuli and Mama's bums and whistling at them in the street, but Sindi's rear end was still unblemished by those two round bruises that said someone thought you were hot stuff. But why would tsotsis reset the alarm?

Besides, their clothes were gone so it was obvious nothing bad had happened. She threw back the blankets. They'd gone somewhere without her and she wanted to know where.

She ran next door in her nightie, but standing on Auntie's doorstep, her resolve wavered. Auntie never got out of bed before nine. She wouldn't welcome a seven-am wake-up call unless something terrible *had* happened. Sindi stuck a finger in one ear and pressed the other to the door. All she heard was a rush of noise, like the thrum of ocean waves inside seashells, and a rustling she could not identify. An insect in the wood, perhaps.

Defeated, she turned towards home and saw a man standing on the other side of the road, staring at her. She scowled at him. The hair on the back of her neck prickled. What was she thinking, standing in the street in her nightie? She wasn't the kind of girl to parade around half-dressed. She'd seen the kind of trouble that invited, the kinds of men. She tugged at her frilly hem. She didn't even like the nightie. It was one of a two-pack, another two-for-the-price-of-one birthday present – except this time it was from Auntie, not Mama.

The man stepped into the road, but he did not take his eyes off her to look for traffic. If she didn't wake Auntie, something terrible would happen. Her knuckles connected with Auntie's door, rat-tat-tat. She imagined the man behind her, his breath hot in her ear. She knocked again, harder, with both fists. *Please wake up, please wake up, please wake up.*

The door swung open. "Oh, it's you." Auntie sneered down her nose as if she'd just discovered dog pooh on her doorstep. "What do you want?"

Fear tied her tongue. She swung around, gesticulating. The man was walking up the road, towards the train station.

"Great timing. Come to spoil things for your sister again, huh?" Auntie leaned against the doorjamb, holding the door close to her so that Sindi could not see past her into the house. With her other hand, she clutched the neckline of a silver satin dressing-gown that looked like a costume from *Star Trek: After the Rapture*.

Sindi frowned. On top of the pink chiffon head-wrap that held Auntie's curlers in place, perched at a jaunty angle, was a conical hat. One of the many left over from the twins' birthday party.

"What's with the ha–"

A squeal of delight from within the house cut her off. A bright peal of laughter followed, the kind that had once spilled from her sister's mouth on a daily basis. It chimed with her memory, conjuring a flirty girl always ready with a practical joke, but quick to sour and bring out her fists if the joke was on her. All that remained of that Thuli were the quick fists.

"What's going on?"

Auntie clicked her tongue, angling her head for dramatic effect. The hat's thin elastic strap cut into her cheek. "Don't stand on my doorstep in your see-through nightie asking me questions about things that have nothing to do with you. People are going to think I'm running a brothel. Sies. I can see your tetties. Go home before someone calls the police." She stepped backwards and slammed the door.

Sindi's cheeks burned. They were conspiring against her, Mama and Thuli, Auntie too. But she wasn't going to run home with her tail between her legs just because Auntie told her to. She eyed the beer crate next to the step, the one Auntie liked to sit on when she rubbed Intensive Care into her arms.

Sindi circled the house, arm slung through one of the crate's handholds. The view into Auntie's house was obscured by lace curtains, but the kitchen window had been stripped of its frill when Auntie accidentally set fire to it. She'd been quick to extinguish the flames with the pot of pork-knuckle soup she'd been making for supper, but had taken out several panes of glass when she let go of the pot. The bottom two-thirds of the window had been boarded up, so Sindi stood on the crate and peered through the cracked panes at the top.

Mama sat at the kitchen table with Auntie. She was dressed for work and also wore a party hat. Sindi couldn't see Thuli. She eyed the remains of their breakfast congealing in a pan on the stove. It looked like one of Auntie's special-occasion bacon, egg and banana fry-ups, probably with vetkoek and syrup too. And, if that were not enough proof that Thuli was Mama's favourite, her twin chose that moment to twirl into the room. The skirt of her dress flared around her as if she were the stamen and stalk of an exotic flower. Although she couldn't see the velvet roses embossed onto the cotton from where she crouched at the window, Sindi knew that when her sister turned they'd catch the light, creating a shimmering garden of white on white. The most beautiful dress Sindi had ever seen.

Mama clapped her hands over her mouth. "Look at you, all grown up." She pulled Thuli close and Sindi had to strain to hear. "Things have been hard for you, I know. I've seen how Sindi and her friends treat you, but it will get better. These things between siblings pass. That person Sindi is pretending to be, that's not who she really is. You can only pretend for so long. One day, the truth comes out, and you're sorry for the bad things you did to the ones you love. One day, the past catches up and overtakes you."

"Sizane, enough with the heavy stuff, I want to see Thuli jaiva in her new dress." Auntie began to sing: "Like a virgin, touched for the very first time . . ." Her voice was flat and out of key, but Thuli shook her hips and stuck out her bum like she was on *Idols*. "Like a vi-ir-ir-ir-gin, feel your heartbeat next to my-i-i-i-ine."

Sindi sat on the crate and swiped at her eyes. That dress was meant to be hers. She'd seen it in Maponya Mall a few weeks back when they'd gone to buy shoes. She was the one who held it against her to show Mama just how beautiful it was. She was the one who'd spent weeks dropping hints, only to be let down two mornings ago when she'd seen the tiny bag waiting for her on the kitchen table. She fingered the six plastic bangles on her wrist, each a different acid colour. Her disappointment had been made bearable by the fact that Thuli had got the same.

Tears spilled onto her cheeks. Even when she thought she was ahead, fate was waiting to drag her down. Come Friday, Nandi would dump her and, when the sgqebhezanas got an eyeful of that dress, Thuli would be everyone's new best friend. What would she be left with? Nothing. A big fat zero.

She slipped the bangles off her wrist and dropped them one by one onto the ground so they overlapped like the Olympic rings. If there was an Olympic event for moegoe losers, she'd win gold. The bright bracelets looked even more tacky in the dirt, if that was possible. She imagined Thuli prancing home to show off her new dress, and she placed the heel of her bare foot against the pink bangle and ground it into the dust. She wouldn't give Thuli the satisfaction of being there to watch her gloat.

Sindi dressed hurriedly, then sprinted a couple of blocks before ducking between two shacks to catch her breath. As much as she didn't want to be there when Thuli came home with her new dress, she didn't want to stand around in the schoolyard with the sgqebhezanas, concealing her feelings behind a fake smile. She took a meandering back route the rest of the way to school and was relieved to find the playground deserted when she finally got there. Head down, she hurried across the courtyard and ducked into the shadows under the stairwell. With no watch, she had no way to tell how much time had passed since the bell. She wanted to wait a few minutes to make sure the class had started before she went up. That way, she wouldn't have to talk to Nandi.

She leaned against the wall and let her feet slide away from her, only pushing with her toes for traction when the muscles in her thighs began to tremble. Through her uniform, the cold brick pressed into her flesh, a rough contrast to the slippery brace of her soles. She closed her eyes, focused on the solidity of the wall. Immovable. Safe. After a while, she could no longer feel the tension in her calves, and began to imagine she did not need feet to remain vertical. The bricks would hold her up. She could hang on the wall like a photograph.

The distant babble of teachers filtered into her calm, dark place, reciting lessons she'd learned years ago when she'd been in a class on the ground floor. She remembered how it felt when Mrs Bart, their grade-one teacher, separated her from Thuli and put them in different groups on opposite ends of the classroom. *You need to learn to use your own tongue, Sindisiwe.* The expanse of floor between them had seemed infinite as Sindi stared across at her sister who, even on that first day, giggled and chattered as if freed from a heavy weight. For Sindi, it was a physical wrench that robbed her of her only way to communicate and made her invisible. She used to think Mrs Bart was responsible for her broken voice. If only she could still lay the blame at her door.

Other voices penetrated her stillness. Closer: hushed whispers, a giggle. She heard her name and then a finger prodded her, sending an electric jolt between her ribs. Her feet lost their precarious grip and slid out from under her, but the wall was not as keen to let her go. The brick ripped fabric and skin, digging in even after her coccyx slammed into cement. Laughter exploded around her.

"Yo yo yo, Sindisiwe. Why you hiding under the stairs?"

Through a blur of tears she looked up at the sgqebhezanas, elbowing each other with relish. "Nice pink pantie, girlfriend," Pumi mocked.

She yanked the hem of her dress over her underwear and tried to stand. Her legs vibrated violently as her feet scrabbled for purchase. All she could do to reduce her humiliation was bring her splayed legs together and wait for them to go. But they were in no hurry. Pumi crouched in front of her, enveloping Sindi in her scent of cigarette smoke and deodorant, both pungent. "We thought you were A for Absent, too babalaz' after your party, but here you are, hiding under the stairs. Who you waiting for?"

"Nnn_no. . ."

"N-n-no one. Of course not, no boy is going to swap spit under the stairs with you, not unless he wants his tongue tied in n-n-knots."

Another burst of laughter. Sindi blinked hard, but a single tear escaped and rolled down her cheek. It clung to her jaw just long enough for everyone to notice, then dripped onto her hand.

"Shoo, Sindi. We're just teasing, neh. Don't be a crybaby."

"I'm n_not."

The sgqebhezanas shuffled their feet, cutting eyes at each other.

"Pumi, we better go, before Miss gets back from tea and notices we're not there."

Pumi stood. "You coming?" She grabbed Sindi's hand, pulling her to her feet.

Sindi followed the sgqebhezanas around the building to the narrow path between the school and the back fence. They were headed away from their classroom, planning perhaps to take the opposite staircase to avoid the office. In her mind's eye, she counted the doors they'd have to sneak past on the third floor to get to their classroom at the end: six. Six chances to be caught by a teacher, rather than two chances to be caught by the principal or the secretary. The stupid sgqebhezanas were increasing their risk of detention by four.

The others passed the second stairwell without taking it. Sindi hesitated. "Hey, guys . . ." she began.

They ignored her and hurried along the rear wall of the hall. Maybe they were heading to the prefabs for a smoke, though Pumi stank like she'd just had one. Sindi was in enough trouble already without being dragged into sgqebhezana mischief. She took the stairs two at a time. Two, four, six, eight, ten, twelve, before the *tic-tac* of high heels descending at a rapid pace sent her scuttling back down. She scrambled after the sgqebhezanas, cursing her luck.

They doubled back along the front of the hall, and Sindi saw a queue of bored grade sevens, leaning against the wall. The line snaked to the stage door.

"Nandi's keeping our place," Pumi explained, pushing through the clot of students in the doorway.

The gloomy corridor beyond smelled like a full ashtray left to stew in the rain. The hall was the only part of the original building that hadn't been razed to the ground during the D-Day riots. The community had insisted it be preserved, but no amount of renovation could erase the stink. The scent of mildew and disuse became more acute the further in Sindi went, scanning the blank grey faces for her friend. She saw Thuli first. Standing just behind Nandi! Had she already been replaced? She clenched her clammy hands into fists, trying to summon the bravado for a fight, but the sgqebhezanas passed Thuli without even glancing her way.

"Hey, where were you this morning?" Nandi took her hand.

The knowledge that she would soon lose Nandi's friendship made her touch unbearable. For the umpteenth time that morning, Sindi felt a prickle of tears. She tucked her hands under her armpits and shrugged, cutting eyes at Thuli as if to say that she could discuss nothing with her sister nearby. Thuli watched their silent exchange, frowning in a way that could be mistaken for concern if Sindi hadn't known better.

"What's going on?" Sindi asked. Over Nandi's shoulder she could see Thuli's eyes still seeking her out. She sneered, enjoying the wounded expression that flashed across her sister's features before Thuli mirrored her scorn.

"Government health drive. All grade sevens have to get some vaccination before high school. It's taking so long though, only six students have been in so far. At this rate, we'll be standing here all day."

Just then the blue door at the end of the corridor opened and a girl exited, rubbing her shoulder. All eyes focused on the door. An endless minute passed before a nurse appeared, holding a clipboard.

"Next."

The queue was torture: standing there while Nandi chattered on, as if their friendship wasn't about to be over in a mere five days. Four and a half, really.

"Next."

Two hours later, Sindi finally went in through the blue door and came out clutching her arm. Not that it hurt. Sindi had felt the iciness of the alcohol swab, the sharp jab of the needle and the nerve ache as the vaccine penetrated her muscle – but in a detached way, as if her arm belonged to someone else, a starring in a movie she was watching. The thing that did hurt, the thing responsible for the tears she was struggling to hold back, was the knowledge that it was over. Nandi was friends with the person Sindi wanted to be, not the person she really was. It was like Mama said. One day, the truth comes out. One day, the past catches up and overtakes you.

Four days before the end of the world, Sindi arrived at school after the bell again, and spent break locked in a toilet cubicle. Throughout the long day she kept her head down, barely acknowledging Nandi's whispered asides. When the final bell went, she swept her things into her bag and took off before her bewildered friend had time to ask her what was going on.

At the end of second break on Wednesday, two and a half days until the end of the world, Sindi slid the lock of the toilet cubicle and found Nandi waiting for her at the basins.

"You okay, Sins?"

Sindi bent over the basin. "I'm fine," she mumbled, shrugging Nandi's hand from her shoulder, "I need to get to class." She did not look back to see if Nandi followed.

By Thursday, one day until the end of the world, the cold silence between them felt heavy and final. Nandi's nostrils twitched and she refused to look at Sindi. When the bell went, it was Nandi who swept her things into her bag and stormed out.

That night, Sindi's guilt and restless limbs kept her awake. After several sharp kicks from Thuli, she blanked her mind and channelled her agitation into her fists, holding her body rigid long enough for her sister's breath to even out. Only then did she allow thoughts of Nandi back into her mind.

Nandi had shared things with Sindi, secret things she said she told no one else, not even the sgqebhezanas. Like how her Auntie Doreen did it up against the outside wall with her boyfriend when she thought everyone was asleep, and not always with the same boyfriend. How her parents sometimes fought, calling each other names and blaspheming so that she worried they would go to hell. How she sometimes whispered in her grandmother's ear that she should die, even though her dad said Gogo understood. Maybe because she did.

Sindi absorbed these intimate facts, but never shared anything in return. Not that Nandi had ever asked her to. And now, faced with the possibility that her own darkest secret might be revealed, she was shunning her only friend instead of trusting her. She was willing to toss Nandi's friendship in the trash without explanation. Just like that. When tested, she behaved exactly like her fickle twin.

On Friday afternoon, the day the world was set to end, Sindi waited behind the prefab shed at the far end of the playground. Being neither athletic nor interested in looking sophisticated for boys, she'd never been to Smoker's Corner before, and had only thought of the place because all the kids who usually hung out there, like the sgqebhezanas, would be at the mall making eyes at each other. She peered through the darkened window at the sports equipment stored inside the shed. The folded nets and balls, crated according to shape and purpose, were at odds with the debris of cigarette butts, spent plastic lighters and blackened matches clogging the gutter in the alley behind it.

Since she'd slipped the note to Nandi that morning, her stomach had been in knots. She felt a wave of nausea whenever she thought about it. What if Nandi didn't come? Would that be worse, or better? Her stomach clenched violently. She took a deep breath and began to count the butts bleeding yellow onto the rain-soaked cement, but her eyes kept darting to where she knew Nandi would appear. If she came. After losing track three times, she gave up and fished a piece of discarded string from a puddle and began to work at the knot in it.

236

"Hi." Nandi stood suddenly in front of her with her arms across her chest as if barring the way to her heart.

"Hi_hi." Sindi smiled. Nandi's lips remained rigid. Perhaps this wasn't such a good idea.

"You said in your note you wanted to explain why you're being such a bitch."

Sindi had never used the word *bitch*, but she supposed it was fair. She nodded.

"Well, I haven't got all day. I still want to practise my solo for tonight. The one you said you'd come see, but I guess you're not into it any more."

"I do have to tell you sss_asomething, and it does have to do with that."

"I knew it. You're just a heathen like all the others. I thought you were special."

"I . . ."

"You what? Huh?"

How was she going to tell Nandi anything if she kept interrupting her? She clenched her fists.

"You're just like everyone else. I made friends with you when nobody would, reached out to you after your own sister stabbed you in the back and . . ."

"Nandi, let me speak!" she shouted, freed from her stutter by anger.

The telling was not easy. It took almost an hour to tell Nandi everything: the trip to Eston, her grandmother, what had happened to Sindi as a baby. She left out what she'd done at her grandmother's grave and the fact she'd snooped in Nandi's diary, sins Nandi might consider unforgivable. But she told the truth about her soul.

"If I come to church with you, everybody will see that I'm empty."

Nandi leaned against the prefab shed and studied her as if trying to see through her flesh. She'd expected an explosion, thought Nandi would shout and tell her she was going to hell, but her chatterbox friend was silent. Unable to stand the scrutiny, she picked at the knot in the wet string. It had started to drizzle again. She could feel the dance of fine drops on the back of her neck.

"I saw," Nandi finally said, "that night at Saviour's. When I saw you and Thuli coming out of the shop. I was going yell, but then my head felt hot and one of you went black and there was a light shining on the other one. I knew God was giving me a message."

Sindi couldn't look at her. If she did, Nandi would see that Sindi already knew.

"Even if your grandmother was right and twins only have one soul, you are meant to be saved. That's what your name means, Sins. God wants all His souls to go to heaven. God will save you."

The knot in the string loosened. She jiggled it, pulling the two pieces apart.

Nandi took her hand. "Look at me." Nandi's lips were soft, but her eyes glinted as if made of metal. She gripped Sindi's hand so tightly her fingers hurt. "Thuli's the bad person, not you. She's going to hell. Don't worry, we'll figure out a way to save you. God wants it."

Hell's Gates

In spite of Nandi's reassurance, Sindi still didn't want to go with her to church and have a whole lot of Believers stare through her like an empty glass.

"That's okay, Sins," Nandi said, though she hardened her lips as if it weren't. "I probably shouldn't bring someone without a soul to church anyway."

That Saturday, a heat wave began. It would bring the drought that people eventually came to call the Long Dry. For five weeks, the mercury never dropped below 30° Celsius, and the unseasonal heat sent dormant mosquitoes into a breeding frenzy. At night, the insects swarmed through open windows to feast while the twins kicked and elbowed each other in the steamy dark. Each morning they woke slick with sweat, bruised and itchy. A week into the wave, Auntie returned from a rousing sermon at church convinced that the end of days was upon them. She took one look at the twins, pocked from relentless scratching, and told Mama to get her house in order. She said that hell's gates had opened up and two of Satan's minions had taken possession of the girls. Mama threw a bottle at her.

Just when Sindi thought her discomfort couldn't get any worse, the walls of the zozo began to sweat, releasing a chemical stink similar to the fumes rising from the road in front of Saviour's. There, the tar felt soft underfoot, and if she stood in one place too long, her feet burned as if the soles of her shoes were on fire. She began to dream of drowning again, but this time she sank into molten pitch instead of the ocean's cool depths.

Two weeks after Sindi's confession, the mercury rose again and Nandi received an apocalyptic message that the sun was going to explode. Sindi got the details the following Monday at school, and later, at Nandi's house, it was all Nandi and her mother could talk about. Apparently, Nandi had fallen to the floor during a frenzied worship-session at church, when the Holy Spirit had come down and taken hold of the entire congregation. Nandi's eyes had rolled to white, which meant that her spiritual vision had opened up – *three years earlier than most.*

When Nandi was revived, she spoke in tongues: an ability she claimed she could now summon at will. She gave Sindi a demonstration in a toilet cubicle at break. Unfortunately, the sgqebhezanas came in to refresh their make-up at the pinnacle of her performance, and ambushed her as she exited the cubicle, rolling their eyes and spouting gibberish.

With her spiritual vision unlocked, Nandi began to receive an almost constant stream of divine missives. Most arrived in the form of dreams, but sometimes she read messages in newspaper headlines or saw patterns in shrubs – a bit like when Moses spoke with the burning bush, she said. After the toilet incident, she highlighted certain letters on a page of her history textbook to spell out *Pumi is evil and going to hell.* Most recently, the Angel Gabriel had informed her in a dream that Thuli was actually a demon who had infected Mama's womb during pregnancy and stolen Sindi's soul. In order to save Sindi, they needed to transfer it back before the sun exploded.

"But how?"

"I've been thinking," Nandi said, "we should speak to Ben."

"Ben?"

"Ben who works at Saviour's."

"Why? Shouldn't we rather sss_aspeak to ss_asomeone at your church?"

Nandi sighed and shook her head. "The Father can't save your soul if you don't have a soul to save. Besides, there's a reason God chose to reveal your problem to me, Sins, right before He opened my celestial eyes. I'm supposed to save you. Don't you see that?"

"But why Ben?"

"He's from Nigeria. They say he knows stuff."

"He's just crazy."

"People say that about the Father."

Sindi nodded. People did say that about the Black Preacher. And worse, but she didn't like to tell Nandi what, in case it upset her. "Okay," she said.

They began stopping by Saviour's Pit Stop every day after school, but Ben, who for years had been as permanent a fixture as the old fuel pumps, was never there. Joe resisted all Nandi's attempts to interrogate him, refusing to be drawn on Ben's whereabouts. Before turning to serve his paying customers, he dismissed the girls with annoying and mystifying statements: "Where is anyone really, in the great scheme of things?" or "Here today, gone tomorrow, nothing is forever. We are all in the ever-repeating moment of now. Yes?"

After two weeks of this, Nandi dragged Sindi back to Saviour's late one afternoon and made her hide behind the pumps. She instructed Sindi to watch the shop, but Sindi's eyes kept drifting upwards. Being so close to her mechanical demons made her hair stand on end. There was something behind the murky glass. She could feel its suspicious regard. It was biding its time, waiting for her to look away long enough for it to snake a rubber hose around her neck.

"Let's get out of here, sss_asomeone's going to see us." She tugged on Nandi's sleeve.

"Don't be such a wuss, Sins," Nandi hissed, peering at the shop through the loop in a hose. "This is important. Last night my dad said he came to fill up his car, but Joe's run out of diesel."

"Sss_aso?"

"So, Ben's going to have to come in and make more."

"What m-m-makes you think that?"

Nandi gave her the eye-roll, the same way Thuli used to when Sindi said something stupid. "Duh, it's his job."

Sindi's fingers curled into her palm. Thuli she could've smacked.

An hour later, there was still no sign of Ben. Joe locked up the shop, folded his lawn chair and hooked it over his shoulder. Sindi's calves ached and she saw no point in staying crouched. She stood, sending a hot rush of pins and needles through her feet. "This is dumb. Joe's going home and Ben's nnn_not coming. Let's get out of here."

Nandi pulled her down. "He's not going home. Look."

Joe removed the padlock from the corrugated-iron gates and disappeared through them into the backyard with his chair. A moment later, he reappeared, rolling an oil drum towards the Chicken Licken takeaway next door.

"Ben's sss_astill nn_not coming."

"Maybe, but I'm going to get Joe to tell me how to find him if it's the last thing I do."

In the yard, Joe's old yellow Merc slumped on its brick pedestal. The contraption of oil drums, plastic bottles, rubber hoses and PVC pipes he'd constructed to distil b-diesel from Chicken Licken's deep-fat fryer leavings was still there, sheltered under a sheet-iron lean-to. The drums looked as if they'd been in a fire. Against one wall was large wire-mesh locker. The generator that ran the pump was bigger than she remembered. She'd heard the old generator had exploded a few years back, when Ben had first come to work at Saviour's; that explained the blackened oil drums. Besides the generator, not much had changed since she'd last been in the back yard, when she and Thuli were still small enough for Joe to lift into the red leather seats to play driving-driving. Thuli never let her steer. A smile played at the corners of Sindi's mouth. She'd been around Saviour's far longer than Nandi – ever since Mama brought them to the city when they were just a few days old.

"What nn_now?"

Nandi narrowed her eyes to slits. "Now we wait."

Joe returned, rolling the drum. Grease trailed from its ill-fitting cap.

Nandi waited for him to padlock the gates, locking them in, before she stepped out from behind the Merc and demanded to know Ben's working hours. "We have important things to do," she told him haughtily. "We can't be wasting all our time coming around when Ben's not here."

If Joe was surprised by their presence in his yard, his face did not reflect it. His eyes were shielded by mirrored sunglasses, but Sindi could feel them on her. She squirmed under his scrutiny.

"You are right," he drawled eventually, "life passes in the blink of an eye. You should not squander the few moments you have on earth. Come, Sindi." He lumbered towards the locker and opened it. Sindi followed him, glancing nervously at the round dial of the thermometer as she passed the still. The needle sat at zero.

"Okay, girls, we going to need a few things to get you started."

Sindi eyed the drums of chemicals lined up along the bottom shelf. A row of skull-and-crossbones stared back at her with empty eye-sockets. *Flammable*, she read. One shelf up was an assortment of glass beakers and flasks like the ones in the science classroom at school. Joe picked a round-bottomed flask, then rummaged through the safety glasses and gloves on the top shelf. He took down a can of Cobra wax and a bunch of rags, stiff with white wax. These he handed to Sindi.

"Polish the Merc and I'll tell you what you need to know. Fair trade, no?"

Nandi narrowed her eyes at him as if trying to see into his soul. She nodded slowly.

"Okay then. You polish, I talk." While Sindi pried the lid off the Cobra, he settled his bulk into the lawn chair, placing the flask on the ground next to him. "If Ben were here, this is what he would tell you," he began. And then launched into a meandering lecture on the merits of turning one's passion into a business.

"This has nothing to do with Ben," Nandi cried after ten minutes. "You're wasting our time."

"This is everything to do with Ben. Polish and patience is what you need, not time."

Nandi gave Sindi an exasperated eye-roll, but they continued to smear wax onto the old car's hull. Another ten minutes passed, Joe droning on.

"And that," he concluded, "is how I went from cruising the town in that beauty to selling b-diesel to run clapper-trappers." He lapsed into silence and tilted his head towards them as if awaiting a response.

Nandi threw her rags to the ground. "What's your point?"

"Ah, there is no point, and that is my point. You can pour all your love into something, walk your path with righteousness, and still every road is a dead end. There is only now. A single moment. Now. Ben is not here now. Okay?"

"This is ridiculous," said Nandi. She stomped to the gate and rattled the chain, then turned and glared at Joe. He tossed a bunch of keys to her.

"It's the one marked with red nail-polish," he said.

She found the right key and inserted it into the lock. Her hands were trembling with rage. "Come Sins," she said, dropping the bunch of keys to the ground and marching off.

Before following, Sindi folded her cloth and placed it carefully on top of the Cobra tin.

"Why do you call your friend Sin?" Joe yelled after them. "She is a child of God, not an act of wickedness."

Sindi turned and gave him a grateful smile. He was standing next to the b-diesel still, decanting fuel from a tap at the bottom of the largest drum. The needle on the thermometer sat a third of the way up the dial. Joe held the round-bottomed flask up to the light, so that for a moment his head seemed to be contained within a circle of glowing, golden liquid. She frowned. The drum he'd used to collect oil from Chicken Licken was lying on its side, lidless and empty. She could not recall him getting up out of his chair to pour the oil into the still. Nor had the generator been powered up. It would have drowned out his voice.

Nandi stomped across the veld in a huff. When she reached the road on the other side, she stood waiting for Sindi to catch up, hands on hips, jiggling her foot. "You know, Sins, I don't think you're taking this seriously enough. You're going to hell. Do you even understand what that means?"

"It's not m_my fault Joe won't tell us where Ben is."

"Isn't it? I get the feeling he knows you don't believe. If you believed, he'd tell us."

Sindi stared at the pavement. She did believe, but the truth was that she didn't like to think too deeply about her soul, or lack of it. She felt powerless to do anything to save herself. She went along with Nandi's plans to keep her friend happy, but really, she'd have preferred Nandi to stop harping on about it. She was going to hell, and if Nandi's prophesies proved right, she was going soon. She just wanted to have fun, like they'd had before her confession behind the prefabs. This constant searching for Sindi's salvation just made her think of the eternal fires: fires of sulphur and brimstone that Nandi said she'd burn in if they failed. She was starting to wish she'd never told Nandi anything about it.

"Look, Sins, I got to go. I'll see you in school tomorrow, okay?"

Sindi nodded, a little hurt that Nandi hadn't invited her to watch TV like they usually did in the afternoon.

The next day, Nandi seemed to have forgiven her, and asked Sindi around to her house after school. But instead of flopping down on the couch to watch TV, Nandi sent Sindi to wait in her room while she went to the garage to get something from her father's toolbox. She returned with a craft knife.

"I've been thinking," she said, "if we became blood-sisters, God wouldn't abandon you. He wouldn't send the sister of His chosen one to hell."

She clicked the blade of the craft knife out two notches and drew the blade quickly across her palm twice. She sucked her teeth as blood welled from the vertical and horizontal incisions she'd made.

"Hold out your hand," she said. Sindi did as she was told. Nandi must really love her if she was willing to bind herself to someone soulless. They pressed their bleeding palms together and Nandi recited the pact of sister-hood she'd composed. By the time she'd finished, their blood was tacky and their skin resisted separation.

On the six-o'clock news that same evening, it was announced that the mercury had risen to 42° Celsius, the highest temperature ever recorded in the city. The news anchor cut to an interview with an environmental scientist who said that, as predicted, government's choice of profitability over sustainability had proved disastrous, and not even the most drastic of measures could stave off catastrophe. Back in the studio, a government climate-analyst shifted his tie from side to side. He cleared his throat several times before saying that the heat wave was part of a natural cycle that occurred every six hundred years. Then he called the environmen-talist alarmist.

When Sindi left Nandi's house after the bulletin, the sky was shot with crimson. "Wow, a message from God," Nandi said. "The Lord is going to send us a way to save you soon."

Sindi looked at Nandi's incisions, then at the sky, but couldn't see any-thing she could interpret as a sign.

As she walked home, she swung her arms to make the wound on her palm throb. People sat outside on chairs and beer crates to escape the heat that radiated from the corrugated iron and turned their shacks into ovens. It was a relief to tune in to their conversations and not think about how doomed she was.

All the way home she picked up similar snippets. Everyone was talk-ing about the scientist on the news, and that gave her something else to worry about. Who to believe: the scientist in Bermuda shorts or the gov-ernment official? When she thought of men in suits, she thought of Auntie's boyfriend on his way to court in scuffed shoes, and Gogo Nkosi's lodger standing in the dock. Also of the Black Preacher and Nandi's father.

Which made it fifty-fifty, baddies and goodies, if she discounted Auntie's opinion of the preacher and put him on the side of good.

She expected the talk around their kitchen table would be more of the same. Mama moaning about the heat and blaming government corruption for it. Auntie fanning herself with the latest copy of *True Love* magazine, a self-righteous smirk on her face. There would be beer. Beer had always been a given on a Friday, but with the heat wave it had become an everyday thing. As soon as Mama arrived home, Auntie would come over and remark that it was thirty degrees in the shade again, and Mama would send one of the twins for a quart from Ma Elias'. They had to run back with it before the condensation on the bottle evaporated.

Lost in thought, she opened the door of their zozo and was blasted by heat. She stepped into the soupy interior. The curtains were drawn, and the sudden change in light made her vision swell. She put out a steadying hand while she waited for her pupils to dilate. The wall felt sticky against her palm, as if the wood had begun to sweat the glue holding the planks together. The usual odours of creosote and alcohol-soured perspiration were more pungent, but there was another smell, something familiar yet new to the household. She sniffed. The metallic tang made her clench her slashed hand.

As her eyes adjusted to the dimness, Sindi saw someone sitting at the kitchen table, head in hands. "Mama?" she whispered.

Mama looked smaller than she should be, shrunken, as if in the hours since Sindi had last seen her she'd caught some illness that had rapidly eaten away at her substance.

Things that eat a man from the inside.

Mama made a small *hic-hic* noise, a sound Sindi could not immediately place. She cocked her head to listen. The sound repeated at breathy intervals, increasing in volume. Mama had not cried since the funeral.

Sindi lunged for the light switch. Halfway across the floor, her foot snared. She tripped and stumbled sideways into the table. The pain made her hiss, but it did not slow her down. Her thumb found the switch, flicked it. Light flooded the room. It made Mama familiar again, the kitchen strange, as if she'd stepped into someone else's house and found her mother seated at their table.

A chair lay on its side among shards of a broken coffee mug, the red one Mama liked to drink beer out of. Books spilled from Thuli's schoolbag, which she must have hung over the back of the chair when she came home from school. The strap was twisted into a loop, and there were dark blotches on the canvas, coin-sized marks like when the lid of a khoki pen accidentally comes off and the fabric sucks the nib dry, but they were the colour of Auntie's nail polish. Scabs on Thuli's bag. On the floor too.

Sindi thought of the wall, sticky against her skin. She held up her hand in front of her face. There was a dark-red stain on her palm.

"Where have you been?"

Sindi separated her fingers and peered at Mama between the Vs. Even at the funeral in Eston, when she thought Mama's grief might shred her insides, she'd not looked so broken. Her eyes were like fermented fruit, her lips glistened with snot. She clutched an envelope, twisting the paper as if trying to wring liquid from it. Knuckles bulging, rubbed raw. Bloody.

Blood. The smell. The mottling on her palm where it had lifted from the wall, like a faded tattoo of a heart, anatomically correct. Like Thuli's heart, red and rapping and made of glass. Too close to the surface to survive a bullet. An image flashed into her mind. Thuli lying on the floor, dark liquid spilling from her skull like on *Real Crime Stories* on TV.

She pushed the curtain aside and flicked on the bedroom light. Mama was shouting, words her brain refused to decipher as she struggled to make sense of the scene in front of her.

The wardrobe door hung off its hinge. Thuli's dresser drawer had been pulled out and emptied, the rail in the wardrobe stripped of her clothes. All Thuli's things were gone, except for the dress from the secret birthday party. It lay on the floor in two crumpled pieces like half-formed twins.

Shreds of cotton patterned the carpet, as if following the trajectory of a missile that had ripped through the dress. Thuli was not there, but that just increased Sindi's anxiety.

"You little sluts," Mama slurred, her breath hot in Sindi's ear. That was what she'd been shouting, that they were sluts and had been allowed to run wild too long. That she was going to teach them.

Mama's breasts pressed into her back. Her hand slid from Sindi's right shoulder to her left so that her forearm pushed against Sindi's throat – not enough to cut off her air, but enough for Sindi to feel the threat of violence coiled into her muscles. Sindi froze. Tsotsis hadn't broken in and done this. Whatever this was, Mama had done it, and she was going to do it to Sindi too.

But even as Mama's hand pressed down on her shoulder, so hard she thought her legs would give out, Sindi did not want to believe. Mama had not suffered a black mood since Eston. That savage part of her seemed to have been buried in the field with the old woman's body.

Later, Sindi would not be able to recall who began to cry first. She remembered watching her tears spill onto Mama's skin, and Mama's gulping sobs jerking against her back, but not who started. She remembered the dead weight of her mother collapsing drunkenly against her, as if fury had been the only thing keeping her upright. The tension leaving Mama's body transferred to Sindi's, wiring her ligaments and bunching her muscles; it gave her the strength to direct her mother to the mattress, where she collapsed and curled into herself. Sindi waited until she'd passed out, then took off Mama's shoes and placed them side by side at the foot of the bed.

If anyone knew where Thuli was, it would be Auntie. But Auntie's house was shut up against the night. Light bled through a crack in the drawn curtains and she thought she heard a man's voice, but when she knocked he stopped talking. She waited. Knocked again. No one came.

Back in the kitchen of the zozo, she scanned the chaos and was glad

Auntie had not answered. Sindi wouldn't have known what to tell her. She knelt in front of the kitchen cupboard and took out the bucket, the Jik, a few old cleaning rags that Mama wouldn't mind her throwing away. She found the broom and mop in the corner, upright and untouched, the only witnesses. She wanted to ask them, *what happened?* Instead, she turned the broom on its head and swept up the bits of glass and fabric. She packed Thuli's books into her bag, righted the chairs and hung the bag over the back of one. She closed the empty drawer, but she could do nothing about the wardrobe. The door tipped heavily towards her when she tried to straighten it, and she was afraid it might fall on her. Then there was only the blood. And the letter.

She held the letter up to the light. Something bad, she was sure. She could just make out the dark twists of someone's handwriting, a few short lines. She read the brief message: Mrs Nxumalo was requested to go to the school to see the district nurse. It didn't make sense. How could such simple words turn everything upside down? She folded the crumpled letter back into the envelope and put it in her pocket. Her fingers rested lightly against it as she walked to the bottom of the road and filled the bucket at the government tap. People still sat outside talking, as if nothing had happened. A neighbour, she could not see who in the dark, called out to her: "Tell your mama to come out and join us." Water slopped onto her shoes.

She found a single handprint at the door. Strange that she'd rested her own palm against it, the only mark on the wall. She dabbed at the wood, lifting off the mark, then dropped the cloth into the bucket. Tendrils of blood seeped into the water, dancing away from the cloth like delicate fronds of seaweed. She dunked the mop, but found only a few sticky patches on the floor needing attention. As she worked, the water took on a pinkish tinge. At the height of her terror, she'd imagined pools of red, but this was more the result of a bloodied nose. No big deal.

There was no blood in the bedroom. She laid the two pieces of the dress side by side on the bed, smoothed their jagged seams with her palm. They did not fit together. Ruefully, she recalled the pieces she'd swept up. Mama must have torn bits off after she'd ripped it in half. She folded the halves into each other, so they wouldn't feel lonely, and pushed them into the gap between the mattress and the wall.

After she'd emptied the bucket into the street, bolted the door and opened the windows to let the unbearable heat and suffocating smells out, the house was the same as it had been that morning before she left for school.

If she didn't look at the wardrobe, it was the same.

She switched off the light and lay down on her side of the bed. Mama was snoring and everything was the same.

Sindi woke to the smell of frying eggs. She found Mama in the kitchen and they sat across from each other, Mama bleary-eyed, her breath fumy. Sindi eyed the empty chair. Thuli's schoolbag was no longer there.

Two fried eggs wallowed in oil on her plate. She punctured the centres with her fork, watched the glossy yellow bleed into the thick white bread, soak in, congeal. She stared at her plate until her food was cold and sticky. Like blood. Except egg retained that bright colour when it crusted: yolk-yellow, wet or dry.

"Got to go." She was at the door before Mama could scold her for not eating her breakfast.

"Sindisiwe?"

She rested her fingers on the handle, ready to bolt. "M_M_Mama?"

"I don't want to hear her name."

She walked to school with her hand in the pocket of her tunic, cupping the envelope, the paper clammy with her sweat. Neighbours gave her puzzled looks and she wondered if they knew where Thuli was. If they knew, and it had been something bad, someone would have called the police. Sindi fingered the torn edge of the envelope. Thuli must have run away. For some reason, the visit to the nurse had sent Mama into a rage and Thuli had run away.

What could possibly have made Mama so angry? Sindi thought about the questions the nurse had asked her, about boyfriends and other embarrassing things. The nurse had tested her blood on a stick that looked like the pregnancy test Pumi once lifted from her mother's handbag. Pumi had peed on it and they'd crowded around her while she held it up to the light. Giggling, they'd squinted at the results window. A faint pink line had appeared almost instantly. Negative. Not pregnant.

"You can't be sure with a pee test," Nandi had told Pumi. "Auntie Doreen says that blood tests are much more accurate."

That's why the nurse wanted to see Mama: Thuli was pregnant. She'd run away because she was pregnant. She imagined Thuli in her new white dress, meeting a boy at Maponya Mall. She imagined them kissing, his hand on her bum.

No wonder Mama had been so furious. Mama had gone to see the nurse, then come home in a rage and turned the house upside down when she discovered Thuli's things gone. She must have been so angry she punched the wall, scraping her knuckles. Probably sliced her hand on the broken coffee mug too. She could imagine blood dripping from Mama's fist onto Thuli's bag, the floor.

A pregnancy explained everything: Mama ripping the dress, calling them sluts, not wanting Sindi to speak her name. How disappointing for Mama to discover her favourite daughter had no good in her, just like Nandi said. Served her right. She thought of the dress, *her* dress ripped in two. The dress was the real victim. The dress, and Sindi.

When she arrived at school, Nandi was leaning on the gatepost, pointedly ignoring the sgqebhezanas. She frowned when she saw Sindi. Without saying a word, she took Sindi by the elbow and ushered her to the toilets.

"What happened?" Nandi whispered, leading her to the basin furthest from the door.

A girl standing at another basin gave them the same puzzled look Sindi had been getting all morning. Maybe she knew too. Nandi scowled at the girl, and hemmed Sindi in, shielding her. When Sindi saw herself in the mirror, she understood her friend's concern. Her tunic and shirt were rumpled, her sleeves flecked with brown stains. There was a smudge on her cheek and her hair was sticking up. She'd slept in her uniform, and it was obvious. She hadn't checked in the wardrobe mirror before she left home – she didn't like looking at the broken door.

"Thuli's run away," she whispered.

Nandi's eyes widened. "Serious? What happened?"

"She m_met a boy at Mma_ponya M_mall and they've run away together. She's pregnant."

"What? No way, Sins. She's such a grenade."

"It's true," she snapped, offended. If Nandi thought Thuli was ugly, then so was Sindi.

"I just don't believe it, Sins. Even if there was a boy willing to do it with her, no way he's going to run away with her."

Sindi pulled the envelope from her pocket. "They did. He loves her and they're going to get m_married. They left a letter."

Nandi squinted at the envelope. "Sure that's from her? It looks official."

Sindi frowned at her mother's name printed in formal block-letters on the blue paper: Mrs S Nxumalo. She slipped it back into her pocket. "It is. I've read it. She m_met a boy at Mma_ponya M_mall. They ran away together." Her voice was shrill.

"Okay, chila. Let me see it."

Sindi shook her head. "It's personal." She slipped the letter into her pocket and turned away so she didn't have to read the disbelief on Nandi's face. She tidied herself up as best she could, tugging on the hem of her tunic to straighten out the creases.

"What are you going to do?" Nandi asked as they hurried down the corridor to class.

"Nnn_nothing. I'm glad she's gone."

"I mean about your soul. If Thuli's run away, what will you do?"

Sindi shrugged. There was nothing she could do.

That afternoon, Sindi told Nandi she wasn't feeling well and went straight home after school. Before going into their zozo, she stopped outside Auntie's door and listened. She could hear TV blare and maybe voices, but Auntie did not come when she knocked.

At home, she poured a glass of milk and sat at the kitchen table alone. Mama would not be home for two hours and the house seemed quieter than usual. With all Thuli's stuff gone, it was almost like she didn't exist any more. Sindi drank her milk, then went into the bedroom and pulled the two halves of the white dress from behind her bed. She put her arms through the sleeves and lay in the middle of the bed with the dress on top of her, like a paper doll in cut-out clothes. She was not entirely convinced by Nandi's dream that Thuli was a demon and not really her sister; but still, she closed her eyes and imagined being an only child. She woke with her hand clutching the letter.

Auntie did not come around to share a quart of cold beer when Mama returned from work, and Sindi wondered whether they had fallen out too. Auntie had a hot tongue, always quick to lay blame. Perhaps she thought it was Mama's fault that Thuli got pregnant. Mama prepared dinner for two and they ate opposite each other with only the clink and scrape of their cutlery to break the silence between them. Mama did not mention Thuli or the events of the previous night, and neither did Sindi. They went to bed early, straight after washing the dishes.

Sindi put on her pyjamas and hung her school uniform in the wardrobe. What if Mama went through the pockets of her tunic and found the letter? She glanced surreptitiously at Mama, then folded the letter into her hand and took it to bed with her. She fell asleep clutching it under her pillow. Reaching for it as soon as the alarm went off the next morning, she was both relieved and disappointed to find it still there.

She walked to school alone, daydreaming she wore the white dress and was Mama's first-born and only daughter, a fantasy she managed to spin out until Miss Patterson called Thuli's name at roll call.

During break, Pumi and the sgqebhezanas sauntered over to where she and Nandi sat.

"I heard your sister's been baking a bunny at the mall. Is that true, S-S-Sindi?"

Sindi glared at them.

"So what if it is? What's that got to do with us?" Nandi said.

"Just being friendly, sista. Chila. But I'm wondering, who is this invisible boy she hooked up with? I've never seen Thuli at the mall. Have any of you?" Pumi snapped her fingers over her shoulder. The sgqebhezanas shook their heads as if they were a chorus of puppets on one string. "So I'm thinking, maybe Miss-Speaking-in-Tongues is speaking in lies."

"I don't lie. Tell them, Sindi."

"Yes, tell us S-S-Sindi. Or even better, show us the letter."

Sindi stuck her hand into her pocket and clutched the letter tightly. "N_n_no. Go away."

"O-o-okay then. But you know, Nandi, lying is a sin. And so is gossiping. See you in hell." They walked away laughing.

"I can't believe you t_told them."

Nandi shook her head, her eyes narrow. "I can't believe you think I would. It wasn't me."

"Who was it then? I didn't t_t_tell anyone else."

Nandi snapped the lid on her lunchbox and shoved it into her bag. Her lips were sealed in a hard line when she stood up. She looked down at Sindi, face contorted with rage. "I made friends with you when no one else would. And I've stuck by you even though it's probably a sin to be friends with someone with no soul. I even gave you my blood to try and save you, and now you turn on me like Pumi's dog. Why don't you go lick Pumi's backside? You're just like all the others."

Sindi watched her storm across the playground, walking faster than she'd ever seen Nandi move before. She pulled the letter out and stared at Mama's name. Yesterday morning, when she'd told Nandi about Thuli, that other girl in the toilets must have overheard them.

The bell went. Lunch break was over. Sindi folded the letter and put it back into her pocket. Nandi had been a really good friend to her. There was no way she'd tell the sgqebhezanas. She stood and walked to class alone, praying that Nandi would forgive her.

Nandi refused to acknowledge Sindi's apology. She gave her the silent treatment until the end of the day, when she said she would forgive Sindi, but that it would take her some time. At the school gates, Nandi said good-bye and they hugged awkwardly. When Sindi tried to pull away, Nandi tightened her embrace and held on. A little too long, considering how pissed she was.

Sindi walked home, feeling blue. When she found the door of the zozo unlocked, her heart sank even further. The past two evenings, tiptoeing around trying not to draw Mama's attention, had been awful. After her fight with Nandi, she just wanted a few hours alone.

Mama was not in the kitchen. Strange sounds emanated from the other side of the wardrobe, like someone was dragging furniture around. She swung the curtain aside, and found the way barred. There was something propped up against the wardrobe, tilted at an angle so the thick plastic it was wrapped in ballooned towards her. She flattened the plastic against the yellow foam inside, and peered at an unblemished mattress.

"Don't just stand there with your lip hanging loose, come help." Auntie and Mama manoeuvred the new mattress to the floor, to where Sindi's bed had been just that morning.

She stepped tentatively into the room. Her bed had been pushed to Mama's side of the room. The white dress was gone. She knew, looking at the black bin-bag in the middle of the floor, that she would not see it again.

Who was the mattress for? Definitely not Thuli. Mama had removed all trace of her twin and had even banned Sindi from speaking her name. No way she'd be getting a brand new mattress. Nope, not Thuli; though Sindi could not imagine another person moving in with them. Perhaps it was Auntie.

Auntie definitely had problems, judging by the sight of her. She usually took great care with her appearance, applying plenty of foundation, lipstick and green or purple mascara. But today she looked haggard, her cheeks and strong jaw shadowed, her eyes puffy. She had a doek wrapped around her head, but she had no curlers in. As fond as she was of Auntie, she didn't relish the idea of sharing their cramped zozo with her. If Auntie moved in, Sindi decided, she'd run away, just like Thuli. And she'd leave a letter.

She reached into her pocket, right down, until her fingers picked at the lint in the seam, then she turned the pocket inside out, unwilling to believe the story her fingertips told. She felt suddenly disconnected, as if her feet had lifted from the floor and she was floating skywards – like those people she'd seen on TV, the ones who'd had near-death experiences during surgery. They'd looked down and seen themselves lying on the table – slit open *from gills to gullet*, one had said. She'd thought that would be scary, but looking down at herself getting smaller and smaller wasn't frightening at all. The further she drifted, the safer she felt. It was as if the letter had anchored her to the earth and all her troubles. T for Trouble. T for Thuli. That's all Thuli had ever brought. Ever since Sindi could walk, Thuli had led her astray. With the last thing tying her to her twin gone, she was free to float into the clouds and disappear. Sisterless, soulless, bodyless. Stratus without cirrus.

"Sindi? Sindisiwe? Ai, what's wrong you, girl? Fast asleep half the time."

Mama tugged at her sleeve and she plummeted down, down, down. She blinked hard.

"Sindisiwe, did you hear me?" Mama frowned at her. "Go next door and tell your sister to pack her things. She can come home tonight."

End of Days

"Mama says you can come home now."

Thuli sat on Auntie's couch, staring at the TV. She gave no indication that she'd heard what Sindi said.

"Mama says you can come home now," she said again, louder.

Slowly, Thuli turned and looked at Sindi over her shoulder.

Sindi took a step backwards. Thuli's cheek was swollen, the area around her eye purplish-black. She had a fat lip, split down the middle, just like Sindi's lip that time she'd tripped over Thembi.

"She says to pack your things, she'll come get you," Sindi said, her voice cracking.

"What's wrong, Sisi? You sound like you feel sorry for me."

Tears stung Sindi's eyes. No matter how much she hated Thuli, she would never have wished this on her. Mama had only ever slapped or pinched the twins before. She reserved her fists for men who got too fresh at Ma Elias'. But Mama hadn't bruised her knuckles on the wall. "Does it hurt a lot?"

Thuli scowled at her. "Like you care? As if you and your fototo girlfriend had nothing to do with it."

"Me? What did I do?"

"Save the innocent act for someone who believes you. Just go away and leave me alone."

Sindi balled her hand into a fist. "It's not my fault you go around doing bad things with boys. You're such a slut." But Thuli had turned the volume on the TV up, drowning her out.

Sindi stormed from Auntie's house and slammed the door. How dare Thuli blame her? She shook with rage. Wait until she told Nandi. They'd come up with a plan. They had to. If Thuli polluted her soul any further, Sindi would never get to heaven.

The next morning at breakfast, Mama asked Sindi to get the money-tin down. Sindi watched her mother count out the rent, wrap it in a Checkers packet and hold it out to her.

"Take this to Joe. And get me some Grand-Pa Headache Powders and a Coke, I can't trust your sister any more," she said, even though Thuli was sitting right there.

Throughout the previous evening, Mama had spoken to Thuli through Sindi, though Sindi didn't bother relaying the messages as she wasn't speaking to Thuli either. Relieved at the chance to get out, Sindi stuffed the packet into the waistband of her jeans.

Outside, her lungs heaved. The tension in the zozo since Thuli came back had sucked the oxygen from the air. Sindi struggled to breathe when Mama and Thuli were in the same room, as if the weight of her sister's sin pressed down on her chest. To make matters worse, Thuli was coughing and sneezing and wiping her nose all the time. Sindi didn't want to catch whatever Thuli had. No one would want to come near her then. She wished she could run away.

Determined to escape for as long as possible, she took a long route to Saviour's, in spite of the wad of cash stashed under her clothes. She fantasised about taking the money and using it to get her own place – but where would she get the next month's rent, and the one after that? It wasn't as if she could find a job, with her stutter. No, running away was out of the question. She thought of the white dress, the one that should've been hers. She could buy ten dresses like that one with the money. She should just head over to Maponya Mall and blow it all on shoes and dresses. That would teach Mama to pick favourites. But then she'd probably come home and find their stuff on the pavement. Evicted. Nandi would definitely toss their friendship aside if Sindi was homeless.

An hour later, Sindi crossed the veld between the township and Joe's. There was no one in the forecourt but the pumps. She could feel their accusing gaze as she walked towards the shop, facing straight ahead, eyes focused on the tip of her nose. It was like they could read her thoughts. Thinking sinful thoughts is as bad as doing them, Nandi had told her. *God sees.* If she looked at the pumps, she was sure she'd see the word *thief* spelled out in the glass windows, like when you wrote *hello* on a calculator using a 4, a 3, two 7s and a 0.

Joe's chair was empty. He was not behind the counter either. She did a quick scan of the aisles, her eyes lingering over the chocolate bars, then decided against helping herself: she already had one foot in hell. She was about to try the workshop when she heard someone singing.

"Emi, oru, abiku, O, catch a emi by the toe, hold on tight and don' let go, if up to heaven you want to go . . ."

"Hello?"

"Emi, oru, abiku, O . . ."

Ben, the elusive Ben. She recognised his voice. She cocked her head to pinpoint where it was coming from, and crept around the counter.

"Catch a emi by the toe, hold on tight and don' let go . . ."

She found Ben hunched under the counter, arms wrapping knees like a kid playing hide-and-go-seek. The strangest thought flitted across her mind: that all the times she and Nandi had come looking for him, he'd been hiding right here.

Ben looked up and gave her a grin. "Little sister, where you been?" He unfolded upwards and dusted himself off.

"Why are you hiding?"

"Who said I hiding? I'm not hiding. I'm fixing the Hurricane."

"Where have *you* been?"

"Me, I been home, little sister. A man must go home sometimes."

She nodded. That made sense. He'd gone to Nigeria. He probably had family there, children. Nandi would be pleased he was back. She'd stop at her friend's house on the way home to tell her, and they could come back here together to question him. Then Sindi frowned. What if he disappeared again before she got back with Nandi?

"Can ss_someone without a ss_asoul get to heaven?"

Ben gave her a quizzical look. "Excuse me? Come again."

She swallowed hard. "How can ss_asomeone . . ."

"I hear you, I just didn't think I hear you right. Everyone got emi, little sister, emi and oru. Two souls. One for spirit, one for mind. But it's not your soul that get you to heaven, it's your actions." He turned and wiped the counter with his sleeve.

Sindi narrowed her eyes at him. He was lying. He knew she didn't have a soul and he was lying to her. "That ss_asong you were ss_asinging, what does it mm_mean?"

"The song? That song about hitching a ride all the way up on somebody else's soul."

"What for? Why would anyone nn_need to hitch a ride if everyone got a ss_asoul?"

"For those that got business there before they die." He shrugged, as if going to heaven was like going to the bank. "Now, if there's nothing you want on earth, then be on your way, I got work to do."

She gave him the rent money and left. All the way to Nandi's house, Ben's stupid song was stuck in her head. So much for Nandi's grand plan: Ben didn't know anything about anything. *Catch a emi by the toe.* Dumber than dumb. Kids' stuff. Like that rhyme they'd learned in school when they were small. *Eeny meeny miny mo, catch a tiger by the toe.* As if a tiger wouldn't claw your face off if you tried. Besides, Auntie said they taught it wrong, that it was supposed to be nigger, *catch a nigger by the toe.* So Thuli had made up a rap version, *eeny meeny bitches ho, catch a nigger by the toe,* and their teacher pulled her by the ear all the way to the toilets and made her eat soap.

Sindi stood at Gogo Nkosi's gate, trying to summon the courage to go in. She wished Nandi had come with her, but Nandi was afraid of being seen entering the home of a sangoma – a witch, she'd called her. She said the word *witch* with the same venom she reserved for the words *heathen* and *slut*, even though consulting Gogo Nkosi had been her idea.

The last time Sindi was in Gogo Nkosi's garden, Jimmy Normans lived in her backyard shack and Dora was alive. She had a vivid memory of standing between the rows of cabbage and morog while he joked that Gogo Nkosi would chop her up for stew if she caught her there. Sindi shuddered. She'd liked him so much.

This would not end well. She'd protested when Nandi first mentioned her new plan. It was a bad idea, a very bad idea. But Nandi had given her the disappointed eye-roll. "It's your last chance at salvation, Sins," she'd said, "and to be honest, I can't keep hanging around with someone who doesn't care about her soul. The Father says we need to free ourselves from the influence of sinners in order to keep the bonds of our spiritual family sacred. I'm going to be a Mother for the New Mankind, you know. We can't be friends if you don't sort out your problem."

It was now or never. If she stood there much longer, thinking about the lodger or Dora or Gogo Nkosi's chicken-head-detaching axe, she'd lose her nerve.

The gate was secured with a wire loop. She unhooked it and lifted the gate over a ridge of hardened ground. The lodger had once whispered to her that Gogo Nkosi made that mound herself: if you were too stupid to figure out how to open the gate, she'd say you were not welcome by the ancestors. The door to Gogo Nkosi's house stood open, but Sindi's knock only attracted the attention of a scrawny hen. It rushed out of the house and began to *tik* hopefully at the ground around her feet. The hen's *puk-puk* had an enquiring tone, and it struck her that the bird might well be Gogo Nkosi. According to Ben, witches could change form and turn into their familiar animal. It kind of made sense that Gogo Nkosi's familiar would be an anorexic chicken – even the wattle under its neck looked a bit like the goitre Gogo Nkosi refused to have cut out. Finding nothing to eat, the chicken gave her a sharp peck on the ankle, then turned and stalked back into the house. Sindi hoped the chicken wasn't Gogo Nkosi, because it didn't seem to like her much. "Hello," she called after it, "Gogo?"

"No matter what anyone has told you, I have never been, nor will I ever be, a chicken."

Gogo Nkosi rested her chin on the handle of her axe. Her wrinkles had multiplied since Sindi had last been there, while the rest of her had shrunk. How long had she been standing at the side of the house, watching Sindi with bird eyes?

Unnerved, Sindi took a deep breath. She'd rehearsed her speech a hundred times in front of Nandi's catatonic grandmother and could recite it without stuttering. "Good afternoon, Gogo Nkosi," she began in a sing-song voice, "I'm doing a school project and . . ."

Gogo Nkosi held up her hand. "Do you have money?"

Sindi blinked. She had not anticipated an interruption. "M_m_money, Gogo?"

"Nothing in this world is free, child."

"But it's for school. You don't even nn_know what I want."

Gogo Nkosi shrugged. "I do not have to. I have a lifetime of experience that tells me no stranger knocks on my door to bring news. So I ask again, do you have money?"

Sindi shook her head.

"Then how do you plan to pay me?"

Sindi looked at her shoes. Of course she would want money. Why hadn't Nandi thought of that? "Sss_asorry Gogo, I'll go and get _asome."

Gogo Nkosi laughed. "And how much will you bring?"

"How m_m_much do you want?"

"That depends on what it is you ask me to do. Come inside. I'll put a plaster on your ankle and you can tell me why you are here. Once I know, I can give you a price."

Although she'd been in her garden many times to visit the lodger, Sindi had never been inside Gogo Nkosi's house. She expected jars of strange things on the shelves and animal remains hanging from the ceiling, much like her grandmother's hut, but the house was disappointingly normal and very tidy. Gogo Nkosi led her to the kitchen and instructed her to sit at the small Formica table. She opened one of the pine cupboards and took out a battered tin that looked as though it might contain something interesting, but it turned out to be a first-aid box stocked with the usual things: Savlon, cotton wool, Disprin, plasters. After she'd supervised the disinfection of the peck wound and the application of a plaster, Gogo Nkosi offered her a glass of water flavoured with honey and lemon. Without waiting for a reply, she poured them each a glass and sat down opposite Sindi. "Now, child, tell me why you have come."

Sindi took another deep breath and began again. "Good afternoon, Gogo Nkosi, I'm doing a school project and would like to ask you a question please. In the newspaper, there was an article about a woman who killed her husband. She defended herself in court by saying that a witchdoctor had stolen her soul and placed in her the soul of a murderer. My teacher has set us the task of discovering what sort of magic was used to take a soul and place it in the body of someone else." Sindi looked down to hide her smile; she'd managed the entire speech without stuttering once.

"Tell me, child, do you always sing when you lie?"

"Sss_asorry, Gogo?"

"As you can probably tell by my many wrinkles, I have been alive a very long time. My years have taught me that there are few certainties in life, but of this I am sure. Black magic has never been taught in school, and you, Sindisiwe, are a liar."

Sindi's cheeks flushed. She'd known it wouldn't work, she'd *known*.

"Yes, child, I know you. You and your sister paid many visits to my vegetable garden, though I conclude from your long absence that it was not my cabbages that held your fascination. Why don't you tell me what it is you really want?"

Sindi bit her lip. She'd never told anyone but Nandi about her problem. What if, once she knew the truth, Gogo Nkosi wanted to fill her mouth with soil? She didn't look capable of holding Sindi down, though she easily wielded an axe that was almost as tall as her. Sindi's sinuses prickled. Gogo Nkosi was her last chance. If she wouldn't help, Sindi might as well be dead.

The three truthful sentences took far longer than her prepared speech, and during the telling of them she did not lift her eyes from the crackled green Formica. She remembered too well the way Thembi had looked at her, and she didn't want to watch Gogo Nkosi's expression change from curiosity to revulsion.

"You want to take the soul of your sister because your grandmother told you that you are empty? Why would she say such a thing?" There was laughter in Gogo Nkosi's voice, an all-too-familiar mocking tone.

"Thuli's nn_not a good person. Nnn_nandi says she's a demon that ss_astole my _asoul before we were born. I just want back what is mine."

Gogo Nkosi laughed again. "Child, go home. Stealing a soul is not a game for little girls to play. You and this Nandi should find something else to entertain you."

Sindi stood. When she walked out of Gogo Nkosi's front door, she would be friendless as well as soulless. She thought of Thuli sitting alone at break, a mirror of what her life would soon be like.

"Stop crying, child. Do you truly believe these things?"

Sindi nodded. "I know it's true. Look at m_m_me. Listen to m_m_me."

Gogo Nkosi sighed. "The power of belief. What you believe becomes true. This dark thing you ask will have a price, child, a very high price."

"I can pay," Sindi said, though she had no idea where she'd find the money.

"Can you? Even I am not sure what this will cost you."

"I'll get the m_m_money."

"I am not talking of money. Go home. Think about what you are asking. Sleep on it. And if, after you have considered this well, you find your heart is still black, bring me R300 and a piece of your sister. But know that you alone will answer for this."

Maybe she just wasn't meant to go to heaven. She turned this thought over in her mind most of the night, and was leaning towards telling Nandi to forget it, forget about Sindi's soul and her salvation, forget about Sindi. Then Thuli got into a fight during first period. She hadn't been back at school five minutes and already she was dragging their name into the gutter.

"Shoo, your sisi's trouble with capital T." Pumi looked impressed in the toilets at break. "I think she broke his nose."

Nandi rolled her eyes. "You're going to end up like her if you don't watch out, Pumi."

"Really? Did God tell you that in a dream?"

"Come, Sins. It stinks in here." Nandi picked up her bag and stalked out.

Sindi followed as her friend marched down the corridor, double time. The encounter with Pumi had clearly unnerved Nandi, not that she'd ever admit it. Sindi suspected that Nandi missed the sgqebhezanas; it wouldn't take long for Nandi and Pumi to make up, if Sindi decided not to go back to Gogo Nkosi.

Nandi finally settled on a sunny spot at the far side of the yard, too hot to attract anyone else. She took out her lunchbox with shaking hands.

"Don't let Pumi get to you."

"Who says she gets to me? I don't care about her." Nandi glared at the sgqebhezanas on the other side of the yard, tearing her sandwich into bite-sized pieces. She chewed, making circular motions with her jaw. It clicked on every rotation. Sindi wished the bell would go. "So, are you going to tell me what happened yesterday? Did you even go?"

"I went," Sindi snapped, "but she wants money."

"Of course she does. Devil-worshippers always want money."

Sindi bit her lip. She wished she had the courage to point out that Nandi's father gave a load of money to their church every month.

"So, how much?"

Sindi told her the sum and Nandi whistled through her teeth. "Wow. Where you going to get it?"

Sindi shrugged. She'd hoped Nandi would offer to help.

"Guess you better figure it out, Sins, time's running out."

Sindi couldn't tell whether she was referring to the end of the world or their friendship. Maybe it didn't matter. Nandi was being such a bitch. Maybe Sindi no longer wanted her as a friend.

"I'm sorry, okay. I'm just really worried about you, Sins." Nandi offered Sindi the uneaten half of her sandwich. "Doesn't your mother keep money in a tin in the kitchen cupboard? She won't notice if you take some."

"Sss_asteal it?"

Nandi shrugged, "It's your soul, Sins. What else you going to do?"

That night when Mama went to bed, Sindi lay in the dark counting out minutes. She still slept on the right-hand side of the old mattress, though Mama had turned it and the indents made by her body and Thuli's were no longer there to sink into. When Mama had been snoring for twenty minutes, she slipped out of bed and took five rand from the tin.

Mama had started drinking again, like she had during the heat wave. Visits to Ma Elias', once a monthly payday event, had become a regular weekend thing. Mama spent both Friday and Saturday nights there, often not returning home until dawn. Sindi felt ashamed of Mama's drunkenness, but it made taking money from the tin easier. Over the following weeks, Sindi managed to squirrel away almost half of Gogo Nkosi's fee.

Success made her blasé. She took bigger and bigger amounts, not bothering to wait until she was certain of Mama's beer coma. At the first snore, she'd slip out of bed and go into the kitchen.

Then, on a Thursday night, with less than R60 to go, Thuli came into the kitchen to get a glass of water and caught Sindi with her hand in the tin.

Sindi froze. She glared at her twin, waiting for her to say something. Thuli let her gaze wander from Sindi's face to the tin and back again. She smirked, poured her water and went back to bed.

"What am I going to do?" she whispered to Nandi the next morning during a maths test. "She's going to tell."

"The wages of sin is death," Nandi hissed back.

Tears stung Sindi's eyes, blurring the numbers on the page. Nandi was meant to be her best friend, how could she be so mean? She clenched her fists in her lap.

There were five minutes left on the clock when Nandi put her pen down. Sindi was still struggling with the first page of problems. The sums swam in front of her, refusing to make sense. She was usually good at maths, better than any of her classmates, because she understood that the subject was about more than adding and subtracting, dividing and multiplying. Mathematics turned chaos into order, the seemingly random into neat equations. There was safety in well-ordered numbers. And she was an A + student.

Nandi frowned at her unfinished paper, then slid her hand under the table and massaged Sindi's fist until her fingers relaxed. Then she put her head down, feigning sleep, and pushed her completed paper onto Sindi's side of the desk. Sindi looked up at Miss Patterson marking homework at her desk. *The wages of sin is death*. Nandi was prepared to cheat for her, to sin for her – and, therefore, to die for her.

That night, she waited until she was sure both Thuli and Mama were asleep. In the dim blue of the streetlight coming through the kitchen window, she counted out the rest of what she needed to pay Gogo Nkosi and stuffed it into her pocket. Before she placed the lid back on the tin, she took out an extra twenty, then took the sharp knife from the kitchen drawer. Mama's sewing scissors would be better, but Sindi couldn't risk opening the wardrobe door and getting the sewing box out.

Thuli slept fitfully. Her skin had a feverish sheen and her sheet was stained with dark-edged irregular circles. There was a sourness to her sweat, an adult smell that made Sindi's nose wrinkle. Thuli seemed to be aging faster than her sister. Her face had lost the plumpness of childhood, accentuating her cheekbones and revealing the woman she'd become. Sindi stood over her with the folded twenty rand note concealed in her palm, wondering if strangers would still know they were twins.

She felt strangely serene when she lifted the upper corner of Thuli's mattress and slipped the note under it. She left a corner sticking out, nothing obvious, just enough to be easily spotted should Mama search the room. In the morning, Sindi would hand the rest of the money over to Nandi to hide at her house. By the time Mama returned from work, the only evidence left would be under Thuli's bed. But, like Nandi said, Mama would most probably think she'd spent the money at Ma Elias' herself, and never bother to look.

Cutting a lock of Thuli's hair proved more difficult. In order to slice through it with the serrated blade, she had to hold the hair taut, awkward with only one hand. To make matters worse, the blade snagged, pulling strands out at the root. Thuli groaned more than once, but she did not wake.

By the time Sindi returned to her bed, she had strands of her sister's hair stuck to her slick palms. She wiped her hands on her pillow, then picked the remaining hairs one by one off her palms. While the dawn turned Thuli's skin silver, Sindi fell asleep and dreamed of Dora's coffin, covered in white carnations. When she reached out to place her own flower on the lid, the coffin opened to reveal not Dora but herself and Nandi, spooning like sisters.

A month had passed since Sindi's last visit, but Gogo Nkosi did not seem surprised to see her. She put the envelope containing Thuli's hair in her pocket and the money in her bra, and told Sindi to return in three days. She did not invite Sindi in, or ask her to repeat what it was she wanted, and Sindi spent the next three days worrying that Gogo Nkosi would do the wrong thing.

Her fears increased when she arrived at Gogo Nkosi's house on the allotted day and found her leaning on the gate, talking to someone invisible. Not wanting to interrupt in case the conversation was supernatural, she stood a little way back and listened to the one side her ears were capable of hearing. After a few minutes, she worried Gogo Nkosi had gone mad. She seemed to be memorising a bizarre shopping list: eggs, umhlovane, powdered baboon finger, and other strange and ordinary things. If the gogo noticed Sindi standing there, she did not show it.

After she'd recited the list several times, she opened the gate and turned to go back into her house. "Come, Sindisiwe," she called over her shoulder, "and close your mouth before you catch a fly."

As Sindi went through the gate, she felt a chill in the air, like passing an open fridge.

"Sit," Gogo Nkosi instructed her. Sindi sat at the green Formica table and watched Gogo Nkosi pour two glasses of iced honey water. When she returned the jug to the fridge, she took out a glass jar with closed screw-top lid and placed it on the table with the two glasses. It contained a brownish mush. Then she sat down herself and said nothing more for five minutes; Sindi watched them tick by on the kitchen clock. The ice in the glasses began to melt. Another minute passed, the longest sixty seconds she'd ever experienced. Gogo Nkosi seemed to be waiting, for what Sindi did not know. She hoped it wasn't more money. Maybe paying up front had been a mistake. Sweat trickled down her neck. Gogo Nkosi stared at her, unblinking. Sindi began to squirm.

"What do you nn_need eggs and u_u_um . . ." she stumbled on the unfamiliar word.

"Umhlovane?" Gogo Nkosi picked up her glass and took a sip. "Something is eating my cabbages. Rats, I suspect. Umhlovane will kill whatever it is."

"And the eggs?"

"Bait."

Sindi imagined Gogo Nkosi mixing the poison. "What about the baboon's finger?"

Gogo Nkosi narrowed her eyes. "You're a nosy child. Let's worry about your prescription and leave the needs of others to me."

Sindi eyed the jar. Moisture had condensed on the glass. She reached out to wipe a clear window with her thumb.

Gogo Nkosi slapped her hand. "Let's not hurry towards this dark place. You have time enough to go there." She reached into the folds of her housecoat and drew out a small penknife, opening the blade and placing it on the table next to the jar. The oiled blade was mottled by oxidation, the bone handle polished and yellow.

"This thing you want to do will not be easy. You need to carry out my instructions carefully: if you fail in a single step, there will be a heavy toll to pay. So I ask you again, child, are you sure of what you do?"

Sindi nodded.

"Say it, the amadlozi must hear your speak."

"I'm sure, Gogo."

Gogo Nkosi nodded. "Take this jar. Only open it when you use it, not before. Once it is open, the magic will be released. Spread the paste over your sister's body, beginning with her head. It will separate her soul from her flesh. Once you have done that, you must work quickly." She picked up the knife. "Give me your hand."

Sindi held out her hand. Gogo Nkosi grasped it firmly and leaned towards her.

"Cut a door into your hand, so that your sister's soul will have somewhere to enter your body." With the tip of the knife, she lightly traced a rectangle on Sindi's palm. "Cut deep enough to draw blood – the blade must be bloodied for the next step. Do you follow me so far?"

Sindi's heart was pounding, but she felt as though Gogo Nkosi's words were being burned into her. She nodded.

"Okay then, child. Using the same knife, beginning and ending at the head, cut around your sister's body. All the way around. Make sure your cut marks cross over."

Sindi frowned. "I can't cut her, Gogo, she won't let m_m_me."

"No, child. Cut the air around her body. Do not cut her. If you open her body, her soul may slip straight back in. Have you followed me so far?"

Sindi nodded.

"Then repeat everything I have told you."

Sindi read the words burned into her mind back to Gogo Nkosi.

"Very good. You must want this very badly, child. Do you not realise how heavy a burden another's soul can be?" She shook her head, and continued. "Once you have cut her soul from her, it will come out of her. Souls always take the shape of a creature that flies, a bird perhaps, or an insect. I cannot say for certain what it will be. That depends on your sister's nature, but since you are twins I shall judge her by you and guess that it will be a wasp or some other evil thing. You must catch it. Once you have it in your hand, it will enter your body through the door you have cut in your palm and the dark deed will be complete."

She let go of Sindi's hand and closed the blade of the knife, placing it on the table between them.

"Now, drink your water and be on your way."

Sindi downed the honey water. She picked up the jar and reached for the knife.

"Leave the knife, child, it belongs to me."

"Where will I get a nn_knife?"

"Any knife will do. The knife is a symbol. The gesture creates the magic, not the object itself. Get it from the same place you got the money, steal it from your mother."

Sindi put the jar in her bag and turned to leave. There was no point in lingering. Gogo Nkosi did not like her, that was obvious, but she didn't need the approval of a *witch*.

At the door, she hesitated. "What will happen if I can't catch it?"

Gogo Nkosi sighed. "I do not know the answer to that, child. There are souls that wander this earth, unable to move on to the kingdom in the sky. Lost souls. Perhaps your sister will become one of them and remain here on earth. Perhaps this will kill you both. I do not know the price. That is why I cannot understand why you are so willing to pay it."

PART 5

The Legend of Thulisile Nxumalo

The Road

I stand on the shoulder of the Ring Road in a twilight haze, blinking-blinking. My heart leaps. I know this place, this rush-hour time. I look to the embankment, where my sisi might be sitting, watching traffic. Stalks of sun-bleached grass stand upright and still, waiting for feet to beat them to chaff. Exhaust fumes grease the back of my throat, but there's no cars in either direction, just white lines and rubber burns. The dry rush of air in my nostrils is the only sound.

I scan the horizon. The sky, low and clear, intersects the road too soon: blue and grey curve suddenly away, as if the world has shrunk.

"Hello!" I yell. My voice bounces off the blank road and blank blue, *hello*, *hello*, *hello* – as if I'm inside a bottle or one of those plastic domes like the one Uncle bought me on the promenade that day we went to the sea. He placed it in my palm and closed my fingers around it. I hated that mermaid straight away, her green tail and naked titties and painted smile like Next-Door-Auntie's asking-for-it shebeen-night lips.

Shame-shame.

"Hello," I yell again, and again the mocking *hello*, *hello*, *hello*, followed by a silence empty of even the white buzz of background noise.

That day we went to the sea, Mama said to stay in one place if we got lost: someone would come and find us. I sit on the shoulder of the highway and wait. The light sinks. Dusk quickly becomes night and doubt begins to gnaw at my hope. The sky is darker than any I've ever seen. There are no indigo edges where the sun should have set or Mama Moon risen, no reflected orange glow from the city's streetlights. Just stars like polished coins, evenly spaced out. They make me lonely.

"What are stars, Joe?" The week after Dora's funeral, while Sindi stuffed her pockets with rolls of Wilson's XXX, I leaned on the counter at Saviour's and pointed at the picture of an exploding supernova on the front page of *The Daily Voice*.

"They are the souls of dead kids waiting to get into heaven," said Joe, "and the moon is the hole in the sky they need to go through to get there. She opens wide if the kids have been good, but if they've been bad – like maybe a thief – she shuts tight so they have to squeeze."

"What about falling stars?"

"Ah. These are souls returning to be rebirthed. For incarnation."

"Auntie says they're bits of space junk burning up in our atmosphere. She says there's more broken satellites orbiting the earth than petrol cars in government scrap yards."

"Does she? Your Auntie tells tall stories."

That night, Sindi and me lay on the floor in the bedroom, staring out the window at the skinny moon hovering in a slice of sky above the RDP houses across the road. "Joe tells tall stories," I told her.

"'Bout what?"

"The stars. If they were dead kids, there'd be a fat one."

A star falls, tailing light. I wait for it to fizzle out, but it keeps coming, brighter-brighter. I watch its downward arc. Bigger and bigger, until it hits an overpass with a flash and hope sparks fresh. Maybe Joe didn't lie.

I run along the deserted road to the overpass. It's dark under the bridge. Water pooled against one side reflects starlight, enough to see there's no one here either. I step into the purple shadows and stare at my face in the mirror surface of the pool. I think of the summer thunderstorms that used to rumble in when me and Sindi were still pinkie-linked, before the Long Dry. I think of the puddles the steaming streets couldn't suck up fast enough, and how we used to hop-frog through them on the way home from school. Crouching over, the brief unsteadying press of my sisi's splayed hands on my back. It hasn't rained in a long time.

I leap into the air. The still water twins me, teeth bared in a grimace of rage, knees bent to absorb the impact. None comes. The last thing I see are squiggles of silver light before I'm swallowed whole.

"Move."

Someone jabs me in the back. I shuffle forward, releasing dusty odours from the carpet beneath my feet. I feel wobbly inside, as if I've just woken up, trailing fragments of a bad dream.

Where am I? My brain sorts the papery scent of books from the chalk of mouldy sandwiches forgotten in the bottom of canvas satchels stained with the ink of leaking pens. School. But there's hospital in the air.

"Yo, this is taking foreeeeeever."

I glance over my shoulder. A queue of listless students unwinds behind me. I catch Dumisile's eye. He grins. I turn away quick, cheeks flushing.

I'm second in line. Nandi is first, shoulders square, head forward like she's determined not to speak to me. Her cornrows are braided round the curve of her skull, like mine used to be when Sindi plaited my hair with a crochet hook. The wobble in my gut is ironed flat by hate. I want to yank the ends of those stupid plaits so hard they tear from her scalp.

The blue door at the end of the passage opens and Sindi comes out. She hurries past, clutching her arm.

"Next."

A thin woman in a navy uniform stands in the doorway. She has wiry arms and big hands like Next-Door-Auntie, man-hands. Nandi steps forward. The woman smiles encouragingly. "Thulisile Nxumalo?" she asks, glancing at her clipboard.

"No, ma'am, Nandi Sithole," Nandi says.

"I want Thulisile Nxumalo next."

I shoulder Nandi as I push past her. She gapes like a fish. I give her the finger and close the door behind me.

I'm standing on the school stage, with the emerald curtains drawn and the stage lights on. The spotlights seem to penetrate the stage, creating bright holes in the polish-darkened boards. All around, things that have been set out to create a makeshift medical surgery float in darkness. The nurse seems to glide across the stage, disconnected from the earth.

"Hello, Thuli. I am Sister Bongi, the district nurse. Please sit down over here."

I sit opposite the nurse. There's a file on the desk with two white labels stuck to the front. One has Sindi's name written across it in block letters, the other has mine. The nurse flips through the folder.

"I'm going to ask you some questions," she says, without looking up. "All your answers are private. I won't tell anyone what you say. It's important that you answer honestly. How old are you?"

I stare at her pen poised on the edge of a blank page and my mouth goes dry. I eye her glass of water, wishing there was one for me. The nurse looks up. "This is not a test, there's no wrong answer."

"Thirteen."

"Of course, you're twins. Have you started your menstruation?"

"'Skies?'"

"Your menstrual cycle." Her voice rasps, like Mama sharpening the kitchen knives with sandpaper. She takes a sip of water. "Do you know what I'm talking about?"

I shake my head.

She sighs. "Your period, Thuli. Your mother should've spoken to you by now."

I shake my head and look down, cheeks hot. "Mama doesn't like to talk about stuff like that."

"Nobody wants to talk about sex or menstruation or pregnancy. It makes my job very difficult."

I wish she wouldn't talk about it either. It's embarrassing.

"Your sister hasn't started her period yet either."

I shrug. If Sindi started her period, she wouldn't tell me.

"Okay, Thulisile, I have a lot to get through today. Let's carry on. Do you have a boyfriend?"

I shake my head.

"Have you ever had a boyfriend?"

I think of the time I held Dumisile's hand under the desk in grade four, how hot my palm got in his grasp. After break, he sat next to Vanessa Naidoo and told everyone I sweated like a pig. I shake my head.

"Good, so you've never had sex?"

I stare at the curtains: there could be an audience on the other side. The ripples in the velvet make me think of the sea. I don't want to remember the feeling of the waves breaking over me, so I think of Vusi. He said he did it behind the hall with Dora, poor dead Dora who can't say she didn't.

"No."

"Good girl. Come over here please. Take off your jersey and hop up on this table."

I follow her and do as she asks. There are two unmarked boxes on the table, an empty stainless-steel bowl, a packet of cotton-wool balls and a super-size bottle of Savlon. The nurse pulls a pair of latex gloves from one of the boxes. They turn her hands white and leave powder on everything she touches. She takes a blister pack from the other box, peels back the foil and empties some small objects into the bowl.

"What are those things for?"

"I need to test your blood," she says. From the bowl, she takes a grey plastic rectangle with a black knob one one side. "This is called a lancet. Hold out your hand."

She swabs the tip of my index finger with Savlon. "I want you to squeeze your finger until it throbs." She presses the lancet against my fingertip. I suck my teeth as a needle pierces my skin. "Hold still." She tosses the lancet into a bin and picks up what looks like a miniature version of the thing Mama used to give us sunlight-soap enemas when we were small-small and stuck.

"What's that for?"

"Don't worry, the worst is over. This is just a pipette to suck up some of your blood, then I'll drop it onto the test stick. That's it. Not so bad, neh?"

I watch her drip my blood into a hollow at one end of a little white plastic stick, followed by a few drops of clear liquid from a small bottle.

"Okay," she says, pressing a Savlon-soaked cotton-wool ball against my finger, "now we wait fifteen minutes for the result and I'll give you your vaccination."

She takes the stainless-steel bowl with my test stick back to her desk and begins sorting through folders. Some have a red stars stuck on the top corner, and those she puts on one side. The rest she piles on the floor. My answers are private, she'd said. But she'd written down everything, and even now she's filling the silence with the scratch of her pen.

"Five more minutes."

I dab at my forehead with the cotton wool, and wonder why the nurse doesn't turn off the spotlights. Circles of sweat stain the navy fabric of her uniform black.

There's no clock for me to watch the time, nothing to look at besides the box of latex gloves and the box of test packs. I kick my legs and accidently knock over the bin. Used lancets, pipettes and test sticks spill onto the floor. Sister Bongi looks up.

"Sorry," I mumble, and climb down to right the bin. While I'm picking up the mess, I slip a test stick into my pocket. I sit back up on the table and, when the nurse has focused on her folders again, I peek at the result windows on the white stick. One is blank, the other has a red chevron. I wonder whose test it is, and if they passed or failed.

"Okay, Thulisile, let's look at your test." She holds it with straight arms like Next-Door-Auntie's boyfriend reading *The Daily Voice*. She frowns, brings it closer, shakes her head. She looks at me the same way Mama does when I've done something to disappoint her and I know I've failed. I want to ask her what the test is for, but the look on her face stops me.

"Thulisile, I need to see your mother." She sticks a red star next to my name on the front of our folder. "I'm going to write her a letter and give it to your teacher. You must collect it tomorrow and take it home."

"I didn't do anything."

"No?" She narrows her eyes as if trying to see inside me. "Just give the letter to your mother. It's very important."

"Okay."

"Okay, you can go."

I slide off the desk and grab my jersey. At the door, I remember the vaccination she's supposed to give me. I turn to ask her about it and see her drop my test into a plastic zip-lock bag.

"What is it?"

"Nothing, sorry." I open the door, and step through. The latch clicks shut. I swing around, lurching for the handle. There's nothing behind me but road, road, road.

I walk. Light passes, dark passes. The change happens in a flash of grey, as if someone flicks a switch that turns blue to grey, then grey to black. I've stopped thinking in terms of night and day, dusk and dawn, of twilight, of hours. I've stopped trying to find the sun or Mama Moon in the flat sky, free of stratus, cirrus, cumulonimbus.

I walk under overpasses with no on-ramps or off-ramps. There is a row of houses on either side of the highway, same-same beige walls, same-same red roofs. I try to climb up to them, but the embankments are steeper than they look and the soles of my baby-dolls slip on the dry grass; one of my feet is always on the road.

I am not on the Ring Road, I figured that out the first time it got light, but there is nothing to tell me where I am. The billboards blur when I try to read them, as if I'm looking at them from a speeding car. I stand for an hour and stare at a sign spanning the highway, but the words shift and change before my brain can turn them to sense.

As the sky begins to dim again, I stop. I sit down in the middle of the road and stare at the blank grey strip of it, not moving, not blinking, until my body begins to harden and I too become concrete.

"Thulisile, wake up!" Someone pinches me. "This is a geography lesson, not a sleeping lesson." Miss Patterson stands in front of me, arms folded across her chest. Giggling ripples around the class. I wipe a string of drool from my chin.

"Sorry, teacher," I mumble.

"See me after class," she says, but when the bell goes a few minutes later, I pick up my satchel and head for the door.

"Thulisile!"

I stand in front of Miss Patterson's desk while the rest of the class shuffle out, giving me looks. Chalk dust and her perfume mingle in my nose, making me feel a little sick. I've loaded my tongue with a lie, but it turns out it's not an excuse for falling asleep I need.

"I gave you a letter last week to give to your mother. Did you give it to her?"

The letter is under my mattress. I don't know what it says because even though I'm not planning to give it to Mama, I'm too scared to break the seal on the envelope in case she finds out. If I don't open it, I can pretend I've just forgotten to give it to her.

"Yes, ma'am."

"You did?" she narrows her eyes. "She hasn't made an appointment yet. The nurse will be here for three more days. It is very important, Thulisile, that she sees the nurse. Please, remind her."

"Yes, ma'am."

She pulls in her lips until she has no mouth. "See you tomorrow."

I walk home, kicking a stone along the road. It's so hot, watery lines rise from the iron roofs of shacks. The heat makes my legs feel fat and my bag too heavy. When I get home, I find Nandi leaning against the wall.

"What do you want?"

"None of your business."

"It's my house," I snap, annoyed by the smirk on her face.

"Not only yours. I'm waiting for Sindi."

"Go wait somewhere else," I swing my satchel onto my other shoulder. It almost hits her, but she sidesteps neatly. "Sindi doesn't really like you. She just hangs out with you because she's got no one else."

"Oh, who told you that?"

"I know," I say. "She's my sister. I can tell."

Nandi rolls her eyes and laughs. "Your sister? True sisters aren't so mean to each other."

"What's that supposed to mean?"

"Nothing," she sings, "I'm just saying, real sisters, blood sisters, are nice to each other." She holds up her hand. Two thin cuts crisscross in the centre of her palm.

I drop my bag. Nandi doesn't move. Her smile is frozen on her lips, but I can see by the way she presses her back to the wall that she's scared of me. I step into her, so close I can smell her cherry chewing-gum. "What do you mean?" I repeat the question through my teeth.

Her hands clench at her sides, but the smile stays put, like it's stuck on. "If you were a true sister, you wouldn't have been so ugly to Sindi that Christmas when you went to Eston. You wouldn't have taken sides with your horrible auntie against her."

Anger sours my throat. It's true, but if Nandi hadn't come between us, we'd have made up long ago. She whispers poison into Sindi's ear, things about me that feed her anger. I bring my fist to her chin, slow, because waiting for a smack is worse than getting one. She flinches. I draw back, but before I can land the punch the door opens and Sindi comes out with Mama. I drop my hand and step away.

"What are you doing?" Mama narrows her eyes at me.

"Nothing," I say.

"Nandi?"

Nandi shakes her head, but Mama grabs my ear and twists it anyway. "I didn't raise you to fight in the street like a dog," she says. "Now go inside before I give you a klap."

I lie on my bed, hating Mama and Nandi and even Sindi. My bad luck that Mama came home early. But then it dawns on me that it's a good time to give her the letter. She's already angry. Also, Next-Door-Auntie is here.

Mama and Auntie sit at opposite ends of the table, drinking Black Label from coffee mugs. They always sit in the same place, always use the same mugs, Mama a red one and Auntie a white one, as if the chairs and mugs have labels. Auntie's telling Mama about the latest goings-on in *Generations*. Mama says she should get a job and stop staring at the TV all day: "It's unhealthy."

The bedsprings have pressed diamond-shaped creases into the envelope. I try to smooth them out before I slip it onto the table in front of Mama.

"What's this?"

"Letter from school."

"You in trouble again? Haibo, Thuli, what's wrong with you?"

"I didn't do anything."

"You never do anything," she says, tearing one end of the envelope and sliding out a single sheet. Ready to run, I watch her scan the letter. When she's finished reading, she puts it back in the envelope and tucks it into her bra strap. "When did you get this letter?"

"Today."

"Today? Thuli, don't lie. When did you get it?"

"Miss Patterson gave it to me today," I tell her, hoping she won't see my teacher.

"This letter wants me to go see the district nurse. Last week, Thuli, last week."

286

I breathe a sigh of relief. Maybe it's too late and the nurse will be gone. "Miss Patterson said to tell you sorry, she forgot to give it to me."

"The nurse is only there until Friday. I have to work. When did they think I could go, hmm?" She pushes back her chair and stands, fastening the buttons on her work blouse. "Lucky for you, I came home early today."

Next-Door-Auntie clicks her tongue. "That bladdie teacher," she says, as if she has a kid and knows all about our school. "I'll walk with you."

I eye Auntie's hair curlers, wondering if she's going to put on a shirt or just go in her bra and skirt.

Mama says not to leave the house, but after ten minutes pacing-pacing, I have to get out. It's too hot. I want ice cream. I can easily get to Saviour's and back in half an hour, long before Mama gets home.

The Pit Stop is quiet. I can't see Ben and there are no customers. I wander up and down the aisles, then loiter at the fridge, staring at the Cornettos and fruit lollies. I imagine sliding the door, the glass steaming up as hot air mixes with the cold inside. I glance at Joe. He's leaning on the counter, holding *The Daily Voice* like he's reading it, but I can feel his eyes boring into me from behind those mirrored sunglasses. I'm a terrible thief; I don't have Sindi's nerves. Defeated, I slink out.

Outside, the air above the road looks like water. The tar's gone soft in places and stinks like our house. I wonder if I should tell Joe. Auntie says landlords should maintain, but Mama says she can't bother him after all he's done for us. Maybe he'll rent us another zozo, a bigger one, with more rooms, one for just me so I don't have to listen to Mama snore, so I don't have to fight Sindi for bed space. I'd sleep on the floor if I had my own room.

There's a squeaking, like the Legend's propellers turning in the wind, but there's no breeze. I follow the noise to the yard gate. Through the open gap I can see Ben pouring oil leavings from Chicken Licken's deep-fat fryers into the b-diesel still.

"What you doing?" I ask, kicking the ground with my toe.

"This, little sister, is magic," he says, steadying a jerry can against his shoulder. Thick brown oil swirls in the neck of a plastic funnel. It goes *gloop-gloop*.

"Thought you were making b-diesel."

He laughs. "You too sharp, little sister. Indeed, I am making diesel, but this process, turning chicken fat into b-diesel – that, little sister, is magic. You want to learn some real magic?"

"Sure." What else am I going to do?

"Then learn from the master." He puffs out his chest like he does when he's about to tell one of his stories. Auntie says she's never heard so many tall stories from one man. Mama just rolls her eyes, which means men tell Auntie plenty tall stories.

"First you filter the oil. You don't want bits of burnt chicken in your diesel, you don't want potato chips. You want your oil clean and nice, like you want your lady. You get it?"

I nod.

"Second, you must settle the oil. You don't want no water in your oil, that make the oil explode during the heating process. This oil here," he says, waving the empty jerry-can in front of me, "already been filtered and settled."

I reach for the can, but he snatches it away. "Uh-uh, little sister, nobody touch the oil but me or the boss, though I don't trust the boss. He cuts corners." He tosses the can to one side and digs a box of matches from his pocket. "Now we heat the oil to exactly thirty-five degrees, no hotter, no colder." He turns on the gas. It hisses, catches with a blue whoosh.

"What now?"

"We wait. When the oil just right, we add a little bit of methanol, a little bit of lye." He rolls two drums into the shade, and we sit on them, watching the oil warm. "In Nigeria," he tells me, "people live by magic. Not like here. Here, everybody heathen." He spits, bends to dip his fingers into the glob of saliva on the ground and makes a cross over his heart. "Here, nobody even leave an offering to the King of the Road. When I first come to work for the boss, I try to correct these heretical ways. I put a plate of food out in the forecourt every morning, for the King you know, this being a business dependent on the road, the customers being users of the road. But the boss, he say it attract the rats. He say stop."

He jumps up and taps the dial of a thermometer. I kick my heels against the drum, rat-a-tat-a-tat. I feel strange inside, like there's a bubble swelling in my stomach. Then I realise I'm happy, or the closest I've been to happy since Eston. Thinking of Eston makes the hole inside open up. I shake off the black mood before I fall in.

While the oil heats, Ben tells me the story of a spirit boy – an abiku, Ben calls him – who kept dying and coming back, and how his restlessness drove his parents mad. I'm so wrapped up in the story, I don't notice the time passing until the day is almost gone. I run home in the twilight, cursing Ben.

I know something is wrong the minute I step through the door. Auntie sits next to Mama, her face pale-pale. She's patting Mama's shoulder, but in a distracted way, like her mind is drifting to a great sorrow. I can't see Mama's face because it's buried in her hands, but from the way her body's shaking, I know she's crying. The last time I saw Mama cry was in Eston.

"Mama?" I whisper, afraid that something bad has happened to Sindi.

Mama looks up. Her eyes are swollen and red. Snot bubbles from her nostrils, her top lip glistens like a slug. "What have you done?"

"Mama?"

She stands. Auntie grabs her arm, but Mama takes a swipe at her. Auntie falls off her chair. My schoolbag, slung over the back of Auntie's chair, vomits books and pencils onto the floor. Mama's across the kitchen in two strides. Standing over me, she looks bigger than normal, a sci-fi monster from TV. My brain says *run* but my legs are too heavy.

"What have you done?"

"Sizane!"

Mama brings her fist down on my head. "Thirteen years old, *thirteen*! You dirty, dirty girl, what have you done?"

I hunch as blows rain down on my head, my face, my body. Her accusations and Auntie's protests mix together until I can't separate the word *dirty* from the word *stop*. The world is full of noise. Someone is screaming, I can't tell if it's me or Auntie. Then everything goes black, and I'm falling.

Pain makes red flowers when I try to move, throbbing roses that blister and burst behind my lids, turning pink and pretty for a moment before blowing out to a bright, aching white. I can't open my eyes, but sometimes I hear voices. Men's voices, though maybe one is a woman, someone I know, but I can't remember her name.

"She's gone too far, I'm calling the gata."

"Don't talk crazy, man. You can't bring the police here."

"What if she dies? They'll say I did it, they'll send me back to Sun City."

"Shh, she won't die."

There are other sounds too: a teaspoon clinking against a mug, the theme tune of *Generations,* dogs barking. I pick odours from the air: pap sticking to the bottom of a pot, boiled cabbage, fried meat, the powder-soap scent of Coty perfume. I try to cling to these things, ground my floating senses in them, but most of the time I just fall, dizzyingly, through darkness. Then I wake up and wish I hadn't.

The light is made of knives. My eyes bleed tears. I touch my fingers to my cheeks and pain blades from my shoulder into my arm, setting my fingers on fire. My entire body hurts. Even my toes scream, trying to get my attention above all the other shouting-yelling-howling parts of me. My spine aches. I try to sit to change position. The world spins. Everything is a dazzling blur. I retch.

"Thuli, oh baby, don't cry." A fuzzy shadow hovers over me, blocking the light. I'm so grateful. Auntie dabs my tears with sandpaper. Agony explodes in my face and I want her gone. I close my eyes, shut her out, fall.

Mama says you can come home now.

I stare at the TV.

I can't believe my sisi took three days to come to see if I'm okay. Three days since I woke up on Next-Door-Auntie's brown couch. It bites, even though we're not close any more, even though that's my fault. If Mama had done this to her, I'd have held her hand until she woke up. I'd have forgiven her.

I gave her an eyeful, holding the pose. The worst side, my right side. She looked like she was going to cry. The first time I saw my face in the mirror above Auntie's dressing table, I almost cried too. Vrot-plum face.

Does it hurt a lot?

Like she cares.

"I won't go home," I tell the TV, "I won't ever go back." But where else is there for me to live? Auntie and her boyfriend don't want me around. I hear them talking about me at night.

I find plastic shopping bags under the sink and pack my things into them. My stomach burns with angry fire.

"Come, Thuli," Mama says when she finally arrives.

Come, Thuli, as if "come" is a magic word that puts everything back to normal. But nothing is the same. At home, the bedroom furniture has been rearranged. Our bed has been pushed onto Mama's side of the room and a mattress, brand new and still covered in plastic, has taken its place. Mama doesn't take the plastic off when she puts the sheet on, and that night when I lie in my new bed, sliding my hands against the polycotton, it makes a *shh-shh* noise. I rub, up and down, up and down, hushing myself to sleep.

"Wake up, it's time for school." Mama nudges me with her foot.

My body aches, from the flu and Mama's beating. I haven't been to school in over a week, but not because Mama cares: she just didn't want Miss Patterson to see the bruises. The swelling has gone down and the bruises are starting to fade. I guess that's why Mama decided I'm ready to go back. I dress slow, hoping she'll change her mind and let me stay home. She doesn't, even though I linger. By the time I'm ready, Sindi's long gone. I drag my feet down the road and get there just as the bell goes, but no one seems in a hurry to get to class. They stand there like they've been waiting for me, staring and whispering, but no one speaks to me.

In class, I sit right at the front so I don't have to look at anyone. I take out my pencil case and book, watch Miss Patterson clean the whiteboard. I can hear them whispering about me. I'm relieved when a scuffle breaks out at the back of the class. At least all eyes are off me for a bit. I turn to watch. Two boys are fighting over a chair. They pull it back and forth between them. The chair's legs scrape against the floor, squealing in protest.

"Stop it." Miss Patterson raises her arm above her head as if to throw her yellow duster at them, then she sees me.

"Oh," she says. Her lips move like she wants to say something more, but nothing comes out. Everyone looks at me again. Their eyes drill holes, they stare so hard.

"Okay, boys," she says finally, "break it up. Sandile, sit down, and Jonas, sit next to Thulisile."

Jonas makes a big show of dragging his feet to where I sit. He slings his satchel over the back of his chair and kicks it as far away from mine as he can. When he sits down, he angles his body away from me. For the first few minutes, he holds his breath as if I stink.

My eyes sting. I bite my lip. Miss Patterson writes a list of words on the board and orders us to copy them down while she goes to the office. She's not gone a minute when a scrunched-up ball of paper hits me on the back of the head.

"Skhebereshe!"

I put my pencil down and turn around.

"What did you call me?" I spit my question at Dumisile. I know it's him even though he's pretending to look at his book. Another missile bounces off my nose. Somebody laughs.

I stand so fast my chair clatters to the floor. No one laughs now. No one says anything. They're all cowards. Made brave by their silence, I stride over to Dumisile's desk and lean on it. "What did you call me?" I growl through my teeth.

Dumisile rocks back on his chair. "If I see a pig, I call it a pig," he grins.

"I am not a pig," I hiss.

"No, even a pig is cleaner than you, skhe-be-reshe." He draws the syllables of the insult out. I stare at his smiling face tilted upwards by the angle of his chair, and without thinking about what I'm doing, I lunge over the desk and slam my fist into his nose so hard his chair falls backwards. The floor knocks the breath from his lungs. He gasps, and quick, before he can recover, I jump on him and start throwing punches. All the anger I've been holding in my stomach boils up into my fists and I hit and hit and hit and hitting feels good.

My edge doesn't last. Dumisile's much bigger than me. He throws me off and we both stagger to our feet. Blood pours from his nostrils. Sneering, he wipes his hand across his nose, but before he can call me a whore again, I go for him.

Pain blurs my vision. I hit the floor, scramble, but before I can get up he's on me. He straddles me and clamps his hands around my throat. My blood pulses to the rhythm of our classmates clapping, egging him on. The world is full of noise again. Dumisile's fist comes down. I feel my nose, still bruised from Mama, crunch and a thick warmth flows down the back of my throat and over my lips.

"What's going on here?"

Miss Patterson pulls Dumisile off me. As I stagger to my feet, I see Nandi and my sisi sitting side by side at their desk. Sindi has her head down, hands over her face. Nandi's smiling like a dog with meat for dinner. I sneer at her, but her smile just grows bigger. She slips an envelope from her book and holds it next to the desk, so I can see it but Sindi can't if she looks. It's the letter the nurse sent to Mama. "Everybody knows," she mouths the words, slow. "Everybody knows."

I want to rush them and push their desk over, force Sindi to look at me, but Miss Patterson has me by the collar. She drags me and Dumisile to the front and makes us face each other. Our noses pour. Dumisile's fist is red with my blood. I don't remember biting him, but there are teeth marks in his palm. He sees the semi-circles at the same time as me, and starts to cry. *You baby.* I grin, baring my bloody teeth to the class. I win.

"Miss, miss, I need to go to the nurse."

Miss Patterson's eyes go wide. "Dumisile, how could you be so stupid?" She lets go of me and hurries him out the classroom. "That's what you get for fighting, neh," I hear her say as they leave.

With Miss Patterson gone, there's no reason to keep standing in front of the class. I right my chair and sit down, pinching my nose.

"Hey, don't bleed on me," Jonas sweeps his things off the desk and moves to Dumisile's empty chair.

The door to the principal's office is closed. It's painted the same government blue as the stage door, where I saw the district nurse. Looking at it makes my gut tilt. I jump when the door finally swings open.

"Come. You can come in now."

I stand in front of the principal's desk with my hands behind my back. I've been there so many times I know not to sit down unless he says.

"Thulisile Nxumalo, back once more? Your teacher tells me you've been fighting again." He doesn't look up from his papers.

I nod. There's no point denying it: my bloodied shirt and torn sleeve tell the story.

"Well," he says, "speak up."

"Yes, sir, but I didn't start it."

"Of course not." He puts the lid on his pen, it clicks like a disapproving tongue. "Is it ever your fault?"

I know I'm not supposed to answer, but still, I want to tell him that this time, it really wasn't. There's little point. If I tell him what Dumisile called me, he'll just say that rubbish about sticks and stones.

"Thulisile, this is a very serious matter. I cannot allow you to come to this school if you're going to get into fights. Not any more. I cannot allow your behaviour to endanger other pupils. Do you understand?"

Tears prickle hot in my sinuses. I bite my lip to stop them. I don't understand. I don't. Dumisile is bigger than me. I was in more danger from him.

"Well," he says, "I'll give you one more chance, but I'm going to write to your mother to make sure it doesn't happen again."

I wait on the bench outside the office for the school secretary to type the letter. There's no way I'm giving it to Mama. After what happened last time. No way.

"Your mother must sign this letter and you must bring it back first thing in the morning, before you go to class. Understand?"

I take the envelope from the school secretary's hand. No one's going to miss me if I never come back to school. No one wants me there anyway. If it's a choice between getting an education and living, I choose life.

"Understand?"

I nod.

I don't bother going back to the classroom to pick up my bag. I walk out the school gate, tearing the letter into pieces. The wind blows the scraps across the courtyard. I understand.

That night I dream of a road. I walk and walk and walk and wake in a sweat. The sheets are twisted, trapping my limbs, my skin sticks to the plastic. I'm afraid to close my eyes again. I wait for light; when it comes, I put on my uniform and leave the house. I stand on the pavement for a while. My eyes burn from lack of sleep and my skull is full of wool. I don't know where to go, so I just walk. Soon walking feels like dreaming and I need to stop before my fear eats me. At the Spaza I duck between the shacks and head for the veld that lies between the township and Saviour's.

There's no one in the veld. Where are all the homeless kids? The emptiness reminds me of the dream. Under the tree, I clear a spot of broken bottles and glass and sit there, waiting-waiting for the day to pass. I'm so tired, but I don't lie down. I'm scared if I close my eyes I'll fall into a road and I won't ever be able to get home. Home is bad, but the dream is worse.

After a while sleep threatens to win and I have to move. I risk being seen and cross the road to Saviour's.

"Lookee what the cat drag in," Ben says. I'm ready to lie, but neither Joe nor Ben asks why I'm not in school.

"Get the cat a chair," is all Joe says.

I slump into the chair, too tired to speak. Within minutes my head's nodding against my chest. I jerk awake, move to the edge of the chair and sit upright.

"Why don't you sleep if you so tired?"

"Bad dreams."

"Ah. You want to tell me about it?"

I shake my head. *Talking about bad things makes them real.*

Joe grunts. "Sometimes if you talk of bad things, it makes them float."

"Float?"

"What's the right word? Like air."

"You mean invisible?"

"No, no," he flicks his fingers, "twinkle, twinkle little star."

"Oh, light."

"That's it. Light."

I consider it. Maybe he's right. Face your fear, make it disappear. Gogo Nkosi's lodger used to say that. "I keep dreaming I'm on this road," I tell him, "I can't get off it and there's no cars or people or anything else. Just me. I walk and walk and walk, but I never get anywhere."

Joe nods. "Kid, you are the wrong way around."

"'Skies?"

"You," he says loud and slow. "You are the wrong way around."

"I don't understand."

He waves his hands in the air then points at my collar. "Like your shirt, the label is outside." I stare at my cuffs. My shirt is inside out, as is my tunic. Even the seams in my socks face out.

"How?" How could I have put on all my clothes like that without noticing?

"Nothing is real, Thuli." Joe says. "You are not here and you are not there. You have walked too long in the now, never looking to your past even though you have no future. You are the dream, we are nothing but memories."

His voice bears down on me, adding to the weight of my restless night. I slump into the chair, but even as my muscles soften into sleep, my heart is clapping so hard it fills the world with noise. "Don't let me sleep. Please Joe. The road never ends."

"It ends," Joe says. "Everything does."

Mumbling, Mumbling about the Dead

I sit under an overpass, rolling stones into a storm-water drain. On the Ring Road, streetlights buzzed, insects scratched, cars whined past, millions of sleeping people breathed in, breathed out. Those sounds joined together to create a background hum, a song of life I hadn't known was there until it wasn't. Here the silence is vast and any sound I make is bigger than it should be. My stones clatter across the concrete like hail on a tin roof. I can even hear the path the well-aimed ones cut through the air as they drop to the bottom of the drain, like someone inhaling to whistle, and the hard recurring bounce when they hit. The drains are empty: nothing cushions my stones. No carpet of dead leaves and litter, no dead girls.

I think about Dora a lot. Poor Dora, stuck in a drain for weeks, like I'm stuck on this road. Poor Dora with her pink coffin almost as wide as it was long. Nobody liked her, though we all pretended, after, that we had, because she was dead and it felt wrong to say mean things.

Dora was a Catholic. I thought Auntie was the only Catholic I knew, until Dora died and we went to Regina Mundi for the funeral. The priest said she'd gone to heaven, but I didn't believe him. After the funeral, Auntie came to our house, dressed respectable in her dark skirt and white blouse. She called that outfit her church clothes, though the skirt was so short you could almost see the curve of her bum cheeks. While Mama made tea, I bent close to Auntie and asked if she thought Dora went to heaven. I whispered the question into her ear because Sindi had just caught a smack from Mama for speaking bad about the girl.

"Of course," Auntie snapped, clicking her tongue. "All children go straight to heaven."

I eyed Mama, but she didn't seem to be paying attention. "What about if Mama died, would she also go straight to heaven?"

"Ai," Mama swung around, "I'm not going to die."

"Everybody dies, Sizane," Auntie told her, "even you."

"And then," Mama asked, "will I go to heaven?" She put Auntie's tea on the table.

"You? No way." Auntie tapped the side of her mug with a teaspoon. "First you'll go to purgatory to pay for your sins."

Mama laughed. "Maybe *you* will," she said, "but me, I'm going straight-straight. Do not pass begin, do not pay a fine, all the way up."

Auntie sniffed. "And why you and not me?"

"Because you are Catholic," Mama settled into her chair, "and me, I don't believe in that religious nonsense."

I look for another stone. I'm bored of my game, but there's nothing else to do. I spot a small pebble at the bottom of the embankment and lean over to pick it up. It sits in my palm, an almost-perfect white oval, its purity marred by a spot black as a blood-fat tick. Beyond the shadowed underpass, the light seems sharper, bright-bright. There's a harsh glare on the concrete, cold and chemical like fluorescent tubes on white tiles. It disorientates me: for a moment, forever, I think I'm in the hospital late at night, staring up at the neon strip lights. I hear the squeak-squeak of rubber trolley-wheels as I'm pushed down a corridor, away from Mama, away from Sindi mumbling-mumbling about the dead, and then they're gone and I'm alone.

The bleak memory settles, making me colder than I've ever felt before, colder than the stone clasped tight in my hand. I rub the stone between my palms, but if there's heat in me the stone doesn't want it. I toss it away. It hits a bridge support on the other side of the road and bounces back, landing smack in the centre of a white line.

I stare at the stone. Strange how it stopped, just like that. As if it can read my thoughts, it trembles and rolls towards the drain. For a moment, forever, the stone hovers. Then it drops. I cock my head, listen for the bounce, but the almost-whistle goes on

and

on

and

on.

The storm drain is set into a raised strip of concrete at the edge of the road. I lie on my belly and peer into it. Solid black. The rectangular inlet is narrow and I have to turn my head to the side to fit. Grit scrapes against my cheek as I wriggle in up to my shoulders. I rotate my head ninety degrees and look down. Eyes wide, I still can't see, but there's a faint drone in my ears, a familiar sound that makes my heart skip. There's somebody down there.

Being a late bloomer might not attract boys the way titties do, but it has one advantage. Anywhere my head fits, the rest can follow. I clasp the verge and pull myself into the drain, slow-slow. Soon, my upper body is hanging down inside the drain and just my pelvis and legs are pressed against the concrete. I reach out with one hand, feeling for the bottom of the drain, and my balance shifts, tipping me forward.

"Thirsty." I move my mouth to form the word but the voice that speaks belongs to a gogo. My lids peel apart. A box of Omo belts out a jingle on the flatscreen, dancing from stain to stain. The blue-white flash makes my eyes water.

There's a packet of cold-and-flu tablets on the coffee table, and a glass of water, half full. A fly circles the rim of the glass, tongue flicking to feast on the gluey leftover of my spit. It's disgusting, but I'm so thirsty I don't care. I bring the glass to my lips, tilt it. Water spills out the side of my mouth onto the brown fabric of Auntie's couch. Auntie's taking care of me during the day now, while Mama's at work.

"Watch out, sleeping beauty." Auntie snatches the glass. "Here, let me."

She helps me to sit, leaning in so close I can count the freckles between her titties. I drain what's left in the glass and close my eyes.

"Don't go back to sleep." Auntie prods me in the ribs. "Your ma's going to be here soon to take you home. You want some tea?"

I shake my head. The thought of drinking a cup of Auntie's too-sweet soupy tea makes me want to vomit. "Just water."

She goes to the kitchen to refill the glass. The water cools my throat but turns acid when it hits my stomach. "I think I'm going to be sick."

"The pot's there," Auntie says, nodding towards the corner by the window. She helps me up and leaves me kneeling over it. It's one of Mama's pots, the big one with the melted handle. There's an inch of pee in the bottom. I retch. My vomit is hot and clear and bitter and dilutes the yellow. I push Mama's pot aside and rest my head on the floor. The carpet smells musty, but it's cool against my face. I want to stay there.

Auntie doesn't like it. "Dogs lie on the floor," she says, "dogs and drunks. Which one are you?"

I force myself to stand and walk back to the couch. My knees ache, my head aches, even my fingers ache. I sit on the couch and stare at the TV.

Auntie's lips are pulled tight and she's giving me looks by the time Mama comes to get me. Auntie doesn't like me to stay late in case her boyfriend comes around. He moved out six weeks back, said he wanted a place of his own, but I heard Mama tell Auntie that she'd seen him at Ma Elias', dancing with someone else. Still, some nights he comes knocking, so Auntie wants me gone, just in case.

Past six, Mama comes. Auntie's got a hundred complaints ready to deliver, but she swallows them when she sees Mama's face. Slack eyes, raw cheeks.

"What happened to you?"

She takes Mama by the arm and they disappear into the kitchen. Auntie puts the kettle on. I can hear crying over the hiss of the kettle and the clink of teaspoons. I know it's Mama because she tries to swallow her crying like she does at night when she thinks me and Sindi are sleeping. I shift, uncomfortable.

After a time, long-long, Mama tells her bad news. Thembi called. Uncle died last week. "What must I do? Thembi is too sick to bury him and she has no money. I can't go there and leave my child. I have no money to spare. My baby is sick too. What if she needs hospital? Who will take her?"

I stare at the TV. Deep down, in my secret place, I feel a stabbing pain like somebody sticking a knife in. Uncle's face appears on the TV screen close-close. I see the blackheads on his nose, smell his rotten-cheese breath, taste it on my tongue.

"Oh, Sizane," Auntie's shrill voice cuts into my thoughts, "I'm so sorry."

"No, it's me that's sorry," Mama says, "for all the wasted years. For all the time my girls could have had an uncle, a family."

I push the blanket off my knees and walk old-man-slow to the kitchen. I stare at Mama until she feels my eyes and looks up. "I'm glad," I tell her in my old-woman voice. My words slap them silent and I know I shouldn't say it again, but I do. "I'm glad."

Auntie's face turns black. She raises her hand, but before she can strike me, Mama grabs her wrist. "What are you glad for?"

"I'm glad Uncle is dead and there is no one to bury him. And I'm glad you ran away from there. I wish I never met him."

"How can you say such a thing?" Auntie is shouting; her voice fades out with the colour on Mama's cheeks.

Mama's eyes seem to sink deeper into the creases that have formed around them these past months. She looks like Gogo, and I only ever saw Gogo after she was dead. Mama stands. The metal legs of her chair grind the RDP concrete of Auntie's kitchen floor, and she walks towards me with heavy feet. I shrink back. She'll hit me hard, but I don't care. Uncle is dead and I'm glad.

"I'm glad," I say again, though I know those are probably the last words I'll ever say.

Mama's hands close over my shoulders. She pulls me towards her. Her chest heaves against my cheek.

I sit in a cast-iron bath with the sun beating down on my head. Hills unroll before me like the mounds of fresh-dug graves.

"How does a girl get so dirty?" someone says.

I peer over the edge at Thembi, crouched next to the tub. The ground seems further away than it should be. She looks up at me and clicks her tongue. "Dirty," she says, striking a match. She lights a fire beneath the tub and stokes it with a stick. The metal begins to glow like rat-eyes reflecting headlights.

"Help me," I plead.

She stands so that her face is level with mine. Seawater spills from two pits where her eyes should be. Her skin is wood splintered by damp. "I am helping you," she says.

Flames lick my fingers. I rock the tub.

"Sit still, dirty girl." She slaps my cheeks with a burning stick. "How can I wash you if you won't sit still?"

My skin begins to melt and the acrid stench of burning plastic fills my nostrils. I want to tell her there's no water in the tub, but my tongue has swollen like a hot sausage I can't spit out. "Hmmmhmm," is all I can say.

"What did I tell you about speaking with your mouth full?" Mama stands over me, holding a kettle. Steam spirals from the spout, wrapping her head in white snakes. They dance around her, hissing: "Dirty, dirty, dirty."

I wake drained and thirsty. The sun streaming through the window onto my face tells me it is afternoon. The last thing I remember is Mama leaving for work. I must have slept all day.

Sheets lie in a pile on the floor. My vest has ridden up my back. I've been fighting in my sleep again. I sit. The plastic protecting the mattress from me clings to my skin, only letting me go when I bend toward my toes.

I shuffle on my bum to the edge of the mattress and sit there until I catch my breath. Then I kneel on the floor next to the bed. As soon as I push onto my knees, angry black dots attack my face, pricking and buzzing like vengeful ants. I clutch the mattress and wait for the dizzy to pass; then I shake out the sheets, trying not to look at the stains. Something leaks from me when I sleep. Night sweats, the nurse at Bara said, but the marks left behind dry darker than sweat.

I try to tuck the plastic under the mattress. It's stretched thin and doesn't fit snugly any more. There are holes where my toenails have ripped through when I kick out against my dreams. I don't care about the plastic any more, or what it means that Mama won't let me take it off; but maybe when I sleep, some part of me that still does care wakes up and tears at it.

I make the bed and go through to the kitchen for a glass of water. The effort saps all my energy and by the time I reach the table my breath comes in short jags. Mama has left a plate for me. Just looking at it makes me feel sick, but if I don't eat it she will shout and after she has used up all her shouting, she will cry. I reach for the jug of water, so thirsty, but I can't lift it.

There is a movement at the window, someone passing. It's too early for Mama to come home, but maybe Auntie has come to check on me. I watch the door handle; it doesn't move, but I hear voices.

"What are you waiting for? Gogo Nkosi gave you that muti ages ago. If you wait much longer, it will be too late. Don't you want to go to heaven?"

Nandi. Hate twists my gut.

"When m_must I? In the day, she goes nn_next door, and Mama is here with her at nn_night."

The door opens and Nandi comes in, as if it's her house to enter as she pleases. Sindi follows. They stop when they see me. Nandi raises her eyebrows and gives Sindi a sideways look. "What you doing here?" she asks me.

I glare at her, but the effort drains me. I blink, reptile-slow, and look away.

Sindi pulls out a chair and sits in front of me, resting her chin on the table. "Where's Mama? She come home early?" She seems friendly.

I shake my head, smile. I can't help it; maybe the same part of me that tears the plastic still hopes things will go back to the way they were, before Nandi. "Auntie had to go to the clinic."

Sindi cuts eyes at Nandi. I should've known better than to trust her. I stand, resting against the table for a second in the hope that she'll help me back to bed. She doesn't move. The kitchen swims. I know I should wait before walking, but I don't want Nandi to see how weak I am. I step slow and careful. The edges of the room darken and the walls begin to dissolve inwards. A numb tingly feeling floods my face, like the time me and Sindi stole half a quart from Next-Door-Auntie's boyfriend and downed the bitter lager behind her house.

The curtain brushes against my face. I swipe at it. Black closes over me. I manage to take a few more steps into the room and stand, swaying-swaying, until I hear the curtain swing back against the side of the wardrobe. Then I sink to the floor, everything spinning.

"Go on, do it. Before she wakes up. I've lit the candles. What you waiting for?"

"I'm nn_not ready, just wait."

"For what? Your mama's going to be home now-now. Do it."

Through my closed lids, I sense the sun has gone. Someone puffs cherry breath onto my face. A hand presses something cold onto my cheeks, my forehead, my mouth. Sticky, like mud. It seeps between my lips, bitter, unlike their sweet breath. My skin begins to burn. I feel like my face is on fire, but after a few seconds the heat dies down and my skin just tingles. Then my face disappears.

The hand moves down my neck to my shoulders, my chest. Heat and numbness follow. *Fight*, says a small voice inside me, and I know whatever they are doing is bad and I should struggle against it; but it's nice, not feeling.

The hand reaches under my vest, presses lightly against my belly. Her palm feels like an iron, dial set to cotton hot, my skin like nylon. She spreads the hot mud stuff over my stomach and between my legs. The burning down there is so bad, worse than anywhere else. The hand lifts away. I scream, but my scream is trapped, rasping in my throat like sandpaper. My jaw snaps, teeth slice into my tongue. Blood floods my mouth, copper and mouldy cheese, like Uncle's breath. *Fight*, the voice in my head is yelling now, but I can't move.

"Put more on, on her legs."

"There isn't any mm_more. Shut up."

"Okay, okay, I'll get a knife." I hear the curtain thud against the wardrobe, once, twice and she's back. "This is the sharpest one I could find."

"M_m_maybe this isn't s_s_asuch a good idea. M_maybe we should sss_astop."

Sindi's stuttering gets worse when she's scared. Knowing she's scared turns my guts liquid.

"It's too late for her. Look at her. Look. She's not going to be around much longer. If you don't do this, you'll go to hell."

"M_maybe I'll go anyway."

"Don't be stupid. Think about all the bad things Thuli did. She's going to hell for what she did and she'll take your only chance of eternal life with her."

In the silence that follows, I can feel Sindi's reluctance. My heart slows. She doesn't want to do it. She doesn't want to hurt me.

"Pass m_me the knife."

The knife slices skin. It hurts, but the hurt is far away. Sindi presses her palm against my stomach again. Blood pools in my bellybutton.

For a moment, forever, she stands like that, waiting and silent, then something deep inside me rips and I feel like I'm being torn in two, divided like the segments of an orange, one for me, one for you.

Then her hand is gone and I'm standing outside of my body and there's no more pain and no more fever ache. I'm light and free, floating-floating. Everything is bright and white and I'm spiralling down a tunnel toward a glowing silver hand. A voice, my sisi's voice, calls me. I look at the hand and see that it's a door and I want, more than anything, to go through the door.

'It stinks in here. What are you girls doing?' Far behind me, at the dark end of the tunnel, Mama is shouting. "Why is Thuli on the floor?"

The tunnel pulsates in time with my heartbeat. Red cracks appear in the tunnel walls, then it breaks apart. The silver hand draws back and sinews the colour of ox-liver snake from my body and drag me down into aching, burning flesh.

Everything hurts. Mama lifts me off the floor with arms that feel like the zigzag edges of a hundred saws, packed tightly together. She puts me down on my bed. The sheet has a million tiny mouths full of razor-sharp teeth.

I watch Mama lean over me to open the window. The room is filled with smoke and smells of dead leaves and green grass and extinguished candles.

"Are you trying to burn the house down, you stupid girls?" Tendrils of white hang around Mama's head like the steam snakes from my dream. The cooler evening air draws them out the window, where they hang briefly before disappearing. "What's on your sister's face?" Mama grasps my chin and turns my head.

Behind Mama, Sindi is staring at me with scaredy-cat eyes.

"Come back," I whisper, "we can be together." But she looks away, and I can't keep looking at her, knowing she doesn't want me. I turn to hide in the darkness beyond the window.

There's a bright dot out there. As I stare it enlarges, bigger-bigger. The edges push outward and it morphs into a misshapen, winged thing that whirrs through the window in a halo of dust.

The moth lands on the mattress next to my head. The fat segments of its body are thick with fur the colour of my unwashed sheets and the markings on its wings look like sweat stains. The moth walks in frantic circles like it's lost and angry at being lost. Then it stops, pulsing-pulsing, and stares at me with eyes like Auntie's black-plastic pearls. I open my mouth to scream; the moth rushes me and slips between my lips.

My body lurches like I'm a girl with two fingers in a plug. Through a shrinking circle of light, I see the moth escape through the window. Then everything is black and Sindi is screaming.

"It's my fault. She's going t_to die."

Mama and Sindi stand over me in a too-bright place that smells of blood, shit, alcohol, antiseptic. Bara.

The last time Mama brought me to Bara, they kept me in a room full of skinny people with hollow cheeks and swollen eyes, and I thought I would never leave.

"Mrs Nxumalo? We have to take her now."

Mama squeezes my hand. I didn't know she was holding it until she let go. I look past the orderly at Mama and Sindi huddled together, getting smaller. Mama is crying. Over the coughs and squalls of sick babies, I hear Sindi mumble: "I killed her, mm_Mama. I killed her."

The wheels of the gurney sing like a mouse, *squeak, squeak, squeak*. There's a jolt and we pass through green doors into a corridor. The doors swing closed, taking Mama and Sindi away. I stare at the ceiling, at the strip lights going by like the white lines on a highway, faster and faster, 90 kilometres per hour, 100, 120, 140, 160. "Don't leave me," I whisper, but it's too late. They're gone and I'm moving away from them at 200 kilometres per hour, over the edge into the never-ending bright white, falling-falling, alone, alone, alone.

The King of the Road

I am a dream, drifting-drifting. I am a dream, unreal, made of memories and briefly sighted things. I dream of floating,

down,

down,

down into the cold damp where it smells of earthworms, like afternoons after rain. I sink into a pit, long and narrow, sides dug straight, lower and lower, where I settle, slow-slow, like dead wood ticking with beetles. The damp begins to leach away and soon there is nothing in the deep but dust and darkness and the smell of things long gone, legs curled, wings crisped. I lie among the unremembered like an odd sock, a missing button. I am the dream that clings for the briefest moment between sleep and waking, then slips away, its shape forgotten.

Everything is white. I sit and a sheet drops from my face into my lap. I'm on the highway again, on a gurney parked at the bottom of an off-ramp. I pull the drip from my arm, swing my legs over the side and take a deep breath. The air makes no noise in my nostrils. My chest doesn't rise and sink. I'm still. Dead still.

Just beyond the off-ramp, the highway disappears. There's no grey strip of concrete winding into a 2D landscape of cardboard cut-out houses. Ahead is a blur, kind of like looking through Next-Door-Auntie's greasy bifocals.

In contrast, the off-ramp cuts upwards in a sharp line. I shield my eyes with a flat hand and squint into the glare. I can just make out a blue-and-white airplane squatting on the forecourt roof of a service station.

I begin the climb to Saviour's like my baby-dolls have springs in their rubber soles, but the hill is steeper than it looks: by the time I reach the top, the sky is bloody and my legs are limp as cooked spaghetti. The air crowds me, pressing against my skin like a sweaty blanket. After the not-hot not-cold of the empty highway, the heat is dizzying. I stumble across the forecourt and sink onto one of the pump islands with my head between my knees. The stink of b-diesel teases my nostrils, not strong-strong like I remember. There are other smells too: slap chips maybe, with lots of salt but no vinegar, and something swampy.

The dizzy passes, but the sky is still the same whore-lipstick shade when I raise my head. I scan the place and my silent heart sinks. Saviour's is walled in by fields. My old neighbourhood is gone, and as far as I can see there's just sugar cane, sugar cane, sugar cane. Same-same wherever I look, like someone cut out a picture from a magazine and pasted it over and over. Fields as fake as the cardboard cut-out houses.

"Hello!" I yell. The only reply comes from a discarded Chicken Licken bucket tumbleweeding across the deserted forecourt. It comes to a stop against the leg of the lawn chair parked outside the shop. I press my face to the shop window but it's too dark to see inside and the door is sealed against my tugging. Defeated, I sink onto the exhausted webbing of Joe's chair and stare at the litter of takeaway containers trapped between the pavement and the road, then beyond to the fields where once there was the veld and houses and life. Nothing moves. This place is dead quiet. Just like the road. Just like me.

I don't want to be here any more, I don't want to be alone. I jump up and grab the door handle again, pulling with all my fear. The seals give, *kiss-kiss*, and crumbs of rotted rubber pitter-patter around my feet.

The temperature inside the shop was always higher than outside. When I step through the door, the heat jumps me like an oros tsotsi on payday.

"Anyone home?" My voice rattles against empty shelves. As my eyes adjust to the dimness, hope sinks. Everything is blanketed in dust. I creep up and down the aisles feeling like a thief, though there's nothing to steal.

310

A dead fly rots in a pool of stagnant water at the bottom of the ice-cream fridge. I slip behind the counter. Grimy cobwebs of spun sugar coat the stainless-steel bowl of the Hurricane machine. My fingers stick to the tacky black switch as I click it on, longing to break the heavy silence. Nothing happens.

"Emi, oru, abiku, O . . ."

I spin around and squint into the shadows. There's someone hunched into the corner singing so soft-soft it's almost silence. If I hadn't heard that song a thousand times on the road, the words would be impossible to make out.

". . . catch a emi by the toe, hold on tight and don' let go, if up to heaven you want to go."

"Sindi?"

"Emi, oru, abiku, O . . ."

"Sindi," I say, sharper this time, but she doesn't skip a beat.

". . . catch a emi by the toe . . ."

I take a step towards her. Behind us the door opens, *kiss-kiss*, shifting the light and luming her up. I lurch backwards, fingers curled in disgust. The singer is a half-formed thing, like a rough sculpture fashioned from lumps of clay.

"You took your time, little sister. Thought you'd never get here." Ben clutches my shoulders to steady me and draws me away from the thing in the corner.

I expected it to be dark outside by now, but the sky blushes and the fake fields surrounding Saviour's Pit Stop still glow a brilliant, golden green in the long dusk rays.

"What happened to the shop?" I ask, not wanting to ask about the creature in the corner that stole my sisi's voice. I'm not ready to know the answer to that question.

Ben sighs. "The boss get hungry. We been waiting for you a long time, little sister. Long time."

He checks his watch, then turns and walks across the forecourt like he's got somewhere to go. A feather drops from the sleeve of his blue over-alls. I pick it up and twirl it by the quill, wondering at the size of it. The plumage is gunmetal grey with an oily green sheen, but it's too big to have come from any pigeon I've ever seen.

"You coming?" Ben jerks his head. "The boss next door."

He leads me through the forecourt, past the watching pumps and a boarded-up storefront to Chicken Licken. Inside, stale spices and rancid oil assault my nostrils. A sunken-eyed woman stands over the fryer, her orange uniform darkened by grease. My stomach turns as I watch her lift a wire basket of chicken bits from the oil and empty the contents into a family-size bucket.

"One Soul Mates Classic LekkerBig for the King of the Road." She slides the bucket down the counter and cuts resentful eyes at me. "What can I get you?"

I glance up at the menu above the counter. An opaque layer of fat makes it impossible to read. I shake my head, step back. "Nothing," I mumble.

Ben taps me on the shoulder. "Bring the chicken, the Boss back there."

Joe's asleep at a table in the window. He's different from the Joe I used to know, who never wore anything but shorts and T-shirts, day in, day out. This Joe's dressed in a dark suit that was probably once sharp, but the sleeves on the jacket have split down the seams and the front is covered in greasy stains. Joe's never been a skinny, but I wouldn't have called him fat-fat. Now, he's gone so oros his beer-belly cheeks swallow his nose. Perched on the wide expanse of his face, his mirror-sunglasses look like sequins. I cut eyes at Ben.

"Like I said, little sister, we been waiting long," he shrugs. "Hey Boss, wake up, she's finally here."

Epilogue
Lifesaver

The mid-morning sun bounces off a small collection of offerings, making her eyes water. The rays paint the glaze on the ceramic vase with gold, imbue the dusty fabric petals with shimmer. In a sealed Consol jar, Lifesavers glow like jewels: doughnut-cut sapphires, citrines, cherry-flavoured rubies. A day too bright for grief, like the yellow morning of Thuli's funeral.

She moves the gifts aside to sit in their place at the head of the grave. She does not remember the cement gravestone from her last visit, on her fourteenth birthday: the only birthday she has marked alone. The mound of earth her twin displaced was naked then. Now the site is flat, the cement block at the head solemn. It's as if, in the years of Sindi's absence, the fact of Thuli's death has become more definite, hardening as her body disintegrated.

Could it be two whole years since she'd left Mama – passed out, sleeping off another night of drunkenness and accusations and weeping – to bring Thuli that jar of Lifesavers? Mama had stopped speaking to Sindi by then, unless her tongue was lubricated by alcohol, which made her cruel. Nandi no longer spoke to her either; she'd made up with the sgqebhezanas, stopped going to church and started wearing lipstick. She'd hooked up with Dumisile, last thing Sindi heard. Auntie tried to be there for her, but she said that every time she saw Sindi, it was like seeing a ghost.

Sindi stayed in the graveyard all that night, begging Thuli to speak to her, but her sister was silent. Unforgiving. Sindi woke from a dreamless sleep with her arm flung over the mound, numb and cold. If Thuli would not come to her, she decided, then she would go to Thuli.

Two years since she walked away from the grave and just kept going.

She read the date off *The Daily Voice* in the supermarket yesterday. At least she thinks it was yesterday. Time still feels slippery.

Two years. That makes her sixteen, she supposes. Sweet sixteen and never been kissed.

Is it Mama that erected the headstone? Brings gifts? The plot is cared for, recently swept. Sindi's footprints disrupt the lines a broom has left in the sand. After the funeral, Mama swore that the next time she set foot in a graveyard it would be to join Thuli. Sindi leans against the gravestone and closes her eyes, pushing back so the raised edges of the letters and numbers bite through her T-shirt and claw at her flesh. She wants to vanish into her sister's name, the date of their birth and Thuli's death, but the pain grounds her, slowing her escape.

The dream has become more difficult to recall with each passing day. It's been a week since she woke in the prefab hut at the old refinery, spooned by Loveday's warm body, waist encircled by Loveday's pale arm. Loveday said she'd been asleep for days, mumbling the same thing over and over. She'd been dreaming.

Eight days, seven nights. Each night when she closes her eyes, she covers her face with her hands and whispers the dream into her empty palms, trying to summon it, as if reciting a spell. She covers her eyes now, tilts her head back so the sun hits her face, and begins.

"In the dream, I crouch behind the Hurricane machine, playing hide-and-go-seek. I'm not supposed to be behind the counter. Ben and Joe are gone and there is nothing on the shelves. Gone, gone, gone, everything is gone."

Sunlight filters through her splayed fingers and her eyelids, turning her vision orange, red, yellow. She presses the tips of her index fingers against her eyes. Spiralling fractals pulse purple and green, in time to her heartbeat. Slowly, an image begins to condense in the centre of the spiral, and soon she can see the interior of the shop. It looks long abandoned, like the Mid Illovo Spar.

Things that eat a man from the inside also eat young girls.

She views the dream from inside herself and out. She is crouching behind the counter and Thuli is calling her name. She can see herself clearly, but struggles to make her sister out, as if Thuli is standing behind clouded glass. There but not there. Spookasem. Ghost. Like that one time she thought she saw Thuli's spirit in the bathroom mirror at Brother Moses' house. She recalls the sinking disappointment when she realised it was just her own face, obscured by steam.

Irritated, she pushes the intruding memory aside and presses her eyeballs harder to refocus on the dream. She pictures herself, following Thuli from the shop. But that's her mind pushing in again, planting lies. She bites her lip and scans her memory for something true. She is in the shop, crouched behind the counter. Then she is behind a pump, watching Thuli share a bucket of chicken with a very fat man.

"Joe and Thuli ate chicken," she whispers. She knows the man is Joe because mirrored sunglasses cover his eyes, and he's wearing the same suit he did at the funeral. Thuli is dressed in her school uniform, the green and maroon New Tiyang Primary tie in a neat knot at her throat. During Thuli's ceremony she'd felt so numb, she had to think of the white dress to summon tears. Thuli should have been buried in that white dress, not her school uniform; she hated her uniform.

From her position behind the pump, she watches Joe stand and dust crumbs of batter from his lap. He takes Thuli's hand and leads her to the men's room. Déja vu. She remembers from childhood all the crazies that walked into the men's room at Saviour's and never came out, when she and Thuli used to play spy.

Joe opens the men's-room door. There is a man waiting inside. She recognises the man, though there is no crease running through the centre of his face where Mama folded the photo. She watches Thuli step over the threshold. She calls her name, but Thuli does not look back; she closes the door behind her.

To her left, Sindi hears a rattle. Not part of the dream: another intrusion. She opens her eyes. Blinks. Loveday is holding the Consol jar. She looks sheepish, caught out.

"Didn't think she would mind," says Loveday. "There's probably sweets in heaven." After a pause she adds, "Sorry."

Sindi takes the jar. If Thuli were alive, she'd slap Loveday through the face. The lid has corroded; she has to hold it between her knees and use both her hands to twist it off. It opens with a grinding sound that sets her teeth on edge. There's a flurry of rust flakes when it finally gives, sprinkling the sand with tiny scabs. Sindi shakes the sweets onto the ground in front of her and begins to divide them.

"One for me," she says. "One for you."

Acknowledgements

I am grateful to Peter Straus, my agent, and Felicia von Keyserlingk at Rogers, Coleridge and White Ltd. Also to James Woodhouse, Ester Levinrad and all at Kwela Books.

I owe a great deal to Henrietta Rose-Innes for her insightful editing and her patience, as well as her understanding of my obsession with symmetry – you made me brave; Maria Rejt for her acuity regarding the very first draft, long, long ago; Alison Burns for her encouragement and mentorship; and Dewi Pritchard for his brilliant suggestions about the structure, his candid comments and his unfailing belief in this even after I'd given up – without him, *Sister-Sister* would have remained forever in a drawer.

Thanks, too, to Sheryl Kavin, Lisa Lazarus, Karyn Reynolds and Candace di Talamo for taking time out of their busy lives to read the manuscript. Also to Alison McQueen, who read several drafts over a five-year period, always with the exuberance of someone who had never seen it before.

Many have been generous with their time and knowledge. Thanks to Geora Zadok for exploring the concrete highway with me; James te Riele for an aerial view of KwaZulu-Natal and Nongoma; John and Jackie te Riele for sharing their extensive knowledge of sugar-cane farming; Michael Westwood and Glyn Craig for instructions on how to make radios from post-apocalyptic junk and copper wire; Michael Westwood for overseeing the distillation process of a fictitious fuel; the Starfish Greathearts Foundation (http://www.starfishcharity.org/) and Heartbeat (http://heartbeat.org.za/) for showing me their projects; and Erin Sweeny for the misspellings in Nandi's diary.

The scamto slang was sourced from *Township Talk: The language, the culture, the people* by Lebo Motshegoa (Double Storey Books, Cape Town, 2005) and *Kasi Slang* – an online archive of words collected by the *Sowetan* (http://blogs.sowetanlive.co.za/slang/).

On the epigraph page, the stanza from "Ode on Melancholy" by John Keats (May 1819) is the version given in *Keats: The Complete Poems*, edited by Miriam Allott (Longman, 1975). The line from *The Famished Road* by Ben Okri comes from page 121 of the 1992 Nan A. Talese/Doubleday edition. The King of the Road in *Sister-Sister* owes his existence to the same.

Much love and thanks, finally, to Julian and Amber-Jane, and the rest of my family, for tolerating the crazy and the endless repetitions of *the end*.

RACHEL ZADOK was born in Tel Aviv in 1972 and raised in Johannesburg. In 2005, she was a runner-up in the Richard & Judy How to Get Published Competition and her first novel *Gem Squash Tokoloshe* was published later that year. *Gem Squash Tokoloshe* was shortlisted for the Whitbread First Novel Award and the John Llewellyn Rhys Prize, and longlisted for the IMPAC award. In 2011, she launched Short Story Day Africa, an initiative to highlight African short fiction. Her writing has appeared in the *Observer*, the *Jewish Chronicle*, the *Independent* and *African Violet and Other Stories*, the 2012 Caine Prize Anthology. Rachel lives in Cape Town with her husband and daughter, and occasionally blogs.